Clement Was Oblivious To Everything

except the woman he was holding pressed against him with the flat side of his ax. He drew in her scent. Faintly sweet, faintly spicy, it smelled ... warm. The scientist in him shuddered at the crossing of sensory data, while another part, a part he scarcely recognized, stirred.

Reaching out, he recognized the delicate shape of humerus, clavicle and scapula and closed his fingers firmly over her shoulder. She was rigid.

"Exhale," he ordered, and she did, in a long, shuddering gust. Personal space forgotten, he leaned closer as, without his glasses, he attempted to examine her face.

Only gradually did he become aware of the soft mewing sound issuing from her throat. He wasn't hurting her. Hands that could hold a butterfly safely would never hurt a woman. But he was becoming increasingly aware of her *femaleness*. A certain softness in the mammary region ... the distinctive conformation of the pelvic girdle ...

Suddenly Clem stiffened. To his dismay, his mind wasn't the only part of him that noticed the differences. His body was starting to react with rather amazing enthusiasm!

Dear Reader:

As you can see, Silhouette Desire has a bold new cover design that we're all excited about. But while the overall look is new, two things remain the same. First, we've kept our eye-catching red border. You can be sure to always spot Silhouette Desires on the shelves! Second, between these new covers are the high-quality love stories that you've come to expect.

In addition, the MAN OF THE MONTH program continues with Mr. September, who comes from the pen of Dixie Browning. Clement Cornelius Barto is a unique hero who is sure to charm you with his unusual ways. But make no mistake, it's not just *Beginner's Luck* that makes him such a winner.

October brings you a man who's double the fun, because not only is Jody Branigan an exciting hero, he's also one of Leslie Davis Guccione's Branigan brothers. Look for his story in *Branigan's Touch*.

We at Silhouette have been happy to hear how much you've all enjoyed the Year of the Man. The responses we've received about the special covers— and to each and every one of our heroes—has been enthusiastic. Remember, there are more men ahead in 1989—don't let any of them get away!

Yours,

Lucia Macro
Senior Editor

DIXIE BROWNING

BEGINNER'S LUCK

SILHOUETTE *Desire*

Published by Silhouette Books New York

America's Publisher of Contemporary Romance

SILHOUETTE BOOKS
300 East 42nd St., New York, N.Y. 10017

Copyright © 1989 by Dixie Browning

ISBN: 0-373-05517-X

First Silhouette Books printing September 1989

Books by Dixie Browning

Silhouette Romance

Unreasonable Summer #12
Tumbled Wall #38
Chance Tomorrow #53
Wren of Paradise #73
East of Today #93
Winter Blossom #113
Renegade Player #142
Island on the Hill #164
Logic of the Heart #172
Loving Rescue #191
A Secret Valentine #203
Practical Dreamer #221
Visible Heart #275
Journey to Quiet Waters #292
The Love Thing #305
First Things Last #323
Something for Herself #381
Reluctant Dreamer #460
A Matter of Timing #527

Silhouette Special Edition

Finders Keepers #50
Reach Out to Cherish #110
Just Deserts #181
Time and Tide #205
By Any Other Name #228
The Security Man #314
Belonging #414

Silhouette Desire

Shadow of Yesterday #68
Image of Love #91
The Hawk and the Honey #111
Late Rising Moon #121
Stormwatch #169
The Tender Barbarian #188
Matchmaker's Moon #212
A Bird in Hand #234
In the Palm of Her Hand #264
A Winter Woman #324
There Once Was a Lover #337
Fate Takes a Holiday #403
Along Came Jones #427
Thin Ice #474
Beginner's Luck #517

Silhouette Christmas Stories 1987

"Henry the Ninth"

DIXIE BROWNING

writes about her contribution to Silhouette Desire's *Man of the Month* program: "When I was first invited to take part in this project, I thought, why not? If any woman ever had a head full of heroes, I do. It's about time one of them got more than second lead.

"But why did I have to choose Clem? Granted, the man was a challenge. If I didn't give him his chance, odds are that no one ever would, but the poor darling is practically inarticulate! Did you ever try to make conversation with a man who hasn't a clue how to go about it? And as for romancing a woman—!

"Well, I'll just leave you to be the judge. I still haven't recovered."

One

Clement was half asleep when the answering machine clicked on, and a disembodied voice filled the room. "Hattie? It's me—Martha. I'm on my way, but so much has happened that I might be a day or so earlier than we'd planned, if it's all right. Something's come up—there's this man, and—oh, I can't go into it now, it's too wild. But if I get in a real bind, I might call for you to come get me, and you're to let me know if it's inconvenient, because I can always—uh-oh, I'd better run. The others are waiting, and there he is again."

Lying on his back, nude except for his glasses—he always put on his glasses when the phone rang—Clement considered the words he'd just listened to. And then he considered the voice. It wasn't the first call the machine had taken from one of his great-aunt's flaky artist friends, but this one was . . . different somehow. Something in the voice intrigued him. Breathless was not quite the word to describe it, although there was an element of breathlessness—as if the caller had been running. The voice was young, southern and definitely female, but there was something else. And it was that something else that bothered him.

It was some time later that it hit him. The something else. She'd been nervous. In fact, she'd sounded almost...frightened.

Clement wasn't the sort to resent having his sleep disturbed by a late-night call. In the first place, it was proof that the phone he'd dropped, broken and repaired was still working. In the second place, he'd always had an inquiring mind, and in the third place, he was rather desperately hoping to hear from his Great-aunt Hattie. She had dragged him away from his work and up to her lair more than a month ago to stay there and keep her pipes from freezing while she cruised the Greek Islands with a bunch of her wacky friends.

All in all, it was a fitting end to a lousy year. Two of his best assistants had quit, supplies he'd requisitioned six months ago had yet to show up and to top it off, Charles Danforth had left, casting Clem in the role of acting administrator.

Protesting hadn't done a bit of good. He was about as effective at registering protests as he was at dealing with bureaucracy. Hell, he couldn't even communicate outside the laboratory, everyone knew that. But as senior member of B.F.I.'s Research and Development Department, he'd been nailed when Danforth had left on short notice to go with Lavorly Laboratories. They'd needed someone in a hurry, and Clem's reflexes had been slow, thanks to a cold that had come and gone all summer and then had finally turned into pneumonia. He'd agreed to fill in during an emergency that showed no signs of ending.

Even with his assistant doing most of the work, the stress had been intense. He'd succumbed to another round of mycoplasma early in October. Coughing his head off, he'd dragged around the lab, dragged around the office, doing a lousy job of everything. And since he hadn't taken a day of vacation in the six years he'd been there, no one could complain when he'd left.

Administrator! He wasn't sure if the job required an imbecile or a genius—all he knew was that it wasn't for him. If B.F.I. didn't find someone else to take over he'd hire out as a street sweeper! That, at least, wouldn't require him to file an endless stream of meaningless reports, which no one bothered to read. Or to attend endless meetings, listen to reams of drivel, while the real work he'd been hired to do grew stale.

Clem was not a social animal. Due to a combination of factors, he had never developed an easy way with people, and forcing it only made matters worse. Hattie Davenport was the only woman outside the laboratory—or inside, either, for that matter—with whom he could carry on anything resembling a normal conversation. They'd been friends since he was six years old, and being rather peculiar herself, she'd never considered him in the least bit strange.

Clem had missed her after she'd retired from teaching art and moved away to live in this Victorian hideaway in the Blue Ridge Mountains, where the nearest neighbor was four miles away over a rugged cross-country path. But he'd understood her need for solitude and self-sufficiency. At seventy-nine, Hattie was far more capable of looking after herself than he was at thirty-two, a fact of which both of them were aware.

He was pretty sure she'd had an ulterior motive for insisting that he house-sit for her while she went on her annual "one last fling." The pipes were in little real danger this early in the season, and her houseplants could be replaced. And few burglers ever made it this deep into the wilds of Buncombe County.

No, he knew Hattie pretty well after all these years. She'd decided it was time to Do Something About Clement again. Stranding him here with no way out had been her effort to force him to become more independent and self-reliant, and he'd been just miserable enough at the time to agree with her scheme. Up to a point.

But the point had long since been passed. He'd run out of things to read at the end of the first week. After going through the stack of technical material he'd brought with him, he'd been bored into exploring the countryside. It was a new experience—dealing with nature in the raw. To his surprise, he discovered he'd been missing an exhilarating adventure by spending his whole life indoors.

Within a week he was hiking miles each day, most of them vertical. He discovered wood chopping. There were fireplaces in most of the rooms, and Hattie's groundhog kiln devoured wood by the cord. He'd exercised, eaten and slept more than he had in years, and in his spare time he'd read through all the old newspapers and started in on Hattie's meager library, which consisted of art books, cook books and nineteenth-century erotica.

That had been a mistake. He was restless enough as it was.

Physically, Clem was completely recovered from his pneumonia. In fact, he'd never felt so fit in his entire life. He even looked different. The short brush cut that he'd found most practical and the neat beard he'd worn for the past half dozen years had grown all out of recognition. He was shaggy, his clothes no longer seemed to fit and he'd developed an astonishing supply of muscles and calluses!

If that added up to self-sufficiency, then Hattie had done her job well. But a man could walk only so many miles, chop only so many cords of wood, sleep only so many hours a day. The restlessness, that deep-seated, nameless emptiness that had been a part of him for as long as he could remember, was getting worse without his work to keep it at bay.

Clem checked the answering machine after coming in from a long hike, hoping for a call from his secretary saying that they'd found someone to take Danforth's place. He needed to continue his work on research. Four projects were sidelined until he could get back to them, and one of them had begun to look promising. But for reasons that were beyond him, the management at B.F.I. was being extremely negligent. It was as if they no longer cared whether new products were in the works or even if those being tested were given approval.

He'd tried calling, but even the switchboard was fouled up. His secretary, Ed Malvern, had been out every time he'd managed to get through, and finally he'd given up in frustration.

The second call came just before dark. It was the same voice. Soft, hesitant, it stirred an unfamiliar feeling inside him that had nothing to do with the words spoken.

Odd, he thought. Judging from the constriction of the larynx, she was either extremely self-conscious or extremely frightened. "Hattie, it's me—Martha. Be looking for me. I'm going to watch for a chance and slip away from the tour. If I can hitch a ride I will, and I may not have time to— Oh-oh, someone's coming! I'll tell you all about it when I see you."

Clem analyzed the message, more intrigued than he cared to admit even to himself over a few words spoken by a stranger. And a woman, at that. She was planning to visit his great-aunt. Evidently, she was expected, but certainly not so soon. Hattie was no stickler for detail, but not even she would invite a guest and then leave home.

Whoever the woman was, Clem devoutly hoped she would find it impossible to slip away—*slip away?*

What an odd way of putting it. Well, intriguing voice or not, Clem didn't wish her luck. If there was one thing he could do without, it was people, and especially people of the female variety.

It wasn't that he was a misogynist. The plain truth was that for all his accomplishments—seven degrees by the time he'd reached twenty-three, including bachelor's degrees in computer science, biology, mathematics and linguistics, master's degrees in chemistry and philosophy and a doctorate in chemical engineering, followed by two years at the prestigious Hastings Institute and an enviable position at Beauchamp Forbes International—the plain truth was that women intimidated him. They scared the hell out of him. When it came to social intercourse, he was a dropout.

The progeny of two brilliant minds, Clem often suspected his parents had produced him to test certain genetic theories of their own before going on to more interesting projects. He'd been pushed hard for the first few years by both parents, then left in the hands of tutors and nannies. He thought of them as teeth, hands and eyes, and for years he'd had bad dreams about a particularly stern individual who had ruled his life until he was seven, when he'd been fortunate enough to escape to boarding school.

At the age of thirteen he'd taken his first degree, but when it came to peer relationships, he hadn't even left the cradle. After a few painful and unsuccessful attempts to fit in, he'd given up trying. His work had benefited, though his personality and disposition had suffered.

Periodically, Hattie, his only other relative, would drag him off to a decent barber and a haberdasher, then fling him in the direction of some hapless female of her acquaintance, hoping nature would take its course.

He'd hoped so, too. God knows, he didn't enjoy being a hermit, and the only thirty-two-year-old male virgin extant.

For that matter, he couldn't even swear he was still a virgin, which only made matters worse. Oh, he had all the right inclinations, there was no doubt of that. But at the thought of doing anything about it, he invariably froze up and broke out in a cold sweat. Even if he'd been given the opportunity, he very much doubted that he'd have been able to rise to the occasion.

It was much simpler to avoid temptation. Not that it came his way too often. Now and then one of the newer female members of the staff would make an overture, but lately even that had ceased. He wasn't a particularly handsome man. His hair was too short, his glasses too thick, and he seemed to have developed a perpetual scowl somewhere along the line, probably from years spent hunched over a book or peering into things that bored the hell out of every woman he'd ever met outside the lab.

So he'd stopped trying. He'd let his beard grow, given up on the idea of trading in his glasses for contacts and accepted his fate. Periodically Malvern would remind him to get a haircut, and he always had it cut extra short so that he wouldn't have to go so often. Hattie deplored it. Personally, Clem considered it remarkably efficient for a man who had never been notably practical.

"There's got to be a woman somewhere who can speak your language," Hattie had cried in exasperation when her last effort had failed. It had been doomed from the start.

The woman, a potter, had been even more shy than he was, and she'd smelled like mildew.

"Give up, Hattie," he'd told her. "I can't dance with them, I can't talk to them—I haven't seen a film in years, and I didn't understand the last few I saw. I'm content the way I am. Why ruin an evening for some perfectly nice woman?"

"It's a waste, and I never could abide the waste of good raw material," Hattie had grumbled. "One of these days you'll fall in love, and then you'll wish you'd got in a bit of practice instead of wasting all your time in that stinky old laboratory."

Hattie had been married four times and had had numerous affairs, or so she claimed. "You're the romantic in the family, Aunt Hattie. If only you weren't my relative, I'd steal you away from your potting and painting and meddling," he'd once teased.

The funny thing was, he'd always been perfectly articulate with Hattie while he hadn't spoken more than a dozen words to his mother, a renowned physicist, in years. And with all other women, he was a total basket case.

Another phone call came the next day. Clement had just taught himself the fine art of rappeling, and was daubing an antiseptic cream on an assortment of scrapes and cuts. He let the answering machine take over. Having given up on hearing from Malvern or Hattie, he preferred to minimize the risk of having to converse with a stranger, and some of Hattie's friends were pretty strange.

It was the same woman, and she sounded, if anything, even more harried than the last time. "Look, Hattie—oh, drat this machine! I hate talking blind, but I know how much you hate to stop what you're doing to answer the phone. Anyway, this man I told you about? Well, I can't take it another day. He just won't quit, and I've told him— Oh, Lordy, here he comes!''

For a long time, Clement sat on the Turkish leather ottoman and pondered this latest message, his long legs sprawled across the dusty parquet floor. There was a considerably higher stress level this time. Whoever the woman was, she was really frightened. Of what? A man. What man? Why was she frightened? Was it because of something the man had done, or something she had done?

The small puzzle, on which he would never, under ordinary circumstances, have wasted a second thought, engaged his mind all through dinner, which consisted of sliced pineapple and Brunswick stew, eaten directly from the cans. Dishwashing was not one of his major accomplishments. There was a machine, but it was obscenely noisy and seemed wasteful for one person.

As for cooking, he could manage if he absolutely had to, but he preferred not to bother. There was a country store with a good supply of canned goods within comfortable hiking distance. He wouldn't starve.

The next call came the following morning just as he stepped out of the shower. Not bothering to dress as he was alone in the house, Clem sat on the foot of the bed and waited.

It was much like the others. She was frightened. She was wondering why Hattie hadn't once answered the phone, if she'd forgotten inviting her. She thought perhaps she should forget about visiting now and go on home.

''Yes, please,'' Clem muttered at the dusty black instrument. He was glad she'd decided not to come—otherwise he might have had to pick up the receiver and actually speak to her. He racked his mind for a clue as to who Hattie might have invited to visit, but if she'd been expecting a visitor, she had forgotten about it and forgotten to warn him, as well.

The last thing he needed was to have some semihysterical woman show up on his doorstep.

After an invigorating hike into town for milk and eggs, Clem tackled his daily stint of wood chopping. It was really rather surprising how quickly he'd taken to the unaccustomed physical regime. The only subject he'd ever done poorly on was physical education. Not the theoretical part, but the rest of it. He'd suffered from asthma as a child, and by the time he'd outgrown that, he'd shot up so that he was all uncoordinated limbs. Add to that a lack of motivation and an extreme astigmatism and it was no wonder he hadn't turned out to be a star athlete.

He took off his shirt—he'd brought along half a dozen, and he'd somehow managed to split a seam or pop a few buttons on each. Positioning the chunk of pine on its end, he lifted the ax over his head and brought it down in the exact center. The two halves fell apart, and he shoved them aside with his foot and reached for another section of firewood.

Martha glanced over her shoulder and spoke quickly into the phone, dismayed to find herself connected to the answering machine again. She was beginning to believe she'd dreamed up Hattie and the invitation to visit her on her way from Louisville to Winston-Salem. Darn it, if she weren't so anxious to get away without being followed, she'd forget the whole thing and go directly to Winston.

"Hattie, this sort of thing just doesn't *happen* to people like me. You probably think I'm imagining the whole thing, but I assure you I'm not. Look, if you're there, I'm coming as soon as I can get away without being followed, and if you're not, I'm probably coming anyway because I don't know what else to do. So if it's not convenient, then I'm sorry. You should answer your phone now and then so people would know what to plan on."

Hanging up the phone, she peered through the sparse crowd at Mack and Ida's Truck Stop. He was still there, pretending to be interested in a display of the owner's bowling trophies.

The creep! If Jack were here, he'd—

No, he wouldn't. Her brother Jack was many things, but foolhardy he was not. He'd likely tell her she was imagining the whole thing and he'd probably be right. Either that or he'd tell her to hand over her emerald and get on with finding herself a job and a place to stay. Again, he'd be right.

Briefly she considered asking one of the drivers at the counter for a ride into Winston. Or anyplace where she could catch a bus. But at this point she was tired and edgy— edgy, nothing, she was just plain scared! And the last thing she wanted to do was to climb into an eighteen wheeler with another stranger. She'd had enough of those.

Hattie was a known quantity. They'd been friends, despite the differences in age and background, since the well-known art teacher had taught a course in watercolor at the Yadkinville Community Center. As soon as Martha had been old enough to drive, she'd taken the truck once a week and driven to Winston to study basic drawing, clay sculpture, landscape and more watercolor. If Hattie taught it, Martha took it. The two of them had developed a lasting friendship that had continued through intermittent letters even after Martha had dropped out of school and gone to Kentucky to look after her brother's children when his wife had died.

Martha had really looked forward to seeing her mentor again, but it was beginning to seem less and less likely. Hattie seemed to have forgotten all about her offer to meet

Martha at the last stop on the tour and drive her to Cat Creek for a few days' visit. Which was rather unfortunate, as she desperately needed a friend at the moment. The trouble was, if she walked into a bus station and bought a ticket for Winston-Salem, Hubert Odwell would be right on her heels. Sooner or later he'd catch up with her, because he was greedy and unscrupulous and he'd obviously pegged her right off for a pushover. He was probably right, too, she thought with a sigh.

Along with twenty-three other amateur rock hounds, Martha climbed aboard the chartered bus, glancing quickly over her shoulder as she mounted the high step. There he was, standing beside his rusty blue sedan picking his teeth as casually as if he hadn't followed them all the way from Hiddenite to Black Mountain, stopping at every site along the way.

He'd claimed to be some sort of an expert, and a few of her fellow tour members had taken their finds to him to be evaluated. Martha hadn't, but only because she was reasonably certain she'd found nothing of any value. Nor was she expecting to. She'd simply been having fun, relaxing for the first time in years.

But that was before she'd found the emerald.

She was beginning to wish she'd never found the darned thing, but she had, and she was too stubborn to give in to that creep! It was just her luck that Odwell had happened to be with her when she'd found it. He'd approached her several times, as he had most of the others, seeming to have a decided preference for women. Maybe he thought they were better gem hunters than men. Or luckier. More gullible, probably.

"Hey, you're not giving up, are you, little lady? I told you most of these places was salted. I'll show you where the good stuff is, I got my car right over there."

"No, thanks, I'll stick with the group. I'm perfectly happy with what I've found." And she was. While once she might have envisioned discovering a fortune in gems—what child living so near the mountains of North Carolina hadn't heard fantastic tales of fabulous sapphires and emeralds plowed up in a field?—she'd long since outgrown that stage. Reality had a way of dulling even the most vivid imagination.

"You give up too easy, little lady. Don't be that way—ol' Hubert can show you a place where you can really strike it rich."

"Look, would you *stop* calling me little lady? And would you stop following me around? Go find the Hope Diamond or something. I've got a headache and I'd like to be left alone!" Normally the most peaceable of women, Martha had been pushed beyond her limit. She'd swung around to confront the man, only to find him right on her heels. To keep from colliding with him, she'd thrown out her arms, and her shoulder bag had slipped off her arm and struck a tree, scattering her belongings in a wide arc.

"Oh, blast! Now look what you made me do!" She'd dropped to her knees on the gravel and leaned over a low barricade. If she'd been ten feet further to the right, she'd have lost everything over a sheer drop. As it was, the contents of her purse had landed in leaf-strewn mud, under scrubby bushes and gnarled roots.

Her wallet was closest, and she'd snatched it and rammed it into her bag. Then she'd begun collecting her address book, her hair brush, sunglasses, Chapstick and an assortment of other paraphernalia. She'd found her tube of tea-rose hand cream under a witch-hobble plant, her pen caught in a clump of snakeroot and then she'd started searching for the matching mechanical pencil.

Virgil Jones, a man she'd considered herself practically engaged to until two months ago, had given her that set. Not

a wildly romantic gift, but then she evidently wasn't the sort
to bring out the romantic side of any man. Certainly Virgil
hadn't thought so. If she'd been smarter, she might have
tumbled earlier to the fact that Virgil hadn't considered her
his equal, either mentally, socially or in any other way.

"Need some help?" She'd felt Odwell's hand on her upturned bottom and swung around to glare at him just as her
fingers closed around a gritty-feeling cylinder.

"No, thank you," she'd said through clenched teeth.
"I've found it. If you want to help me, just go away and
leave me alone, will you?" She brushed off her pencil and
started to drop it into her purse when it dawned on her that
her pencil was much more slender, much smoother—and it
had a clip on the side, not an irregular lump.

Slowly, she'd opened her hand. And then she'd gasped.
The rock lying across her palm had been a green crystal
partially encased in dull matrix, its surface rough and coated
with mud. Even so, there'd been no mistaking its brilliant
green purity.

"Hey, hold on a minute, what have we got here, honey?"
Odwell had moved closer, reaching for her hand. "Looks
like we made us a lucky find, don't it?"

Acting instinctively, Martha had shoved the crystal into
her purse and clamped the worn leather satchel under her
arm. "*We* found nothing. Thanks to you, I lost part of a pen
and pencil set that was given to me by someone I—I hold
very dear!"

Dear? Since their last disastrous evening together, when
he'd told her that she was a nice girl and that she'd make
some lucky man a fine housewife—*housewife!*—she'd held
Virgil Jones about as dear as she held weevils in the pantry.

"I'll give you ten dollars for it, sight unseen."

"My *pencil*?"

Odwell's pudgy red face had taken on a less genial cast. "Yeah, your pencil, honey. You know what I mean—that chunk of pretty green glass you just hid in your bag."

"Oh, for pity's sake," she'd exclaimed nervously, "it's just a—a souvenir. You don't find emeralds in a parking lot."

"Around these parts, you find 'em most anywhere. And I was with you when you found it, so half of whatever we can get for it belongs to me."

The man was crazy! Edging toward the bus, Martha had watched him warily. "That's ridiculous. Whatever I found—and I'm not saying I found anything, mind you—belongs to me. If you'd seen it and picked it up, I certainly wouldn't—"

"A hundred. That's my top offer, lady, and I'm only doing that because I took a real liking to your looks."

Martha might not be the world's most experienced woman, but she was no fool. Her looks were about as exciting as day-old bread. Average height, average build, average reddish-blond hair, brows and lashes. Her most striking feature was probably the pale brown colour of her eyes, and that only because they matched the million or so freckles that covered every exposed part of her body.

"Huh!" she'd snorted, warily edging toward the door of the bus. That door had better have a lock on the inside, because if it didn't she was going to sit on the horn until someone came to her rescue.

"Just leave me alone, will you? It's nothing!"

"Lemme see. I know minerals, and I can tell if we got ourselves a genu-wine emerald or just a pretty paperweight."

She'd struggled with the door—how the devil did these things work, anyway? And then, to her monumental relief, she'd heard the others converging on the bus, wearily comparing sunburned arms and the results of their afternoon dig.

"Ready to head for the motel?" Oscar, the driver, was a real expert when it came to maneuvering the lumbering bus around hairpin turns, but he wasn't the least bit interested in dirtying his hands in the hopes of finding a fortune in precious gems.

"I'll see you later, honey," Hubert Odwell had promised, and Martha, shivering in earnest, had tried to ignore him.

That was how it had started. She'd waited until her roommate had gone to sleep to call Hattie, but all she'd gotten was the answering machine with her friend's zany instructions. Which hadn't been what she'd needed at that point.

The tour, which had gotten her back to North Carolina from Louisville, Kentucky for half the regular bus fare, thanks to a friend at the travel agency and a last-minute, no-refund cancellation, had been a real pleasure up until then.

And dammit, she hated to be forced to cut short her first real vacation in so many years because of a sleazy character who was probably more of a nuisance than a genuine threat. By tomorrow, she told herself again and again, he'd have forgotten her and latched onto some other poor soul.

Only he hadn't. And seeing that rusty blue sedan turn up at stop after stop had only increased her nervousness.

The tour plan had been to visit eight different mining areas as they worked their way southwest, more or less following the Blue Ridge Mountains but coming down for the most promising locations. Such as the one where she'd found the emerald. The tour was to end in Asheville, where she would have been met by Hattie, and they would have spent a few days together at Hattie's home in what she'd laughingly referred to as the suburbs of Cat Creek.

Only everything was going wrong. First there was Hubert Odwell, and then she'd been unable to reach Hattie. And now she didn't know quite what to do.

Fortunately, Clement's sense of hearing was considerably more acute than his sense of sight. Because he'd lost his glasses again. It happened with depressing regularity whenever he was doing anything active, which was most of the time, lately. Bent over a microscope in a climate-controlled environment, they were perfectly secure, but on a sweating face when he was wielding an ax, nothing was safe.

The vehicle, whatever it was, was barely up to the strain of such a steep grade, from the sound of it. Tires slid on gravel, and he could hear pebbles striking a surface far below the road—a drop of some hundred or so meters.

The road ended at this place, so it couldn't be a passerby. Which could mean only one thing—Hattie was home. Praise Paracelsus! As much as he'd enjoyed it, he wasn't sure he could survive much longer. Considering he'd never even been to summer camp, it was a wonder he'd managed to do as well as he had.

Which had no doubt been the whole point of Hattie's experiment.

The truck stopped directly in front of the house, disgorging a single passenger. Either that or the pink wraith that moved away from the large white vehicle was a ghost, and while, scientist or not, Clement didn't dismiss anything as impossible, he rather hoped it would turn out to be the corporeal entity of his great-aunt.

Shirtless, ax in hand, he made his way cautiously as far as he dared. "Hattie?"

Unfortunately, the truck roared off at that moment, and her reply was lost. She was obviously waiting for him to fetch her luggage, but he didn't dare go forth, not until she'd helped him locate his spectacles. He'd slid down too many embankments, tripped on too many rocks and roots to risk moving far in his present condition. "I was beginning to wonder if you'd deserted me altogether. I'll get your luggage if you'll find my glasses for me. I think they're over near the woodpile."

Again her answer was lost in the noise of the departing truck—a delivery van of some sort, from the shape of it. "How was Greece? By the way, you're expecting a visitor. She called several times, and I gather she'll be arriving any time now. Thank God you're back, because if I had to deal with this weirdo, I'd probably end up crawling into that hole in the ground you call your kiln."

The dim figure at the far edge of his vision hadn't moved. Nor had she spoken. Or if she had, Clement hadn't heard her. That was when it occurred to him that something was definitely out of kilter here. If she wasn't a ghost and she wasn't Hattie, then the only other person he could think of who might be arriving on this forsaken slab of rock was—was . . .

Oh, God, not her. Not some hysterical female stranger, and him not even able to see her! He could feel the hair on his arms prickle as his skin tightened. Every muscle in his body contracted. In fact, contracted with considerably more efficiency than many of them had ever manifested in the past. All those hours spent climbing, hiking and wood chopping had evidently reconstructed him to a certain extent, at least physically.

But he was still so much dead meat when it came to actually interacting with a strange woman. She would have to go. That was all there was to it, because he wasn't up to dealing with her, and he damned well wasn't up to explaining why!

"Hattie, where the devil are you?" he muttered under his breath.

Hefting the ax, Clem started toward the fuzzy pink figure, feeling his way cautiously over the rough terrain. The sooner they reached an understanding as to who was going and who was staying, the better he would like it. He'd been feeling pretty good about himself, all things considered, and then she'd had to come along and ruin it.

Two
———

Martha stared uncertainly at the tall, bearded man in the rumpled white pants. His bare chest was patterned with dark hair, as were his arms. He had large, capable-looking hands. One of which happened to be holding an ax.

Her pulse tripped into double time. Drawing a deep, calming breath, she glanced at the cloud of dust thrown up by the bread truck that was roaring off down the grade. If there was still the slightest chance of catching it . . .

There wasn't. She turned to face the bearded stranger. "What have you done wi— Where's Hattie? Oh, no, you don't!" She held up a hand, palm outward. "Not one step closer, do you hear me? I'm not kidding. I've got a voice like a fire siren, and I promise you, I'll scream if you . . ." She swallowed hard.

The stranger held his ground, his face—or as much of it as she could see—expressionless. There was something about him—about the way he was looking at her. As if he weren't quite right in the head, or his eyes wouldn't focus or something.

This was the last straw. Dammit, she just wasn't cut out for this kind of thing! Some women thrived on adventure, but her biggest adventure had been winning the fat calf contest at the county fair.

It had to be that green rock she'd found—the thing must have a curse on it. First that creep Hubert Odwell and now this wild, ax-wielding mountain man.

She mustn't antagonize him. In spite of appearances to the contrary, he might be entirely harmless as long as she didn't get him excited. "Mrs. Davenport is expecting me," she said carefully. "I'm a friend. *Friend*," she stressed, as if trying to convince a headhunter to lay down his poison blowgun.

Oh, glory, she was actually shaking in her mud-stained Nikes.

Clement recognized the voice. He also recognized the fact that the poor creature was still terrified of something, and that bothered him. Had the man who was terrorizing her followed her here? He hadn't noticed anyone else, but there could've been an army out there, and as long as they remained silent, he would never know it.

She needed reassurance. He could offer her that much, at least. "You're safe here. Come closer."

"Uh, no, thanks. I think I'll just mosey on back down the mountain and call Hattie later on. She's obviously busy on some project or other—all I've been getting is her answering machine." Martha's eyes widened as the man took a shambling step toward her. He was roughly the size of a telephone booth, and for all his soft, oddly hesitant voice, there was nothing soft or hesitant about that ax. She glanced at her toilet case, which was perched precariously atop her battered old suitcase. Her emerald was wrapped in a tissue and buried under a layer of tea-rose talcum powder. She could dash past him, snatch it and—

To heck with her emerald. She could move faster unencumbered. With a lot of luck and a head start, she might even be able to outrun him, although those legs of his were long and looked uncomfortably powerful. Still, she was no slouch—she hadn't spent the past three years keeping up with a pair of hyperactive youngsters for nothing.

"Er, um . . . mumble, mumble, mumble," said the man, and Martha took a step backward and felt her foot slide on a bed of small pebbles.

"Where's Hattie?" she challenged once more.

"You're the same one. You're still frightened."

"I am not," she denied automatically. Boldly, she met his eyes, hoping to intimidate him into backing off. Before she realized it, she was caught. Trapped by—by what? A pair of blue eyes? She'd seen blue eyes before, she scoffed.

Yes, but never that sparkly, intense shade of blue. And never with that deep-set quality of—

Of what? Vulnerability? That was ridiculous! She'd never seen a less vulnerable man in her life.

"Yes," the blue-eyed man said calmly, and she scrambled desperately to remember what they'd been talking about. "It was fear I heard in your voice each time. It's still there."

All right, so she was a bit uneasy and he knew it. That couldn't be helped. His own voice was certainly calm enough. Deep and quiet, and sort of . . . hmm. It was only her imagination that made it sound like the sort of voice Virgil called "cultured." The word had always reminded her of buttermilk.

Okay, so maybe there was a brain cell under all that hair. The brightest ones were sometimes the first to go sailing off the deep end. Even those from the very best families, like that case in the news just last month. In spite of what Virgil claimed, money, education and breeding were no guarantee of anything except membership in a few stodgy clubs.

Clement could feel her uneasiness, even though he couldn't see it. He ventured a step closer, then another one, because she was standing entirely too close to the far side of the drive. "Hattie's in—uh, she's still in Greece," he said, thankful he had taken time to familiarize himself with this portion of the property. "I thought you were she. That is, I thought the truck was Hattie. I mean, mumble, mumble, mumble."

Exhaling, he felt a trickle of sweat form in the hollow of his cheek just below the beard line. He shoved a hand roughly through his hair, leaving one dark shock to flop forward onto his brow.

Actually, he was doing pretty well, considering that he couldn't see more than a foot beyond the tip of his nose. He'd sounded almost coherent there for a minute, too. Evidently, his social skills had improved right along with his physical prowess.

"You know Hattie Davenport?" She sounded almost suspicious.

"Great-nephew. Paternal grandmother's—um, sister. You know."

The blur became a bit less blurred as he moved a step closer. He halted. While he was increasingly curious as to her looks, he had always preferred that his personal space remain inviolate. Unfortunately, handicapped as he was by his temporary lack of vision, he might be forced to compromise.

The woman stepped back again, much too close to the edge of the drop, and Clem braced himself for what must be done. Personal space or no, he could hardly allow her to fall off the mountain. Besides, he needed to see who he was dealing with. If he ever located his glasses again he was going to weld the damned things onto his head! He couldn't see to split wood without them, but as soon as he worked up a sweat, they slid off.

"You mentioned losing your glasses?" the woman said, and he wondered if she were telepathic. Testing him for weakness, more likely. He had mentioned having lost his glasses when he'd thought she was Hattie.

A sloucher by habit, Clem drew himself up to his full six feet four, frowning in the general direction of the pink wraith. Why was she testing him? Surely she didn't distrust him. He didn't expect her to be drawn to him, but any fool could see that he was perfectly harmless.

Squinting against the late-afternoon glare, he did what had to be done. "Barto. C. Cornelius Barto."

That should settle matters quickly enough. His latest piece on bipolarization of mutagens had come out just last month in the *Hastings Quarterly*, and before that there'd been that paper on the philosophic rationalization for biogenetic engineering. Clement had never been one to boast of his accomplishments, but if this woman didn't recognize his credentials, his obvious respectability, then it was up to him to enlighten her.

No response. Not a word. All right, so perhaps she'd missed it. Some people's taste in reading matter—Hattie's, for instance—didn't run to scientific journals. "Well?" he demanded. It was her turn now. Who was she? How long was she planning to stay?

She took another step back, and Clem, with uncharacteristic impatience and total disregard for any possible danger, acted. Praying he wouldn't trip on the rock-ribbed, root-threaded terrain, he lunged forward and slung the ax around behind her, cutting off her retreat.

Over his own accelerated heartbeat, he could hear the erratic sound of her breathing. A series of small, shallow gasps, then nothing.

Thunder rumbled in the distance. A wren scolded noisily. A gust of wind stirred the dust, sending down a shower of colorful confetti from various deciduous trees. Clement was oblivious to everything except for the woman he was holding pressed against him with the flat side of his ax. His nostrils flared as he drew in her scent. Faintly sweet, faintly spicy, it was a vaguely familiar scent. It smelled . . . warm.

The scientist in him shuddered at the crossing of sensory data, while another part of him, a part he scarcely recognized, stirred, sat up and began to examine the infinite possibilities of such a mixture.

Reaching up, his hand struck a bit of warm, firm flesh and hung on. He recognized the delicate shape of humerus, clavicle and scapula and closed his fingers firmly over her shoulder. She was rigid. Paralyzed with . . . fear? Dear Lord, what did she think he was going to do to her, bite off her head? He'd probably saved her life.

"Exhale," he ordered, and she did, in a long, shuddering gust. "Now inhale." She gasped. "Slowly!" he barked, and gradually her breathing began to level out. "That's better. Now turn your head to the light so that I can see you better."

He leaned closer, until his nose was practically touching hers. Until he could see the widening of pale amber eyes surrounded by remarkably dense gold-tipped copper lashes. The sclera was clear, almost blue-white. While he watched, her pupils began to contract, then quickly expanded until all but a rim of the iris was hidden.

Hmm, interesting response, he thought with slightly less than clinical objectivity. Considerably more distracted than usual, Clem, through force of habit, set about cataloging the remaining physical data before him. If the thought occurred to him that his reaction was totally out of character he dismissed it. Personal space forgotten, he clutched her shoulder, holding her pressed against him with the ax as he attempted to assay her face.

Only gradually did he become aware of the soft mewing sound issuing from her throat. He wasn't hurting her. Hands that could hold a butterfly without ruffling a wing would never hurt a woman. All the same, he took care.

How exciting were the complex curves of a woman's facial structure. Far less angular than his own. And not only her facial structure, for he was becoming increasingly aware of her *femaleness* pressing against him. A certain softness in the mammary region . . . the distinctive conformation of the pelvic girdle . . .

Suddenly, Clem stiffened. To his dismay, his mind wasn't the only part of him that noticed the difference. His body was starting to react with rather amazing enthusiasm. Praise Paracelsus! What a time to get—what was that term he'd heard recently?—turned on. He was struck with remorse when he noticed her eyes widening with panic.

"Please," she whispered.

Frantically, he sought the words to reassure her. "Oh. Yes. That is . . . yes," he stammered. Still holding her with one hand, he dropped the ax. They were mere inches from the edge. He'd paced off the distance in case of just such an occurrence as this.

"No, not precisely like this," he qualified in a distracted murmur. Clement often spoke his thoughts aloud. Or fragments of those thoughts. No one, to his knowledge, had ever been frightened by the sound of his voice before.

The woman trembling under his hands was obviously terrified. "Would you please let me go?" she whispered.

"I'll leave right now, and I promise you, I won't tell anyone where you are. I *promise*."

Clement frowned. Nothing she'd said made sense. Leaving was impractical, and revealing his presence here was irrelevant. Fear, he supposed, could manifest itself as confusion. Solicitously, he drew her away from the edge of the drop, allowing one hand to linger comfortingly on her arm. Her biceps were slender, but surprisingly firm. How remarkable—he would have thought that biceps would be genderless, but hers felt decidedly female.

On a subliminal level, Clement was aware that he was reacting in a thoroughly unscientific way to this unexpected stimulus. "I gave you my name. You didn't."

"My name? It's M—Martha. Eberly."

Of course. She'd given her name when she'd called, but he'd been more interested in the quality of her voice than in her identity. "Martha," he repeated, testing the feel of it on his tongue. He decided it was a fine name, a womanly name, and was unaware of having reacted in a completely unscientific manner. "Come inside, Martha. The water's cold."

Martha stood her ground, her eyes never leaving his. Dimly, she remembered hearing something about not looking a strange dog directly in the eyes, but she couldn't help herself. His were mesmerizing.

However, if he thought he was going to drown her, he was sadly mistaken. She hadn't escaped from Hubert Odwell only to let herself fall into the hands of some overgrown fruitcake with wild-blue-yonder eyes and dubious intentions. "Yes, of course—inside. You go first and I'll follow just as soon as I get my things," she said in her best Aunt-Marty-knows-best tone of voice.

What she'd follow was that bread truck—and so fast he wouldn't see her for the dust! What had he called himself?

C. Cornelius Something-or-Other? Powerfully pompous
name for such a ragtag looking creature. And while he might
not be precisely balmy, she wasn't about to hang around
long enough to find out what his problem was. Any man
who came at her with an ax, even if he only used it to keep
her from falling off a mountain, was definitely not her first
choice for a companion.

Never mind that sexy voice of his that for one split second had made her insides curl up and purr. Never mind that
for a single, solitary moment, she'd had the wildest urge to
throw herself into those naked, sweaty arms and beg shelter from steep cliffs, sleazy con men and all the rest of life's
miserable little surprises. Martha *knew* what her problem
was, and C. Cornelius What's-it was definitely not the solution.

While she was making up her mind how best to slip past
him, he turned away, tripped over her bags, then, after
apologizing to thin air, swung them up as if both were full
of feathers. Her big bag alone weighed a ton. She'd
crammed it with practically everything she owned, except
for her summer things, which were being shipped as soon as
she had an address. As for her toilet case, it was mostly filled
with rocks. She'd kept every tiny, drab pebble from every
bucket of dirt she'd bought over the past two days, dumping them in with her toothbrush, her curling iron and an
unopened bag of disposable razors. Not to mention her box
of tea-rose scented talcum powder, which just happened to
conceal her ticket to future security.

C. C. What's-his-name smiled at her. At least she hoped
it was a smile. Hiding behind all those wild whiskers, it
could easily have been a grimace.

"Come," he ordered.

Come? As in, me Tarzan, you Jane? Marty stifled a nervous urge to giggle. Really, this whole thing was turning into

a farce. Ax or no, the poor man really did seem harmless enough. He was probably just some weird eccentric—Hattie had always attracted unusual people. Granted, he'd scared the socks off her, but he hadn't actually hurt her, and goodness knows he'd had every opportunity. He could've shoved her off the cliff or chopped her up into itty-bitty pieces, but he hadn't. All he'd done was to hold her too closely and stare at her as if he'd never seen a woman before. She knew she wasn't looking her best today, but did he have to look at her that way?

Warily, she began to follow him across the graveled road that curved around to end at a pair of closed garage doors. Dead end. No through traffic. Probably no traffic at all, she thought sinkingly, as hope of hitching a ride out of here began to fade.

Stumbling over an exposed rock, she recovered herself and continued to follow him, not knowing what else to do at this point. She no longer deluded herself into thinking she could run all the way down the mountain. It was late in the day—the sun would have set before she'd got halfway to the main road, and she had no real desire to be walking along the narrow shoulder of one of these twisting mountain blacktops after dark.

Halfway across the steep, wooded yard, she put a hand to her temple and rubbed absently. It was tension, pure tension. No wonder her head hurt. It was just a wonder that was all that hurt.

Come to think of it, it wasn't, but the backache was something she'd brought on herself, leaning over all those buckets of dirt. When she'd thought about rock hunting, she'd always pictured herself using a chisel and hammer or picking up dazzling gems in clear mountain streams. Not pawing through buckets full of gritty mud.

Glasses or no, C. Cornelius was as surefooted as a mountain goat, Martha thought sourly. Slogging tiredly along several yards behind him, she frowned at the way his lower back flexed with each step, like a well-oiled bronze machine. There was a tiny patch of dark hair just above his dirty white pants on either side of his spine and a shadow where his spine disappeared under his waistband.

And then her gaze migrated a few inches downward. He must know those pants of his were indecently snug. Evidently he thought he was giving her a treat. Hmph! She wouldn't give those seams of his much of a chance if he bent over too many times!

It occurred to her that she was indulging in precisely what she'd often accused her friend Linda at the travel agency of doing. Man watching. Of all the ridiculous things—she must be slightly hysterical. Linda would've liked this one. Great buns, she would've said. A real hunk, hair and all.

Frankly, Martha had always preferred a few brains and a modicum of manners, but then, look where it had got her.

He was getting ahead of her. "Hold on, there, where are you going with my bags?" He was halfway up the stone steps, halfway to the wide, gingerbread porch that was guarded by a pair of mossy concrete gargoyles. She challenged him. "Well?"

Lowering her bags to the steps, he said, "Inside."

"I never said I was staying. Where's Hattie?"

"I told you—Greece."

"What if I don't believe you? Maybe this isn't even her house. Maybe you aren't who you said you were. How do I know?"

He came down the steps, stopping on the bottom one. "It is. I am. Where will you go?"

Her shoulders slumped. Where indeed? It was late—soon it would be dark. Not to mention cold. She was miles from civilization and she didn't know a single soul west of Winston-Salem, which was at least three hours away, even if she'd had the means to get there. And to top it off, Hubert Odwell could already have discovered that she was no longer on the bus and be doubling back, asking around.

"All right, but just for tonight," she said grudgingly.

He didn't smile, he didn't speak, he didn't do anything but stare. Marty armed herself with a description in case it became necessary later on. Tall. *Really* tall and bearded, of course, his hair probably lighter than it looked because it was wet with sweat. Dark brown, she'd call it, not black. His clothes, such as they were, were filthy. He needed a bath, too, because there were dirt stains on his arms.

On the other hand, he'd smelled clean enough. In fact, there was something quite pleasant about the way he smelled. Like whatever all those evergreen trees were—sort of resiny, crisp and masculine.

Oh, boy, she was *really* losing her grip! "I'm not sure this is a good idea," she hedged. "I mean, if Hattie isn't even home, maybe I'd better come back some other time." Plastering what she hoped was a convincing smile on her face, she waited for him to offer to drive her to the nearest bus station.

"You'll get wet."

On the point of wondering if the man had a water fixation, Marty heard a crack of thunder that seemed to echo forever. He'd known it was going to rain. These primitive types could probably smell it. And while she still didn't feel any too good about entrusting herself to a stranger—especially a nonverbal, ax-swinging, half naked stranger—she honestly didn't know what else she could do at this point. Maybe he really was a relative of Hattie's. He was probably all right, she told herself in an attempt at reassurance. A bit off the wall, but perfectly safe. Hattie was slightly flaky, but she'd never have gone off and left her home in the care of someone she didn't trust.

A great-nephew? Maybe, maybe not. Hattie had mentioned a nephew once, someone important at Cal Tech. And of course there was the boy whose portrait she'd painted years and years ago. Martha had had a monumental crush on that portrait the summer she was—what? Fifteen? Sixteen? Thereabouts, at least. She could still get a rush just thinking about it, or she would have if she hadn't been so darned tired.

"Well?" she demanded, shifting her weight to the other foot.

"Yes?"

He wasn't going to give an inch. Maybe English wasn't his first language. Maybe he—oh, what the hell! "Okay, I'm stuck here for tonight, but first thing tomorrow, I'm calling a cab."

Thank the Lord for that emerald. She had a hunch she might need it to get her out of hock after this miserable adventure.

Clement smiled. He wasn't a smiler by nature, but he'd thought it might put her at ease. "Coffee," he said. She'd decided to come inside. Good. Because he couldn't very well have left her outside, and he hadn't the slightest notion of how to get her moving again.

"You said the magic word," she told him in the voice he'd once thought of as breathless. It was more of a huskiness— an uncertain quality. Just as Clem was leading the way up the old stone steps lightning split the sky, and he hastened to reassure her. "Lightning rods."

"I know, Hattie sent me a picture when she first moved up here. I thought the house looked like a wedding cake."

"No, it's a house."

"I didn't mean it literally," she said dryly.

"Oh. Yes."

Actually, with a bath, some decent clothes and a marathon session with a barber, he wouldn't be half bad, she told herself as he let her into a rather gloomy foyer, with a curving stairway on one side and a velvet-draped arch on the other. However, if he could provide her with a cup of coffee and a place to catch her breath until she could find a way to get out of here, he could shave his head and wear a hula skirt for all she cared.

"I have food, too."

"How nice," she said with a weak smile. She would humor him. He was trying to offer hospitality.

"You can sleep in my bed."

"Whoa! Hold it right there, friend." Poor Hattie. If this really was one of her nephews, no wonder she'd kept the poor soul under wraps. He was certainly nothing like the one in the portrait. Hattie had once described that one as a gentle soul who was too brainy for his own good and misunderstood by most ordinary people. Martha had had to hide an overwhelming desire to snatch up the portrait and shield it from a cold, cruel world. The feeling had persisted even after she'd learned that the subject had an I.Q. that rivaled the national debt and was stashed away in a brain trust somewhere up north.

"Um—sleep," she said. "Well, really, maybe I'll just have a cup of coffee and be on my way." Fine, just great, but where? How?

"Hattie's room is closed. Damp. I don't mind damp."

Ushering her inside, Clement heard his guest exhale noisily. He'd forgotten the altitude. While it wasn't all that high, some people might find it a problem, particularly if they came from somewhere near sea level. "Seashore?" he asked.

"See *what*?"

For two cents he would give up trying to communicate with her. She was evidently no better at it than he was. Strange woman, he mused, setting her luggage on the stair landing. But then, what did he know about women? Perhaps they were all strange, and he'd just never noticed. It wouldn't be the first time he'd completely overlooked the obvious while in pursuit of the obscure.

"Water first? It's ice cold. High in mineral content, but harmless. Or coffee? Without my glasses, I don't do that very well, but there's food."

By George, he was becoming positively garrulous! He only hoped she wouldn't be bored by all this chattering. Personally, he was rather impressed with himself.

Martha. Martha Eberly. Interesting arrangement of syllables. But the most remarkable thing of all was that something about this woman was bringing out a whole new facet of his personality, one he had never suspected he possessed. A savoir faire, so to speak.

Clem smiled broadly, feeling happy, relaxed and closer to confident than he ever remembered feeling outside his own territory. "Sit," he said. "You can read labels. Wait right here—don't go away, I'll be right back."

Read labels?

He was back in less than a minute, his arms loaded with cans. Some he could recognize by the shape—the canned ham and sardines. But Martha Eberly might not care for sardines. Perhaps she'd prefer the pâté. There were crackers somewhere that were probably not too stale.

Perhaps the crab soup with sherry... "There's wine to drink," he remembered suddenly. "I don't know about what goes with what. I seldom bother." He never bothered unless he was out with Hattie, and then she selected, but only after a long discussion with the wine steward, which,

ften as not, ended in that gentleman's agreeing to sit for
er.

With a smile, his second in mere minutes—gad, he must
e delirious!—Clem dumped the lot onto an inlaid walnut
able and waited for her to choose. A guest for dinner. *His*
uest! By damn, but he liked the sound of that. Last year
e'd invited a visiting biophysicist to an awards dinner, but
he'd preferred to attend alone. So had he, actually. It had
aken him more than a week to get up his nerve to ask, and
e'd only done it because Ed Malvern, his secretary, had
mplied that, as senior member of the team, it was his duty.

But this was different. Never once had he considered en-
ertaining a woman in his home. He maintained a small
partment near B.F.I., but he spent very little time there, as
here was a comfortable cot in his office, a shower adjoin-
ng his lab and food and drink machines in the basement.

Standing awkwardly beside the table, he continued to
vait, occasionally shifting his weight from one foot to the
ther. He rammed his hands into his pockets and then took
hem out again; crossed his arms and then uncrossed them.
Ie'd give anything to be able to see her. She hadn't spoken
word. Was she waiting for him to tell her what to do?

It was too dark! "More light?" he asked eagerly, and
witched on a tassled floor lamp. "If you don't see any-
hing you like, I could, um, go to the grocers. Only he closes
t six, and it's a four-mile walk."

"Don't you have a car?"

"I don't drive."

"You don't drive?" She sounded amazed.

"I learned once. I had little natural aptitude."

"That doesn't usually stop people."

Clem considered her words and found that he concurred.
Iattie, for instance, could barely see over the dashboard,

and she was constantly using her hands to talk when sh drove, pointing out landscapes she'd like to paint.

The silence stretched out uncomfortably while Clemer waited for Martha to tell him what she wanted to eat. H stroked his beard. Beards, he had discovered, had their uses one of which was to provide a barrier behind which to hide Just now, his was also providing an outlet for nervous e ergy.

Was she waiting for something? Was it his turn to speak He'd made a statement; they'd concurred; end of discus sion. As there was still one outstanding question on the ta ble, the next move was hers. If she didn't make it, he hadn' the faintest idea of what to do or say next.

"Do you need to use the bathroom?" A stroke of ge nius, he prided himself. Just when the conversation had be gun to languish.

"What? Oh—please."

She got to her feet. He could see her shape, her colo shades of pink, coppery on top and paler down below. Pin feet.

"Well? Do you have a tourist map, or am I on my own?'

Clement seldom recognized sarcasm. This time, he di Whereas, ordinarily, it wouldn't have bothered him, agai this time it did. "I'm sorry. I'll show you," he said with a the dignity he could muster, which was considerably mor than he knew.

He took her arm. He was not a toucher—never had been Nor had he been the recipient of many touches, other tha inadvertent ones. He was conscious of a strange, pricklin sensation that spread from the small area where his han came in contact with her arm. He wasn't at all sure wha caused it—even less sure if he liked it. It felt as if it might b dangerous if allowed to continue unchecked.

"How much can you see without your glasses?"

They were passing through a dining room that looked like a cross between a studio and a flea market. Clement made his way easily, being familiar with the hazards. "Considering the degree of refraction necessary to—"

"I'm not interested in degrees or refractions, I only wanted to know if you're totally blind or not. I hate to go off and leave you here alone if you're really helpless. Don't you have another pair of glasses?"

"No, I'm not. And yes, I do, but they're back in Winston-Salem in my office."

They came to a halt before a door near the back of a narrow hallway. "Can't you send for them?"

"Yes."

"Well, have you?" He detected exasperation in her tone and wondered why his lack of vision should matter to her.

"No."

One hand on the painted china doorknob, Martha stared at him, wondering if he were deliberately trying to tie her brain into knots. Was it some kind of psycho thing he was pulling? "Is it that you *can't* talk, or that you just don't choose to? Listen, C. Cornelius Thingamabob, or whoever you claim to be, I'm too tired to play your childish little games. This was supposed to be my vacation—well, sort of, anyway. And for days all I've done is ride in smelly, noisy buses, dig in buckets full of dirt and sleep in crummy motels with a woman in the next bed who snores like a freight train. I haven't eaten since yesterday, and my head hurts, and I don't care who you are or what you've done, just leave me alone!"

Dead silence reigned for perhaps a full minute. Martha wondered if he were going to kill her on the spot or wait until she'd washed some of the road dust off her face and hands. And then he began to speak, and she could have curled up and died unassisted.

"I'm sorry. Yes, I can talk, but I'm not very good at it
The problem is partially genetic, partially environmental,
suspect. It's too late to do much about it now. I—I'm sorry,
Martha. Tell me what I can do to make you comfortable
and I'll do it and then get out of your way. Eat. Stay the
night. Stay as long as you like. I won't bother you again.''

Three

———

Martha stayed in the bathroom as long as she dared. She eyed the sleek, putty-colored shower unit longingly, wishing she could step inside and let the water flow over her body until all her worries and all the dirt she'd collected from traveling dusty roads at breakneck speed swirled away together down the drain.

Instead, she finger-combed her hair and sleeked the front away from her face with damp hands. Neat but not gaudy, she summed up. That had been her mother's highest accolade. Martha had worn gingham and starched pinafores when every other child in her class had worn jeans. She'd had her face scrubbed raw the first time she'd dared smear on a daub of lipstick, and after that she'd had the good sense to wait until she got to school to paint her face.

Neat but not gaudy. Ignoring the mirror, she dried her hands. Neat she could manage pretty well, at least on most occasions. As for gaudy, that was still her secret ambition, but at the moment she'd settle for neat.

Outside the bathroom, which Hattie had enlarged from a tiny powder room, Clement waited for his guest to emerge. He'd promised to leave her alone, and he would, but first he needed to show her where he'd put her bags.

"Upstairs," he said the minute the door opened.

"Who? What?"

"Um—your bags. Hattie's room. I lit a fire."

"A *fire*?"

He could actually feel her fear, and in his eagerness to re-assure her, Clement reached out and caught at her arms—or what he hoped were her arms. One hand brushed against something remarkably soft, but the contact was so fleeting there was no time to evaluate the other properties of the surface.

"Don't touch me!"

Perplexed by her strange attitude, Clem stepped back. "No. I won't." He heard her sniff.

"A fire?" she repeated.

"Fireplaces. Two upstairs. Living room and dining room downstairs. Same chimney. And the kitchen goes up—" He was talking too much. God, why couldn't he learn to say what he meant and shut up, instead of garbling the information and then tripping over his clumsy feet trying to re-capitulate?

"You lit a fire in the fireplace in Hattie's room," Martha interpreted. She moved away from him. "For me? Thank you."

"I—um, it's too soft. The bed, that is. You're not very padded—pressure points, I mean. But if you'd rather..."

"It'll be just fine," Martha assured him, anxious to reach a room with a door she could shut and lock. As blind as he was—and she was pretty sure he wasn't lying about that—he

could hardly see to find his ax. And if she dragged something heavy up against the door from the inside, there was
no reason she shouldn't have a good night's sleep before she
started looking for a way back to civilization. She'd hardly
slept at all since she'd found that darned emerald.

Clement allowed her to go first, and she could feel his eyes
on her backside all the way up the stairs. Whether he could
see or not, she'd be willing to bet he was staring holes in her.
Her spine stiffened and she was extra careful not to wiggle
her hips.

"First one on the right," he said in that oddly attractive
voice. "I closed it. Um, to keep the heat in."

And she would close it to keep possible intruders *out*. She
might be stuck here for the night, but come morning she was
going to find her way back to *somewhere* if she had to roll
downhill all the way. Hubert Odwell or no Hubert Odwell.
C. Cornelius or no C. Cornelius. Evidently Hattie was not
quite as sharp as she'd been four or five years ago. It was a
bit disconcerting, to say the least, to arrive for an invited
visit only to discover that her hostess had forgotten all about
inviting her and gone traipsing off to Greece.

Her bags were just inside the door and seemingly intact,
but the room itself was a shocker. Along with a small tile-
faced fireplace, a square four-poster that sagged like a
hammock and an armoire that could easily have housed a
small family, there were paintings from floor to ceiling. All
styles, all periods and all levels of expertise. Including the
portrait of Hattie's brainy great-nephew, which made her
catch her breath. She stared at it for a long time before
looking away. After all these years, it still had the ability to
make her feel soft and trembly inside. Hattie had to be immensely talented as a painter, because Martha was not a soft
and trembly sort of woman.

A connecting door revealed another bath, this one replete with a lovely bathtub encased in golden oak. Unfortunately she wouldn't be staying around long enough to enjoy it.

Two hours later Martha huddled in the center of the massive bed, wondering how she was going to get through the night. Her headache hadn't gone away. It had simply shifted from the back to the front, which meant that on top of an overdose of tension, her sinuses were starting to act up.

And dammit, she was hungry! It was her own fault, which didn't make her feel one whit better. C. Cornelius had offered her supper. That is, if the dumping of a dozen or so cans in front of her could be construed as an invitation. She'd declined. In fact, once she'd gained the security of Hattie's bedroom, she'd refused to come out again.

Not that he'd insisted. Evidently, when the man had promised to leave her alone, he'd meant it.

For a little while she dozed, her dreams a jumble of chase scenes on hair-raising mountain roads and trying to pack tons of clothes into a tiny toilet case only to have them fly out and scatter all over the edge of a parking lot full of rusty blue sedans. But she was wide awake again when a soft rap on her door sent her heart banging against her ribs.

"Are you awake?"

She didn't move a muscle. The chair she'd jammed under the doorknob wouldn't have kept out a determined housefly.

So he'd finally shown his true colors. Just when she'd been ready to accept him as one of Hattie's harmless, if eccentric, friends, if not actually her nephew, he was trying to sneak into her room at—goodness, what time was it?

Squinting at the luminous dial of her old high-school graduation watch, Marty discovered that it was barely ten o'clock. It felt like the middle of the night, but then she'd been up here for hours.

What now? What could he want this time of night? He'd promised to leave her alone, and she had definitely planned to return the favor. So maybe she'd panicked and acted a bit silly. And yes, she might even have glanced once or twice at his—ah, masculine assets. That still didn't give him any right to—

And anyway, his back had been to her. He couldn't have known what she was looking at.

Hearing his retreating footsteps on the stairway, she filled her lungs with slightly musty air. Whew! That had been a narrow escape. It was her own fault for getting herself into this position, but quite honestly, she hadn't known what else to do. She'd had the devil's own time finding someone who even knew where Hattie Davenport lived, much less someone willing to drive her all the way up. And the thought of walking out to the main road, if one could glorify a narrow, twisting cow path with such a term, had been too much to contemplate.

Martha waited for an hour to pass. And then another one. She was wide awake. Her headache had settled down to a monotonous throb, but her stomach was rumbling like a coal car.

A quarter to twelve. The witching hour. Better a witch, or even an ax murderer, than slow starvation. To function halfway decently, the female body—at least this particular model—required three squares a day, plus frequent doses of peanut-buttered Oreos. Plus, in times of stress or pollen, as many aspirins as the law allowed. Martyrdom had never held much appeal for her.

Nor had freezing to death, Martha conceded quickly as she eased one bare foot from under the covers. The minuscule fire had long since gone out, leaving the room icy and dank. Either the house wasn't insulated or the incredible bearded hulk didn't know diddly about fire building.

Her bathrobe, if she remembered correctly, was on the bottom of a ton of neatly folded clothes, wrapped around her precious collection of family photos. If she unpacked, she'd just have to repack, and it was hardly worth the effort, especially as she might have to make a fast getaway.

Besides, how long could it take to sneak down to that shelf full of pill bottles she'd seen in the downstairs bathroom, snitch a couple of aspirin and then circle by the kitchen for a jar of peanut butter and a spoon? Hot, sweet, milky tea would be great, but there was no point in pushing her luck.

Her eyes strayed to the large vertical portrait of a young man in unfaded jeans and a white shirt, his dark hair flopping over one deep-set, brooding eye. "What about it?" After all these years, she couldn't remember what Hattie had called him. Something short that had reminded her of an old Red Skelton character. Corny, short for Cornelius? Hardly! She'd definitely have remembered that.

Cautiously, Martha moved the chair, opened the door and checked for any sign of life. No lights, no sounds—nothing. Either upstairs or down. Moving silently across the bare hardwood floors, she glided down the stairs, using the banister for guidance, then wondered how on earth she was going to find her way through a dark, unfamiliar house that was booby-trapped with easels full of paintings and sculpture stands full of bronze busts, clay heads and marble thingamabobs. Not to mention a wild assortment of furniture that ranged from moth-eaten antique to classic art deco to city-dump chic.

She'd hand her that—Hattie had always had the courage of her convictions. One of the things that had drawn Martha to the eccentric artist all those years ago had been the fact that the two of them were so completely different. As a teenager and the motherless daughter of a small-time Yadkin County farmer, Martha had accepted her lot in life. Hattie, at whatever age she'd been then—one could never be quite sure—had accepted nothing. Her philosophy, which she'd shared at the drop of a hat, had been that if you didn't care for the hand you'd been dealt, you could toss it on the table and draw again. Life was a game, and most of the cards were wild.

Perhaps it had worked for Hattie. For Martha, it simply hadn't. For Martha, all the cards had been wild and she couldn't even find the game, much less try to play it.

"Ouch! Hellfire and tornadoes!" She hopped on one cold foot and nursed a toe of the other. What idiot would plant a chair right where people were supposed to walk?

If she hadn't been such a wimp, she'd have grabbed one of those cans C. Cornelius had tossed at her, then she wouldn't be creeping around in the dead of night in a booby-trapped house with an ax wielder probably breathing down her neck.

Dammit, she wasn't even dressed for the part! Weren't heroines supposed to wear something virginal and wispy? Wasn't a hero in a white hat supposed to swoop up in the nick of time and save her and her emerald from fire-breathing Odwells?

"What kind of heroine wears a yellow cotton nightgown from J. C. Penney?" she grumbled. "On sale, yet!"

Clement crawled forward, lowered his right knee onto a sharp rock and swore. If he ever found the blasted things, he was going to staple them to his temples. After that he was going to call his office and have Malvern mail his other pair. If he could get through on the blasted phone, that was.

And if he survived the night. In lieu of a robe, he'd worn an old lab coat over his pajamas. The first thing he'd learned was that lab coats were not designed for crawling. He'd left it by the wayside. The next thing he'd discovered was that pajama tops were just as much of a handicap to a man on his knees. The third time he'd crawled into his shirttail and practically strangled himself, he'd shed that, too. So now he was freezing to death, lacerating his hands and knees, and for all he knew, his damned glasses might be anywhere within a radius of fifty feet.

He'd located the chopping block by feel, then ventured out from there. It was slow going; and not just because of the darkness. He wouldn't have made much more headway in broad daylight. As it was, he used the flashlight as a dowsing rod, hoping to hear the clink of glass against metal.

His fingers encountered a jagged splinter and he swore. Somehow he'd managed to collect splinters on parts of his anatomy that had barely even seen the light of day. Not to mention the cuts, bruises and abrasions. Once he found the things, he'd probably have to fill Hattie's bathtub with an antibacterial solution and soak for a week.

If it hadn't been for the headache that always resulted from going without his glasses, he would have waited until morning to start searching, but he couldn't sleep with a headache and he was afraid to risk fumbling blind among Hattie's pill bottles for a remedy. She never threw out anything. The last time he'd looked for a simple antiseptic he'd had to paw through everything from outdated estrogen to something called Porter's Healing Oil.

Playing the flashlight across the ground at a low angle, Clement squinted into a darkness made even more mysterious by myopia and astigmatism, hoping to catch a glint of reflection from his lenses. It was hopeless. He'd have better luck trying to find a needle in a haystack. At least he could have used a magnet and been reasonably sure of eventual success.

He uttered a four-letter word that would have stunned his peers. It was one he'd never before had the courage to use, and he discovered that, as a relief valve, it was surprisingly effective.

However, it did little to solve his immediate problem.

Sighing, he clicked off the flashlight and tilted his head back, staring at a soft glow he assumed must be a cloud-covered moon. He couldn't even see the damned moon! He despised this feeling of helplessness, always had. He'd felt it too many times in his life, and no matter how he insulated himself with degrees, accomplishments and accolades, it had never ceased to bother him.

After a while he'd learned to curb his vulnerability by keeping to the relatively safe limits of laboratories, libraries and home.

If it weren't for Hattie, he'd probably have turned into a real recluse by now. She was the one who insisted on his getting out into what she called the real world now and then, and because he cared for her deeply, he made the effort.

But he hated it. He was always eager to get back into his comfortable shell. What was it they called those decapod crustaceans that took refuge in the cast-off shells of various univalve mollusks? Hermit crabs. Yes, he could empathize with those homely little fellows. All those long legs tripping over one another...

All of which was doing nothing to solve his immediate problem. He'd barely got to his feet when, without warning, the follicles on his scalp contracted. Blinking owlishly in the darkness, he swung around, tripped on a chunk of split oak and landed on his backside.

"Aha!"

The triumphant cry came from somewhere near the garage. Twisting to one side, Clement palpated his bruised gluteus maximus. Before he could determine the extent of his latest injury, he sneezed.

"I don't know how you found me, you rotten little creep, but I'm warning you—if you don't get out of here this minute, I'm going to wake everyone in the house, and you'll be sorry you ever even *thought* about stealing my emerald!"

It was his paranoid houseguest. He sneezed again.

"You can't fool me, Hubert Odwell. I know who you are, and—and so does the sheriff! I gave him your license number, and that phony business card of yours, so if I were you, I'd get a move on. People around here don't take kindly to crumby jerks who prey on women and try to steal from them."

"Martha—"

"Hush! Don't even try to talk me into anything. I don't want to hear a word out of you, and by the way—it might interest you to know that I'm armed. You have thirty seconds to get in your car and get out of here, because if I lose my temper, I'll *use* this thing!"

"I can't drive. I told you that."

"You can't dri—C. Cornelius? Is that *you*?" Her voice dwindled off like a stuck balloon. "Oh, glory," she murmured.

"I didn't mean to frighten you."

"What are you doing out here? Stargazing?"

"Glasses. Feeling for them. I don't want to mistake estrogen for acetaminophen."

"No, no, of course you don't," Martha murmured soothingly.

Irritated, he wondered if she thought he was going to resort to violence over a pair of lost spectacles. Dammit, he'd told her precisely what he was doing and why. It was only in a social situation that he found it difficult to articulate coherently. "This isn't social," he argued. "You do understand that, don't you?"

"Oh, yes. Yes, I do, I understand perfectly." She was backing away. He could hear the sounds quite clearly.

Bending over, Clem felt for the flashlight, which he'd dropped when she'd startled him. It had evidently rolled away. "Although relatively speaking, I suppose it is," he murmured, wanting to keep her there. Even though she was somewhat strange, he found himself drawn to her for reasons that escaped him completely. Normally, he'd have hid out in the woods all night to escape such an encounter.

"Is what?" she asked warily. At least she'd stopped retreating.

"Social." He moved forward, hands held out in front of him like a shield. "That is, depending on one's—"

"Stay back! Stay right where you are. Social or not, that's far enough!"

He could see her now. At least he could see a faint pale column against the inky shadow of a yew tree. He wasn't nearly close enough. Clem found himself wanting to touch her again, to smell that faint fragrance he'd detected earlier. He wanted to know who she was and what she was doing there and where she'd come from and what she thought about—about everything. He wanted to *talk* to her, wonder of wonders! That in itself was a problem. How was it possible for a man to spend his entire life in pursuit of knowledge and not learn the basic art of communicating with another human being on a personal level?

Hell, even the birds and bees managed *that* much!

"Would you please read labels for me?" he blurted. If he could get her to do that much, it would be a beginning. Quite aside from the fact that he needed her eyes, he rather desperately needed to keep her around long enough to examine and evaluate his startling physical reaction to the sound of her voice and the scent that seemed to surround her. It had never happened to him before—at least not in a long, long time.

"Labels? You mean like *food*?" she asked, and he detected a slight lessening of wariness.

"Medication first. On the shelf. Going without glasses gives me a headache. Without them, I can't read the labels."

And then she was beside him. Taking his arm, she urged him toward the house, and Clem let his hand slip down and clasp hers as they moved cautiously through the dark yard. "Watch that branch," she warned, her voice husky against the crisp night air. "For pity's sake, C. Cornelius, why didn't you say so in the first place? And you can't even see to find them, either, can you? But why on earth did you wait until the middle of the night?"

As Clement could no longer recall the line of reasoning that had led him to sit in the darkened study for hours after she'd locked herself into the bedroom upstairs, he didn't bother even to attempt a reply.

She led him to the house as if he were a small child and she were his nanny—although come to think of it, his nanny had used a harness on him until he'd refused to wear it. From then on, he'd heeled at command rather than have her drag him along.

Two hands, palm to palm. It was a strange sensation. Clement couldn't decide if he liked it or not. The trouble was, he seemed to be losing control of the situation.

"If you'll share your headache remedy with me, I'll read you all the labels you want, but you really should have a spare pair of glasses. Or contacts."

"Yes."

"Back to monosyllables." She opened the door and guided him over the sill. Clement could have told her that he was fine on familiar territory. Like any sight-impaired person, he'd made a point of familiarizing himself with the house in case of such an event.

"Come sit down over here and tell me where to find the aspirin." Leaving the rolling pin on the table, she led him to a hideous purple plush chair and he let himself be led, not sure whether he was enjoying the attention or frustrated by it.

Frustrated by something, that was becoming increasingly clear. Maybe she was right to be wary around him. "Acetylsalicylate or acetaminophen. Not the ibuprofen—that's for Hattie's hands."

He missed her presence for the few moments she was gone, and the fact intrigued him. It was totally foreign to his nature, for he was the quintessential loner. Impatiently he waited for her to reappear. He didn't even know what she looked like—not really. He knew only the sound of her voice—he liked it very much. And the way she smelled. He definitely liked that!

"You're back," he said, and felt an immediate rush of embarrassment at so gauche an observation.

"I'll get us some water. Or milk, if you have it. I skipped too many meals today. Normally I eat like a horse, but what with one thing and another..."

"There's milk. There's food, too."

She laughed, and every sensory organ in his body registered the effect. "So you keep trying to tell me, but so far, I haven't got closer than the outside of a can."

"Martha Eberly," Clement repeated after he'd taken two of the capsules and downed a glass of icy well water. "Will you talk to me?"

"Talk to you? About what?" Martha set her glass carefully on an enameled table.

Clement tried to think of something fascinating to say. What did men talk about with women? Women who weren't scientists? "You're *not* a scientist, are you?" he asked, although he was fairly certain of the answer.

"A scientist? Goodness, no! I'm not anything—at least not yet."

There didn't seem to be a lot he could say to that. She'd effectively shut off any discussion of work. He couldn't very well ask her about her work if she didn't have any, nor could he discuss his own. It would turn into a monologue, and a technical one at that, and then she would either walk away or say something cutting, and this time, he didn't want it to end that way.

He'd once invited a woman to a movie and they'd gone for three hours without exchanging a single word. A month later he'd worked up his nerve and asked her out to dinner and she'd said no thanks, she'd rather spend a lively evening alone watching dust settle on her furniture. It had been a year before he'd tried again. The next time he'd chosen a woman who had talked nonstop about football players and clothes, and he hadn't bothered to ask her out again. Not that she would have gone.

Martha sighed.

Clement sighed. If only he could have seen her, he might have gauged the situation more accurately. However, she was still here. She hadn't walked away yet, and that was a favorable sign, wasn't it?

Taking courage from that small fact, he said cheerfully, "Well. What would you like to talk about?"

"What would I— How about food?"

"All right." Food? What was there to say about it? He'd much rather know about the man who'd frightened her and why she was here and where she'd come from and where she was—

"We're going to *talk* about it? Is that *all*?" she exclaimed.

She sounded exasperated, and for the life of him Clem didn't know why. He'd thought things were progressing unusually well. Here they were, seated across the table from one another, having shared a companionable dose of acetaminophen, yet she seemed—tense.

"Uh—all? No. You go first—what do you find interesting about food?"

Hmm... Not bad for a beginner, he thought a little smugly. Conversation wasn't all that difficult once you got the hang of it—make a statement and then follow up with a question. That way, there was a reciprocal interchange of ideas instead of the dead end at which he so often found himself stranded.

He could tell she had leaned forward. The pale blur shifted. "The lack of it, at the moment," she snapped. "It's all I can think about."

Evidently she didn't know the rules of conversation. First a statement, then a question. What was he supposed to say now?

He cleared his throat, then he sneezed.

"Bless you," she muttered. "Do you have a cold?"

He beamed. They were off again!

"Why, thank you. That's very kind of you. No." *Now, ask her something, wonderboy!* Like what makes her smell the way she does. Like why the touch of her hand on his arm should cause a physiological reaction in practically every system in his body, with the possible exception of the digestive system.

Intellectually he knew the answer, yet for some reason the data kept falling apart in his mind when he attempted to analyze it.

"As I was saying," Martha went on a bit grimly, "I never sleep too well on an empty stomach."

"Physiologically, the favored position is supine, not prone. That is, you should sleep on your back, or at least on your side. You see, the cervical vertebrae—"

"Stuff your cervical vertebrae! I'm hungry, dammit!"

Clement blinked at the outburst. Had he offended her? His usual offense was boring his partner, but she didn't sound bored. She sounded . . . "Hungry?"

"Famished."

He groaned. Of course she was. That's what she'd meant when she'd mentioned missing meals. Myopic and astigmatic eyes glinted blue with flecks of gold as Clement rose and held out a hand. "I, too. Hungry, that is. You choose, I'll open."

"I thought you'd never ask." She got to her feet and peered toward the kitchen with a look of anticipation. "Better yet, how about I cook, we both eat. You do have eggs, don't you?"

"Yes."

"Bacon?"

"No."

"Oh, well . . . Bread?"

"Frozen."

"It'll thaw. I'm a great hand at thawing. How about cheese?"

"Yes. Interesting mold patterns. A type of penicillin, you know."

Martha halted in the door of the kitchen. "Mold? Um— what kind of cheese is it?"

"The label says Rocquefort."

Her hesitation was barely noticeable. "Scrambled eggs with Rocquefort it is. Sounds heavenly."

But Clement, hungry though he was, was momentarily distracted by the clean, feminine scent that eddied around her. She was yellow from the floor up, but still pale copper on top. Her arms and her face were pink, as if she'd recently been exposed to an excessive amount of ultraviolet radiation.

"Look, you're going to have to tell me where things are. How's your headache, by the way?" She brushed past him and he heard the whisper of fabric on flesh. He swallowed hard, rooted to the spot and tingling with a variety of sensations he'd have given his eyeteeth to explore. "Um—what are you wearing, Martha?"

"I'm glad you asked that question." She placed several things on the counter and shut the door. "My nightgown."

"You are?" He beamed, feeling as if he'd just been knighted. "It was a good question then?" He could visualize her smiling, hear the sound of it in her voice, and it pleased him inordinately. Really, they were getting along superbly! She was obviously a very perceptive woman.

"I'm glad you asked because if you'd been able to see what I was wearing, I wouldn't be wearing it. What I mean is, I wouldn't be here. Like this, I mean. Good Lord, I'm beginning to sound like you."

"You are? Is that good?"

She shoved a bowl in his hands and said, "Beat these. Gently, now—don't slosh. Will coffee keep you awake, or would you prefer hot milk?"

"I want to stay awake. I could talk all night, couldn't you?" He felt something cold and wet land on the top of his foot. The bowl was abruptly removed from his hands, and he could hear her stirring gently with a whisk. Maybe he'd been a bit too enthusiastic. He hoped he hadn't made too big a mess of it.

She handed him a paper towel, and he wiped the egg off his foot, hoping he hadn't spilled it on his pajamas, as well. Damn—he'd left his shirt outside. He would never have risked offending her again by appearing half naked if he'd been thinking straight.

"No, C. Cornelius, I couldn't talk all night," she said, sounding distinctly unoffended. She was a kind person, he decided. "As tired as I am, I'm even hungrier than that. So let's have our supper and get to bed, because tomorrow I need to get an early start if I'm going to find a ride to Asheville in time to catch the bus home."

Four

———

Clement was determined to keep her there. He didn't know how, much less why. All he knew was that it was vitally important that she stay long enough to—

Long enough for him to...

Swearing softly, he shoved both hands through his hair, raking it from his brow. It occurred to him that he'd needed a haircut when he'd left Winston. By now there was no telling what he looked like. No wonder she'd been wary of him.

Martha. Who was she? Intellectual curiosity had driven him since he'd barely been able to walk, only this was something entirely different. After a few hours in her presence, he was possessed by a compelling urge to explore every facet of her mind and body.

It wasn't going to work. In fact, it was scary as hell! Trying to relate to a woman who didn't really interest him turned him into a tongue-tied jerk. What would happen with a woman who mattered to him?

Clem wanted badly to think he'd made real progress tonight, but ruthless self-honesty was too ingrained. He'd managed to get through an hour without making an absolute ass of himself.

On the other hand, for him, even that much was a considerable accomplishment.

He paced in a well-worn pattern. He'd always paced when faced with a conundrum, and this one had him stumped. Why Martha Eberly? Why some woman whose voice he'd heard a few times, whose face he had yet to see clearly? Why not the lovely young biochemist who'd come to work for B.F.I. last fall? He'd spent three months working up enough nerve to ask her out to dinner, then been so relieved when she'd turned him down that he'd gone home and drunk himself into a stupor—a matter of three beers.

Martha. The name suited her. There was a gentle quality about the name and about the woman. He didn't know how he knew, but he'd felt it right from the first. Strength and vulnerability—fear and daring. And compassion. Look at the way she'd taken him on in the backyard, after seeing the flashlight and thinking an intruder was snooping around, about to break into Hattie's house.

And the way she'd taken his hand and led him inside.

She was warm and soft, and she smelled like fresh baked bread and roses, with a hint of something more intimate that stirred him in a way he hadn't been stirred in a long time.

Clem told himself sternly that it was purely a matter of hormones. It had to be. But regardless of the cause, it was a definite fact, which was unfortunate, as he didn't have a snowball's chance in hell of alleviating the attendant discomfort. He'd always had excellent control over both his mind and his body, but something told him that control of his was going to be severely challenged before Martha Eberly turned tail and headed down the mountain.

Clement tugged at his beard. If he'd been slated to have that sort of relationship with a woman, it would have occurred before now. He was thirty-two years old. All the longing and all the luck in the world couldn't alter the fact that he hadn't the least idea of how to ask a woman to lie down and let him—

That is, to take off her clothes and allow—

Well, dammit, what did a man *do*? How did he go about setting the scene? And if, wonder of wonders, the woman proved willing, what then? Who undressed first? Was it a mutual or a reciprocal arrangement? Besides, how did he know he could—that is, that *it* would—

Oh, the devil! His head was pounding again, and he hadn't a chance of getting to sleep in this frame of mind.

It was inevitable, perhaps, that Clem's mind would home in on the single most painful memory in a voluminous and orderly mental file. A memory that should have been discarded years ago.

He'd been in grad school at the time—about fifteen and incredibly naive. Due to his age, he'd been put in a freshman dorm. If the term "wimp" had been popular at the time, it would've been used to describe him, but there'd been others, equally descriptive, and he'd been called them all.

How many times had he wished he'd been born with the I.Q. of a chimp? Or better yet, a tortoise. Bright enough to manage survival and procreation; incapable of worrying about much else. By now he might even have been married to Georgina Duffy.

Black hair, blue eyes, with a pouting mouth and a body that had temporarily nullified roughly a hundred thousand dollars worth of education from his mind the first time he'd ever laid eyes on her, Georgina had been a waitress at the student union. Clement had cut classes, meals and everything else just to watch her move around the room. The first time she'd smiled at him, he'd gone catatonic.

His condition, of course, had been pathetically obvious to his roommates, Rolf and Bucky, both of whom had been in their early twenties. Always the butt of jokes, he'd suddenly become the chief source of entertainment on his hall, and with his usual denseness, he'd quite misunderstood. Like a fool, he'd smiled and lapped up the unaccustomed attention.

It had been a cinch for them to talk him into attending the post-game party at the home of one of the students. All they'd had to do was to tell him Georgina would be there. If they'd spread it on too thick, told him she was panting to get to know him better, Clement wouldn't have gone within a mile of the place. He'd been quite content to worship quietly from a safe distance. It was all he'd known how to do.

But they'd played it just right. Rolf had given him a pep talk and Bucky had talked him out of wearing his beige suit, pin-striped shirt and knit tie. Together they'd fixed him up with a pair of faded jeans that were long enough and a Hawaiian print shirt.

Once there, they'd settled him in a quiet corner where he could watch the goings-on without getting in the way and offered to bring him a drink.

"Fruit punch? You gotta be kidding," Rolf had said. "Hell, man, we got to celebrate! I'll bring you a beer, right? Forty-six to zip, man! Did we stomp their tight ends into the mud, or what?"

Clement, who was far more familiar with tithonometers than he was with tight ends, had maintained some vestige of self-preservation. "I'd better stick with the punch. I'm still underage, you know," he'd said, blossoming under the rare camaraderie.

That was the night he'd learned about vodka. That was the night he'd learned about a lot of things. By the time Georgina had migrated over to his corner, he was leaning against the wall, grinning foolishly. The grin didn't waver when she stopped in front of him, although when she leaned forward and breathed on his lenses, fogging them up, his knees had threatened to buckle.

"Come on, honey, you need to get out of this hot ol' place and breathe a little cool air."

He didn't remember going with her. Nor had he been aware of all the snickers, the swift glances. Looking back, he was surprised he'd been able to navigate on his own. Or perhaps he'd had some help. What he did remember was a dimly lighted library with a leather sofa that had felt shockingly cold to the touch. He remembered Georgina's fingers on his chest—she'd been saying something about loosening his buttons and his belt so that he could breathe. He remembered more or less collapsing so that his cheek was pillowed on her chest, which was even softer than it looked. Her perfume had been strong and cloying, and he remembered turning so that his nose would clear the swell of her right breast.

The next thing he remembered was waking up to see a ring of faces, male and female, all around him. Georgina had been trying to talk over all the laughter, but she'd been giggling too hard. "Oh, come on, guys, haven't I earned a beer? Leave the poor baby alone."

There'd been an immediate outcry, and she'd waved it down. "All right, all right, so what d'you want, a demo or a blow-by-blow description?"

Clement had prayed to die. It was either that or disgrace himself even further by throwing up on his borrowed shirt.

"Hey, take it from me, guys, it takes more than brains to—"

There'd been a chorus of irreverent comments, and someone had shouted, "Come on, Georgie, what's his I.Q.?"

"A lot bigger than yours, Bucky boy," she'd retorted, and there'd been another roar of laughter, and some squeals from the female members of the group.

It had been then that Clement had realized that except for his shoes, socks and the lurid shirt, which barely managed to preserve his modesty, he was stark naked. Just as another roar of laughter broke over him he'd felt the first wave of nausea.

"Okay, okay, you've had your fun—I know I have," she'd purred, and Clement hadn't waited to hear any more. He'd leaped off the sofa and windmilled his way through the crowd, uncaring of his near-nude state. He'd been sick as a dog, and it was only because he hadn't been able to lift his head off the pillow the next morning that he hadn't left school, the country and possibly the universe.

He'd like to think that he'd proved something by staying on after the most humiliating experience of his life. But in the end, all he'd proved was that he couldn't tolerate alcohol and he was a dead loss where women were concerned. Either he didn't have what it took to please them or he didn't know how. The result was the same. Since then, he'd never risked another disaster.

The positive result had been that he'd been able to throw himself wholeheartedly into his studies at a time when most boys his age had been distracted by more exciting pursuits.

Martha lay awake until the eastern sky began to turn gray. Hattie's soft mattress was a swaybacked nightmare for someone used to flat and hard. Every bone and muscle in her body ached. She hadn't been able to get comfortable enough to sleep, and the more she lay awake, the more she worried.

Worry had always come easy to Martha, starting from the time when her mother had been diagnosed as terminally ill. Later she'd worried about her father, who had relied on her mother far more than any man should have done. She'd worried about her brother, Jack, who'd hated farming and joined the army with a view to earning himself a college education.

Finally, after Jack had been educated and married, with a family of his own in Kentucky, and her father had sold his tobacco allotment, got rid of all the stock except for a cow, a few laying hens and three coon dogs and retired to the front porch rocker to wait for his heart to stop ticking, she'd worried about her own future.

And felt selfish and unworthy for doing so.

Rubbing gritty-feeling eyes, she sat up in bed, taking perverse pleasure in the bite of cold air through her thin cotton gown. She had truly done all she could have done... hadn't she? After Papa had died and the farm had been sold, there'd been enough money to get her started in school, although she'd already been having second thoughts about majoring in art. By that time, Hattie had retired and moved away, and with her inspiration reduced to the occasional letter, Martha had just about decided on a business major when Jack's wife had gone into early labor and died giving birth to a daughter. Martha had dropped everything to go take care of her two-and-a-half-year-old nephew and her newborn niece.

And despite the tragic circumstances, she'd loved it. She'd done a pretty good job, too, considering she'd never been around children all that much. But growing up on a farm, with both parents ailing in their last years, she'd learned about care giving. In the midst of juggling meals and laundry and a thousand other tasks, she'd often been frustrated, often impatient with her own shortcomings. But in retrospect, it had been deeply satisfying. So much so that she'd all but decided, now that Jack was remarried and she was no longer needed, to go into nurse's training.

And then she'd found that blasted emerald, and having found the thing, she refused to allow some crook to steal it from her. She had about four hundred dollars left from her part of the sale of the farm—Jack had needed a down payment on a house, and she'd gladly lent it to him, but she still had her training to pay for. Four hundred dollars wasn't nearly enough, and she'd lain awake nights wondering where she was going to get the rest, because with a new wife and two children, it would be years before Jack's paycheck would stretch to loan payments.

Worrying? Martha was an expert at worrying. Which was obviously something C. Cornelius didn't believe in. Up here all alone, blind as a bat, unable to drive or even to communicate effectively, it was a wonder he'd survived! Not that he looked all that helpless. He didn't look helpless at all, in fact. But it was pretty clear that the man needed a keeper.

Unbidden, a vision of his tall, beautifully constructed body took shape in her mind. Her breath quickened. What on earth was she thinking of? He'd wrapped an ax around her backside and scared the wits out of her! He was wild, bushy-headed, totally unpredictable, and if her brain hadn't slipped into neutral, she'd have been out of here so fast!

All right, to be ruthlessly honest, which she always tried to be and occasionally succeeded, Martha knew that it hadn't been paralysis that had kept her from running away when he'd let her go.

There'd been something about him...something sort of...

Which was ridiculous! No woman with a grain of common sense would admit to being attracted to someone like

C. Cornelius. Because even if he did turn out to be Hattie's nephew, he must be some sort of black sheep. She'd only ever heard of one nephew, the one in the portrait. The brainy one. And if C. Cornelius even *had* a brain, he managed to keep it pretty well hidden.

On the other hand, he was sort of sweet. And his rear end was worthy of attention by even the most seasoned man watcher. Which she wasn't.

Martha's gaze strayed to the portrait on the opposite wall. She could recall the first time she'd ever seen it in Hattie's west end house in Winston. She'd been smitten and painfully transparent, no doubt, because Hattie had answered her unasked questions, telling her that the subject had been something of a prodigy.

At the time, Martha hadn't even been sure what a prodigy was, but she'd been deeply impressed by the sensitive face, the long jaw and the deep set, brooding eyes.

What had Hattie called him? Lordy, it had been so long ago! She'd fallen in and out of love with any number of movie and TV stars since then. And Virgil, of course.

It had been something distinctly ungeniuslike. Hank? Clyde? Clem! That was it—Clem. Martha remembered being disappointed at his name. She'd rechristened him Ian in her mind—or had it been Sean? And then Hattie had moved away, and she'd forgotten all about him until she'd seen the portrait again.

It was gradually growing light outside. Pale yellow warmed the gray, pushing back the darkness. Mist hugged the ground, blackening the tree trunks, and reluctantly Martha eased herself out of bed and hurried into the cold bathroom. There was an electric strip heater, but it was no match for the high-ceilinged room. There was also a radiator, which, like the one in her bedroom, was barely lukewarm.

Speed and a tub of hot water would have to serve. And serve quickly if she intended to walk to the nearest town, check on buses and hire someone to come haul her luggage in to town.

After turning on the hot-water faucet full blast, she dashed into the bedroom and was digging a set of clean clothes out of her suitcase when she heard the bellowing sound from downstairs. Clutching a set of underwear and a pair of white socks, she went to the door, opened it a crack and listened.

"C. Cornelius? Was that you?" she called hesitantly. And then, when there was no reply, she yelled louder. "Cornelius! Are you all right?"

"No!"

Oh, Lord, what had he done now? Praying that he hadn't retrieved his glasses since she'd last seen him, she hurried downstairs, following the sound of his angry voice.

"Damned antiquated system," Clement grumbled as he slapped the walls in search of a towel, which he finally located by tripping on it. He muttered something profane about modern plumbing, touched briefly on the Greeks and the Romans and jammed his toe against the edge of the door. It was bad enough that the second bathroom upstairs hadn't worked in years. It was even worse that any time two people attempted to use the remaining two at the same time, one of them risked either frostbite or scalding. Hattie had explained the vagaries of the plumbing system to him, and during the week she'd spent getting him acclimated before she'd left for New York and ultimately Greece, they'd worked out a schedule for bath taking.

"Cornelius! Where are you?"

Not content merely to freeze him to death, she had now come to gloat! Unthinking, Clement threw open the bath-

oom door and glared at the pale shape hovering in the dark
allway. "It was *my* turn!" he announced indignantly.

"Oh, my Lord," whispered the shape.

Either she was praying or she was in shock. That partic-
lar tone of voice was difficult to interpret. As random
atches of soap suds slowly slid down his chest and his right
high, Clem continued to squint at her.

And then it suddenly struck him that just because he
ouldn't see her, that didn't mean she was similarly handi-
apped. With a strangled sound, he slammed the door be-
ween them and leaned against it, breathing raggedly. Was
e out of his moth-eaten mind? He'd lived alone for so long
e could no longer even be trusted among civilized people!

Several minutes later, chastely saronged with a mono-
rammed mauve-on-purple towel, Clement opened the door
a crack and peered out. The fear of seeing a ring of grin-
ing faces was subliminal, but very real nevertheless.

"Martha?" he whispered experimentally.

No response.

Thank God! If he'd actually thought there was the
lightest possibility that she was still lurking in the shadows, he would have barricaded himself in the bathroom for
he next six weeks.

Where the hell was his bathrobe? Or rather, the lab coat
hat substituted for a robe?

In the backyard, of course, along with his pajama top and
is damned glasses. Which, by now, were probably broken
r trampled into the ground.

Clem hadn't thought to bring a change of clothes with
im when he'd hurried down for his regular early morning
hower. Having had the run of the house, he'd tended to fall
nto a few bad habits, at least one of which he was going to
ave to shed immediately.

And dammit, the minute Hattie got back into the coun try he was going to prevail on her to drive him into town where he could get himself a decent bathrobe! And a few new shirts in a larger size. And—well, hell, why not? A pair of blue jeans. The pale, streaky kind with the label on the rear end.

Clement headed for the back stairs, praying he wouldn' be discovered. His beard dripped on his chest, and a drop of cold water wove its way through the thicket there and headed south. The towel felt clammy on his backside. It barely covered him. There wasn't a real man-size towel in the entire house, and he wasn't built for tea towels.

He'd thought he'd made some real progress last night, but he'd really blown it with this stunt. He should've kept his mouth shut and gone ahead with his cold shower, even though the immediate need had passed. She couldn't know that when anyone turned on the hot water upstairs, it in stantly shut it off all over the rest of the system.

And if she was still here by the time he got dressed, he'd probably need another ice-cold dousing. Maybe it was for the best, he told himself, knowing full well that he was way beyond any pretense at intellectual honesty.

By the time Clement worked up his nerve to go down stairs again, fully dressed this time, he had put his embar rassment behind him. He'd had a lifetime of experience in putting embarrassing episodes behind him. Embarrass ment was merely a state of mind, accompanied by certain characteristic physiological changes—most of which he'd learned to control before he'd reached voting age.

"Well," he said calmly to the unfamiliar yellow blur at the head of the table.

"There's coffee made, and I can scramble you another egg. There are more in the carton."

"I do eggs quite well." He refused to have her think of him as helpless, along with everything else. All right, so maybe he hadn't managed to extinguish quite all of his embarrassment.

"Without your glasses?"

"It's a simple matter of putting them in a pan, running water over them and increasing the temperature until the protoplasm is sufficiently coagulated. It's all in the timing—allowing, of course, for the altitude." Which should show her that he was in no danger of starving if she walked out.

But in spite of what he'd told himself, Clem knew that he wasn't about to allow her to leave. For reasons he didn't dare go into, it had become vitally important to him that she stay on. At least until he'd proved that he wasn't a complete ass.

He could hear her stirring her coffee, and the aroma of it made his nose twitch. He walked directly to the cabinet that held the cups, took down a large one and set it on the table. Right on top of the cup and saucer she'd already laid out for him. Something broke.

"Sit *down*!" Martha barked. It was a soft bark, but it didn't lack authority for all that. "You stay put until I get back, you hear me?"

Clement sat. Had he thought he could control his emotions? He was in worse shape than he'd been seventeen years ago, when he'd slept through his own debauchment and awakened to discover himself surrounded by an appreciative audience. He had a subliminal vision of waking up one morning to see Martha standing over him, laughing her head off because he'd tried to make love to her and failed miserably.

Oh, hell, he had to get out of there. He would walk, run, climb—anything, as long as it took him away from this woman!

Jumping up, he felt a sharp pain in his right heel and heard something grate on the floor. Before he could react to either, the door opened and she was back. Clement dropped into the chair, resigned to his ignominious fate.

"They were right where you left them," Martha announced. "Muddy, though—no wonder you couldn't find them. I'll just rinse them off. It must have rained in the night."

"I didn't leave them, I knocked them off and then couldn't see to find them," he muttered sullenly.

"Whatever. Here you are, Cinderella—a perfect fit." She slid the pair of plastic-rimmed spectacles on his nose and hooked the wings over his ears, and Clem remembered, chagrined, that he'd been intending to get new frames for several years. These had been mended in three places with adhesive tape. Tape that was now grimy and frayed.

Martha laid a hand on his shoulder. If he'd been hooked up to a voltmeter, the needle would have jammed. "You ought to get a hanger for them next time you go to town. Who's going to find them for you after I leave?"

"You're not leaving." So much for subtlety.

She snatched back her hand, and Clement settled the glasses properly on his nose and turned an apologetic look on her. "Not yet? Please?" He couldn't let her go until he made sure he could find her again. If she would allow him to escort her wherever she was headed, then he'd have an address—something. Or even time enough on the way to convince her to stay with him.

Why hadn't he stuck with driving until he'd mastered it? Any idiot could drive. Statistics proved it. It would have been the perfect solution. He could practically hear himself saying nonchalantly, "Stick around for a few more days,

oney, and I'll drive you wherever you're going and help
ou get settled. You'll need someone to carry your bags for
ou."

"What?" Martha exploded. "You told me you didn't
rive, and I believed you! And all this time you were lying
o me, and here I've been—"

Oh, hell, he'd done it again. Spoken his thoughts aloud.
ome men weren't fit to be let out without a leash and a
uzzle. "No! I mean, I don't. Drive, that is—no car. Hat-
ie's is—but I can't—if I owned a car, I'd give it to you.
lease believe me, Martha."

She slid into the chair across from him, and Clem stared
t her raptly, seeing her clearly for the first time. She was
uite simply the most beautiful creature he had ever beheld
n his long and uneventful life.

"Stop staring, you're making me self-conscious. How can
believe any man who says one thing one minute and an-
ther thing the next? And any man who'd offer to give his
ar to a stranger is wacko. C. Cornelius, if you expect a
erson to believe anything you say, try leveling off at a sen-
ible altitude and sticking to the simple truth for a change,
kay?"

"Yes," he said dutifully. "There's my name, to start
vith."

"C. Cornelius? I thought it was sort of pretentious. What
lo your friends call you? C? Neil?"

"My—uh—associates call me Clement. Or Dr. Barto. Or
ir. But Hattie calls me Clem," he added with a hopeful
xpression that elicited a soft groan from the woman across
rom him. "If you don't like it, you can call me something
lse," he added quickly.

Martha hadn't missed the evasion. The man didn't have
ny friends—not real friends. At least, no one who came to
nind immediately. But worst of all—or best of all, she
vasn't sure which—he was Hattie's Clem. *Her* Clem of the

sensitive face and the vulnerable mouth and the deep, brooding eyes, only now all that was hidden behind thick lenses and that gosh-awful beard. That hauntingly beautiful boy in a man's body.

And it was *definitely* a man's body, all right! Martha had seen all the evidence she needed to on that score. Those broad shoulders, the narrow hips and long legs—and that fascinating pattern of wiry black hair that collected most heavily in the one area where she hadn't dared to allow her eyes to linger.

She looked at him as searchingly as he was studying her and decided that never in her life had she met a lonelier, a loster, a more endearingly vulnerable man.

For the moment, it completely escaped her that she couldn't wait to get away from him. Besides, it was only common decency to stay long enough to be sure he could look after himself until Hattie got home. She owed her old friend *that* much, at least, for befriending a naive young girl fresh off a tobacco farm and teaching her about art, about people and about life outside Yadkin County.

Suddenly embarrassed to realize she'd been staring, she asked the first thing that popped into her head. "Why did you tell me your name was C. Cornelius?"

Clement shrugged. "I don't know."

"I think I do. You were hiding. It doesn't take a psychologist to know that you'd do almost anything to keep strangers from getting too close to you. Any man who's reluctant even to share his first name..."

"It sounds childish when you put it like that."

"Even the glasses. And that gosh-awful beard."

He lifted a hand to cover his chin. "You don't like beards?"

"I don't like them or dislike them," she dismissed, "but how do you ever hope to make friends when you won't even share your face with them?"

"I don't— It's, uh—grown since I got here. I, um—didn't bring a razor."

"Well, I did. And there's bound to be a pair of scissors around here somewhere."

"Samson."

"Beg pardon?"

"Hair."

"Are we back to monosyllables again? Look, I'm not threatening to cut off anything, I was only making an observation. If you're finished with your coffee, I'll wash up. Or did you want something more?"

Clem's stomach tightened in anticipation, and he quelled it with a silent command. He wasn't about to allow her to cook for him, not when she already thought he was a dead loss. One way or another, he was determined to repair his reputation before she got away, because he couldn't bear the thought of her remembering him as a clown who couldn't take three steps without tripping over his own feet.

If she remembered him at all.

"Which way is town from here? I thought I'd go find out if a bus does come through, and then see if I could hire someone to drive me back and pick up my bags."

Clement began to panic. "You don't mean town."

"I do mean town."

"Asheville's too far. There's Cat Creek."

"I thought this *was* Cat Creek."

"Post office."

"Bus stop? Good glory, I'm beginning to sound just like you!"

Clement stood up, his smile a well-kept secret under his overgrown beard. He had his vision back, and Asheville was too far to walk, and he was reasonably certain that no bus came within ten miles of Cat Creek township. With advantages like those, he could conquer the world!

Five

They'd gone less than a mile when Martha stopped suddenly. If it had happened three weeks ago, Clement would have plowed into her and sent them both tumbling down the steep grade, but almost a month of daily hiking and climbing, not to mention the fortresslike stack of wood he'd split, had done wonders for his coordination.

"Did you change your mind?" he asked. The trail was easy here, and he'd allowed her to push past him and lead the way. For now.

"I walked right off and forgot all about it. I can't believe I did that!" Eyes wide in her flushed face, she grabbed one of his arms and shook it. "Clement, don't you understand? Anyone could walk in off the road and steal it. You *did* lock up, didn't you?"

"Lock what?" Was she feeling all right? She looked all right. God, yes—she looked extremely all right!

"The doors. The windows. What does a person usually lock when he leaves a house to go out?"

"I don't know."

She gave his arm another shake. Actually, it was not at all an unpleasant sensation. In fact, he discovered that he rather liked being touched, in any way at all, by her. Clement smiled at her—she was quite strong for someone so small. Her head only came up to his pectoral region.

"What do you mean, you don't know? You don't remember whether or not you *locked up*?"

"I meant that I don't know what people usually lock up when they go out," Clement explained patiently. "I suppose it depends on what they value most. But my memory is adequate—quite good, in fact."

The sound that emerged from somewhere in the region of her throat was part groan, part scream. "For once, can you concentrate on a simple question long enough to give a simple answer? Did you or did you not lock the house before we left?"

"Yes, usually I concentrate quite well, and my answers are always direct. And yes, I did."

Abruptly, she let go of his arm and sat on a mossy slope, drawing her knees up. Clement watched as she lowered her head so that her chin rested on her crossed arms. He felt a strong need to touch her hair, to experience for himself the texture that could gleam with metallic brilliance yet look as soft as a vapor.

Instead, he cleared his throat and turned to stare across the ravine to the ragged blue skyline in the distance. He'd been talking quite freely, in complete, coherent sentences. And yet something was still missing. Try as he would, he couldn't seem to get the knack of conversing. The flow was lacking—the easy give-and-take that went on among the more junior members of his staff.

Choosing a place several feet away, he lowered himself to the ground and sat awkwardly, hands dangling from his widespread knees. "Who is Hubert Odwell, Martha?" He'd planned to wait until he'd gained her confidence before prying into her personal affairs, but he couldn't afford to wait any longer. She was frightened. Both evidence and instinct told him that Odwell was responsible for the way she overreacted. "At least tell me why he's following you."

She looked stricken. "How do you know someone's following me?"

"The phone calls."

"But I never mentioned his name—I know I didn't!" She was twisting her hands, and Clem reached out and covered them both with one of his.

"Last night," he said in what he hoped was a calming tone. "When you thought I was an intruder, you called me Hubert Odwell."

She sagged, but she didn't try to pull away. Gradually, the panic faded from her eyes, leaving only a tired sort of wariness that made him want to gather her into his arms and say something poetic and heroic.

Which would, of course, have the effect of making her laugh. Laughter was better than fear; unfortunately, he could think of nothing either heroic or poetic at the moment. "He frightens you?"

"Oh, it's crazy. You wouldn't understand."

Probably not, he thought, absorbing the pain. It was nothing he hadn't heard before, but he'd wanted her to trust him, to turn to him instinctively. To see him as strong and capable and—oh, yes, as desirable, too. That most of all, perhaps.

"Probably not," he said with quiet dignity. "It's generally accepted, however, that talking a problem through helps clarify and organize the thought processes. I, um—do it myself, on occasion.''

Brilliant! Tell her how you talk to yourself. When she's done laughing at that, you can tell her about the way you sometimes watch the woman in the next apartment coming home from the supermarket, and how you pretend she's your wife, hurrying home to be with you. Oh, yes, a bit of voyeurism should instill an inordinate amount of confidence!

''That is, I sometimes try out a phrase or two aloud,'' he mumbled, ''but only on rare occasions when I, um—have trouble consolidating my er—um . . .'' He cleared his throat and tugged at his beard. If he'd been wearing a tie, he would've straightened it.

She was going to ignore him. Why shouldn't she? They were, after all, strangers. At least, *he* was a stranger. Somehow, *she* had become much more than a stranger. Electromagnetism? A biochemical reaction? Pheromones? At this point, Clement didn't really give a hang about causative factors. Whatever it was, it was happening. And it was completely outside his extremely limited experience.

He stole a look at her, noting the pure line of her profile. If there were a universal prototype for feminine beauty, he decided, it would be Martha Eberly. Withdrawing her hand from his, she lifted her head, staring over a hardwood forest that still glowed with a remnant of fall color. Watching her brought an ache to the region of his solar plexus that was oddly pleasant.

From a distance came the grinding sound of a truck straining to climb a steep grade. Clem strained along with it. *Come on...come on...this way. Look this way. Easy now, all you have to do is turn your head a bit. Just a bit more, that's it—pretend we're friends and you've something to say to me.*

Praise Paracelsus, she was going to *talk* to him!

"There's this man—Odwell…" Her voice dwindled, and Clement waited. *There was this man? Yes? And what happened?*

"He was following you," he prompted when it seemed as if she'd forgotten he was there. It occurred to him fleetingly that the more reluctant she was to talk, the more articulate he seemed to become, which in itself was a remarkable phenomenon.

"Not me—my emerald." Her gaze flew to his face, and he was struck by the sight of the slanting November sun gilding the very tips of her lashes.

"Go on," he said in what he hoped was a reassuring tone. *Her emerald?* "He was following your emerald. Uh—any particular reason?"

"Clem, do you know anything about law? I don't mean malpractice, but mining laws. Or—well, not exactly mining… *finding* laws."

"Huh?" Now which one of them was sounding incoherent? "Sorry, I'm a research chemist, not a lawyer. Naturally I've read some law, but only as a matter of interest."

"Well, maybe you can tell me— You see, I found it, but he was with me. Well, not exactly *with* me—I mean, he was a pest. He greeted every new load of diggers with this spiel about being some sort of an expert, handing out crummy business cards and offering to evaluate their finds. You know the sort of thing."

Clem didn't, but he wasn't about to say so now.

"There were plenty of samples and charts and things available—I mean, it wasn't as if any one of us expected to find anything really earthshaking. I was only along for the ride, and because it was sort of fun, and it would get me close to Hattie's, and I hadn't seen her since I moved to Louisville, but—so anyway…"

She was digressing wildly, and Clement loved every dangling, disorganized moment of it. He edged closer, close enough so that now and then he caught a drift of her fresh-bread-and-roses fragrance. She was doing remarkable things for his self-esteem, not to mention his libido. "Yes? He offered his services and then what?"

"And I said no thanks, but he turned up at the next stop, and went through the same thing. He was...overfriendly. You know? The sort of person you want to wash your hands after touching. A real creep."

Clement swallowed and turned to gaze over Cat Creek Valley, a shallow, laurel-filled gorge that angled diagonally down the side of the mountain. After a few moments, Martha went on speaking, and he listened, but some of the brilliance had gone out of the noonday sun. He would hear her out and advise her—help her if he could. But there was no point in pretending she could ever take someone like him seriously. And he didn't think he could survive her ridicule.

"I was on my way to the bus—you know how it gets chilly once the sun goes down—when he came up behind me and started in about showing me this place where I could find some really good stones. And when I turned around to tell him I wasn't interested—or had I already done that? I don't remember," she said distractedly. "Anyway, my shoulder bag flew off and everything got dumped, and when I was looking for my pencil—it's part of a set, and I'd just as soon lose the whole thing, but anyway, there it was. This emerald. This enormous, beautiful crystal in some sort of pinky colored rock—matrix, it's called, but I don't know if that's the name of the rock or just what they call the stuff gems come wrapped in."

Once more she fell silent. Obviously, she'd forgotten he was even there, which was just as well, because at the moment, Clem was having the devil's own time keeping his mind on her rambling tale and off her small, flawlessly constructed body.

On the other hand, he couldn't afford to jeopardize the ground he had so unexpectedly gained. It wasn't every day that a beautiful woman confided in him. Or even every decade. "This emerald. You say he's claiming it?"

"Half ownership. Because he was with me—he says—when I found it. He says there's some kind of law, which I don't for one minute believe, do you? Have you ever heard of a law like that?"

"Does this Odwell fellow have any connection, contractual or otherwise, to the property where you found the stone?"

"No way. In fact, when I complained, the proprietor of one of the mines said they all hate that sort of thing, but unless he actually breaks the law, there's not a lot they can do, since they're open to the public and he's part of it. The public, I mean."

She sighed, and Clem fought and overcame a powerful need to gather her in his arms and protect her. "He's followed you ever since?"

She nodded. "I know it's silly, but he really scares me. I can handle anything—well, almost anything—but I'm no good when it comes to dealing with . . . with crooks."

Neither was Clem. He'd never been forced to. But he was damned well going to handle this crook if it was the last thing he ever did. And if it came down to a fight, well, then . . . He would rely on his excellent reach and his knowledge of physics. Unless Odwell was taller and longer in the arms, and had a phenomenal understanding of leverage points, that should give Clem the advantage.

However, he would just as soon try logic first. "Mail it," he said decisively.

"*Mail* it! Mail what?"

"The emerald."

"Where? Back to where I found it? Thanks a lot!"

"Does it mean that much to you? Money, I mean?"

"Spoken like a rich man." Her eyes passed disparagingly over his torn shirt and stained whites. "I don't know what they pay you at that brain trust of yours, but for your information, I don't even have a job. All I've ever done is farm, keep house and take care of people, and believe me, the salary is lousy and the benefits are even worse! Don't get me wrong—I loved doing it, I really did, but now I've got to find something else. I'm twenty-nine years old and—well, anyway, that emerald just happens to be my social security, my insurance policy and my—" She shook her head. "Oh, for pity's sake, shut up, Marty," she muttered in an undertone.

"No, please. I'm interested in all you have to say."

She sent him a look of disbelief. "The point is, I need it. If I'd never laid eyes on the blessed thing, I'd have been just as happy—happier, in fact. But since I did, no crooked little weasel is going to steal it from me!"

"Then mail it. If not to your own address—"

"I don't even have an address."

"Mail it to an appraiser. I believe that would be the most logical step to take."

"Lovely. And just where do I find this person?"

He was on solid ground, at last. While he hadn't the least idea of how to go about dealing with the likes of Hubert Odwell, the wife of his secretary worked in a jewelry store in Hanes Mall. Malvern had mentioned having his mother's diamond rings appraised for insurance purposes recently by a member of the staff there.

He told her about Malvern and his wife, Virginia. "I'm sure she would be able to help."

"How do I know I can trust her?"

"Do you trust me?"

She waited so long Clem wished he could retract the question, but finally she nodded. Not effusively, but it was a definite affirmative.

Clem restrained the broad grin that threatened to break through his usual stoicism. "Well!" he said, the one word jam-packed with satisfaction.

"At least it's better than doing nothing," Martha conceded. She shook her hair, and a whiff of her fragrance reached out to him, jangling his senses until he could scarcely think coherently. Driven by the heady intoxication of success, Clem cautiously slipped an arm around her shoulders and urged her against his side.

Careful—easy does it. Scare her away now, that's the end of everything.

Her voice muffled against the clean, soapy smell of his collar, Martha said, "Look, thanks for not laughing at me. This whole crazy thing sounds like one of those wild adventure movies—women finding jewels and being chased all over two continents by wicked little men in dirty white suits who need a shave." She caught her breath. "Oops—nothing personal."

If she'd called him a registered, certified, homicidal maniac, Clem wouldn't have taken offense. He was in heaven. He was actually *holding* her! She was actually leaning her head on his shoulder, of her own free will! He felt like stepping over the mountain and handing all of Cat Creek Township to her as a gift!

"We—um—there's no reason to go to town now, I suppose," he suggested.

"No need? What do you mean, no need?"

"I mean, now that you've settled the business of what to do about Odwell and your emerald, we'll have to go back and get it, and then you can stay and wait for Hattie to come home.''

She pulled away and stared at him. ''Stay? Of course I can't stay. I've still got to check on buses and find a way to get my luggage to the bus station. I appreciate your suggestion about the emerald, because frankly I didn't relish the idea of carrying it with me while I get myself settled—probably in a motel for a few days until I can get established and all. You know how flimsy those door chains are—one snip with a pair of bolt cutters and it would be hello, Hubert, goodbye, social security.''

Clem took a moment to follow her progress from Cat Creek to a motel in Winston-Salem. And while he was reasonably certain she wasn't going to find the answer to her transportation needs in a town of some thirty-seven souls, he decided to let her find it out for herself. It would allow him more time to work out a plan.

''Yes, of course,'' he said. Reluctantly he stood and extended a hand, which she ignored. He watched her rise as gracefully as a dryad and brush the dust from the seat of her yellow pants.

Neither of them spoke for the next two miles. The going was rough; he could hear her behind him, panting and sliding on the rocky trail. He wanted to swing her up in his arms and carry her—

Carry her somewhere where they could be alone together until he'd convinced her that they belonged together. She was the best thing that had ever happened to him in this lifetime, and she hadn't even happened. Not in any real sense.

But she was going to.

''Whew! I didn't know I was in such bad shape,'' she panted, pausing beside a thready little waterfall that trickled down a rocky, laurel-hung slope. Clement turned just as she scooped up a handful of water and splashed it on her face, then dipped up another palmful to drink. "This stuff's safe, isn't it? I grew up drinking from a creek that ran right through a cow pasture and lived to tell the tale."

"Unless there's a concentration of certain minerals that can be toxic when taken in excess. Or—um, extensive development higher up that isn't visible from here."

"Killjoy. It tastes great, anyway—I'll risk it. How much farther do we have to go?"

Clement didn't answer. He was too busy studying the patterns of wetness on her yellow cotton shirt—some made by perspiration, some by the recent splashing. She'd worn a sweater when they'd started out, but it had become first a cape and then an apron, worn over her hips.

Her body intrigued him. Not because it was a woman's body and most of what he knew about women's bodies had come from textbooks, but because it was hers. He found himself wanting to know everything about her—physical, mental, spiritual and emotional. And if there was something beyond those qualities, then he wanted to know about that, too. "Oh—what? Less than a mile. The other side of this ridge, then more or less directly down. First there's the creek."

"Cat Creek?"

"Yes. There's a bridge, but the creek itself is no more than a trickle. I presume the bridge was constructed for the times when the creek is in spate." Dammit, why did he always sound as if he were lecturing? "What I meant was that the creek is usually dry—"

"That's what you said."

"Not what I said—the way in which I said it. You might have noticed that I'm not an eloquent man." He held back a briar cane and waited for her to come abreast. Just as she reached him, she came to a dead stop and smiled into his eyes.

"Believe me, I'd noticed," she said gently. "You've improved enormously just since last night, though. I think you must be shy."

Terminally, he wanted to say—only somehow, not with you. And right now he seemed to be entering a new phase of his painfully slow metamorphosis. "I—uh... Catalyst," he gasped. "You, that is. I mean, people—oh, sacred Sarpedon," he muttered, and plowed ahead in silence until he was stopped by a particularly vicious cane briar that had flopped across the trail.

It caught him on the thigh and dug in. When he tried to unhook it from his pants he snagged the back of his hand and swore a little less carefully.

"Here, let me," Martha said, kneeling beside him. "Wow, you really set the hook—ah! There, that does it." She took his hand and examined it, frowning in a way that made the smiles of all other women suffer by comparison.

Clem went into cardiac arrest. By the time he'd recovered, she had cleaned his scratches with a small scrap of lace-trimmed linen and tucked it back in her pocket.

"Um...cold water. Blood stains. The creek," he stammered.

She was getting better at interpreting his non sequiturs. "It's an old hanky. It doesn't matter. Just my one-woman stand against being pushed off the planet by garbage dumps."

"Biodegradable is good," he said gravely.

"Reusable is better. Come on, let's go. If there's a bus today, I'd hate to think I missed it because I stood around arguing the merits of biodegradable over reusable." Laughing, she gave him a gentle push, and Clement had no choice but to move on.

Maybe the bridge would be out. Maybe there'd be a rock slide on the gravel road and the creek would be flooded from the rain they'd had recently and the bridge would have washed out. Then they'd be stranded together until it could be put back in order—which could take forever, as Cat Creek bridge was hardly a priority item on the agenda of the department of transportation. He doubted if the department even knew it existed.

His well of loquaciousness had dried up. When Martha's foot rolled on a stone and she recovered, laughing, Clem absorbed the heady sound of it into his bloodstream. He wondered how she'd sound played back at half speed, with all her sub- and supra-audible notes in evidence. And then, waiting for her to negotiate a particularly tricky patch of trail, he wondered how she would *look* played back at half speed.

The thought was mind-boggling.

"Clement?"

"Yes?" His voice was muffled, and she peered into his face. "Thanks for letting me talk. And for suggesting what you did. Of course, I'll probably just take it with me when I go, because nobody in his right mind would bother to follow me all the way up here. Would he?"

How would he know? He was no authority on criminal thought processes. But she needed reassurance, and he was something of an authority on that. On the need, at least. "Of course not. Logically, Odwell would be better served to stay and wait until someone else makes a find. Without appraisal, he can't know the value of your stone—it might be badly flawed. It might not even be valuable at all."

"Oh *ho*, that's all you know," she chortled. "I'll show it to you when we get back. I owe you that much."

She didn't owe him anything. What Clem wanted from her had nothing to do with her possessions. He had more

han enough to take care of them both if he never worked
nother day in his life, thanks to several rather favorable li-
ensing agreements from patents taken out before he'd gone
o work for B.F.I. Now, of course, B.F.I. had full rights to
ll his discoveries.

When he didn't respond, she swung along beside him, her
and occasionally brushing against his. Clement steeled
imself to ignore it. He was beginning to suspect he already
vas in way over his head.

"You know, it's sort of funny, really," Martha mur-
nured.

"Funny?"

"Ha-ha funny, not weird funny. I mean, first I find this
abulous gemstone, and then someone tries to steal it from
ne, and then I escape for help, only I end up in a place right
•ff the cover of a Gothic novel, and there's this great
•earded, brooding stranger who greets me with an ax, of all
hings. Dr. Barto and Mr. Hyde? I mean, it's positively
Transylvanian."

Clement didn't particularly care for the picture she'd
•ainted, accurate or not. He'd thought they'd moved be-
ond the awkward beginning. "I believe Transylvania
County is southwest of here," he said with all the dignity he
ould summon.

"Oh, lighten up, Clement. Just because you're a re-
earch scientist—" And then she giggled. "A research
hemist! Oh, glory, it's perfect, don't you see? For pity's
ake, where's your sense of humor? I thought you were
Hattie's nephew. She's always saying that if you can't laugh,
ou can't love, and if you can't love, you may as well take
n garbage."

"That makes absolutely no sense at all."

She was taking two steps to his one to keep up, and she
aught at his hand, crushing it playfully in hers. "Oh,

Clement, you know how Hattie is—she says things for effect. It's part of her style."

He knew that. He also knew he was behaving even more like an ass than usual. From an auspicious beginning, he'd suddenly found himself back at the bottom of the heap, and he didn't even know how it had happened. Except that it was somehow connected with that infernal sensitivity of his— that horror of being laughed at that had plagued him for the past fifteen or so years.

"What's the matter," she teased gently, "don't you even believe in laughter?"

"I'm perfectly capable of laughing when something is genuinely amusing." God, what a stilted prig he sounded! She'd be justified in kicking his tail off the next cliff they came to.

"Well, as we've already discussed the subject of garbage, I guess it's love you don't believe in."

Suddenly he was far sweatier than the sixty-five-degree temperature and the forty-three-percent humidity could possibly account for. "There's the creek," he muttered, stepping ahead of her as if to test the narrow wooden bridge.

She caught up with him easily. Ignoring the precariousness of the ramshackle bridge, she hurried after him. "Clem, wait—darn it, I'm sorry if I touched on a tender subject, but you're not the easiest man in the world to get along with. Okay, so your love life is none of my business. Sorry I mentioned it. I was only joking, you know."

Clement wanted to shake her. He wanted to hold her in his arms and force her to stay there until he could say what was in his heart and mind. Didn't she understand, the very thought of love—the emotion she mentioned so casually— terrified him! He didn't know what it was—there was no scientific evidence it even existed. All he knew was that since yesterday—since she'd come into his life—he'd found himself wanting something he couldn't begin to describe, and he hadn't the foggiest notion of how to go about getting it.

"You can see the roof of the post office from here," he informed her stiffly. "Watch that root up ahead—the ground drops off rather precipitously on the other side."

Martha sighed and did as she was told. She maneuvered the twisted root and the scooped out hollow just beyond it easily enough, though her mind was somewhere else. What was wrong with him? He was a strikingly attractive man—or he might be if he trimmed that beard of his. But he acted as if women were an alien species, one he might study under a microscope but would never dream of considering as equal.

Was that it? Was he another Virgil? A man who believed that a woman without a college degree and all the trappings was not to be taken seriously?

Or had a woman hurt him so badly he'd hid out here in the mountains to lick his wounds?

She could picture some women being put off by his rough exterior and his almost crippling shyness. Right at first, she'd been rather alarmed herself. But somewhere along the line the portrait of the young Clem and the tall, awkward man hiding behind a beard, an initial and a pair of thick lenses had melded into a man she'd instinctively trusted. And was fast coming to like. Like, in fact, rather a lot.

How strange. She hadn't known how she felt until she'd put it all together in her mind, but it was just as he'd said—verbalizing helped one to understand.

And then she came to an abrupt halt. "That's *it*? But where's the town?"

They had reached a badly graded road overlooking a small cluster of buildings. No more than a dozen at most. Asphalt squiggles gleamed like giant snail tracks on the surface of the narrow blacktop that ran through the middle of Cat Creek Township. A flag hung limply outside an un-painted building that looked as if it were held together by an assortment of faded signs.

There were three cars and four trucks in evidence. No people. No sign of a bus or even the bread truck that had delivered her to Hattie's house the day before.

"We can ask at the store about buses and registered mail," Clement said. "It serves as the post office."

"It looks like one of the paintings in the dining room—all those rooftops and the kudzu vine turning everything into green sculpture. Are you sure this is the closest town?"

"Yes."

She gave him a suspicious look. "Have I done something to make you angry, Clement?" For some reason, he'd withdrawn into his shell again. Maybe she shouldn't have teased him about his sense of humor—especially since he didn't appear to have one.

"Angry? Of course not. If you're ready, shall we go on down?"

Touchy. Distinctly touchy. Maybe it had something to do with his shyness. Or his love life? Lord knows what little time bomb she'd inadvertently tripped over. She only knew she missed the bumbling, hesitant giant with the sweet smile and the shy looks. She'd come to trust him. She liked him. What's more, she'd sort of gotten the impression that he liked her, too, but evidently she'd been wrong. It wouldn't be the first time, nor likely the last.

"You need milk," she said. "And why not check on the mail to see if there's any word from Hattie, as long as we're here."

"Milk," he repeated. "Mail."

"And buses," she reminded him. Not waiting, she started out along the steep, graveled road toward Lick Munden's Superette.

The man behind the counter stared at a spot over their heads, fly swatter in hand, and muttered an obscenity. Then he shook his head and laid down his weapon. "He'p you?" he inquired laconically.

Clement spoke up. "Mail. Milk."

"D'livery truck just left. Got in half dozen boxes o' choc'late mint ice cream. Ain't tried it, you ort to. 'S good."

"It would melt," Clement told him.

"Eat it here. I got a spoon in the back." He snatched up his swatter and went after a droning bluebottle fly, muttering threats as he rounded the scarred counter.

"No, thank you," Martha put in hurriedly. "We'd better get the mail and the milk and get on back. I—it looks like it might rain again."

The storekeeper turned to stare at her. "You with him? Up to Davenport's place? Man askin' jest yestidday who was stayin' up yonder. Told him all I knew was what I saw, and I ain't been up there since Old Man Mooney died and sold the place to a flatlander."

Martha went cold. She saw Clement's lips twitch in amusement at the order in which the events had supposedly taken place, but she was beyond appreciating the fact that he did, after all, have a sense of humor.

Odwell was still after her. Somehow, he'd managed to track her this far, and if he was nosing around Hattie's place, then he might even *be* there by now!

She pushed in front of Clement and leaned across the counter. "Do any buses come through here?"

"Nope. Nearest bus station's Asheville, I reckon."

"How far is that?" She had a sinking feeling it was *too* far.

"Straight line or road?" Lick Munden stepped over to a boxlike enclosure at one end of the cluttered counter, donned a green plastic visor and began to sort through a small bundle of mail. Martha was all but hyperventilating by the time he selected three letters, carefully putting the rest back. Then he removed the visor, hung it on a nail and came back to the center of the counter.

"Never mind about Asheville," Martha said tensely. "This man who was asking questions—was he driving a rusty blue sedan?"

"Might be. Didn't ask."

"Was he—uh—kind of short, with sandy-colored hair slicked back and a round, red face?"

The storekeeper's glance passed up the length of Clement's six-foot-four-inch frame. "Wouldn't call him perzackly tall. As to his hair, couldn't say. Wore a hat. Face 'bout as round and red as the next feller, I reckon. He weren't nobody I knowed by sight."

Clement, who had been silently observing Martha's increasing agitation, moved to stand protectively beside her. To his astonishment, he felt her small fist slip into the hollow of his palm, and he gripped it tightly. "If this man should return," he said in a tone so authoritative he barely recognized it as his own, "I would appreciate it if you wouldn't mention having seen us."

"Ain't no skin off my nose what you and your missus does. Me, I mind my own business."

Clement did his best to control the sudden rush of warmth that flooded over him at the reference to Martha as his missus. "Then you—uh—you'll respect our privacy?" he asked, forcing his features into a semblance of gravity.

"Said so, didn't I? Here's Miz Davenport's mail—milk in the cooler."

They'd barely stepped down off the stone-slab stoop when Martha said tersely, "He knows. How could he possibly know where I am? I made sure he was following the bus before I even started asking around for a ride."

"We can't be certain it's Odwell."

"No? And I suppose you're used to having people snooping around asking questions about where you are and what you're doing?"

The more upset she became, the calmer Clement grew. Who was that guy—Jack Bond? Agent double-oh something? This must be what it felt like to know one was equipped for the most hair-raising eventuality. Actually, it was quite satisfying. Downright exhilarating, in fact.

"Uh—what? Oh," he stammered, landing back on earth with a tooth-rattling thump. "No, not really, but that doesn't mean the man is Hubert Odwell."

"Of course not, it's the I.R.S. You're being audited, right?"

"Not that I know of, but I'm quite certain my accountant would—"

"Clement, get serious! You can't really be that dense, can you?"

After that jibe about his sense of humor, he couldn't resist. "My density is subject to fluctuation under conditions of stress."

She blinked, but bobbed right back. "All right, you're far from dense. Look, I'm not sure what your problem is, but whatever it is, you've got to admit that there can't be *two* strange men asking questions."

"It's conceivable."

"Which means I've got to get out of here," she said, ignoring his response.

Clem turned and clasped her shoulders, his deep-set eyes brilliant behind his rather smudged lenses. "It means nothing of the kind. No one knows where you are. Munden isn't the sort to give out free information. Besides, if you leave— if you move into a motel—who will look after you?"

Her mouth fell open as she stared up at him, and the sigh momentarily robbed Clem's mind of any thoughts of emeralds and prowlers—as well as his own dismal record with women. He leaned closer. He could actually feel her breath warming his face. His mouth was dry, his hands were damp and his heart was foundering under the strain. So close...Another few inches and his lips would touch hers.

No, dammit, another few inches and she'd be battling her way through his beard! He hadn't trimmed the thing in weeks, hadn't bothered to look in a mirror in longer than that.

"Uh—that is, yes... *well*," he said, stepping back.

"Clement, what am I going to do?" she wailed softly.

"Forget about it. For now, that is. Never worry over a problem in an untimely manner. It's exhausting and it does nothing to address the problem."

"Whew! I never know which one I'm going to be dealing with next, Barto the brilliant or Clem the closemouthed."

"Sorry—it isn't deliberate." He achieved a creditable smile, which was better than getting all stiff-necked again. He could be a real idiot when the occasion demanded—and even when it didn't. "Martha, I want you to know that you'll be quite safe with me. I've trained my body to do without sleep for thirty-six hours, and I promise you, I won't leave you unguarded for a single moment."

Martha looked at him in astonishment. "Are you serious? You *are* serious. Oh, lordy, Clement, I was only joking. It's my problem, not yours."

Struggling to determine the best way to reassure her—he could hardly tell her that he would willingly pledge the rest of his life to fulfilling her slightest whim—he said, "I make you uncomfortable. I'm aware of that, and I'm sorry, but still intend to look after you. While you're here. Visiting with Hattie. At her house, I mean."

He gazed down at her helplessly. If she laughed—if she ridiculed his offer—he didn't know what he'd do. He was offering more than he'd ever dared offer to any woman before, more than he'd ever dreamed he could. Only how could he tell her so without frightening her even more? He'd only met her yesterday.

"Oh, Clement," Martha said softly, and she leaned her head against his chest for the briefest moment.

His heart stopped, flopped and resumed its frantic pace. Not a single one of his seven degrees could help him when it came to interpreting her smile. He only knew that no one had ever smiled at him in just that way before. Or with the same cataclysmic effect.

"You really haven't changed all that much from the boy in the portrait, have you?" she murmured, easing herself from his arms.

Six

On the way home, Clement pondered various methods of keeping Martha from finding a way to leave him. If she were determined to go, he could hardly keep her there forcibly, yet he knew he had to explore this extraordinary thing that was happening to him, and to explore it, he needed her there. Because she was at the core of it.

But how?

Threats? She could conceivably strangle while laughing at his attempts to play the tough guy. Threats were out. Bribery? What could he possibly offer that she would want, except for her freedom? Perhaps a road map and the keys to Hattie's car. Still, there had to be something he could do—some simple thing that he'd overlooked just because it *was* so simple.

Systematize, Barto, Observe, analyze, compile your data and extrapolate from there, starting with your obvious strengths and advantages.

His scowl deepened. All right then, he decided impatiently—he'd start with his *dis*advantages. That shouldn't present any problem.

One, he had problems communicating. He'd made remarkable progress since she'd come, but it still wasn't enough. He couldn't talk a fly into a sugar bowl.

Two, he had an unfortunate way of becoming aroused when he was with her, which embarrassed him and was hardly likely to instill confidence in her, should she ever become aware of it.

Numbers three through seven—he didn't have the sort of looks a woman liked in a man, his clothes were a mess, he needed a haircut and a trim and his damned glasses made him look like a myopic frog.

When he could find them, that was. He didn't even want to know what he looked like fumbling around without them.

And then it hit him. His eyes. His glasses. She'd said she hated to go off and leave him alone without them...no. That would be dishonest.

Preoccupied, he strode ahead, as if his longer legs stood a chance of catching up with the answer to all his problems.

"How about blazing a trail as you go, speedy. If I don't make it back by the end of the week, you might send out a posse—or better yet, get in touch with Hubert. We know he can always find me."

Clement waited for Martha to catch up with him. His face flaming in competition with the surrounding fall foliage, he stammered an apology. "It's the stairways. I mean, I don't care for elevators. Uh—that is—"

"If there's an elevator up this damned mountain, Clement Cornelius Barto, and you've been leading me on this chase for nothing—"

"No! That is, it's in the Grayson Building. Where I work, that is. Nine of them, and three in my apartment—floors, that is. But it's not only that—I've been doing a lot of other climbing. Mountains, I mean. Actually, not an entire one. Only portions of the same one. I think."

"Then don't let me—whew!—hold you back," Martha panted. "How about sending out a—Saint Bernard when—you get home. Or—whew! Better yet, a donkey!"

"You're exhausted."

"I'm *not* exhausted, but I've—I've got a stitch."

A stitch. "A stitch?"

"I'm tired! Winded! Pooped!" She pressed a hand against her side, and Clement closed his eyes briefly and called himself every derogatory name he could think of. "Sit on that rock." Taking her arm, he led her carefully to a worn boulder that projected above a bed of dry leaves. She sat, reminding him again of a lovely dryad, and he dropped to his knees beside her.

"Breathe naturally," he commanded, his voice rough with concern.

"That's easy for you to say!"

He gave her a few moments and then he said, "Listen."

Martha drew in several more deep breaths, wiped her brow and then looked at him expectantly, as if waiting for him to continue. "I'm listening. You're going to tell me there's a taxi stand around the corner, right?"

"Sorry. Birds."

She frowned. "Birds? Where? I don't hear any birds."

Neither did he. For once, the birds remained stubbornly silent. In all the times he'd trekked this same trail, never once had his presence stilled the cheerful cacophony that usually echoed across the ravine.

To fill the silence, he said, "I don't know their names. From their point of view, that's probably irrelevant. I've found that I like being able to hear them without having to know their names. There's a sort of..."

"There's a sort of?" she prompted when he fell silent.

"Um—well, a freedom in it. Not having to know their names, I mean. Forget it—you wouldn't understand."

"Like eating cold spaghetti for breakfast."

"Spaghetti?"

"That's freedom. When you've cooked a proper breakfast for everyone within range every single day for the past eight or ten years, and then one day you decide, what the dickens—let's all eat cold spaghetti."

His smile dawned slowly as he realized that she did indeed understand—although her metaphor was not one he would have chosen. "Right. They're spaghetti birds."

"Clement, could we open the milk? I'm parched."

He practically tripped in his haste to oblige. "I'm sorry I don't have a glass—you go first. Have all you want."

Martha laughed, and he fancied he could detect a faint echo of the sound from the dense forest surrounding them. He watched her tilt the jug, entranced with the line of her throat, the swell of her breasts and the faint shadow of her closed eyelids.

When he came to his senses again, she was holding the half-gallon jug out to him, an opalescent ring of milk showing above the bow of her upper lip. "What are you staring at?" she asked, recapping the milk and putting it down when he continued to ignore her outstretched arm.

"The turbid medium theory. Milk over pink skin. Or a red bowl. Or, um—a wood floor. Portrait painters make use of it to achieve depth in skin tones. It's what makes the sky appear to be blue when there's no blue pigment at all in the sky—only the warm light of the sun filtered through layers of atmosphere."

"What brought on all that?" Martha asked slowly.

Clem's gaze moved from her mouth to her eyes and back again. "The milk. Around your mouth."

The tip of her tongue darted out to circle her lips, leaving behind a sheen of moisture, and suddenly, his breathing grew labored. He shifted his position.

"Stop staring at me that way! Am I breaking out or something?"

"Martha, um ... do you like kissing?"

She almost fell off her perch. "Do I like *what*?"

"I'm sorry, I shouldn't have asked that."

"Probably not, but you did. What I want to know is ... why?"

"Why what?"

She stood abruptly, and her foot struck the milk jug, toppling it several feet down the trail. "Clement, what is it with you? First you can't talk at all, and then you spout off like a textbook on the wildest assortment of topics, and then you—you sound like a—an I don't know what! How old are you, anyway?"

"Thirty-two and a quarter." He was standing, too, his face a study in consternation. "I shouldn't have asked you that."

"You're certainly old enough to know better. A man doesn't go around asking strange women if they—well, you know. Or maybe you were joking?"

"No. Well, do you?" he persisted doggedly.

"Of course I do! That is, sometimes I do. Oh, for goodness sake, it all depends."

"On what?"

The sun slanted through a break in the trees, highlighting a patch of wildflowers, an eroded granite outcropping and one extremely dusty plastic jug of milk. Clement stared at them unseeingly. One foot dug a shallow furrow in the path. She was right. It was a stupid question, and he was old enough to know better. Thank God he hadn't come right out and asked her if she enjoyed the physical act of love. Because he really wanted to know. What he wanted to know even more was if she enjoyed it enough to risk doing it with him.

Oh, lord, this was getting out of hand! He couldn't even talk to the woman without making a fool of himself, and already he was worrying about how he was going to go about making love to her!

In fact, he was worrying so much he was becoming acutely uncomfortable. Physically. This was embarrassing! The last time he'd suffered such pronounced symptoms had been when Danforth's secretary had come by to pick up his requisitions and noticed a run in her panty hose. She'd proceeded to investigate the source right there in his laboratory. She'd kept sending him funny looks, as if daring him to do something. What had she thought he could do about it, produce a fresh pair out of a test tube?

This time he couldn't very well relieve the immediate physical manifestations by running down nine flights of stairs to the coffee machine in the basement and back up again.

"On how I feel about someone, of course."

The words startled Clem from his mental miasma. She was obviously responding to something he'd said, but what? He did some quick backtracking, matching question to answer, and ended up feeling more discouraged than ever. Her feelings toward him were clear enough. The kindest thing would be to let her go, although he wasn't quite sure how to go about it short of calling a cab from town to drive her to the airport as Hattie had done.

"I'm sorry," he mumbled.

"Sorry for what?"

Forcing a smile he didn't feel, he explained. "Logjams. Sometimes big chunks break through, sometimes small trickles. Actually, my thought processes are remarkably clear. They just get muddied up somehow in translation."

He waited for her to laugh. Or to call him a nerd, a nut case or any of the usual terms he was accustomed to hearing. Usually, but not always, spoken in an undertone. He'd actually thought he was improving, but it wasn't going to work.

"You're talking about your shyness—the way you sometimes seem to have trouble making yourself understood."

"Sometimes? That's like saying it sometimes snows in Siberia."

But Martha was beginning to understand this great, woolly teddy bear. Right now he was all bent out of shape because he'd blurted out a sophomoric question about kissing. And because he was aroused. If he even suspected she'd noticed that, he'd have turned every color of the rainbow instead of merely red.

Lord knows, if it had happened when he'd first confronted her with that ax in his hands, she'd probably have sailed right off that cliff at the edge of the road. She wasn't cut out to be a sacrificial maiden. But since then, she'd come to know him better. And the really shocking thing was that his physical reaction didn't shock her at all. Just the opposite, in fact. She found it almost stimulating. All right—she'd found it *extremely* stimulating.

Martha had entertained a few sexual fantasies of her own when she hadn't been too exhausted with having to work on the farm, look after Papa, go to school and study art in her spare time. A good many of them had even been about this very man. Or rather, about a brooding young man in an unforgettable portrait.

But she was an adult now, and she'd learned the hard way that fantasies were strictly a hothouse product. They withered fast in the cold air of reality.

As Clem and Martha sat on the rock together, steeped in the fragrance of resinous forest and sun-dried grasses and wildflowers, Martha's sexual awareness gradually began to fade, to be replaced by something more easily acceptable. Certainly a lot more comfortable.

The old tenderness she'd felt for Hattie's portrait had returned full force, with overtones of something deeper, richer, warmer. A moment's nostalgia, brought on by all the rush and confusion of the past few weeks, she told herself. Hardly surprising after all she'd been through. It was quiet and peaceful here, and Clem was a comforting, undemanding presence beside her. Almost too undemanding.

Suddenly Martha, who had never in her life asked a man out, never called first or kissed on a first date—or even *had* that many dates, at least as far as variety was concerned— felt a sudden, startling urge to turn and take C. Cornelius Barto in her arms, to succor him, to smooth that unruly forelock from his face and—if she could find a mouth under all that beard—to kiss it!

Whoa, lady! Both feet on the ground! She could hear her father's voice as if he were right there beside her, and she heeded the voice of caution by force of habit.

Coercing her protesting muscles into action, she said, "I reckon we'd better get moving. I'm not even sure I can get up."

While she was trying to convince her leg muscles that it was their duty to lever her butt off the rock, Clement arose with a lithe movement that could have made her hate him. Was it her fault that housework and keeping up with two small dynamos didn't exactly put her into Jane Fonda condition? Just because *he* could leap tall buildings in a single bound...

Except for a few groans, a grunt or two and a lot of huffing and puffing, the journey continued in silence. Martha allowed her mind to drift, too tired to call it to heel. It drifted frequently to Clement Barto. Slightly less frequently to Hubert Odwell—she was really going to have to settle matters with him, and she wasn't quite convinced that getting the emerald out of her possession would do it. What if he didn't believe her? They never did in the movies.

The sun was grazing the tops of the trees on the western side of the ridge by the time they sighted the house. Martha, doing her best to ignore screaming muscles and swollen feet, muttered, "If by some miracle...I make it as far as the bathtub, I'm going to...take up residence there for the next two weeks. Whew! I warn you, Clement...don't even try to evict me for anything short of a...four-course dinner!"

Clement grinned at the slight figure plodding up the last stretch. "Eggs or cans?"

A scathing look told him what she thought of her choices. "Just keep an eye out...for buzzards circling overhead, will you? And next time you need milk..."

He could hear her labored breathing, see the look of exhaustion on her face, and even sweaty, dusty and flushed with exertion, she was the most beautiful creature he had ever beheld, real or imaginary. Suddenly infused with fresh energy, he said, "Your emerald. We'll have to go back to mail it."

"Don't even think about it." Martha groaned, pausing to eye the last uphill stretch. "Clem, I've been doing some thinking..." Leaning against a locust tree, she waited for him to join her. "Slow up, darn it! You've walked circles around me and—" Pant, gasp. "You're not even breathing hard! What are you grinning about, you hairy hyena? If you're waiting for me to fall at your feet, forget it. I might be a weakling, but I'm a proud weakling.''

Clem's laughter echoed off the surrounding slopes. When he could speak again, he did his best to salve her ego. ''You're just not used to the altitude.''

''This isn't exactly...Mount Mitchell. A few years ago...I could have kept up with you ... but I ... must have gotten soft.''

''Soft,'' he repeated, and the thought of her softness had an immediate and not unexpected effect on him.

''In the body, not the head,'' she retorted. ''Soft meaning weak—not soft as opposed to hard. Although I guess— oh, forget it!''

He only wished he could! Hunching his shoulders protectively, Clem drew one knee up, bracing his foot on the rough bark. He forced himself to think of cold showers, icy mountain streams. When that didn't work, he turned his mind to one of the more fascinating projects he'd had to sideline when he had taken over Danforth's administrative duties.

Unfortunately, his senses had a mind of their own, and they were reveling in the sweet-spicy fragrance of her heated body, the zephyr sound of her breathing. He thought of the milk that had rimmed her lips and licked his.

Soft as opposed to hard. God! The very concept sent him reeling!

She broke through his feverish daydream, scattering the pieces before he could snatch them back. ''If you're still waiting for me to keel over, forget it,'' she said dryly. ''Just give me another minute...to catch my breath...and I'll race you to the front door.''

Clem prided himself on his fast recovery. ''I'll even give you a head start, since you're handicapped.''

"Oh, for pity's sake, I am not! My feet hurt, that's all."

"No, I meant your legs."

Bottom against the tree, Martha leaned out, twisting around so that she could glare at him. "What's wrong with my legs?"

"They're too short. I mean, they're quite sufficient—that is, they're certainly in proportion—" With a short oath, he turned and swept her off the ground mail, milk and all. "I haven't even seen your legs—" Yet, he qualified silently. "But I'm sure mine are longer."

Martha registered a single squawk of protest then sagged in his arms, and Clem savored the moment. He almost hated to begin the journey. Once begun, it would quickly end. On the other hand, holding her this way was having a rather predictable physiological effect. Cold sweat. Palpitations. Dry mouth. Etcetera.

He started walking. And then he started worrying. What if he tripped? What if he gave in to the overpowering need to lower her to the ground and kiss every square—and rounded—inch of her marvelous body, short legs included?

He felt an arm slide around his neck and he trembled. Common sense told him that she was merely anchoring herself in case he dropped her, but then, common sense was one area in which he'd always been lamentably weak. If it couldn't be taught in a classroom or a laboratory—and that particular commodity couldn't—then he hadn't learned it, because he'd wasted ninety percent of his life in one or the other.

At first she was stiff. Laughing, she demanded to be set down, but bit by bit she ceased protesting and began to relax. Before Clem had gone a third of the way, her cheek was resting in the curve of his shoulder, making him feel handsome, charming and every bit as masterful as Petruchio at his best.

"Watch that root. If you fall, I fall," Martha said a little breathlessly, and his arms tightened imperceptibly. Ease up, you fool, he cautioned himself silently. Don't scare her now—not when things are just beginning to look promising.

Not until they were at the front door did Clement reluctantly set her down. She sighed and promptly kicked off both her shoes. He was tired, too, but he would have held her willingly for the next fifty years if he could have thought of an excuse that sounded even faintly reasonable.

He seriously doubted that she would care for the real one—that he could never remember anything having felt so wonderful, so right, in his entire life as she did. In his arms. Pressed tightly against his body, her sweet scent warming his nostrils, her lips so close he could have touched them with his if he'd dared.

One day soon he would dare, he promised himself. Somehow, he would learn whatever had to be learned—there were books, weren't there? There were how-to books on everything these days. And once he felt sufficiently knowledgeable, he would ask her—

Ask her what? Hell, he didn't even know the questions, much less the answers!

But he could learn. He had a brain. What was the use of having spent his entire life in pursuit of knowledge if he hadn't learned how to achieve the one thing he wanted more than anything else in the world?

Shouldering open the screen door, Clem busied himself with the massive pewter latch. Dream on, you great blundering ox. And what's she going to be doing while you bone up on the gentle art of wooing a woman?

"Need some help? What's the matter, can't you find the right key?"

"No. Yes."

"Oh, for pity's sake," she muttered tiredly, leaning against the wall, the jug of milk dangling from her fingertips.

Clement was actually trembling by the time he felt the latch give way. He reached out to relieve her of the milk and accidentally knocked it from her grasp. And then he swore softly.

It was Martha who retrieved the milk. Taking his hand in her other one, she led him inside and shut the door. "Men! You're as bushed as I am, only you're too proud to let on. Well, don't be embarrassed—you don't have to prove anything to me. I'm ready for a long hot soak, and then I'm going to dig out my slippers, because I don't think I'll be able to cram my feet into real shoes for a week at least. Next time I start out on an eight-mile hike, I hope someone ties me to a tree."

Taking the guilt for her suffering upon his own shoulders, Clem searched the cluttered files of his mind for something to offer in assuagement. "Soak. Maybe powder—salts? I'm not sure of the proper treatment—"

"Don't worry, I'm going to soak. If I'm not out by Thanksgiving, save me some turkey."

"I promise, I won't even open the can until you're out of the bathroom." His smile was tentative, and his heart soared when she chuckled in response to his feeble joke.

Actually, Clement could have done with a bath himself, but he would have to wait, thanks to the peculiarities of the antiquated hot-water system. Waiting for Martha was a privilege. He would willingly commit to a lifetime of cold showers if he thought it would add to her comfort.

In fact, for his own comfort, he would probably have to. "You go ahead," he said. "I have a something that needs attending to first."

It had been a mistake, Clem admitted to himself some half hour later when he tried to get up from the floor. The minute she'd gone upstairs, he'd stretched out on the rug on his stomach, knowing full well what would happen if he fell asleep in that position. And then he'd fallen asleep.

It had happened. He could barely turn his head.

Levering himself up by degrees, he winced at the assortment of twinges and kinks in his cervical region. That was the part of his spine that caught hell. Too many years spent poring over books and microscopes. Plus the tension. That always got him in the neck.

Using a crawling, sliding technique, he made it as far as the ottoman and then he braced himself to do what had to be done. Head hanging, he laced his fingers together at the back of his neck and began manipulating.

"Another headache?" Martha said from the doorway.

Ducking around, he squinted in the direction of her voice, having removed his glasses for safekeeping. The movement was too much for his spasming muscles, and he groaned. "Stiff neck."

"Need some help? Jack used to collect tension back there from hanging over his books too long. He has rotten posture." She was beside him before he realized it, her hands sliding underneath his. Clem reached for his glasses just as she dug in her thumbs, and she said, "Uh-uh. Leave them off. Hang your head forward and relax, I won't hurt you."

Jack? Who was Jack? Why had she been in a position to offer this sort of service to him? "Ouch!" He yelped when she hit a tender spot.

"Hurt? Good. It means I'm in the right area. I'll loosen you up back here and get the blood flowing again."

"Your hands are stronger than they look."

"I grew up on a farm. I was priming tobacco and milking before I was old enough to read."

"Who's Jack?" Clem's voice was muffled, his head hanging practically onto his chest, but it was working. He could feel the spasms beginning to ease. Her hands were remarkably effective.

"My brother. I've been living with him for the past few years, taking care of my niece and nephew. Jack's a widower." Her thumbs lifted and soothed, lifted and soothed firmly, but without bruising force. "Trina died when Jenny was born, and I went out to Louisville and—that still hurt? No? Good. Anyway, three weeks ago Jack remarried. I stayed while they went on their honeymoon, and now I'm on my way home. I was going to have a little vacation and visit Hattie on the way, but you know what happened then."

He knew. Yet he didn't know anything at all. He wanted to know everything about her. What she read, what music she listened to—if she liked rainy days and cold winter mornings, or blue skies and burnished summer sunrises.

"Ah," Clement groaned. She was working down his spine, the heel of her hands pressing hard and twisting. He could feel a rush of heat mounting in his body that had nothing at all to do with her hands on his back—nothing and everything, he amended. She had the same effect on him simply by being in the same room.

Relaxed after her bath, Martha seemed inclined to talk. "I'll miss the children. I've tried not to think about it because I know it's best for Jack and the kids this way—regular family, with both parents. But I've had Jenny since birth. She's like my own child. Poor Jack—he and Trina married right out of high school—probably too young, but you know how it is."

That was just the trouble. He didn't know how it was. Hadn't an inkling. He did know, however, that the thought of being married to a woman—to *this* woman—of giving her children . . .

Well, it was quite simply the most wonderful thing imaginable in a large and wondrous universe. He would have traded any number of Nobel prizes for a woman of his own. Not just any woman, but *this* woman.

"So this is the way it comes about," he mused aloud.

"The way what comes about? Am I being too rough on you? Sorry. You're so big. I mean your muscles—your shoulders, that is." She stammered to a halt and went on kneading.

How love comes about. How it manifests itself, Clem thought. He almost spoke the words aloud, but caught himself in time. He hadn't believed in love since he'd been fifteen, in spite of the fact that a large portion of the world's literature was based on just such a hypothesis.

Love. He'd considered it a myth, at best—rationalization for the procreative urge, at worst. Other children had believed in the tooth fairy—in Santa Claus. Clem never had. He'd been inclined to suspect a mutant virus whenever he'd seen otherwise sane men and women suddenly lose all semblance of reason over a member of the opposite sex.

"'Love, like a mountain wind upon an oak, Falling upon me, shakes me leaf and bough,'" he murmured wonderingly.

"What?"

Face flushed, he fumbled for his glasses and jammed them on his face. "Um—it's—uh . . . Sappho. Uh, something she said. Wrote, that is. I—um—don't know why it popped into my head. Mountain wind. I expect the wind blowing reminded me of it."

"There's not a whiff of wind," Martha retorted, but her voice was not quite as sharp as it might have been. In fact, it sounded almost gentle when she said, "Clement, do you realize we didn't have any lunch today, and now it's almost eight o'clock? I don't know about you, but I've already worked off a week's worth of calories."

He pounced on the excuse. "Hunger. That's it!"

"Why don't you go get a nice, warm soak to finish what I started here while I fix us some supper? Say, forty-five minutes? Will that be enough time for you to get the rest of the kinks out?"

He was not a tub man, he realized some fifteen minutes later, immersed in hot water up to just below his sternum. Why hadn't he settled for a quick shower? A cold one, at that?

Because she'd told him to get in the tub. If she'd told him to climb into an autoclave and switch it on, he would have cheerfully steamed himself purple. This business of being in love was going to be tricky! It might even be fatal if he didn't learn how to handle it.

Thoughtfully, Clem scrunched down deeper, resting his heels on the brass and porcelain sprockets of the faucets. By George, he had to admit, it did feel pretty good. There was something downright intimate about sharing a bathtub, even if they shared it at different times. He could still smell the spicy, flowery scent of whatever it was she used—soap or shampoo or whatever. Her toiletries were arranged neatly on the marble basin—a bottle with yellow roses on it. A jar with a yellow lid. A lavender razor and a pink toothbrush. Intimate things. Who else knew the color of her toothbrush and razor?

Suddenly, Clem's mind took off on a tangent that sent the blood coursing through his body. His pulses hammered at the mental images that were forming faster than he could deal with them in the steamy atmosphere.

There's no reason two people can't share a bathtub at the same time, if one of them sits . . .

He shook his head. No, not that way. He'd want to see her face and her breasts, not the back of her head and her scapulae. But if she turned around to face him, then where would her legs go? Crossed over his thighs? Along his flanks? In the short, old-fashioned tub, there wasn't room to lie down, even for one. With two people involved, one of them was either going to drown or break a few bones.

To hell with hot soaks! He was going to be in worse shape than ever if he didn't get his mind on something a little less stimulating. A few fractures were beginning to sound like a reasonable price to pay for holding Martha's wet and warm body against his and allowing nature to take its course.

Hastily, Clem pulled the plug, drained half the water out and turned on the cold water full force. Five minutes later, he rubbed himself ruthlessly with a coarse towel and then dressed, popping another button and momentarily jamming his zipper in his haste.

The prosaic smell of coffee greeted him as soon as he opened the door, and he began to breathe easier. Was that ham he smelled cooking? It occurred to him that part of his hallucinations might be due to the fact that his body had not been refueled in some time.

But the scientist in him refused to allow him to get away with such faulty reasoning. His brain might have wandered off the track, but his body knew very well what it wanted. And it wasn't food.

"It's ham and cheese omelets, and they're done. There's cheese toast, too. Sorry if that doesn't suit, but I didn't have a whole lot to pick from. You don't have any butter."

She was still wearing her robe. It was yellow, belted at the waist, made of some soft, corded fabric—chenille, he thought, and he wondered what she was wearing underneath. Hoping the flush he could feel rising up from his collar would stop at his beard line, Clem took his seat at the

head of the table with as much aplomb as he could muster
Unfortunately, his newly discovered talent for creating eroti
fantasies was making it rather difficult. Damn those book
of Hattie's!

Clearing his throat, he said, "The word comes from th
French word for caterpillar, you know."

Martha looked startled. "Omelet? I thought it ha
something to do with eggs."

There went his foot again. "Um—chenille. Your, uh–
whatchamacallit. Robe. The word omelet comes from th
Latin word for small plate."

"How . . . interesting," she said faintly, picking up he
fork.

"No, it's not." Clement took up his utensils, holding th
knife in one hand and the fork in the other, as though the
were weapons. "I don't know anything interesting. Tha
is—everything I say comes out sounding like recycled text
books. Or worse."

"That's not true, Clem. And anyway, it's no great crime
Besides, you're getting better all the time, honestly. Now ea
your toast while it's hot. Cold cheese toast is stringy an
tasteless."

Obediently, he picked up his cheese toast and took a larg
bite, feeling as if he were back in the nursery.

"I added a pinch of cocoa to the coffee." Martha cuppe
her mug in her hands, inhaled and sipped. "I wanted some
thing rich-tasting tonight. We've earned it, don't you thin
so?"

"That was kind of you."

"It wasn't kind at all," she said impatiently. "I did it be
cause I like it! For all I know, you could be allergic to co
coa." She attacked her omelet, releasing even more of it
rich, enticing aroma.

Gradually the stiffness left him. So he'd done it again. Overreacted. It wasn't the first time, and it would hardly be the last. He simply wasn't a social creature, and the sooner he stopped trying to be something he wasn't, the better for all concerned.

Clem felt considerably more comfortable. His stomach, at least, was satisfied. Martha was a relaxing companion. She didn't chatter, nor did she demand of him things that were beyond his capability.

In a way, he almost wished she would.

Blotting his shaggy mustache with a napkin, he managed an apologetic smile. "I'm afraid I need a trim rather badly. Packing—I don't travel much. I forgot some things..."

"I noticed. You're welcome to one of my razors. I have a bag of disposable ones in my toilet case. So much for my stand on ecology," she said with a rueful smile, which he found totally endearing. "Frankly, I was hoping you'd shave while I was here, now that I know who you are. I'm curious to see how much you've changed since Hattie painted that portrait."

Clement's coffee spoon clattered against his saucer. "You know about the portrait?"

She nodded. "For at least the past ten or twelve years. I used to go home with Hattie for lunch sometimes on Saturdays, since I lived out in the country and came in for morning and afternoon classes."

"I'm surprised you recognized me under all this." Clem tugged at a length of curly, reddish-brown beard.

"I didn't at first, but things began to add up. Your name. Your eyes. Something about the way you hold your head— sort of watchful. Like you don't quite trust people."

"I was only sixteen or so," he muttered, embarrassed at her analysis.

"It's a beautiful portrait, Clem. You must be awfully proud of Hattie."

When he didn't reply, she smiled down at her plate and said, "I know she was awfully proud of you. You were the only one of her family she ever talked about. She said you were a genius, but even so, there was an outside chance for you. I never did know what she meant. I'm afraid at that age, I did more looking than listening."

Clement fiddled with a crust of cheese toast, strewing crumbs on the table and knocking his fork to the floor. He mumbled something about the weather.

"What?"

"Nothing!" he practically yelled, and then wished he could evaporate without a trace. "Sorry. I didn't mean to shout."

They sipped coffee silently for a few moments, and Clem searched for a tactful way to ask something that had occurred to him while he was hunting down a pair of hole-free socks.

Was she free? Had she already formed an attachment to any particular man? Did she believe that two discerning adults could meet and instantly recognize qualities in the other that would be a sound basis for a lasting relationship?

Would she lie down with him and let him hold her in his arms, and allow him to make love to her again and again until he finally learned how to please her?

Suddenly he leaped to his feet, tipping his chair and catching it just before it toppled over. "Wait here! I mean, excuse me, please."

Her look of concern would have thrilled him if he hadn't already turned away. "Clement, what's wrong? Are you ill?"

"Wait right there. Don't move! I'll be back in five minutes."

Martha stared at his half-eaten omelet. She wasn't exactly a gourmet chef. Still, no one had ever reacted quite this violently to her cooking before.

Maybe he was allergic. Not to eggs, because they'd had those before. To cocoa? Possibly.

Or to her.

Seven

The scissors were right where he remembered having seen them—in Hattie's sewing basket. And while they weren't exactly regulation shears, they would do well enough in an emergency. This was an emergency. He walked into the bathroom and closed the door behind him. Clement frowned at his image in the mirror. He angled his head this way and that, and then grabbed a handful of beard. No wonder she'd been staring at him earlier. His face looked like the backside of a hedgehog.

And these clothes! Everything he owned had shrunk since he'd been in Cat Creek. Something to do with the water, no doubt. The seams of all his shirts were giving way.

Clement had never given much thought to clothes, other than to wish the laundry wouldn't use so much starch. He limited himself to safe combinations of black, gray, tan and white, according to the season. On the rare occasions when Hattie barged into his life and commandeered him for dinner or an opening, he wore one of the suits she'd picked out for him. His shirts were all of the finest quality. And they all were white. His ties were a blend of silk and wool, and like his socks, they were all black. It was a safe system.

Denim. That was what he needed, he told himself for the second time in as many days. Even old Heinrich, a legend in bioastronautics in his day, lived in denim pants and something that looked like a pair of red pajamas. A running suit, he called it. On Heinrich it looked more like an empty Christmas stocking hanging from a doorknob.

It also looked a hell of a lot more comfortable than over-starched whites or khakis, Clement conceded, making up his mind to augment his limited wardrobe the very first chance he got.

Ten minutes later, he stood frowning at the reflection of his unfamiliar face, parts of which had not seen the light of day in several years. As barbering tools, a disposable razor and a pair of pinking shears left something to be desired, but they'd done the job. He now sported half a dozen nicks, a ragged but manageable mustache and a clean-shaven, if somewhat pale, jaw. Should he have rid himself of the mustache, too? Without the beard, it was too obvious. It seemed to have no purpose other than adornment, and Clem was acutely uncomfortable with the idea of adorning himself.

However, he couldn't quite bring himself to bare his entire face. Besides, the real test was not what he thought of it, but what Martha would think. Would she consider it an improvement? Or would she take one look at his bare face and start laughing?

Oh, hell, it had been a lousy idea! He should have known better. A clean-shaven jaw wasn't going to improve his ability to converse in a suave and debonair manner. That took years of practice, starting, no doubt, in kindergarten.

At five years old, he'd been exploring the fascinating worlds of algebra, astronomy and chemistry, not dancing around the maypole with some pigtailed tadpole in pink ruffles. Nor had he managed to catch up since.

How was he supposed to know what women liked to talk about? Women who weren't involved in his own area of interest, that was. Music? The mathematics upon which some of the major compositions were based was a remarkably fascinating topic—but what if she didn't care for music?

There was always poetry. No! Scratch poetry. Those lines of Sappho's he'd blurted out earlier had embarrassed him and done nothing at all for her. Maybe she preferred the French poets.

Flowers! All women liked flowers, didn't they? He knew a lot about flowers—botanical names, chemical properties... If they got stuck for a topic, he could always bring in botany. Maybe he'd ask her why she smelled like roses and fresh-baked bread instead of chemicals, musk and drycleaning fluid, like most other women.

Hearing a sound outside the door, Clement swallowed hard and gripped the edge of the sink. When it came to conversation, he'd just have to allow her to take the lead. Surely it couldn't be that difficult to carry on a casual conversation. They'd been doing great for a while today.

"Go get 'em, tiger!" he growled at the stranger in the mirror. "Concentrate hard on being casual and spontaneous. Nothing to it!" He raised a fist in a mock salute.

"Clement, are you all right?"

The fist fell and sweat suddenly beaded his forehead. Hell, no, he wasn't all right! He was coming apart at the seams, both figuratively and literally. What's more, he hadn't the foggiest notion of what to do about it. "Right. Uh—I mean, I am. Yes!" *Smooth, Barto—real smooth!*

He flung open the door before he could lose his nerve and then winced at her startled gasp. She didn't like his face. His damned nose was too long, and his jaw was too—too something. "I'm sorry. I thought it would be an improvement," he mumbled. Stepping back, he tried to close the door again.

"C.C. Barto, don't you dare shut that door in my face!" She had her foot in it. Short of sacrificing a few of her slipper-clad metatarsi, there was nothing he could do.

Reluctantly, Clem allowed her to look her fill. Nothing—not even the tandem bout of walking pneumonia that had landed him up here in Buncombe County in the first place—had ever made him feel quite so vulnerable. "I'm sorry. I've startled you."

"No, you— That's not it."

"I shouldn't have. It was a bad idea." He covered his chin with his hand. "Er, um—it was bothering me. With summer coming on and all..." *It's November, cretin!*

Before he could duck inside the bathroom, Martha reached up and brushed her hand down the side of his nude face. Adrenaline pumped through his system. "I wondered if you'd changed," she murmured.

"Changed?" He sounded as if he were strangling. He *felt* as if he were strangling. Her hands were so soft, so...

"From the portrait."

They were standing in the doorway. Behind them was the bathtub where he'd lain fantasizing about her. This was no place to hold a discussion—even Clement was smart enough to know that much. Edging her out into the hall, he leaped on the opening she'd offered. "The portrait! I mean, art. In general, that is. Do you like it? Or would you rather have a cup of coffee?"

Martha's smile trembled on the verge of laughter. The good kind of laughter, filled with tenderness, caring and empathy. All those things she had no business feeling at this stage. It was too soon. Clement was too... different.

Besides, her plans were all made, and they definitely didn't include an involvement with a sweet, slightly dippy hermit, no matter how appealing he was. "Coffee would be nice," she said huskily, "and yes, I've always been interested in art, but..."

It was only a matter of inches. Later, Martha was never certain which one of them had closed the distance. It was as if they were being drawn together by a giant magnet, each one too mystified by the process to do anything about it.

Clement stopped breathing. He wasn't sure, but he thought perhaps his heart might have ceased beating for several moments. He lowered his head, and Martha lifted hers, and he felt her breath touch his lips like a phantom kiss... like a dream.

Only dreams didn't wind their arms around him and stroke his back. Dreams didn't feel cool for one split instant and then melt in his arms, turning him incandescent... and decidedly tumescent.

Their lips met—slid, met again. Clem pressed hard and then drew back, afraid of hurting her. His teeth—her teeth—lips were incredibly sensitive. He broke away, gasping for breath, but he couldn't stay away, and this time he had to know—would it shock her? Would she be repelled?

He had to know how she tasted. He was starving for her.

Instinct carried him tentatively into the kiss—a gentle parting of the lips, a hesitant touch of the tongue, and then the kiss gathered its own momentum, carrying him to a depth that was way over his head. He couldn't get enough of her—the taste, the feel—the very essence of her. His chest was bursting, he was trembling all over, beset by the fierce demands of a body that knew what it wanted and would not be thwarted by mere reason.

The soft chenille cocoon fell away unnoticed. Two of the remaining four buttons on Clem's shirt landed on the carpet. His bare chest strained against the rumpled yellow batiste of her gown, his hands searching out treasure after treasure, marveling over the incredible phenomenon that was Martha Eberly.

His glasses were worse than useless, and he flung them away. Driven wild by the exquisite agony of desire, he came to his senses only enough to realize that he'd been moving his pelvis in such a way, pressing himself against her so that she couldn't mistake what was happening to him.

He was horrified. She must despise him! Making a heroic effort to control his need, he tried to explain, to apologize. "Martha, I—"

"No, don't."

With rough, unsteady hands, he held her away. And then brought her back to him, crushing her fragile femininity against his crude masculinity one last time before he put her away from him. "So sorry, my dearest one," he muttered. "I can't tell you how sorry I am."

She fumbled at the neck of her gown. "Oh, no, it was—I shouldn't have—" Groping frantically for her robe, she tried to think of something that would explain her inexplicable lapse of judgment with a man she'd met only the day before. She knew better, she honestly did. In this day and age—and she was no kid! The trouble was, he was so entirely outside her realm of experience that she didn't know how to deal with him. She'd dropped her guard, and it—whatever *it* was—had hit her before she could duck!

Spotting a glow of pale yellow against the faded pattern of the hall runner, she dived for it at the same moment Clement did. They collided, he steadied her then backed away as if he'd burned his hands.

He looked so full of self-reproach, and Martha, her heart constricting painfully, knew it was going to be up to her to navigate them safely through the next few moments. She tied on her robe, then, spotting his glasses against the baseboard, retrieved them and placed them in his hand. "Clement, have you ever considered getting contacts?"

"Hm—the thing is . . . Contacts? Oh, I—ah . . ."

"Don't tell me, I already know. You can't hide behind contacts, right?" With a sigh she watched as he hurriedly rammed the patched and fingerprinted glasses into place.

Both feet on the ground, Marty. She simply couldn't allow herself to be sidetracked just because she'd run headlong into an old fantasy figure and found him more fascinating than ever. That was all it was, really. It couldn't be anything more, because they didn't know each other, and if you didn't know someone, you couldn't possibly fall in love with them. Infatuation, maybe, but not love.

"Coffee would be nice," she said, forcing herself to a calmness she was far from feeling. In unspoken agreement, they headed for the kitchen. "And yes, now that you mention it, I've always been interested in art. I was never all that good at it, but one of these days, when I have time for a hobby, I plan to take it up again. It's the least I can do, after Hattie invested all that time and effort on me."

Clement was grateful that one of them, at least, had found the way back down to earth. He still had a ways to go yet, but he would follow her lead. She hadn't slugged him. She hadn't laughed in his face. That was a good sign, wasn't it?

"The—uh—relationship between the mathematical basis for certain paintings and some of the major musical compositions is—um, interesting, don't you think so?" He made a pass at his untidy hair and then tried surreptitiously to tuck in his shirttail.

"I'll take your word for it." She rinsed out the coffeepot and filled it with water while Clem took down two cups and two saucers, none of which matched.

His head was still spinning. Had he really kissed her the way he thought he had? Long, hungry kisses? Tongue-searching, teeth-touching kisses? The sort he'd read about in novels? He'd always discounted nine-tenths of the male-female thing as sheer imagination, but it seemed he'd been wrong. If anything, the authors hadn't done their subject justice.

"—because math was never one of my favorite subjects," Martha was saying. "My best classes were art and literature—the inexact sciences, you might say. Although I was good at spelling, too, and that's sort of an exact science."

"It's illogical."

"I know—it's fluky, but I won all the spelling bees, anyway. Well, not all, but most of them. So I thought I'd try nurse's training and maybe later on take up art as a hobby." She spoke rapidly, as if she were trying to fill up the silence. "I never really had enough talent as an artist to make a living at it, and I think it's much better to be a first-rate something practical than a fourth-rate something *im*practical, don't you?"

Her smile was too brilliant to be entirely true. Even in his dazed state, Clem recognized that much. She was nervous, and it was all his fault, and he was sorry, but he didn't think it would help matters much if he told her that she could never be a fourth-rate anything because she was unique. Superb. All the superlatives in the five languages in which he was fluent fell short of describing the wonder and beauty of Martha Eberly.

However, she was obviously waiting for a response of some kind. Clem reached back through the fog and grasped at a straw. "Spelling. I didn't mean you were illogical, I meant that spelling was."

"Oh."

The silence was broken by a rumble of thunder, and a new tension seemed to fill the air. Clem hunched his shoulders, shifted from one foot to the other and in desperation blurted out the first thing that entered his mind. "Are you—um, attached or anything? To a man, I mean?"

She dropped the measuring spoon, scattering coffee over the counter. "Now look what you made me do!" Sweeping the mess into her palm, she dumped it in the trash, still grumbling. "Now I've lost count."

Doggedly, Clement persisted. He had to know. "Are you?"

"No, I am definitely not attached. To a man or anything else!"

"Good." Dragging out a chair, he dropped into it and stretched his long legs across the black and white tiled floor. It was going to be tough enough without having to worry about unseating an entrenched competitor. He wasn't stupid. No man, unless he'd been cloistered from birth, could be ignorant of what went on between the sexes. Academically, Clem was as well-informed as the next man. He simply lacked experience. Hands-on experience, so to speak.

"Good?" Martha had finally managed to get the coffee maker in operation, and now she prowled around the kitchen, looking everywhere but at him. "I'll be twenty-nine years old next Thursday. At that age, most women have formed some sort of an attachment, as you call it."

Clem controlled the urge to leap into the opening and offer himself in any capacity whatsoever, just so long as it was permanent. In a determinedly casual manner, he mentioned the fact that he had an excellent position with Beauchamp Forbes International. "It, um—I mean, I have this

apartment—but I could easily afford a house if you'd—"
The moment he saw the look on her face, he began working on a graceful method of extracting a size-twelve shoe from his mouth.

There were no graceful methods. "I didn't mean that. I mean, I *did* mean it, but not the way it sounded. I mean, it's true—that is, I do have— Oh, hell, could we talk about something else?"

Turning away, Martha snatched the coffeepot from under the filter basket. The last few drops sizzled on the warming element as she filled their cups. "I'll be looking for an apartment, too—that is, unless I can get into a nursing school right away, but I think it's already too late this year, so I thought I'd get a temporary job and find a cheap place to stay somewhere close by, and—do you want cream or not?"

Clement preferred his coffee black. Nevertheless, he accepted both cream and sugar, and stirred vigorously.

"So... An apartment, huh?"

She nodded, seemingly distracted by the pattern of blackberries and blossoms on her cup. A soft flush of color came and went on her face, and Clement stared, entranced, as her freckles disappeared and reappeared. "It's the job that has me worried." She laughed, but it sounded forced. "Know anybody who needs a good farmhand? I'm pretty good on a tractor, as long as it's not too modern. Ours were mostly held together with rust and baling wire."

He tried to imagine her on a tractor and failed. The truth was, he wasn't precisely sure what a tractor looked like, other than that it had two big wheels and two little ones.

He could picture her in a haystack, all right, her face all sun-kissed and pink, her hair tumbled over her shoulders as she held up her arms in invitation. Her full breasts would be trembling with each breath, the rosy tips casting a shadow in the slanting sunlight—and her legs! Elegant high-topped shoes with pointed toes, striped stockings rolled just below dimpled knees and a length of rounded white thigh leading the eyes upward, upward . . .

Clem shifted in his chair as his body reacted forcefully to the image that had come straight out of one of Hattie's books of erotica. The farmer's daughter and the hired hand.

And he knew who he wanted that hired hand to be. He'd have thrown over a lifetime of preparation and all the rewards it had brought him for a single moment kneeling beside the figure in the haystack. The woman with Martha's face—

Not Martha's face! He simply had to regain control of his mind! "Books! That is, have you read any good books lately?" he croaked a little desperately.

She seemed just as relieved to move onto safe, impersonal territory. "If you consider *The Cat in the Hat* and *Three Little Pigs* interesting, then yes."

He'd heard of *Cats*, the Broadway musical, but he hadn't seen it. And the Tennessee Williams novel, *Cat on a Hot Tin Roof*, had made him slightly uncomfortable. As for swine . . . "Orwell's *Animal Farm* was rather interesting," he said, proud to be able to contribute something.

"But hardly in the same category," she said dryly. "Clement, are you really as dense as you seem to be, or are you playing some elaborate game? If this is your idea of fun—trying to keep me off balance—then let me assure you that I'm not enjoying it. I'm tired and sore, and I've got a lot on my mind, and what's more—"

"Game?"

"Yes, game, dammit!"

"I thought we were conducting a casual conversation."

"A casual *what*?" He looked so genuinely perplexed that Martha was inclined to believe him. He really was that dense—at least as far as women were concerned. "Look," she said more gently, "you don't conduct a conversation the way you'd conduct a—a train. Or an orchestra. It—they just happen. Two people start talking, and bingo! Instant conversation." The look she sent him was compounded of disbelief, irritation and something more elusive. "I don't need games, Clem. And I don't need any man complicating my life at this point. It's already complicated enough—so if you're playing games, just stop it, will you?" She didn't sound cross, only tired.

The trouble with a clean-shaven face, Clement decided, was that a man had nowhere to hide. Nothing to twist or twiddle when the going got rough. "I'm sorry. That is, yes. Certainly."

He wasn't at all sure what she meant by game, but if they were playing one, he didn't intend to lose. In fact, if he played it well, they'd both be winners.

"Is it my being here that bothers you?" Martha asked. "Would you feel more comfortable if I hitched a ride down to Asheville instead of waiting for Hattie? I'd planned to go anyway as soon as I found out she wasn't here. I don't know why I'm still hanging around, except that this place is even harder to get out of than it was to get into."

"No!" he blurted, bracing both arms on the table to lean forward. His glasses sat slightly crooked on his nose, thanks to having been dropped one too many times. "That is, I don't know when she'll be back—she was supposed to have been back four days ago. But I want you to stay. I don't want you to go. Not now—not ever."

Thunder rattled the windowpanes and faded away, leaving the house in stillness. No tick of a clock, no hum of a refrigerator to break the sudden tension that held them both in thrall.

"Ever?" Martha whispered, and from the expression in her eyes, Clem knew he'd frightened her again.

"I don't know how to say it right."

"No, no, it's all right. I know you didn't mean it the way it sounded."

He could feel his molars pressing together, feel his deltoids hardening into nerve-pinching knots. His hands were trembling almost imperceptibly, and when he caught her gaze on them, he tightened them into fists. "I meant it," he said flatly. "I'm just no damned good at—at expressing what I feel."

Martha began shaking her head, and he knew in advance he was going to hear a denial of what was happening. "You don't feel anything, Clem. You can't—we don't even know each other. What happened upstairs was—well, it was an accident. It didn't mean anything." She wouldn't meet his eyes, and he wondered if she were afraid of being caught in a lie.

Because it had meant something! He had never been so moved, so deeply affected by anything in his life, and she hadn't exactly resisted him. He'd felt her heart accelerate, heard the soft whimper in her throat when he'd torn his mouth away, afraid he'd gone too far.

"It just doesn't work that way," she whispered. "Not this fast."

"Then how does it work? How long does it take? Tell me, because I have to know!" The width of the table was between them, and Clem wanted to shove it aside. He wanted to touch her, to take her face in his hands and hold it so that he could study every nuance of expression. He wanted to know what was in her mind; instead he knew only that she wasn't telling him the truth. Not the entire truth, and that knowledge tortured him.

"How do I know? There's no time limit, but it just can't happen this fast. Believe me, that much I do know. I was— there was this man, and we thought—that is, I thought we were going to be married."

The table jerked as Clem's hands tightened on its edge. "You love him."

"I thought I did."

The pain of it was worse than anything he could ever remember experiencing, but he remained calm on the surface. If he frightened her now, she would close up, and he'd never get close to her again. "When did you begin to have doubts?"

Her smile tore him apart. "I think it must have started when I told him that there was no longer any reason to wait, since Jack was planning to remarry and wouldn't be needing me any longer. That's when Virgil told me that while he would always be fond of me, he'd never really considered marriage. At least, not with me. It seems I was soothing and restful and undemanding, and Virgil needed those qualities at that particular time in his career. I was exactly what he wanted for a—" She broke off and took a deep breath, still not quite meeting his eyes. "For a brief affair, but marriage was out of the question. We were incompatible."

Clem shoved back his chair and stood. "That lobotomized bastard! What the bloody hell did he mean, you were not compatible!"

She had to laugh. He looked so outraged, as though he'd been mortally insulted. If anyone had cause to be upset, it was she, and even she hadn't reacted this violently. "Compatible as in similar backgrounds," she explained. "Sit down, Clem, before you have a stroke. I don't see why you're overreacting this way—it's nothing to do with you."

"I am not overreacting! And what do you mean, it's nothing to do with me? The man insulted you, and you say it's nothing to do with me?"

Martha got up and took his hand. "Come on into the living room and relax. You're overcaffeinated. Have you ever considered switching to decaf?"

He let himself be led, but he wasn't about to relax. Not until he got to the bottom of this Virgil business. Come to think of it, he'd always considered Virgil's *Aeneid* a rather fulsome piece of work.

"Sit down. Relax. Tell me about your job, Clem."

"You wouldn't be interested. It's dull. That is, most women—I mean, you don't really want to hear—"

She could have chosen to be insulted. They both knew that she could never pretend to be a match for him intellectually. But he wasn't being condescending, he simply considered himself an uninteresting man. "Talk," she ordered.

He cleared his throat, squinted at a cobweb that connected the ornate chandelier to an unframed abstract and then said in a rush, "Molecular biology, recombinant DNA—um, an exploration of certain mutagenic substances. Cancer research, that is. Now, what do you mean, incompatible? Is the man a cretin? Is he blind as well as ignorant?"

Martha had to smile. He was such a bold and fearless Galahad—or was it Don Quixote? Had he cast her as his Dulcinea? "If you must know, Virgil thought he'd do better to marry a woman with a similar background. He's a lawyer. His father was a judge and they were one of the wealthiest families in Kentucky before the war. Between the states, that is. Whereas I grew up on a small farm in Yadkin County—and I do mean small. We kept a few Holsteins, but we could've bought a whole fleet of milk tankers for what it cost to winter them over, and as for the chickens, don't ever let anyone tell you chickens are cost-effective. Not when they scratch up your neighbor's seedbeds and get out on the highway and cause a three-car pileup. If it weren't for the tobacco allotment, we'd have gone under without a trace."

"I still don't see—"

"Background. Education. I never even finished my first year of college before I had to drop out."

"But you loved him."

She smiled tiredly just as a few drops of rain struck the west windows. "I don't know. I thought I did, at least."

Clement closed his eyes as if they pained him fiercely. After a while, he spoke again, his tone subdued. "Did you and he—that is, were you—"

"Lovers? Yes." She said it gently, but the words seemed to echo in the silence.

It was Clem who finally broke it, his voice low and even. "The man was mentally incapacitated. No rational man could ever have let you go."

Martha fought back an overwhelming urge to cry, and that was rather surprising, for she wasn't a woman who cried easily. She'd wept over leaving the children, but she hadn't shed a single tear over Virgil. Which must prove something, only she wasn't quite sure what it was.

"Thank you for trying to salvage my self-esteem, Clem, but it's really not necessary. Whatever I felt for Virgil, it's over now. It was over months ago, before Jack's wedding. I was too busy at the time getting the children prepared and the house ready and all to even think about it. When I finally had the time, I discovered that I couldn't drum up much emotion. Unless it was embarrassment for having made such a fool of myself." She smiled, and he saw whimsy and pain and concern in her smile, and it was all he could do to keep from touching her. "So you see, you don't have to worry about me—I've always been the practical sort. Some people just aren't cut out for great passion.''

A solid sheet of rain suddenly pummeled the slate roof, cascading over the eaves. Wind blew it against the windows and the side of the house. "My shoes!" Martha yelped, jumping up from the table.

"Shoes?"

"They're still out on the porch where I kicked them off, and now they're getting drenched!"

She was halfway to the front door when he caught her. "Let me go! You'll get wet."

They raced out together, and Clem turned back to switch on the porch light. By that time, Martha was already drenched. "Get inside, I'll find them!" he yelled over the deafening torrent.

"Over there—just past that rocking chair." She tried to shield her face against the blowing rain, but it was no use.

Moments before his glasses blurred into uselessness, Clem saw one pink Nike lying on its side at the edge of the porch. The other one was nowhere in sight. "Go back inside, Martha. There's no point in both of us getting chilled."

He spotted the other shoe and took the steps two at a time, leaping over one of the gargoyles that guarded the house. Grabbing it from under the rhododendron, he ducked under the deluge from a leaky gutter and gained the comparative shelter of the porch, totally blinded, totally exhilarated. He felt as if he'd battled a den full of dragons for his lady love instead of jumping over one cracked and mossy concrete gargoyle to retrieve her shoe.

After emptying the sneakers, Clem pushed Martha inside. By then they were both laughing breathlessly, although neither of them could have said why. "You didn't have to do that," she protested.

He removed his useless glasses and placed them—he hoped—on the hall table. "I was afraid you'd get washed down the ravine."

"All the same, there was no sense in both of us getting soaked." They were huddled together on a small Turkish rug just inside the door, and Clement wished he could see her better.

He reached out a tentative hand and encountered her hip. "But then, I've never been a practical man. It's one of my minor shortcomings." They moved closer together as if seeking warmth. Both were shivering, for the temperature had plummeted from its afternoon high.

"Do you have any m-major ones?"

"You mean you hadn't noticed?"

Clement rocked her gently in his arms, his body beginning to stir with its usual reaction in spite of their soggy condition. With his lips, he brushed her hair from her brow, then traced the path of a raindrop down her cheek with the tip of his tongue.

"No. N-nothing major."

He closed his eyes and prayed for guidance. What did he do now? He was suffering the most exquisite torture man could possibly endure, and if he didn't soon regain control of his body, there was no way she could help from feeling—from knowing...

"Clem?" Her breath was like liquid fire against his cold wet chest.

"Hmm?" he murmured, sounding as if he were strangling.

"You know this isn't very sensible. We've already discovered that both of us are—that is, that neither one of us is..." Her face was moving over the front of his shirt, where the buttons were supposed to be and weren't. When he felt her lips on his naked skin, he groaned in agony. Praise Paracelsus, he was going to explode right here in the foyer!

"Immune," she whimpered desperately.

One of his hands had found its way to her nape, and was toying with the hollow valley there, while a flood of damp silk played over his knuckles. Textures. Never before had he realized the importance of textures. She was velvet and silk, and there was a little mole just at her hairline that matched the one above her lip, which was darker than her freckles. He ached to taste them both.

"It's foolish to get involved," she protested halfheartedly. "We don't know each other—I'll be leaving tomorrow—or the next day. We haven't a single thing in common. You're a brain—I'm a pair of hands. We—we can't even carry on a sensible conversation." She laughed shakily, and he felt it to the soles of his feet.

"That's my fault, not yours. So teach me. I can learn. I've never had any trouble learning anything I wanted to, and I really want to learn . . . Oh, God, Martha, don't you know what you've done to me?" Her fingertips found the sensitive spot her lips had also discovered, and he groaned as a battery of avid messages went zinging from nipple to brain, to be transmitted to an antenna midway along his anatomy. One that was receiving those messages with embarrassing enthusiasm. "You've got to admit that we're compatible," he gasped. "If we were any more compatible, I'd be sprawled out at your feet, unconscious!"

Clem thought she murmured something in response, but he couldn't be sure, as her voice was muffled against his chest. It occurred to him that she might be suffocating. "Martha? I'm sorry—can you breathe?"

It was possible, he told himself—in fact, it was highly probable—that she might not be as profoundly affected as he was. There could be dozens of reasons that her fingers were kneading his sides, that she was pressing herself against him that way. "Martha?" he whispered again. *Dearest. Darling. Beloved.* Lines of poetry that had never had meaning for him before suddenly illuminated themselves in his mind.

"I can breathe, Clem, that's not the problem. It's too fast—we don't know each other, and I'm not—that is, I don't—well, Virgil was the only one, and I swore I wouldn't make that mistake twice."

"It's *not* a mistake. Please trust me."

Trust him? Only yesterday he'd come at her with an ax in his hand, and now he was demanding her *trust*?

But that had been a mistake, Clem rationalized desperately. And this was different. Surely she knew that. "Believe me, it's right for us," he murmured into her ear. "I could never do anything to hurt you, don't you know that?"

"We're dripping on Hattie's Oriental rug."

"We're probably generating steam."

She laughed shakily, and he felt as if a weight had been removed from his heart. Easing his grip on her, he said, "Um—I'm not sure I can walk, but we could try to make it as far as the living room."

They made it to the hard Victorian sofa, and Clem wondered if he were feverish, hallucinating or merely losing his mind. By the time they were settled in a cozy tangle of arms and legs, the room, the house—the whole bloody universe, in fact—could have disappeared and he wouldn't have noticed.

Martha was forced to lie half on top of him, because the plush sofa was barely wide enough for two. "I can't believe I'm doing this," she said, the words scarcely audible under the drumming rain. "And I thought I was so practical."

"That's all right, I'm impractical enough for both of us."

"That doesn't make a bit of sense."

"I think I was attempting a jest."

"Ho ho."

"Hmm," he murmured deeply as he adjusted her position. Her head settled sweetly into the hollow between his chest and his shoulder, her hair tickling the sensitive underside of his chin. One of his hands rested oh, so lightly on her solar plexus. If he moved it up just a fraction, his thumb would brush the soft underside of her breast.

Closing his eyes, Clem prayed he wouldn't die or otherwise make a fool of himself before the night was over.

"Any minute now, I'm going to get up from here and go wash the coffee things, and then go up to bed," Martha murmured.

The word bed echoed resoundingly in his head, setting up sympathetic vibrations in the most unusual places. Clement swallowed hard and closed his eyes. Martha breathed through her parted lips in one long, expressive sigh.

"Are you cold?" he asked.

She tilted her head, and he wondered if she were smiling, but he was afraid to lift his own head to see. "No, are you?"

"Did you ever hear the term cold feet?"

"Everybody's heard of cold feet. Probably had them at one time or another, too. Are your feet cold, Clement?"

"Not really. If anything, my temperature is elevated, but—uh, what I mean is—" He steeled himself, and the words came out all in a rush. "Martha, I want more than anything in the world to go to bed with you, but I haven't got the least idea—I mean, does a man ask first, or is there some signal? I'm not sure I...um, know how to do this thing gracefully."

And if she said yes? What then? Did he carry her upstairs, or did they go up side by side? God, he'd probably drop her halfway up the stairs—his legs felt like rubber bands! Maybe he was supposed to let her go first and undress. How long should he wait?

At times like this, he almost wished he smoked. Or drank. He needed a crutch. Those blasted books of Hattie's hadn't done anything but get him primed—they weren't the least bit of good as far as procedure and etiquette were concerned.

Martha exhaled in a long, shuddering sigh. She felt her eyes filling, but lacked the will to lift a hand and wipe them dry.

Clement, man and boy merged into one, filled her with an emotion that was almost frightening in its intensity, its sweetness. She didn't know what it was—didn't trust it. Yet she hadn't the will to resist it.

If it had been anyone else, she'd have been gone in a minute. Either that, or he'd have quickly found himself lying on the floor nursing a badly bruised ego. Reason told her that no man as handsome, as brilliant and as successful as C. Cornelius Barto could possibly be all that naive, but reason wasn't everything. Besides, if it were an act, then it was a darned good one.

"How do you usually go about seducing a woman?" When he didn't reply, she leaned on one elbow to study his face. He was paler than normal, but that could be because he was wet and cold. There were spots of color centered high on his angular cheekbones. Fever?

Embarrassment. "I do believe you're nervous," she said wonderingly.

"Paralyzed."

Trusting her instincts, Martha took the lead. She was as crazy as he was—neither of them had any business playing with dynamite this way, but something about him reached out to her and refused to let go. Lord knows it wasn't pity—no man as sexy as Clement Barto needed any woman's pity.

For Hattie's sake—and for her own, because she needed to be important to someone, just for a little while—and for his, because he was incredibly special—she would help him. She couldn't actually credit that he'd never before made love to a woman—no normal man reached the age of thirty-two and remained a virgin—but if he had a problem, and if she could help him with it, then she would. Because as unlikely as it seemed, she did care for him.

Not even to herself would Martha admit that what she was feeling for Clem Barto was more powerful than what she'd felt for Virgil Jones. Steeling herself, she said, "It's really not all that hard."

"I'm not a complete neophyte, you know," he informed her, and she breathed a sigh of relief.

Or was it relief? Wasn't there just a tiny twinge of jealousy for the woman—or women—who had initiated him into the art of love?

"I have participated in kissing before. On several occasions," he said with modest pride. "But never—um, horizontally."

Martha, her face buried in his throat, closed her eyes and sighed. If she wasn't already in love, she was well on the way. Of all the crazy, impossible things to happen to her at this particular point in her life—just when she'd been on the verge of getting her future back on track after so long.

"As you know—I mean, I mentioned," she stammered. "That is, I told you about Virgil. So you know that I'm not without experience, either." And while her own experience might be slightly deeper, it was not much broader than his. And never before had she felt anything like this aching, longing *need*.

He was watching her, his eyes burning with a dark fire that made her lick her lips nervously. "That is, you have to understand that this doesn't mean I'm staying, Clem. No matter what happens tonight, I still have to leave as soon as I can arrange it. I just want you to understand that."

He was silent for a long time, and Martha was beginning to regret having warned him. Why shouldn't she have this much, she asked herself defensively. What was wrong with spending one glorious night in the arms of a man who was strong and decent, gentle yet oddly courageous? An endearingly innocent man who had only to look at her to set her heart to pounding?

She lifted her head the slightest bit, and her lips brushed against Clem's chin. He took command as if it were the signal he had been waiting for. Turning them so that Martha was lying on the bottom, he half covered her, his weight braced on one arm.

It was a chaste kiss, that first one, because Clem was afraid of frightening her. Afraid of losing control. He was a large man, and he was powerfully aroused, and God only knew what would happen if he lost control.

"Martha, Martha," he murmured against her throat. "What are you thinking?" He needed to know. He hadn't a clue.

She sounded as breathless as he felt. "Of a brooding young man in stiff new jeans and a white T-shirt. His face is all shadowy, and his eyes look so sad, and . . . oh, Clement, sometimes I used to think about him and wonder where he was . . . and who he was with."

His lips brushed hers, pressed hard and long, and he groaned. He was holding her too tightly again, and he eased his hold, murmuring slightly incoherent words of apology as he pressed kisses on her cheeks, her eyelids, her temples.

At last he found her mouth once more, and this time there was nothing at all hesitant in the way he stroked her lips apart. Passion and instinct drove him to explore her in a manner that left them both melting and breathless, their hands trembling and their hips pressing together.

"What are you doing?" she blurted when he began unfastening her top.

His hands stilled, resting palm down on her breasts. "I want to see you. Is it all right?"

"I don't know what's all right and what isn't, I—Clem, are you sure? You know it will only be tonight?"

It would be forever, but he retained just enough discretion not to say so. "You're trembling. Are you frightened?" Her face was so close he could see the shards of color in her irises—copper, gold, bronze. Even as he watched, her pupils expanded until they all but eclipsed the gold ring.

"No. Yes—a little. Are you?"

"A little. No, a lot. But I don't want to stop. This is the most wonderful thing I've ever experienced. I know now how it feels to ride a comet."

She gathered the lapels of her robe tightly around her throat and edged away from him as far as his arms would allow. "Clem, listen to me. One of us really needs to be sensible about this."

"This is the most sensible thing I've ever been involved in," he said, knowing somehow that it was the truth.

"I won't argue with you, but you need to think—while there's still time. A few kisses—well, that's one thing, but what you're wanting is something else entirely."

"I know what I want. Believe me, even I know the difference between a kiss and making love. Theoretically, at least."

"Well...I just want you to know that there could be problems. Have you considered the emotional side of this?"

"Yes," he said gravely. Her elbow was cutting into his biceps, which was the least of his discomforts.

"Oh, lordy, why didn't I just let my darned sneakers wash down the mountain? If I'd gone straight to bed, none of this would have happened."

"It would have happened, only maybe not so soon."

"But that's just it, don't you see? We should give it time!"

"You said you were leaving," he countered, although surely she knew that she wouldn't be leaving now. It simply wasn't possible to walk away from something so powerful, so compelling. "So perfect," he murmured aloud.

It didn't even faze her, his out-of-context comment. That was a good sign, wasn't it? They were growing more compatible every moment they were together. An amalgam of minds.

Martha struggled out of his arms and sat on the edge of the sofa, smoothing her wildly tangled hair. "That's right, only I can't leave until I find a ride or a bus that comes within walking distance, or—well, anyway, tomorrow you can tell me all about yourself, and I'll do the same, and then tomorrow night, maybe—"

"Did you know your eyes look almost black in this light? Actually, there are several possible reasons for the expansion of—"

"Clement! Will you just be quiet a minute and listen to what I'm trying to tell you? We're—well, attracted. That is, we're *mildly* attracted to each other, but it's probably just because we're stuck up here together with no one around for comparison, and—"

"Propinquity, you mean."

"I do? Whatever—the thing is, there's no room in your life for a college dropout whose chief claim to fame is her blackberry cobbler, and there's certainly no room in my life for a man who—well, for any man, and I know I probably led you to think that I—well, all right, I want you, too, but it just isn't smart, and—"

Clement stood up. "Don't be afraid," he said gently. "I'm just as nervous as you are, but I promise you, there's nothing to be afraid of. Come to bed now, Martha."

Eight

By the time he reached the second floor, Clem had had second thoughts, third ones, and was working on a fourth set. Oh, he wanted her, all right. He'd never wanted anything more in his life, but what if he couldn't... What if he *couldn't*? What if he did everything all wrong?

To hell with sublimation, he should have practiced! Most men his age had gone through the experience numerous times, so that when they finally met the one woman in the world who really mattered, they were adept enough not to botch it.

"Martha, maybe it would be better—" Oh, no—even his voice was shaking!

She slid her arm around his waist and led him down the hall to his bedroom. "I'm freezing, aren't you? Is the furnace working?"

"The furnace? Oh—*that* furnace. It doesn't quite make it as far as the second floor. Something about a pump...

Look, Martha, I want you to know that I—that if I—tha is, if we—"

"You shouldn't get chilled," she said gently. "If yo come down with pneumonia again, my Nikes and I wi never forgive ourselves."

The strangled sound he uttered must have sounde something like fireplace, because she crossed directly to when they entered the cluttered bedroom. "Where are you matches? I'd suggest hot coffee, only I don't think you nerves could handle it."

"Martha . . ."

"My friends call me Marty."

"Marty. Come here. Please." He was relieved to hear hi voice sounding somewhat stronger. How was it possible t feel so powerful and at the same time so incredibly weak? had to be a malfunction of the adrenal system.

She found the matches in a brass holder, struck one an touched it to several crumpled papers. They both watche the flames curl around the pine kindling, exploding splin ters until soon there was a roaring blaze licking at the spli oak.

Adjusting the screen, she turned toward him, and Clen thought he detected a trace of nervousness on her face. He eyes would dart upward to meet his, then fall again, linger ing in the vicinity of his damp and rumpled collar.

Not knowing what else to do—although he knew what h *wanted* to do—he held open his arms, and she walked int them.

Clem closed his eyes and rested his cheek on the top of he head. It was like going home, to someone who'd never ha a home. It was shelter on a wild, stormy night. He tol himself he could hold her that way forever, but then a storm of another sort began to gather.

His arms tightened around her. His breath came in long, shuddering sighs. As for Martha, she seemed to have forgotten to breathe altogether. She was plastered so close to his body that it occurred to him that she probably couldn't have breathed if she'd tried.

With a mumbled apology, Clem stepped back. Neither of them was cold any longer, but they were both decidedly wet, and wet clothing was uncomfortable. Wet chenille was also surprisingly cumbersome, and when he reached out and untied her sash and then laid open the two sides of her robe, Martha didn't protest. Her eyes met his and clung there, and in a sudden attack of nerves, he dropped his hands.

"You were beginning to steam," he explained, and she lifted her hands and unfastened the only remaining button on his shirt.

And then somehow, they were bumping elbows, removing clothes and tossing them carelessly toward the cold radiator. They laughed, and the sound was breathless and overexcited. She looked at him, and found him watching her, and both flushed. She'd worn underpants under her gown, and now she stood before him in only those, her arms crossed over her breasts.

"I never knew how beautiful a woman could be—warm and pink is much better than cold and gray."

"Gray?"

"Marble." He swallowed hard, wondering how the world's finest sculptors could have fallen so far short of the mark. "You know—museums. Aphrodite of Melos and..."

But Martha wasn't thinking about sculpture. All she knew was that Clement was the most beautiful man she had ever beheld, with firelight flickering on his long, smoothly muscled body. He looked every bit as hard as any stone figure possibly could, and she was thankful he wasn't made of cold marble.

Cold! There was nothing cold about the look in his eyes as they wandered over her, from her bare toes, curled against the floor, to her hair, which was already drying in a wild tangle. His gaze lingered in the area where her arms shielded her breasts, but he didn't ask her to lower them. Nor did he reach out to her.

And she was positive—well, it was really perfectly obvious—*thrillingly* obvious—that it wasn't because he didn't want to.

Now that she had all but committed herself, Martha was losing her courage. She had never been with any man except Virgil, and even then it had only been three times, because she hadn't been sure it was the right thing to do for so long. And then she'd been disappointed.

Which might have been part of the reason he'd concluded that they weren't compatible.

"Do you—that is, should I have left on my—um . . . ?"

Sensing his embarrassment at having removed all his clothes while she still wore her underpants, Martha forced herself to remove the final barrier. The only light was from the hall and the fireplace, and she prayed he wouldn't see the color that stained her face. Experienced women of twenty-nine did *not* blush. It was merely the radiant heat.

"Oh, my," he whispered reverently, devouring her with his eyes. "Oh, my."

She was inordinantly pleased at his reaction. For the first time in her life, she felt almost beautiful. "Well . . ." she murmured.

"Yes. Well, um . . . oh, my, yes!" Clem said fervently, and she bit her lip, wondering why she had suddenly ceased to be embarrassed.

Because she had. Except for that one swift glance, she had avoided looking—*there*. But she'd looked every where else. And everything she saw made her want to hold this man in her arms, to comfort him and love him and make him believe in himself so that the next time—with the next woman...

She shied away from that thought, finding it unexpectedly painful.

"Martha, I'm not sure of the protocol, but maybe if we were to lie down together—on the bed, that is—then maybe, um..."

"That sounds like a sensible thing to do," she said calmly, waiting for him to make the first move. When he didn't, she did.

The sheets were icy. Gasping, she curled into a fetal knot. When Clem came in beside her, he wrapped his arms around the bundle that consisted mostly of knees and elbows. She was shivering, but he hardly seemed to notice the cold sheets at all.

"You'll warm up in a minute," he assured her, and she nodded, tangling her hair against the pillow. "The nerve endings just under the –"

"Clement. Hush up."

"All right. But I really would like to be closer to you, only I can't if you won't straighten out."

"If I straighten out, my feet'll turn into chunks of ice."

His hands smoothed a tentative path along her back, scalding her wherever they touched. "I'll warm you a place, how's that?"

"Really warm. Hot." She was shivering, but not from the cold.

He extended both his feet and moved them back and forth under the covers. "It's warming up already," he assured her, and she began to unbend, just a bit at first. And then she extended one leg, sliding her toes along his shin. He was warm. He was burning up, in fact. Hair on a man's leg felt strange—exciting. She'd touched the hair on his chest, and it had caused her stomach to quiver. Feeling his shin and then the slight brush of a hairy thigh moving against her own caused a minor earthquake somewhere in the vicinity of her navel.

"Getting warm?" he rumbled against her temple.

She made some sort of noise—it sounded more like a purr than anything else. It felt like a purr. He was stroking her back, his hands moving from her shoulders, lingering to trace her nape with his thumb, to her hips, his large palms curving over them, squeezing gently.

And back again. The heel of his hand raked over the side of her breast, and she wriggled closer, pressing against him. There was really no point in huddling up in a knot, when he had all this heat to spare...

"If you were to turn onto your back just a bit more," Clem murmured, "and I were to turn more like this—" He demonstrated, moving over her so that his face was mere inches above hers.

"Yes?"

"I believe it might be possible to—um—achieve another..."

"Kiss?" she whispered against his lips. Her arms came up around his neck. As he ravaged her mouth in a hungry kiss that made up in earnestness anything it might lack in expertise, Martha savored the feel of his smooth skin, his thick hair, his ears...

After endless moments, he pulled back, staring at her with dark, glittering eyes. "My God," he said reverently. "It's amazing—the wetter it is, the more incendiary it becomes. Did you know that?"

Teetering between tears and laughter, Martha slid one hand between them, raking her fingers through the crisp hair on his chest until she found what she sought. Her own breasts were aching. She couldn't beg him to touch them, but she could show him.

Clem felt lightning streak through his body. He stiffened. All over. "Did that hurt?" she asked softly.

"Hurt. Hurt?" He groaned. "God, no! What happened?"

Encouraged, she deliberately manipulated his nipples into hardened points. "There's this old song," she whispered. "You must have heard it—something about the head bone being connected to the neck bone, and the neck bone being connected to the shoulder bone . . ."

"And the—ah, chest bone?" he panted.

"Connected to all sorts of mysterious parts," she teased.

"Synapses," he gasped, and pressing his throbbing pelvis against hers, he left her in no doubt that his connections were all quite intact. "Theoretically," he began, and she shushed him with a soft, damp kiss.

"At a time like this, do you really want to discuss theories?"

"What I want—Marty, I'm afraid I—that is . . ."

"Darling, I wouldn't be here if I didn't want you." She took his hand and brought it to the vicinity of her breast, leaving him to find his way unaided.

And he did. Unerringly, and with devastating results. A long time later, after he had discovered the joys of touch and taste, sending her closer to the edge than she had ever been before, he rolled away, tossing the covers off and lying there, proudly, primally male.

"Is something wrong?" she asked after watching him— feasting her eyes on his glorious, unashamed masculinity for several moments.

"I'm afraid I might hurt you. Or disappoint you. Marty, I've never felt so helpless in all my life. If I were twenty years old, it would be different."

"For pity's sake, you don't think you're too *old*!"

"Oh, no—hell, no!" He turned to face her then, and without thinking, she lifted the sheet over his flanks. He was damp and overheated, and she didn't want him to catch a chill. "It's just that—well, physiologically, a man of twenty is much more—that is, he doesn't have as much time for doubts to set in."

"You want to back out?"

"Not exactly."

Beside herself with frustration, she tried to be patient, but it wasn't easy. "Then what is it that you *do* want?"

"I want—what I want more than anything else in the world at this moment, is to bury myself inside you and stay there for a week, at least. With options. And to have you want me as much as I want you, and to—"

When she would have interrupted him, he laid his fore-finger over her lips. "And to know that I'm capable of pleasing you the way you please me. To know I can make you feel just half—just a *fraction* of what you make me feel."

"But don't you know? Can't you tell? Clem—" She nipped his finger with her teeth, then, taking his hand, she placed it on her heart so that he could feel the storm raging inside her. There was another way she could show him how ready she was for him, but she hadn't the courage. She was only a beginner herself, hardly up to instructing someone else.

"I do know what goes where—that is, in theory, but in actual practice—when it matters so very much—"

"Clem . . ."

"When I'm afraid I won't be able to—"

"Clem!" And when she had his full, if slightly agonized, attention, she said tenderly, "You do know how to kiss me, so kiss me now. Then if you don't want to go any further, we won't. We'll just hold each other and sleep.'' From the sexual flush blooming on his lean cheeks, and from certain other unmistakable signs, Martha knew that he wanted much more than a little cuddling. She only hoped she was capable of guiding them both through this thing, because never in her life had she been entrusted with such a wonderful, delicate mission.

He kissed her. The kiss grew, and Martha wriggled until she was practically lying on top of him. Her hand trailed over his chest, toyed with the cowlick just below his breastbone, and followed the narrow path to his navel. She felt his abdomen spasm and smiled, even as he nibbled on her lower lip. He was learning. It was all a matter of confidence.

Clem savored her mouth until they were forced to break apart for breath. He found her breast again, marveling over the way it fit into his palm. Instinct guided his lips along the most sensitive area of her neck, into the little hollow at the base of her throat and down over the slope of her breast. He took the crest between his lips. His tongue circled once, and he felt her shudder. Remembering how it had felt when she had caressed him, he was emboldened enough to continue his attentions, and after a while he moved to the other breast lest it feel neglected.

His palm opened over her stomach, and one finger edged into her navel. That, too, he'd learned to his amazement, was a source of remarkable sensations. Encouraged by the way she seemed to melt into the mattress, he strayed deeper under the sheet until he encountered the soft nest sheltered between her thighs.

She moaned softly. Shifting, she allowed him access. With a trembling sort of wonder, he discovered the intricate flower of her womanhood. Textbook anatomy was one thing; a warm and eager body was quite another. When he touched her there, she whimpered.

"Did I hurt you?" He drew back his hand, and she caught it in hers and carried it back to her.

"No—oh, no, please!"

Clem's own condition was rapidly becoming critical. His loins ached with an intolerable pressure. All he could think of was the urgent need to throw himself on her and assuage the awful hunger of a lifetime. But he dare not. In his clumsiness, he could hurt her, and nothing was worth that.

And so he continued to caress her, ever so gently, until suddenly she was gasping for breath, and then she was pulling at his shoulders, pleading incoherently, and he could only guess at what she wanted.

"Please—now!"

There was no mistaking where she was urging him. Shaking with his own need, Clem managed to position himself between her thighs. Carefully, he lowered his trembling body to hers, fully expecting everything to work more or less as it did in the diagrams.

It didn't. Nothing went where it was supposed to go, and when he tried surreptitiously to help the situation, his hands tangled with hers. He felt himself bump against her, and even the bumps were so terribly exciting that he thought he might explode. But suddenly, everything slid into place. Nature's ingenious intent became evident, and he heard a long, low groan.

Hers?

His. Hers was the drawn out, shuddering moan.

"Oh, Clement . . . oh, my goodness, please . . ."

He hadn't the slightest idea what she was begging for, because his conscious mind had long since shut down. All he knew was this fierce, compelling urge, this driving need to—

"Yes, yes, *yes*!"

And they were racing, harder and harder, higher and higher, all incoherent words and shuddering gasps, clutching, stiffening, crying out, then sighing, eyes shut tightly, bodies drenched in sweat.

Heads reeling, barely conscious, they clung to one another, safe, sated, secure for the moment.

A long while later, Clem became aware of something wriggling beneath him. He lifted his weight, and Martha slid out. "I only wanted to breathe a little," she explained apologetically.

"Of course. I should have thought—um, made arrangements."

But he wouldn't let her go. He couldn't. She had given him the single most exquisite experience in his entire life, and he knew he could never let her go now, no matter what happened. "Even if it never happens again," he murmured deeply.

"Even if— Didn't you—I mean, I thought we both . . ."

His heart swelled with love as he heard her stammering. He knew what she was trying to say, and in a minute, he'd think of the proper way to reassure her. His precious little love was sounding every bit as confused as he once had.

"Thank you, Martha."

"Oh, well, you don't have to thank me—I mean, it was— oh, for pity's sake, Clem, a man doesn't go around thanking a woman for—that."

Propping his head at an angle, he stared at her in open amazement. "Why on earth not? No man could ever have been given a more beautiful gift."

She was growing redder by the moment, her freckles taking on a faintly greenish cast in contrast. "You just don't, that's all," she muttered. And then, "But Clem—I still don't understand. I mean, I know you're shy and all, but— honestly, at your age. *Never*?''

He didn't pretend to misunderstand. Sighing, he turned onto his back and stared at the shadowy ceiling. It wasn't going to be easy. In fact it was going to be downright painful. But he could deny her nothing, and she'd asked.

"I was always too young. Well, not always, of course, but my classmates tended to be years older, especially once I got to the university.'' *It had been like spending his entire life in a small, windowless room. Not an unpleasant room, because there were books. But in isolation, nevertheless.* "Because of my age, I was closely supervised. Every minute of my time was programmed, but it was an interesting program—quite stimulating, in fact. On the whole, I enjoyed it immensely.''

"Didn't you have any time for recreation?''

"There were concerts, art shows. Plays, of course. I tried out for sports, but I ended up in traction.''

"Oh, no!'' She held him closer, as if to assuage a boyhood injury. His back had been broken, and he'd spent almost two years in a brace. In his small, pleasant, windowless room.

"At any rate, I graduated from the university at thirteen and went to graduate school immediately. My parents thought it would be best, and I had nothing else in particular to do.''

Martha found his hand and nestled it against her breasts, and there was nothing sexual about the gesture. "But surely there were girls there. And you must have been tall for your age.''

He smiled at the memory of the way he'd been. "The basketball team was interested, but only until they saw me in action. I was completely uncoordinated. My eyes were

already quite bad, and I had trouble walking without tripping over my feet because my head was usually in a book.''

"But the girls," she interrupted. "They weren't blind,
too, were they?"

He chuckled, and the sound reverberated between them.
"I'd have had better luck if they had been. I was a mess,
Marty. My clothes were all wrong—far too neat, I'm afraid.
Early training. My features, which, as you might have no-
ticed, aren't particularly delicate, were even worse on a six-
foot-four, one-hundred-twenty-eight-pound frame."

"But I thought you were beautiful! The portrait, remember? It must've been painted about then."

He caressed her hair, and his finger traced the shell of her
ear. "It was a short canvas, and Hattie's always been fond
of me. She collects strange people."

"Like me."

"And me, though I'm hers by default."

He was silent so long Martha wondered if he'd fallen
asleep. "So there were no girls—no women? Clem, I'm not
prying, I just can't believe that no woman has ever discovered how—well, it just doesn't seem possible, that's all."

After a while, he said, "There was this one girl—her name
was Georgina. She was beautiful—at least, I thought so at
the time. I was—um, I think the proper term is smitten."

"How old were you then?"

"Fifteen, sixteen or thereabouts. My roommates and
some of their friends set up sort of a—ah, surprise for me.
It was at a party and—oh, hell, Marty, I don't really want
to talk about this. It happened a long time ago, and I should
have forgotten it by now. Unfortunately, ridicule—sexual
ridicule, that is—is a little hard to take when you're that age
and awfully unsure of yourself."

"You mean that you and she—"

"I mean that I don't know if we did or not. That was also the night I was introduced to the joys of vodka. I stuck it out for the rest of the term, but I don't think I said more than half a dozen words outside the classroom over that entire period. And I made damned sure I didn't get within range of anything female, especially in a social context."

"But eventually," she urged gently, "you graduated and went on . . . you must have met people. Dated."

"Some. Not as much as you might expect. And maybe I deliberately chose nonthreatening types. I don't know—I do know I took a hell of a lot of cold showers, and I ran up and down several hundred flights of stairs."

Suddenly he grinned and rolled her on top of him. "Enough of this talk, woman. You might have noticed that I'm a man of few words."

"A man of action, in fact," she pointed out solemnly.

"I try." He made a slight adjustment to their relative positions, and a low groan caught in his throat. "Is it too soon? That is, could you—I mean, could we possibly. . ."

It wasn't, and she could, and they did. This time, there was nothing at all tentative in Clem's technique. A brilliant man, he had always had a creative bent, and having been shown the basics, he was more than capable of devising all sorts of delicious variations that left them both limp and satiated a long time later.

The rain stopped shortly after midnight. Just as the sky was beginning to grow light, Martha awoke to find Clem leaning over her, his head propped on one arm. He was gazing down at her with a beatific smile on his face, his eyes dreamy and slightly unfocused.

"Haven't you been asleep at all?" she murmured.

His warm hand slid over her waist and drew her closer. "How could I sleep? Maybe I'll never sleep again. Martha,

I want you to know that I'll do everything in my power to make you—"

She laid a hand over his lips. "Please, Clem—don't."

Instantly the dark blue eyes grew more guarded. His hand grew still on her side. "Don't what?"

"Don't say anything. Not just yet."

"But there's so much to say—so much to plan." He scrambled out of bed suddenly and stood beside her, naked and magnificent. He felt for his glasses on the bedside table and jammed them on.

Nine

—

"We need to talk." Martha sat up in bed and pulled the quilt under her chin, and Clem thought that with her red-gold hair tumbling over her shoulders, her face flushed with sleep and her eyes glistening like polished amber, she'd never looked more beautiful.

Nor more desirable. The last thing he wanted to do was talk. He was still on shaky ground when it came to expressing himself with words, but last night he'd discovered a whole new world of expression. And he hadn't even begun to express all he had to say.

"I'll build up the fire first," he said.

"You'd better put on some clothes."

"I'm coming right back to bed as soon as I throw a log on the fire."

"Put on something anyway, or we'll never get any talking done."

He was willing to indulge her. There'd be plenty of time for making love. They had the rest of their lives. Besides, she was right—there were things to be decided. Such as where they would live. His apartment suddenly seemed small, cold and utterly without appeal. "Do you like apple trees?" he asked, dusting the bark off his hands and retrieving his khakis from the floor.

"Apple trees? Clem, hand me my bathrobe, will you? I can't think properly until I've washed my face."

Still smiling—it seemed to be a permanent condition with him ever since he'd awakened with her wrapped around him, her thigh between his legs and her head tucked under his chin—Clem picked up the yellow chenille garment, unconsciously cradling it close to his face. "Then think improperly. I'll help you get started, all right?"

Putting on his pants, he missed the quick look of pain that crossed Martha's face. "Look, I'd better dash down and turn on the furnace. We'll both be starving in a few minutes, especially after—"

His smile widened into a grin that threatened to lapse into laughter. "Now that you mention it..."

Martha threw back the quilt and slipped on her robe, and Clem watched every move as if it were the most remarkable event he'd ever witnessed. Personally, he'd discovered that euphoria was its own insulation.

"Five minutes?" she said.

"Make it ten. I'd like a quick shower."

"Then make it twenty. I'll have one when you're through."

"We'll meet back here?"

"We'll meet in the kitchen," she said firmly.

Clem was disappointed, but then, perhaps she had a point. Enthusiasm alone wouldn't make up for a lack of fuel. After a hot shower and a big breakfast, they could take up where they'd left off last night. "Twenty minutes—that's my outer limit," he warned, reaching for her to steal one last kiss, but she slipped out the door before he could touch her.

By the time Martha had snatched a handful of clean clothes from her suitcase, trekked downstairs to the only functioning shower in the three-bathroom house, bathed, dressed and hurried upstairs again, the doubts had already begun to erode her small store of self-confidence. What on earth had she been thinking of? She'd never done anything so—so totally irresponsible in her whole life! What had come over her?

With a haste that resembled panic, she set about straightening the contents of her suitcase. She'd ransacked it so many times by now it would almost have been better to dump it out and start over, but she felt an urgent need to see it packed. And closed. And sitting beside the door, ready to go downstairs.

Better yet, being stowed in the belly of a Greyhound bus bound for Winston-Salem.

"Oh, glory, what have I done?" she muttered to herself as she crammed the damp things she'd worn the day before into a plastic bag and tucked them in one corner. They'd probably be mildewed by the time she unpacked again, and it would serve her right. Her brain had evidently mildewed, too!

She heard the stairs creak and knew that Clem was headed for his shower. She'd have to hurry, or he'd come after her, and she'd already proved how staunch her powers of resistance were. Zilch!

While she crammed things in helter-skelter, she worried over what had happened. Never in her life had she done anything so impulsive. She'd always been the practical one.

Always! She'd never even been seriously tempted to sleep with a man before. Even with Virgil, it had been mostly a case of "it was long past time."

She'd always feared a pregnancy she couldn't afford, as well as emotional entanglements she knew she wasn't equipped to handle.

So what had she done? Gone to bed with a man whose portrait she'd fallen in love with when she was a teenager! Let him make love to her until she couldn't think straight, knowing full well that there wasn't a chance in this world they could have anything more than that.

They were too different. He spoke languages she'd never even heard of—knew about things she couldn't even conceive. What on earth would they have talked about? She could tell him how to stretch five dollars' worth of meat into three meals, how to jump start a forty-year-old tractor and how to stop a toddler's tantrum before it built up a full head of steam. Oh, sure, he'd be fascinated by all that! And then he could tell her about the joys of exploring mutagenic whatchamacallits and—oh, hell, she couldn't even remember the rest of it!

It just wouldn't work. In her heart of hearts, Martha knew it wouldn't be fair to Clem. She'd like to think she'd given him the confidence to live a full life from now on—with someone from his own background. At least she could do that much for him, although she suspected she'd be paying for her generosity for years to come.

Half an hour later, she was listlessly scrambling eggs when Clem came into the kitchen. It didn't help her mood to discover that he looked every bit as uncomfortable as she felt.

Dumping the scrambled eggs into an unwarmed bowl, she plucked the toast—also cold by now—from the toaster and wondered how she was going to manage a dignified escape.

Why hadn't she shipped everything, instead of trying to bring so much of it with her? How the devil was she going to get it all down to Lick Munden's Superette? And even if she got that far, how long would it take her to hitch a ride into Asheville?

"Clem, I need—"

"Martha, I thought we—"

They both spoke at once, and Martha gestured impatiently at a chair. "Breakfast is cold."

"No, I'm late."

"That doesn't make sense."

"That I'm late?"

"No, dammit, that breakfast—that just because—oh, nothing!"

"Thank you for cooking," he said politely. He picked up his fork and put it down again.

"It was the least I could do." She hadn't meant that the way it sounded—as if she were grateful to him for anything—but damned if she was going to try to explain that!

"The post office!" Clem pounced on the change of topic like a drowning man would a life raft. "That is, your emerald..."

"There's no point in mailing it when I can just as well deliver it myself. I seriously doubt if Hubert Odwell will be lurking around after all this time." All this time? It seemed like forever, but it had only been a few days. How strange, she mused, nibbling a piece of cold toast, that a person's whole life could change so quickly. She didn't even feel like the same woman who had climbed out of a bread truck to be confronted by a bearded, ax-wielding mountain of a man who had turned her whole life upside down before she knew what was happening.

Martha gave up all pretense of being interested in breakfast. She could no more hide the shadows under her eyes, caused by a lack of sleep, than she could hide her feelings, and she *had* to! Her feelings, at least.

Clem propped his elbows on the table, rested his forehead in his palms for a moment then let his fingers slide through his hair, leaving it looking rumpled and decidedly sexy. "I—uh—seem to have mislaid the ability to organize my thoughts."

"I've never been very sharp before breakfast, either."

"No. Yes. That is—" He finished his coffee and poured a second cup. She was shutting him out. He had to think! All right, if she was shutting him out, then she must be feeling defensive. And if she was feeling defensive, that must mean she was feeling threatened. And if she felt threatened, then she wasn't as unaffected as she'd like him to believe.

The next move was his, Clem told himself. And it had damned well better be a good one, because he might not get a second chance.

But the next move was neither Clem's nor Martha's. The sound of a car grinding up the steep grade had them looking searchingly at one another, then at the door.

"Hattie," Clem muttered. *Not now, dammit. Why couldn't you wait until I'd consolidated my position?*

"He's found me," Martha whispered, shoving her chair back from the table. She hurried out to the foyer, and Clem caught up with her just before she reached the front door.

"Where are you going?"

Eyes blazing with indignation, she told him. "I'm going to tell that nasty little rodent that I'm sick and tired of being harrassed, and that if he doesn't leave me alone this very minute, I'm—"

Taking her by the shoulders, Clem set her firmly aside. "You're going to go upstairs and let me handle this," he said with a tone of quiet authority that would have astonished him had he been aware of it. Not until the words were out had he known what he was going to say, but now that he'd said it, he meant it.

"It's not your battle." Martha wriggled from his grasp and reached for the door. "Clem, I appreciate what you're trying to do, but I'm perfectly capable of looking after myself."

"That's not the point." He removed her hand gently from the knob just as they heard the sound of the car door slamming outside. "Marty, let me do this. Please?"

"I don't even know what you're planning to do," she said a little desperately. "Look, it's not that I relish seeing him again, but if I don't face up to my problems—"

The hoarse sound of a little-used doorbell interrupted, and Clem took advantage of her momentary distraction to open the front door and step outside.

"Odwell?" he challenged, although the man with the alligator shoes and the matching briefcase hardly matched the description Martha had given the storekeeper of the petty confidence man who preyed on gullible amateur rockhounds.

"Barnes—K. Jasper Barnes," the man said. He extended a well-groomed hand, and Clem stared at it in confusion. "You are C. Cornelius Barto, aren't you?"

"Barnes," Clem repeated slowly. He accepted a brief, dry handshake while his brain rapidly processed data. Odwell might have an accomplice, but this man struck him as reasonably honest. Slick, something of a hustler, but basically sound. Certainly not the kind of man who would terrorize women.

On the other hand, when it came to dealing with personnel, Clem knew his limitations. For Martha's sake, he couldn't afford to take any chances. "May I see some identification?"

"Certainly, certainly," the well-dressed young man replied, producing a card case as he spoke. "I'm with Lavorly Laboratories. Danforth said you'd be a good man to bring into the fold. He suggested I contact you." He smiled, and Clem's shoulders settled a notch lower. His fists uncurled. "You're a hard man to locate, Dr. Barto. Your phone's unlisted, your parents' phone is unlisted and this elderly relative of yours that Danforth mentioned—even her number is unlisted."

"Not that it does much good. She always hands it out to anyone who asks," Clem said. He was slightly dazed, having expected to slay a dragon and been confronted with something else entirely.

"Unfortunately, I couldn't reach her to ask," Barnes said with a twitch of thin lips that hinted at a sense of humor. "And your secretary wouldn't give me the time of day. By the way, I believe he's taking a shot at Danforth's position. Can he handle it?"

Ed Malvern? Administrator? "Probably. He's been doing the job since Danforth left."

"If discretion counts, he's a shoo-in."

Clem wasn't particularly interested in Ed Malvern at this point. "You were asking about me at the grocery store in Cat Creek?"

"For all the good it did me. You'd think I was hunting a still or something—do they still have them in these parts?"

"I wouldn't know about that. What, specifically, did you want to see me about?"

"Could we go inside and talk? I have some figures here I'd like to show you, and frankly, I could use a cup of coffee. I've been driving in circles for the past two hours looking for the right turnoff."

Martha had listened only long enough to be certain he wasn't mixed up with Odwell, and that had been long enough for a plan to formulate in her mind. Whoever he was—wherever he was going from here—she was going with him. Sooner or later, he was bound to pass close to a bus station. She didn't know where Lavorly Laboratories was located, but she would take her chances.

By the time she had lugged her large suitcase to the foot of the stairs and gone back for her toilet case, she could hear them coming through the dining room.

"—at least six weeks," Clem was saying.

"I understand. If you've been holed up here that long, then you probably haven't heard about the buyout. B.F.I.'s top management granted themselves close to half a million shares of restricted stock and then put the company up for grabs. The stock's almost doubled in two weeks, and there's no end in sight."

"I don't suppose that will affect my position one way or another," Clem said.

"I wouldn't bet on it. In cases like these—"

"Even so," Clem interrupted as they came into the front hall where Martha stood, purse clutched in her hands, beside her stacked luggage. "I can't give you an answer now. If you'll... *Martha*?"

He felt a knife slide into his heart and twist as he recognized her intent, but the pain that had shown on his face was gone in an instant. Long years of habit set the process in motion. Defences clanged into place, barriers were erected, and by the time he spoke again, his voice was quite calm. Emotionless.

"Martha Eberly—Jasper Barnes. Mr. Barnes will be going right through Winston-Salem on his way to the Research Triangle. I'm sure he'll be glad to give you a lift."

Ten

Moonlight lay over the ground like snow. Clem knew he could wait no longer. He'd waited too long as it was. Scared, eager, half sick with nerves, as long as he'd been preparing he'd been able to fool himself that he stood a chance. At first she'd be surprised to see him, but she'd invite him inside, where he would proceed to demonstrate his new savoir faire. He'd learned a hell of a lot, and he'd changed, in every way but one.

Martha was still the most important single element in his life. The love that had taken him unawares those first few days had grown since they'd been apart until it was a physical ache inside him.

Not until he turned the corner of the street where she lived did it occur to him that she might not be alone. His hands gripped the steering wheel. His speed, which had averaged five miles an hour below the speed limit for residential districts, dropped to ten below.

A car turned off a side street, moved up on his bumper and honked.

Clem gripped the steering wheel until his knuckles whitened.

The house was small. If he hadn't already located it and driven past several times in daylight, he never would have found it. Moss green, with putty-colored trim, a wreath on the door and a half porch that sagged on one corner. She deserved better. He hated to see her living in a place like this.

Clem parked on the street behind Martha's eight-year-old compact station wagon. He knew it was hers, just as he knew she was working for a children's clothing shop in Hanes Mall. He also knew, thanks to Virginia Malvern, that management was impressed enough to have offered her a shot at assistant managership at the end of six months if she would agree to stay on.

He was halfway up the walk when he remembered the roses and had to go back for them. Yellow roses. Like the ones on her jars and bottles. By the time he made it back through the scraggly hedge, up the cracked concrete walk and across the sloping wooden porch, he was beginning to sweat. Why the devil had he dressed up like a damn gigolo? He should have stuck to his old gray suit, with the white shirt and black tie. He should've worn his glasses instead of his new contacts, and he should've let his beard grow back. There'd have been time for a short one, at least.

His knock was more vigorous than he'd intended. It rattled the panes on the glass-topped door.

She came to the door wearing something yellow again—not her bathrobe. A sweater—sweatshirt? And a pair of jeans that fit her like a glove. On her feet were a pair of enormous furry yellow slippers, with ears.

Clem cleared his throat, took a deep breath and said quite calmly, "Good evening, Martha." He'd rehearsed in front of the mirror and chosen the more prosaic greeting over, "Martha! Good to see you again!"

She was supposed to say something back, wasn't she? "I—um, I believe we're going to have a heavy frost tonight. Please say something before I fall apart, will you?"

Six-feet-four, one hundred sixty-two pounds, with seven degrees from the best schools in the country, and he was shaking in his cordovans before a tiny slip of a woman with ears on her slippers!

Clem stared for perhaps thirty of the longest seconds known to man, and then he shoved the bouquet of yellow roses at her, scraping his knuckles on the screen door, which neither of them had opened yet.

"Clem?" she whispered, ignoring the roses. "How did you find me?"

He could only manage to parrot his third prepared statement, which was, "Nice place you have here." It was a lousy place. It needed trees and a lot more breathing space; instead it had neighbors ten feet on either side and a moribund hedge.

"How did you—I almost didn't— Come inside. I mean, won't you— Oh, lord, just *get in here*!"

He got. Crushing the rose stems in his fist, he stepped past her into a tiny, cheerful room filled with photos of children and a couple he thought must be her brother and one of his wives, a middle-aged man on a tractor and a woman in an apron, laughing self-consciously as she squinted into the sun. There was a stack of papers and pamphlets on a footstool, a partially stuffed rag doll lying on the loveseat and a sewing basket nearby. "I brought you these." He shoved the flowers at her, praying she wouldn't notice how nervous he was.

"They're beautiful, but Clem—what happened to you? You look . . . different. How on earth did you find me? I haven't even sent Hattie my address yet. She sounded so strange when I called last week." She got a green vase from the kitchen and arranged the roses, burying her face in them before placing them on the table.

"Virginia Malvern."

"At the jewelry store?"

He nodded. Either his neck had grown in the past three minutes, or his collar had shrunk. He was strangling. "Um, your emerald—that is, she said—"

"That it wasn't an emerald after all. To tell you the truth, I'm almost relieved. I don't think I'm cut out for emeralds."

"Spodumene is nice, too." He didn't know what to say. He'd considered buying her an emerald and substituting it, but a crystal of that size, even badly flawed, would be hard to come by.

"I'm keeping it for a souvenir." She straightened the stack of papers on the stool, and Clem knew very well she was avoiding meeting his eyes.

He refused to let her get away with it. He refused to let her get away, period. "If Hattie sounded strange, it was because she was disappointed not to come back and find us— uh—well, you know."

"She was *what*?"

"Disappointed. That we weren't married." At least he had her full attention now, Clem thought with singular satisfaction. "I think it was part of her annual Doing Something About Clement routine, only as a rule she's satisfied to ruin a single evening.''

''To ruin a—''

''I didn't mean it that way,'' he said hastily.

Martha dropped down onto a cane-bottomed chair and then bobbed up again to offer him a seat, but Clem didn't want to sit. He wanted to hold her. He wanted to take her in his arms and never let her go, but he suspected they needed to talk first. *I know damned well you care for me, because it couldn't have happened between us the way it did if you'd been indifferent. I could actually feel you caring!*

''I can't believe Hattie deliberately went off and—I mean, she knew I was coming—she invited me herself. You mean she got you up there and then stayed away just so that we—'' *She knew how I would react—she's never forgotten how I felt about your portrait. And I thought I'd been so clever about hiding it.*

Clem nodded, wishing he'd taken the time to write out precisely what he wanted to say to her. He needed the right words, needed to state his case in a calm and orderly fashion, because his new finery—the haircut, the contact lenses, the navy-blue briefs instead of the white boxer shorts he'd always worn—they weren't enough. He was going to have to *tell* her how he felt, and he'd probably strangle on the words.

''Warm for December, isn't it?'' He tugged at his tie.

''The furnace is new. You look—'' *Why are we wasting all this time on words? Why don't you hold me? Don't you want me anymore?*

Martha cleared her throat. ''You look wonderful, Clem. Your hair...'' It was styled, not just whacked off. She knew little about men's fashions, but she did know a good suit when she saw one, and Clem's was excellent. On him it was fantastic. The pale blue shirt and the paisley tie enhanced the intensity of his eyes. "What have you been doing with yourself lately?"

"Thank you. Learning. Preparing to move." *Missing you until I thought I would die from it.*

"To move? You're really leaving B.F.I., then?" *Damn you, why did you come back if you're only going to leave again? I was almost starting to get over you—I was going entire days without crying. Come spring, I'd have been almost as good as new, and now I'll have to start all over again!*

"Yes. Yes, I am."

Clem stood and began to pace, stepping over a stack of books and a bowl of pecans. Three strides took him to the far side of the living room, and he turned and confronted her. Sweat prickled on his clean-shaven upper lip, and he rammed his hands into his pockets to hide their unsteadiness. "Dammit, Marty, I've done all I know how to do! If it isn't enough, then tell me what else needs changing, and I'll change it. I can learn."

She was on her feet in an instant. In another moment, he would have had her where he wanted her—in his arms again. He turned away, and it was the hardest thing he'd ever done in his life. "I have to get this said," he told her. "If I lose my nerve—that is, if I get distracted, I might not be able to—that is, I . . ."

"Then say it—please." *Say what I've been waiting to hear, what I need to hear more than anything else in the world.*

Her voice seeped into the deepest recesses of his soul, touching, healing, claiming what was already hers—had been hers since the first moment he saw her. "Martha, I— That is, I can drive now. I buy my own clothes." He wrenched loose his fifty-dollar tie and unfastened the top button of his tailor-made shirt. "I bought a car. I took driving lessons. There was an advertisement for dancing lessons, but I don't even know if you like to dance. I'm not sure I'll ever be very good at it, because coordination isn't something that can be taught, but—"

"Clem."

"—I'm willing to try. And there are bridge lessons. Guitar lessons, art lessons, voice lessons and something called ikebana—"

"Clem!"

"I have money. I met with my accountant to arrange to have everything moved, and I have quite a lot of money. I'll give you all you want—for social security and insurance and that sort of thing—no ropes attached."

His back was turned, but he knew precisely when she came to stand behind him. He could feel her with every fiber of his body. "Strings," she said softly.

"Strings?"

"The phrase is, no strings attached, and I can't take your money, Clem." *I'd rather have the strings.* "It's just not done. But thank you."

He turned to face her then, and she was so close—so close... But still he didn't take her in his arms. "But I want you to have it. I want to give you something, don't you understand? I want to give you everything, but I don't know what you want. You left—"

She broke in. "Not because I wanted to. I did it for you."

His eyes went the color of slate. "God, don't do me any more favors like that!"

"Clem, you're a—that is, you didn't seem to know how—how truly wonderful you really are. I thought perhaps after we'd, um—gotten to know one another, you might want to try—that is, you might meet other women and discover what you'd been missing all these years, and I would never want to hold you back.'' *Don't just stand there, tell me I'm wrong! Tell me you don't want any other woman but me! Tell me you love me, Clem. Please...*

Let me show you, darling. I'll never be able to tell you with words as well as I can show you. Clem opened his arms, and she leaned forward, and they were together. After a month that had nearly torn him apart—a month that had left her thinner, paler, her eyes more shadowed, they were together.

He kissed her lips, her forehead, the velvet mole above her lips, her eyelids. And then he found her lips again, telling her without words how much he'd missed her.

He was intoxicated by the scent of her. By the familiar taste of her, the moist velvet feel of her kisses. Her body against his was so fragile, he felt clumsier than ever, and he took exquisite care when he swept her up in his arms to hold her gently. Without lifting his lips from her, he turned toward the nearest door.

"This is the kitchen," he said blankly sometime later, when he came up for air.

Martha laughed softly. "I know. The bedroom's through there."

He laid her on the bed, and she watched while he removed his clothes. He was a little embarrassed now at the navy-blue briefs. He had a feeling he'd always be the white boxer type at heart, but if he'd thought it would have helped the cause, he'd have worn black tights and a purple cape.

Kneeling beside her on the bed, Clem told himself that he had to do this right—his whole future might depend on it.

Slippers first. And when she was barefooted, he could eas
her jeans down over her hips and slide them off. And then..

Later, he didn't know who removed what. All he knew
was they were wrapped together, bare skin against bare skin
murmured words blunting murmured words as they touched
and kissed and explored.

She was so beautiful—he'd forgotten how beautiful sh
was. Her small, full breasts peaked against his palms, an
he thought he would die of pleasure. When her lips and then
her teeth brushed against his nipples, he closed his eyes i
exquisite pain.

He suckled her, loving the way she gasped, the way he
body stiffened. Loving the way each small sound she mad
registered in the depths of his body.

He was so full he thought he would explode, but he didn'
want it to end. "Forever," he said hoarsely, "or as long a
I can manage."

She seemed to understand, because the hand that ha
been caressing its way down his flat belly began to edge up
ward again. If she'd touched him there, it would've been al
over. "Or again and again?" she whispered, and he though
that was the best idea of all.

Burying his face against her throat, he whispered word
he had not yet been able to say to her face. He worshiped he
breasts, paying homage to each one in turn before strokin
the satin skin above her waist with tiny wet kisses. *I lov
you, Martha Eberly. I've always loved you, and I alway
will.*

When he could stand it no longer, he rose above her
trembling in his need. "Again and again?" he asked, hi
voice barely audible over the harsh sound of his breathing
"Promise?"

Her arms came around him, and she drew him to her, cradling him in her thighs. "Again and again, for as long as you want me, I promise," she whispered.

It was over too quickly, as he'd known it would be, but the shattering intensity of it left them both stunned for a long time. They clung tightly, beyond speech, almost beyond thought.

Gradually, Clem became aware of a coolness on his damp body, and he got up and found a blanket. Covering them both, he gathered her in his arms.

"There are nursing schools in Durham, you know."

"Clem, you may as well know this about me from the first."

"I'd hardly call this the first," he said with a slow, satisfied smile.

She had to smile at that, too. "No, but you see, the thing is, I don't have a degree, and I'm probably never going to have one, because it's not all that important to me. I have friends with degrees who can't even find a job, and other friends without them who're doing just fine, and I think I must fall somewhere in the middle, because—"

"I love you, Martha."

She caught her breath. He could see her eyes darken, and he thought he would die of the waiting before she said, "I know you do, darling. I love you, too, but you have to understand that I'm not going to be a bit of help to you in your career."

"My career is coming along just fine."

"I don't speak a single foreign language, and my cooking is strictly country, and I know that women are supposed to want a career for fulfillment and so that they don't really need a man, and I'm afraid I don't. I used to have plans, but after a while the fire just sort of went out for lack of fuel. I'm sorry, but you may as well know the worst. After all these years, I've discovered that an interesting job is enough, because what I really like doing is looking after children and—and people I love, and maybe gardening, and—and—''

He kissed the hollow of her throat, loving the sweet-salt taste of her skin. "You're distracting me," she said breathlessly.

"Good. That's what I intended to do."

"Did you understand what I said, Clement? I'm probably all wrong for you. We're not at all compatible. You're brilliant and I'm strictly utilitarian. You write articles I can't wade through for publications the library had a hard time even locating, and I read recipes and try to figure out how to use a computerized cash register without setting off all sorts of alarms. Even my emerald turned out to be a perfectly ordinary whatchamacallit.''

"Your chunk of whatchamacallit is a form of green spodumene called hiddenite, and it's only found in one place in the world."

"Beginner's luck. At least no one's chasing me for it. Who ever heard of an international jewel thief chasing after a chunk of whatchamacallit?''

He chuckled, and after a moment so did she. "Marty—if I'm so brilliant, surely you're practical enough to trust me to know what's right for us." Holding her tightly, he rolled her over until she lay on top of him, her small freckled nose mere inches away from his own. One of them—he never knew which one—closed the distance, and it was a long time later before they could talk again.

"Hattie's going to take credit for this, you know," Clem said, tracing her hairline until he found the small mole he remembered.

"So let her. We'll name out first daughter after her if you don't think it might be asking for trouble."

"Just to be on the safe side, why don't we call our first one Martha. Once we get the hang of it, we might consider risking another Hattie."

As moonlight spilled across the foot of the bed, Clem could sense her smiling in the darkness. His arms tightened around her, and he brushed a kiss against her hair. Daughters. The very thought of sharing a future with this woman filled him with an almost unbearable joy, but to think of having *daughters* with her, too! Children of his own, children to love, to laugh with, to teach how to play—

Martha had found what she'd thought was an emerald, but he'd found the rarest jewel of all, without even searching. And his had turned out to be real.

* * * * *

Silhouette Romance®

LONG, TALL TEXANS

Diana Palmer brings you the second Award of Excellence title

SUTTON'S WAY

In Diana Palmer's bestselling Long, Tall Texans trilogy, you had a mesmerizing glimpse of Quinn Sutton—a mean, lean Wyoming wildcat of a man, with a disposition to match.

Now, in September, Quinn's back with a story of his own. Set in the Wyoming wilderness, he learns a few things about women from snowbound beauty Amanda Callaway—and a lot more about love.

He's a Texan at heart . . . who soon has a Wyoming wedding in mind!

The Award of Excellence is given to one specially selected title per month. Spend September discovering *Sutton's Way* #670 . . . only in Silhouette Romance.

 *Silhouette Intimate Moments*®

COMING IN OCTOBER!
A FRESH LOOK FOR
Silhouette Intimate Moments!

Silhouette Intimate Moments has always brought you the perfect combination of love and excitement, and now they're about to get a new cover design that's just as exciting as the stories inside.

Over the years we've brought you stories that combined romance with something a little bit different, like adventure or suspense. We've brought you longtime favorite authors like Nora Roberts and Linda Howard. We've brought you exciting new talents like Patricia Gardner Evans and Marilyn Pappano. Now let us bring you a new cover design guaranteed to catch your eye just as our heroes and heroines catch your heart.

Look for it in October—
Only from Silhouette Intimate Moments!

IMNC-1

COMING SOON...

Indulge a Little
Give a Lot

An irresistible opportunity to pamper
yourself with free* gifts and help a
great cause, Big Brothers/Big Sisters
Programs and Services.

*With proofs-of-purchase plus postage and handling.

Watch for it in October!

LINDA LADD

DRAGON FIRE

AVON BOOKS ◆ NEW YORK

DRAGON FIRE is an original publication of Avon Books. This work has never before appeared in book form. This work is a novel. Any similarity to actual persons or events is purely coincidental.

AVON BOOKS
A division of
The Hearst Corporation
1350 Avenue of the Americas
New York, New York 10019

Copyright © 1992 by Linda Ladd
Published by arrangement with the author
Library of Congress Catalog Card Number: 91-92081
ISBN: 0-380-75698-6

First Avon Books Printing: January 1992

AVON TRADEMARK REG. U.S. PAT. OFF. AND IN OTHER COUNTRIES, MARCA REGISTRADA, HECHO EN U.S.A.

Printed in the U.S.A.

RA   10   9   8   7   6   5   4   3   2   1

For
Ron and Kathy Ladd
Sherry and Angie
and Josh

And with a
very special thank you
to Ellen Edwards
for all her help and support

1

November 10, 1871
Chicago, Illinois

At one end of the congested railway platform, a small figure stood a short distance from the milling crowd. Robed completely in black, Windsor Richmond was oblivious to the cries of porters pushing rumbling baggage carts past her. Instead, she focused her sapphire eyes with steadfast concentration on two tall, black-haired gentlemen conversing together near where a westward-bound train was hissing and spewing clouds of steam in preparation for departure. One of the men was Stone Kincaid, and she had come to kill him.

Windsor impatiently readjusted the bulky black wimple which fell in draping folds just past her shoulders. Since she had donned the somber nun's habit, she had found the clinging headdress and long, full skirt cumbersome and uncomfortable. Even more important, such restrictive clothing impeded the lithe agility she would need to subdue the big American.

Irritated, she longed to throw off the dress and wear only the black silk tunic and trousers she had

on beneath the nun's costume. The attire to which
she had become accustomed while growing to
womanhood in China was so much more practical.
She could not understand why the nuns required
so many layers of clothing. Even harder to understand was the inclination of the American women
to subject themselves to strange binding garments
beneath their voluminous outer garb.

The people of the United States were very peculiar, and though she had lived for several months
in the city of San Francisco, which lay far to the
west of Chicago, she still could not comprehend
many of the American customs. She was eager to
finish her mission so she could return to the peaceful mountain province in northern China where she
belonged.

Her delicately arched blond brows drawn together, she scanned the mob of people rushing
around as if afflicted with wild-eyed panic. She was
constantly amazed by the huge numbers of inhab-
itants in the cities of this land where her parents
had been born. How could these Americans attain
inner peace, living in such loud and chaotic sur-
roundings?

With so many curious eyes forever watching everyone else, Windsor would have to be cautious.
She would have to wait until the precise opportunity presented itself, then she would avenge poor
Hung-pin's murder. Grief grabbed at her heart,
gouging it with sharp claws, further bruising emotions still raw and bleeding from the death of her
beloved blood brother a little over a fortnight ago.
At times she missed Hung-pin so much she felt she
couldn't bear the pain of being without him for another moment.

The inhuman way Hung-pin had been killed was
partly why she felt so compelled to punish his
murderer. Stone Kincaid had forced Hung-pin to
suffer long hours of excruciating agony before his

spirit had fled his body. Windsor shuddered, unable to forget how her friend had looked hanging from the tree limb, the flesh of his back torn away in ragged strips. She would have to remain very patient to exact vengeance for such a heinous crime.

But perseverance was a virtue Windsor had been taught well. When at the age of ten she had been brought to the Temple of the Blue Mountain to live with Hung-pin and the other disciples, the Old One had taken her to a dark, dusty corner where many candles burned and the smell of incense perfumed the air. The wise sage had gestured with wordless eloquence at a fine-spun spider's web suspended like gossamer between the brass candelabra and the stone wall.

For many weeks afterward, she had spent her early morning hours of meditation before the silken-stranded net, observing the work of the swift brown spider. She had taken note of the way he fashioned his beautiful, glistening designs, then backed away until he seemed to disappear, to await his unsuspecting prey. In time, Windsor had understood the Old One's lesson of steadfastness. She would be in no hurry. She would watch and wait until Stone Kincaid struggled helplessly in her own web, like the big green dragonfly had done until the small, clever spider had crept forth and devoured him.

Her interest sharpened as one of the two men she observed looked at an American lady wearing a distinctive scarlet cloak. Windsor had noticed before that he glanced often toward where she stood beside their waiting carriage. The woman in red had accompanied the two men since they had left their gray stone mansion on Lincoln Avenue.

To her surprise, Windsor had found the task of locating Stone Kincaid amazingly simple, considering the size of the big town on the southern shores of the great inland water called Lake Michigan. Upon her very first inquiry about him when she had arrived from San Francisco the day before, the stationmaster at this very railway depot had spoken freely of the Kincaids. He had told her they were a well-known and wealthy family—the owners and operators of dozens of the locomotives that traveled daily in and out of Chicago.

Even more astonishing, the helpful railway employee had had no qualms about giving her Stone Kincaid's address and precise directions to his home! She had walked there, watched, and waited with the patience of her eight-legged friend until the three Americans had led her back to the departure platform.

Yet she did not know which man was Stone Kincaid. They resembled each other very much, both tall and lean with strong, thickly muscled bodies. One of them was dressed much more formally, in a finely tailored, dark gray frock coat and matching waistcoat, with an elegant beaver hat upon his head.

The other man was attired as were many of the Americans she had seen in the streets of San Francisco. Like the gunfighters there, he wore a brown leather vest over a white linen shirt, and he was heavily armed. Two guns were secured in the black-and-silver holsters strapped to his thighs, and he carried a rifle in one hand, as well as a black leather travelling valise. Apparently he was the one ready to embark on the journey west.

Faint scratching sounds captured Windsor's attention. Jun-li is impatient, she thought with a smile, lifting her bamboo suitcase from where she had hung it across her chest by its sturdy leather strap.

"Shh, my little friend," she whispered through the closely woven slats, "I will take you out soon, I promise."

But first she must determine which man was the evil Stone Kincaid. Holding Jun-li's case by its carrying handle, she hurried across the planked platform toward her unsuspecting dragonfly.

"Stone, you're making a hell of a big mistake! Dammit, your obsession with finding Emerson Clan is going to get you killed!"

Stone Kincaid studied the passengers boarding the train to California, only vaguely listening to the familiar harangue that his older brother, Gray, was spouting again with such fervor. How many times since they had heard that Emerson Clan had been seen in California had Gray reiterated the same monotonous arguments? Regardless, nothing Gray said, or could ever say, would keep Stone from tracking down Clan. Stone had been after the murdering bastard for too damn long—since the day six years ago when Northern forces had marched into Andersonville, Georgia, and liberated him and thousands of other Federal soldiers from nothing less than hell on earth.

"For God's sake, Stone, you haven't heard a word I've said, have you?"

With a concerted effort, Stone refocused his attention on his brother.

"You're wasting your breath, Gray," he replied quietly. "I'm going after Clan, and there's nothing you can do about it." He swung an arm toward his sister-in-law, Tyler, where she awaited her husband near their conveyance. "So why don't you concern yourself with your wife and the child she carries? I can take care of myself."

Gray's handsome features softened as he turned his gaze upon Tyler. When a half smile tugged at his brother's lips, Stone inwardly shook his head, having grown accustomed to Gray's besotted, lovelorn expressions since Tyler MacKenzie had waltzed into Gray's life nearly a year ago. A well-

practiced con artist hell-bent on swindling Gray out
of ten thousand dollars, she had ultimately stolen
his heart instead, a feat Stone would never have
thought possible in a matrimony-avoiding bachelor
like Gray.

"My God," Gray said, his gaze lingering fondly
on his petite wife, "I get sick to my stomach when
I think how close Emerson Clan came to hurting
Tyler and the baby."

At Gray's mention of Clan's latest crimes against
his family, rage roared inside Stone with the fierce-
ness of a bonfire. Only a month ago, Clan had been
in Chicago, enticed there by one of Tyler's confidence games.

Designed to help Stone capture him, Tyler's plan
had succeeded, and Stone had reveled at the sight
of Clan thrown into jail. But because of the fires
that were raging throughout the city at the time,
Clan had managed to escape from the authorities
and had kidnapped Tyler, then nearly killed Gray
when he and Stone had tried to rescue her. Still,
Clan had got away.

"And he left a gunshot wound in your side to
remember him by," Stone muttered to Gray, his
voice tight. "Which is one more reason for me to
go after him. He's worse than an animal. He kills
and tortures because he enjoys it. And he'll keep
on murdering innocent people until someone puts
a bullet through his skull. I intend to be the one
who does it."

Succumbing to defeat, Gray shook his head.
"And there's nothing I can say or do to keep you
here?"

"Nope."

"Then be careful, and for God's sake, don't underestimate Clan again. He's the closest thing to a
devil I've ever known."

"He belongs in hell, all right, and that's exactly
where I intend to send him—"

Stone's vicious vow was cut off as he was struck from behind and knocked forward a step. Going down in a low crouch, he spun, his Colt revolver cold against his palm. Dismay flooded him when he realized he had drawn his weapon on a Catholic Sister. The poor woman lay sprawled on the platform, the breath knocked out of her. Appalled, Stone quickly reholstered his weapon and knelt to assist her.

"Please forgive me, Sister. Are you hurt?"

The nun didn't answer his solicitous inquiry, rubbing her arm as Stone drew her to her feet. Standing between Gray and him, she appeared tiny indeed: both men stood well over six feet.

"No, I do not believe I am injured," the nun murmured, rearranging her black skirt and righting the heavy silver crucifix which hung around her waist. "I am the one at fault. I was in a hurry and did not watch where I was going."

Instantly, Stone was struck by her voice. Low and melodious, her words fell upon his ear like the soft, sweetly lilting notes of a harp. A slight accent flowed through her speech, an unusual one that he did not recognize. She looked at him then, and Stone found himself staring into large limpid eyes of deep midnight blue, fringed with sweeping golden lashes. Even more than their beautiful sapphire color transfixed him; he was arrested by what he sensed to be a deep tranquility aglow in their calm, quiet depths.

Uncannily, he was held captive by the most peculiar sensation. With some kind of innate certainty, he felt as if he knew her already, that somewhere long ago, at a time never to be forgotten, he had loved her. Slightly aghast at his ridiculous and uncharacteristic reaction to the woman, he stared at her, deciding she was much too young to be a nun.

"Since my brother here seems at a loss for

words," Gray was saying, effectively snapping Stone's spell, "I'll do the honor, Sister. My name is Gray Kincaid, and this is my brother, Stone."

"How do you do," she answered softly. "I am Sister Mary."

When she rubbed her elbow again, Gray leaned forward, a frown of concern on his brow. "Are you sure you're not hurt?"

"I am fine. I must apologize for being so clumsy."

"No, I'm sure I was at fault," Stone ventured courteously, but he couldn't seem to drag his eyes off her face. Her fine-boned features were small and delicate, and her skin was as smooth and clear as the purest white alabaster, though at the moment, her high cheekbones were flushed with rose-tinged color. His regard moved to her lips. Before he could stop himself, he had mentally tasted them.

Stone quickly jerked the reins of his thoughts. God forgive me, the woman's a nun, he thought, uncomfortable and not a little ashamed of his erotic turn of mind. To hide his own embarrassment, he bent and retrieved the small bamboo suitcase that she had dropped.

"Please allow me to escort you to the train, Sister Mary. I was just about to bid good-bye to my brother."

"You are very kind," the nun replied in her musical voice.

Once again Stone vainly attempted to pinpoint her odd, lyrical accent. A few feet away, the conductor boomed out one last hearty call to board, impelling Stone to stretch his palm toward Gray.

"Take care of Tyler," he told him, grinning, "and let me know how our little sister fares on her adventure in Mexico."

"I'm just grateful that Carlisle has Chase Lancaster looking after her while she's visiting the Perez family in Mexico City. Otherwise, I'd really be worried, considering how often she manages to get herself in trouble.''

Gray's criticism of their headstrong younger sister was mellowed by an indulgent smile, but his expression quickly sobered.

''Watch your back, Stone. This time I've got a bad feeling about you going after Emerson Clan.''

''Don't worry about me. You know I can take care of myself. I'll send word to you as soon as I get him.''

Gray looked no less worried, but he nodded, then politely tipped his hat to the young Catholic Sister. As Gray turned and wended his way through the people congregated to wave good-bye to those boarding the express train departing west, Stone lifted his arm in a farewell wave to his beautiful cinnamon-eyed sister-in-law. Despite Tyler's unsavory past, Stone had become fond of her during the past few months. She had changed a lot since she had married his brother, and all for the better. Gray was a lucky man.

Returning his attention to the black-garbed nun at his side, he clasped his fingers around her elbow.

''Are you traveling far, Sister Mary?'' he asked, guiding her toward the train.

Her head dipped forward in an affirmative nod, making the black folds of her wimple settle around her face. He found himself wondering what color her hair was beneath the somber cloth. Golden blond, he decided, like her eyelashes.

''I am to join others of my order in San Francisco,'' she answered softly.

''Then it appears we'll be traveling companions for the next week or so,'' Stone remarked as they reached the narrow iron stairs leading onto the open-air rear platform of the nearest car.

He assisted the nun up the steps, then swung up easily behind her.

"I must find the conductor and purchase my ticket," she said, gazing up at him. "Thank you for carrying my box. I will take it now. You are very kind to help me."

"My pleasure, ma'am."

Stone relinquished her suitcase and watched as she slipped the long leather strap over her head and across her chest. What an odd way for a lady to carry her bag, he thought in surprise, almost the way a soldier would wear his bandoliers. In fact, he realized suddenly, the suitcase itself was unusual. Most women he knew carried their belongings in decorated bandboxes or tapestry-covered valises.

Without further comment, the lovely Catholic Sister moved away from him and disappeared into the crowded aisle of the first-class coach. Stone grimaced to think of the long journey he faced, hemmed in by so many other people. He disliked enclosed places, and he already dreaded the days and nights ahead of him in the stifling confines of the passenger car.

The engine roared, and, accompanied by clanging bells, waving handkerchiefs, and many shouted farewells, the locomotive's pistons began to pump, chugging slowly at first, then faster as the train moved away from the platform, steam hissing in vapor clouds from the underbelly of the iron engine.

Stone waved again to Gray and Tyler. He would miss them, but more than anything else, he was eager to get to San Francisco. This time he wouldn't make the mistake of turning Emerson Clan over to the law. This time, he would kill him himself. With his bare hands, if necessary.

2

For more than forty-eight hours the train had puffed and chugged its way across the wide, desolate plains, leaving billows of white smoke to drift in great clouds over the tall, waving prairie grasses. Windsor had spent her waking hours observing Stone Kincaid's behavior, biding her time like her friend the patient spider.

Under the thick fringe of her lashes, she watched him now, where he and two other men sat around a small table bolted to the floor at the rear of the car. They played at some sort of strange gambling game with many cards and colored chips. Often, one of his companions would curse about the cards in his hands. Their voices were gruff and argumentative, and the cigars they held between their fingers contaminated the air with a foul smell.

Many of the other passengers also smoked; others spat ugly globs of brown juice into brass spittoons beside each upholstered seat. She could understand why many of the women had congregated in the next car, away from the crude talk. But she could not leave; she had to remain close to her big, black-haired quarry.

Windsor had speculated much about Stone Kin-

11

caid. He did not look like a cold-blooded killer. He was exceedingly handsome of face, his features as strong and powerful as the well-formed muscles of his body. His eyes were blue, like hers, but of a lighter hue that seemed to turn silver at times. At the moment, his eyes were downcast, intently studying the five cards he held spread evenly in his left hand. His right hand, however, lay upon his thigh, close to one of his big black guns.

He seemed a quiet, thoughtful man, who rarely spoke with others, not even to the two men with whom he sported. He kept to himself, but she had noticed how he watched the other passengers and listened to their talk. She must be careful. Had the Old One not told her that a man of sense talks little and listens much?

Often, too, Stone Kincaid absented himself from the stuffy coach to stand alone on the open-air platform at the rear of the car. At such times he stared out over the endless grasslands toward the western horizon, and she wondered if he thought of Emerson Clan, the man his brother had mentioned at the Chicago depot. Why did Stone Kincaid seek this man? Was Clan the reason for the glow of anger she had seen lurking deep in Stone Kincaid's eyes, like goldfish hiding at the bottom of a lotus pool?

But more alarming than anything else about him was the pull of Stone Kincaid's soul upon her own. Windsor had known from the moment they had spoken that their spirits were kindred. Even so, she was pledged to end his life so that Hung-pin's spirit could soar free. Perhaps tonight, the moment she awaited would at last present itself.

For the past two evenings Stone Kincaid had offered to convert her seat into a night berth, but even after all the other passengers had climbed into their narrow bunks, he had remained seated in his upholstered chair. Throughout the night she had peeked out, hoping to find him asleep, but he never seemed to shut his eyes. Stone Kincaid was strange, and very different from the other male travelers.

Sighing, Windsor shifted her gaze and stared out the crimson-draped, plate-glass window beside her. Early that morning they had finally left the rolling plains and entered the foothills of the high mountains called the Rockies. Windsor had been overwhelmed by the wonderful aura of contentment that had washed over her like a foamy tide on a warm sandy beach. She loved the towering peaks and thick green forests hugging the railway bed, so like those in the valley surrounding her temple. She wished she were there now, where she could listen to the wisdom of the Old One. Here, in this curious land of America, she could only rely on herself.

Outside, night had fallen long ago, as black and soft as Hung-pin's hair. The moon had climbed high, full and pale, casting a ghostly light over the dark-shadowed trees alongside the tracks. On nights such as this during her childhood, she and Hung-pin had practiced stealth. At such times the moon had been their enemy, its silvery glow revealing their every movement.

She smiled to herself, thinking about the way they had carefully unrolled the long length of white rice paper, then attempted to tread so lightly upon its thin surface that the fragile paper remained untorn. Many years of diligent practice finally enabled them to conquer the feat. Hung-pin had mastered the art first, of course. He had always excelled in their tasks before she had, especially the more difficult ones. It had been Hung-pin who had persuaded her to come to the United States to meet her American mother. If she had not come, if she had not begged Hung-pin to accompany her, her blood brother would still be alive and well.

Deeply forlorn, she tried not to think about Hung-pin. She repositioned her case, holding it securely atop her lap. Jun-li was restless. She could feel him moving around inside his cage. He longed for bedtime, when behind the barrier of the privacy curtains she could release him from his prison. She felt pity for her little friend because she understood how he felt. She wished to be free from the close confines of the coach.

Outside in the moonlit night, the air would smell clean and feel cool against her face, like the twilight breezes deep in the valleys of Kansu Province. She liked the cold air, but most of the passengers spent much time huddled around the pot bellied stove in the center of the car. They were very affected by the weather, the large Americans. She closed her eyes, pretending she was home again, watching the spider dance along his strands of silk, her beloved Hung-pin at her side.

Stone tossed down his poker hand, bored with the game and even more weary of listening to the two bickering men with whom he played. After so many hours cooped up with Slokum and Ranney, he was beginning to regret his decision not to use his family's private coach for the journey west. Gray had offered him its use, but Stone knew that Gray, as president of the Kincaid Railway Company, frequently used the custom-built car for his own business trips. Now that Gray was married, he would definitely want to take Tyler along with him. Stone certainly didn't blame him.

Despite his present disenchantment with his traveling companions, there were good reasons to associate with the other passengers. Perhaps during their idle chatter they would drop a tidbit of information about Emerson Clan. At the mere thought of his nemesis, Stone balled his fingers into tight fists. Consciously trying to relax his tense muscles, he glanced around until his gaze came to rest on the nun.

Sister Mary sat by herself, her eyes closed, her odd bamboo case balanced primly atop her knees. She guarded her possessions like a she-bear protecting newborn cubs, he thought, allowing himself the pleasure of admiring her face while she was unaware of his interest. Since they had boarded the train together, he had endeavored not to look at her, not to think about her. But how many times had he found himself doing both—wondering what shade of blonde her hair would be if he pulled away her wimple, or how her skin would feel if he traced his fingers down the elegant curve of her cheek.

Disgusted with himself, he jerked his gaze away from her. What the devil was the matter with him? He was not a religious man, nor was he particularly scrupulous, but he sure as hell had never mentally seduced an innocent nun before!

"Ain't so bad to look at, now is she, Mr. Kincaid?"

At Slokum's slyly muttered innuendo, Stone slowly turned his attention to the man across the table. A gut-heavy, slack-jowled Texas cattle agent, Matt Slokum sweated profusely, and an offensive odor emanated from his rumpled brown plaid suit.

"You're talking about a Catholic nun, Slokum."

"May be, Kincaid. But, nun or not, she's bound to have a woman's body hidden 'neath all them black robes she's a-wearin', now ain't she? The right kind of man could show her what she's a-missin' by spendin' all her time prayin' and countin' them rosary beads, if you catch my meanin'."

Stone's eyes narrowed. "I catch your meaning, Slokum, and I think you're being disrespectful."

Slokum's large flat nose wrinkled into an ugly scowl. "You cain't say you ain't hankered to sneak a little bit of a peek under them there skirts, now can you, Kincaid? I done seen you lookin' at her, more'n once, and it weren't no prayerful kind of look in them icy blue eyes of yours." He guffawed, elbowing the skinny man named Ranney, who sat to the left of him. Ranney chuckled; then his round, baby-soft cheeks reddened as Stone silenced him with a cold, unwavering stare.

"Like I said, you're being disrespectful."

Slokum looked down at Stone's hand, where it lay atop his knee near his revolver; then he squirmed uneasily in his seat. "I dint mean no harm." His voice sounded nervous. "Like most ever other man in this here coach, I just got eyes in my head."

"Then keep them there, and keep your god-damn mouth shut."

Stone shoved back his chair, angrier than he had reason to be. Slokum was right. Stone had been thinking impure thoughts about the nun, probably worse ones than either Slokum's or Ranney's. Feeling absurdly conscience-stricken, he gathered his winnings, pocketed them, then glanced out the nearest window. It had grown late; the black night pressed like mourning bunting against the glass.

Several passengers were in the process of converting their day chairs into berths, but Sister Mary made no move to do so. She continued to sit motionlessly, her back ramrod-straight. He wondered if she was praying and what about, then wondered why the hell he cared.

With his brows hunched down, his face took on an annoyed grimace. Maybe it was time he went outside and had a cigar. Maybe the cold night air would cool down his blood and get pretty little Sister Mary off his mind. Despite his resolve to ignore the nun, he found himself pausing beside her chair on his way down the aisle.

"Pardon me, Sister Mary, but if you like, I'll pull down your bed for you."

The nun opened her eyes, and as their gazes met,

Stone felt startled, as if she had grabbed the front of his shirt and pulled him close against her. The woman's effect on him was absolutely uncanny.

"You are very kind to think of me," she murmured in her shy manner, casting her long lashes down over her magnificent sapphire eyes.

"Yeah," he muttered, one corner of his mouth quirking with a hint of irony. She wouldn't think him so kind if she knew some of the indecent thoughts he was entertaining about her. "I guess you'll have to stand up while I fix the bed, Sister."

She rose at once, demurely arranging her drab attire. Slokum was right. What a waste, a young woman as beautiful as she was, garbed all in black, married for life to the Church. She should be in a man's bed, head thrown back, eyes half closed with desire. His loins stirred as that mental image burned like a furnace blast through his veins.

Clenching his teeth, he arranged the two facing seats to form the bottom bunk, then lowered the upper bed, which was suspended by chains from the car's ceiling. Finished, he stood back, away from her, not offering to assist her. In his present, rather inflamed state of mind, touching her was not the thing to do. He waited silently as she placed her bamboo case on the top bunk, then, despite her bulky dress and long veil, stepped up lightly on the lower seat and swung herself with nimble grace onto the top berth.

From the beginning she had aroused his protective instincts. He had considered her far too young and innocent to be traveling alone. He laughed inwardly, thinking what an unlikely guardian he would make for her. The Church would certainly frown on his cold-blooded vow to hunt down and kill Emerson Clan, and poor Sister Mary would undoubtedly wear out her rosary beads pleading for his soul.

"I hope you enjoy a restful night," he said politely. "These berths aren't too comfortable."

"Actually, this is a most luxurious bed for me. I am used to a simple pallet upon the floor."

Sister Mary smiled at him, a lovely, enchanting curve of soft pink lips, and Stone caught himself staring at her in openmouthed fascination, like some stricken swain. But, Lord help him, she had the most beautiful face he had ever seen. Their eyes locked with an intensity Stone understood all too well. Apparently Sister Mary didn't. Her friendly expression faded into vague uncertainty.

"Good night, Mr. Kincaid," she murmured, quickly drawing the privacy curtains together.

She must have sensed his desire for her, he decided, and the realization had obviously frightened her. And his passion had been aroused, all right. Stone still felt the heat warming his mind and body. Dammit, what the devil had gotten into him?

Since he had lowered himself to lusting so single-mindedly after a nun, he obviously was in need of a woman to share his bed. There would be plenty of willing ladies, once he reached San Francisco. Meanwhile, he would do well to stay as far away from Sister Mary as he could get.

By now most of the other passengers were abed; even Slokum and Ranney had disappeared into their draped sleepers. One of the Negro porters was moving about the car dimming the oil lamps, which swung desultorily from the wall holders. Stone frowned, longing to stretch out and relax his tired muscles, but not in some closed-in, coffinlike bunk, one that was nowhere big enough to accommodate his long legs.

Ever since he had been at Andersonville, he couldn't stand any kind of small, cramped place. His lean jaw clenched, held tight as his eyes turned as hard as blue-gray granite. He fought unsuccessfully to suppress a surge of bitter loathing churned up by the mere thought of his incarceration in the brutal Confederate prison camp.

For two long, seemingly endless years, he had fought and scratched to survive while penned up inside the filthy, swampy stockade, and for every day, every moment of that purgatory, Emerson Clan had made damn sure Stone had suffered more deprivation and hardship than any other prisoner.

With a conscious effort Stone thrust thoughts of the prison out of his mind as he settled into a nearby chair. It didn't matter where he spent the night. He wouldn't sleep much. He never did.

A long time later, Stone was jerked out of his shallow, uneasy doze. His own hoarse groan had roused him, and he knew at once he'd had the same damned dream again. Sweat covered his brow, and he focused bleary eyes on the green-shaded lamp swaying in cadence to the rocking motions of the locomotive. The flickering illumination lit the car dimly, and he balled his fists to stop the trembling of his hands.

Not a single day had passed since the war's end that his skin didn't crawl with the dreadful memory, a horror that never, ever left him. There had been three of them—Stone, John Morris, and Edward Hunt. Both of the other men had been lieutenants under Stone's command. Both had been close, personal friends. Their plan had been formulated in desperation, a reckless attempt to escape the wretched, inhumane conditions of the prison. They had labored and sweated for weeks digging the tunnel beneath the stockade.

Like a fleeing snake, a long, undulating shudder writhed down Stone's spine, making his skin grow cold. Again, for the thousandth time, he saw Clan's face at the end of the tunnel, his pale blue eyes glinting with evil malevolence. Clan's cruel laughter had echoed down the length of the narrow passage, just before he had intentionally collapsed the open end and trapped all three prisoners inside, burying them alive.

Horror came spiralling down inside Stone's mind. Hairs stood up on the back of his neck, and cold sweat beaded his upper lip. Even now, as he sat alone in the passenger car years afterward, well and whole, he felt trapped again in the stifling darkness, dirt and rubble raining down on his back, his rasping breath loud in his ears as he frantically fought to dig his way out.

Struggling against the demons torturing his brain, he dragged an open palm down his face. His nightmares would not end until he killed Clan. He knew that. He would do it for John and Edward, who had suffocated to death before Stone could get them out. His desire for vengeance was too in-grained, as much a part of him now as the beating of his heart. Like the most insidious of poisons, his intense hatred for Clan ran in his blood.

Wide awake, he sat up, his eyes focused across the aisle from him where black drapes covered the nun's berth. There was no sound in the coach, just the distant rhythm of wheels clacking against metal. Everyone slept except for him. He could barely remember how it felt to experience a night of deep, restful sleep, instead of lurching awake with a pounding heart, his mind riveted with horror.

Drawing in a deep breath, he shoved himself to his feet. Outside the windows, faint light crowned the horizon. Dawn. He needed to get outside, where he could inhale the crisp mountain air and rid himself of the demons in his head.

3

Separating her curtains a mere fraction, Windsor discovered that Stone Kincaid had arisen from his chair and was on his way down the corridor toward the outside rear platform. At last, she thought, the chance she had been waiting for. Only livestock and purebred horses bound for the liveries of San Francisco traveled in the coach behind them. There would be no witness to her deed.

"Shh, Jun-li," she whispered, her lips close to his bamboo cage. "It is time."

With great care, she hung the case across her body so that both hands could remain free. Stone Kincaid was very strong, and much bigger than she. She must not underestimate him.

Briefly, with unwelcome clarity, she remembered the moment he had bidden her good night. His silvery blue eyes had radiated an intense, inner glow, a knowing, intimate look that made her uncomfortable, even now.

She did not exactly understand the significance of what had transpired between them then, but she knew some unspoken communication had been sent to her. She knew little about men, especially the Americans. Hung-pin and the other disciples at the Temple of the Blue Mountain had been her friends. None of them had ever looked at her the way Stone Kincaid did.

Could it be that he already suspected she was not what she pretended to be? He appeared to be much more intelligent than the other Westerners she had met, such as the loudmouthed Slokum, who was continually staring and grinning at her. But she must never let herself forget that Kincaid was a murderer, and he must be very quick and dangerous if he had been able to capture Hung-pin. Her blood brother had been a master at martial arts, even better than she.

Pain touched her heart. Hung-pin had been bound hand and foot, rendered completely helpless to protect himself before Kincaid and his friends had tortured him to death. Only a coward would take another life in such a brutal way. Windsor's dainty chin angled upward, hardening with resolve. Stone Kincaid would not find her helpless.

Making sure the corridor was deserted, she slid from the bunk without a sound. Standing motionlessly, she listened. Then she pushed Jun-li's box around until it lay flat against her back, where it would not trouble her if she had to use her fighting skills to subdue the big man. With the quiet tread she had mastered long ago atop the brittle rice paper, she glided down the aisle.

She had nearly reached the rear door when suddenly, without warning, the train lurched to one side with such violence that Windsor was thrown backward down the aisle. As she fell, she turned, protecting Jun-li's cage and grabbing frantically for a handhold on the curtains of the nearest berth.

Her quick reflexes saved her from a painful fall as the car jerked forcefully to one side and tilted into a slow, terrifying roll. As everyone and everything not bolted down hurtled toward one wall, Windsor managed to grasp a chair leg. The side of the car hit the ground with a bone-jolting crash and a terrible rending of metal and shattering of glass.

In the aftermath of the derailment, moans and muffled groans filtered through the dust and darkness as stunned passengers began to stir amidst the rubble thrown into their beds. Releasing her hold on the chair, Windsor dropped and landed on the side wall of the coach, now beneath her. She crouched there, trying to get her breath and think what could have happened.

Seconds later, an overturned oil lamp burst into flames close beside her. A whooshing sound followed as a pair of curtains ignited, and she scrambled out of the way of the fire. More hysteria ensued as terrified travelers became aware of the new hazard. Panic took hold as the flames spread and screaming, injured passengers climbed blindly over chairs, berths, and other people, all trying to find a way out of the blazing inferno.

Remaining calm, Windsor ignored the pandemonium surrounding her and slowly inched her way toward the outside door. Smoke hung in a heavy pall throughout the interior now, giving rise to strangled coughing and frenzied shrieks. Jun-li began to scratch and chatter in alarm, and Windsor crept forward on her hands and knees as quickly as she could until she found the outside entrance. The door had been knocked outward on the impact of the crash, and she crawled through the rails of the observation deck to the ground between her coach and the preceding car.

Not until then did she realize that the train was under attack. All around her, hair-raising war whoops filled the air. While she watched, a dozen screeching Indians thundered past her hiding place, the hoofbeats of their horses shaking the earth beneath her. She had heard many stories about the fierce red men who lived in the interior plains and mountains of the United States, but she had never before seen one. Crouching behind the side rail, she hid as several more ponies passed at a wild gallop, the riders half naked and streaked with black-and-yellow paint.

Several yards down the track, a hoarse scream caught her attention, and she saw the white man named Slokum leap from atop the train where he had escaped through one of the broken windows. Caught up in complete hysteria, he rolled bodily when he hit the ground, then rose to his feet and dashed across the fifteen- or twenty-yard expanse between the train and the dense forest vegetation.

Within minutes, a howling warrior rode hard in pursuit of him. As the Indian neared the fleeing man, he swung a long, feather-decorated club, striking Slokum on the back of the head. Slokum fell lifelessly, and the Indian leapt from his still-prancing horse, caught hold of the man's hair, and severed it from the scalp with one swift swipe of his sharp knife.

Bile rose in Windsor's throat at such savagery, but she swallowed down her horror and backed farther underneath the train. She drew up at once as heat scorched the side of her face. The dry grasses beneath the overturned train had caught fire, and it was spreading quickly toward her. Alarmed, Windsor looked toward the safety of the trees. The savage who had bludgeoned Slokum was gone now, leaving the poor man's corpse sprawled facedown, but dozens of other Indians, their paint-smeared faces twisted into grotesque, snarling masks, rode in circles around the train, clubbing and shooting everyone they saw.

Windsor waited a moment longer, but she knew that within seconds the fire would reach her. As a handful of warriors passed with thudding hoof-beats and horrific yells, she bolted for the forest. Ten yards from the train, an ear-piercing yell raised

gooseflesh on her arms, and she turned to face her
attacker, barely able to dodge the galloping horse.

Trained for quickness, she managed to lunge to
one side as the Indian swung his club. The toma-
hawk hit her a glancing blow between the shoulder
blades, sending her down hard. Her temple
slammed painfully against the ground, consciousness instantly dissolving into a burst of bright colors.

When she was able to revive enough to become
aware of her plight, the vicious savage was on his
knees atop her, a long knife raised high above his
head. Still half dazed from her fall, Windsor fought
weakly as he ripped the black wimple from her
head. When her long blond hair tumbled free, his
snarl faded into a look of surprise. Still straddling
her, he pinned down her arms with his knees and
held her by the throat as a second Indian reined
up and jumped from his pony. Terrified, Windsor
began to scream as both men began to tear off her
clothes.

Concealed in a thick stand of cedars near the end
of the train wreck, Stone laid low, now and then
taking a potshot at the Pawnee as they galloped
past him. Since he had been on the outer platform
at the beginning of the attack, he had managed to
jump free before the train had hit whatever barrier
the Indians had used to derail the engine. He had
taken cover before the warriors had caught sight of
him, but he was still in deep trouble.

Turning on one side, he reloaded both of his revolvers from the ammunition he carried on his gun
belt, cursing the fact that his rifle was still inside
the train. As several braves galloped past his hiding place, he rolled back onto his stomach, keeping
his head down. He aimed, fired, and was gratified
when the last rider reeled backward off his mount.

Stone scrutinized the burning railway cars for

any sign of survivors. The Pawnee had found the livestock car and were helping themselves to the horses and cattle, but few of the passengers were in sight. Most of those who had tried to escape already lay dead. He scanned the open ground to the side of the wreck. He froze.

The nun lay on her back a good distance away, struggling against two Pawnee bucks who were tearing off her dress. Cursing, Stone jumped to his feet and began to run. Halfway to her, he raised his pistol and fired. One of the Indians fell; the other jumped to his feet and pointed his rifle at Stone. Stone pulled the trigger again and watched a hole open up in the middle of the Pawnee's forehead.

A shrill war cry sent Stone diving to one side. He rolled, came to his knees, and fired from the hip at the mounted Pawnee thundering straight at him. His shot missed, and the Indian leapt on him, knocking him backward to the ground. Rolling over and over, they grappled for the knife clutched in the Indian's fist as the frightened pony reared and flailed sharp hoofs near their heads.

Summoning all his strength, Stone got a grip on the warrior's wrist, forcing the knife away from his throat as he strove to get his bent knee between their bodies. He shoved hard against the savage's chest, and when the Pawnee was thrown backward, he pulled his gun and fired point-blank into the Indian's stomach.

The savage crumpled, but Stone barely looked at him, springing to his feet and making a grab for the horse. Jerking hard on the halter rope, he sought to control the animal's excited sidestepping, then pulled the mare toward the nun, who had managed to push herself shakily to her knees and was clutching her bamboo case tightly against her chest.

Grasping her by the arm, Stone yanked her to

her feet. Cursing, he realized another wave of
Pawnee was about to swoop around the back of the
train toward them. Turning, he got off a couple of
shots, gripping the reins of the skitterish horse,
then endeavored to swing his leg over the pony's
back. As he pulled himself astride, something hit
him in the back of his left shoulder. It felt as if he
had been struck hard by a fist, and white-hot agony shot the length of his arm.

Looking down, he saw the bloody tip of an arrow protruding from just beneath his collarbone.
Grinding his teeth to fight the pain, he reached
down to the nun with his good arm and swung her
up behind him, struggling to control the dancing
horse with his injured arm. Leaning low over the
horse's neck, he kicked the mare toward the trees,
praying the rolling black smoke from the burning
train and the thick clouds of dust kicked up by the
galloping horses would hide their flight.

Miraculously, they made it safely to the dense
undergrowth, and Stone spurred the horse on,
thrashing headlong through the brush and trees,
unmindful of anything but putting distance between himself and the Pawnee. He rode hard, the
nun holding on to him around his waist. They were
miles from the wreck before he finally slowed the
lathered horse. He turned, searching behind them
for pursuers. Pain seared him from shoulder to
hand. Already his shirt was completely soaked with
blood, and the left side of his body was rapidly
losing all feeling.

Every stride of the horse jolted the arrow jutting
out of the meat of his shoulder, but he forced himself to go on. He couldn't stop now, not until they
found a place to hide. In their haste, they were
leaving an obvious trail, and if the Pawnee scouts
found it, they would track them for days to make
the kill. His blood ran in streams down his chest.

He felt weak and woozy. He wasn't going to last much longer. Painfully, he pulled up on the reins.

"The arrow's got to come out." A low groan escaped him as he shifted positions. "I'm going to break it off, here in front; then you'll have to pull it out the back. Can you do it?"

"Yes." Her voice was completely calm.

Stone took a deep breath, set his teeth, then snapped the arrow's shaft a couple of inches from his shoulder. His mind dipped dangerously with pain, but he fought his way back to consciousness.

"All right, pull the damn thing out."

She did—in one swift jerk. Stone bit off a moan, then leaned forward, sweat drenching his face. He felt the nun press something against the entry hole in his back.

"Here," she said from behind him, "put this inside your shirt to stop the bleeding."

Her voice sounded wavery and far away, but Stone did as she bade, taking the wad of black material she thrust into his hand and stuffing it inside the front of his blood-soaked shirt.

"I'm having trouble holding the reins," he muttered unsteadily. "If I pass out, you need to try to get us back to the last water depot we passed. Just keep moving back the way we came, parallel to the tracks."

For nearly an hour, Stone clung to consciousness, the pain so bad he couldn't think straight. He had to revive himself, he thought blearily. Sister Mary wouldn't have a chance in hell alone in the mountains. By force of will he kept going, until they came upon a clear, swift-flowing stream.

The mare stopped, and Stone slumped heavily forward. The nun slid to the ground, then reached up to help him. As he swung one leg over the horse's neck, he stared dully at her bare head, vaguely aware that her hair was golden blond, just as he had thought. Then, as his boots hit the ground, he knew no more, sliding swiftly into a gaping black abyss where there was no light and no sound, only blessed peace.

"Om Mani Padme Hum, Om Mani Padme Hum, Om Mani Padme Hum . . ."
The queer low murmur filtered slowly through the thick, impenetrable darkness that seemed wrapped like tight black bandages around Stone's brain. Slowly, resolutely, he fought his way upward from the murky depths of unawareness. He tried desperately to open his eyes, but his lids felt as if heavy bags of wet sand weighted them down. Disoriented, he strove to force his groggy mind to clear. What had happened? Why was he so confused?

"Om Mani Padme Hum, Om Mani Padme Hum . . ."
For a few minutes, he listened to the odd sounds, not at all sure if the bizarre chanting came from inside or outside his head. After a moment or two, he began to put things together. He had been on a train headed for San Francisco. They had been attacked by the Pawnee, and he had gotten an arrow in his shoulder. But how could that be? He felt no pain.

With renewed effort, he labored to open his eyes. He was staring at a black-and-white monkey sitting atop his chest. He blinked. Oh, God, I'm delirious, he thought, gaping at the tiny animal in stupefaction. He squeezed his eyelids together. Valiantly, he fought against the fog shrouding his brain. Then, half afraid of what he would see, he ventured another look.

Good God, there *was* a monkey on his chest, a small, white-faced capuchin such as he had seen soliciting coins for organ-grinders on the sidewalks of Chicago. Squinting, he attempted to thrust the strange creature off him, then realized with some

panic that he could not. He was tied down, both
his hands and his feet. Alarmed, he twisted his
body and tried to pull loose from the wooden
stakes hammered into the ground. At his efforts,
the bindings only tightened around his wrists and
ankles.

"*Chee, chee, chee,*" came the capuchin's shrill
chatter as it suddenly scampered away.

Stone craned his neck to one side to follow its
flight. The monkey stopped beside the nun, who
sat cross-legged on the ground several yards away
from him. Her head was bare, the sun glinting gold
off her hair, which was now woven into a long
braid that hung down her back. Her eyes were
closed, her hands lying palms-up atop her knees,
her thumbs lightly touching her middle fingers. The
murmuring was coming from her.

"Hey," he yelled hoarsely, pulling hard against
the stakes.

Sister Mary did not move a muscle. The monotonous droning continued, and Stone muttered an
oath. Dammit, what the hell was going on?

He tensed as the monkey suddenly loosed a
high-pitched shriek. The nun's chanting stopped.
She opened her eyes, stared at the monkey, said
something in a strange tongue, then turned to look
at Stone. Eyes as tranquil as deep blue water observed him dispassionately for the space of a heartbeat; then she rose in one graceful motion. She had
discarded the tattered black gown the Indians had
ripped apart, and now wore some sort of strange,
close-fitting black tunic atop loose black trousers.
She knelt between his outstretched legs.

"Untie me, dammit!" he ground out, feeling like
an utter idiot.

Her eyes narrowed slightly. "You are hurt. I was
afraid you would thrash around and remove the
needles."

"Needles? What the devil are you talking about?"

"There—on your arm. There are more in your ankle and knee."

Stone lifted his head enough to see where she pointed. On his left arm, a long line of fine silver needles angled from his flesh. A few of the pins were affixed with a dark substance that smoldered, releasing minute plumes of black smoke.

"The needles relieve the pain of the arrow wound. When I release you, you must lie very still and not disturb their placement."

"Just cut me the hell loose," he muttered through clamped teeth.

Sister Mary withdrew a short black dagger from the folds of her tunic, the green stones in the handle winking in the sun as she sliced through the black material binding his ankles and wrists.

As soon as he was free, Stone lurched upright, furiously jerking the needles from his arm. Immediately, pure agony ripped through his shoulder. He groaned, then bit off the sound. He glared at the nun, and she stared back without speaking. He clutched his aching shoulder and staggered to his feet.

"I do not understand you Americans. Why do you wish to feel the pain of your injury?" Sister Mary's face was serious.

"I don't like being tied down, and I don't like needles stuck in me. Who are you anyway? You sure as hell don't act like any nun I've ever met." He frowned, wishing he had some whiskey to dull the pain.

"You will reopen your wounds if you move around so much," she admonished calmly as she gathered up the pins he had discarded. "I stitched the edges together while you were unaware."

Stone stared at her, becoming slightly light-headed. He examined the exit wound just beneath his clavicle. The flesh was raw and angry-looking, but it had been sewn with tiny black stitches, as neat as a widow's sampler. His whole left side throbbed like hell.

"I guess I ought to be grateful," he muttered.

"I will insert the needles again, if you wish."

Stone nodded, and the nun moved forward. He watched her withdraw a black lacquered box from her bamboo case. About the size of a deck of cards, the lid was etched with scarlet Chinese symbols. She selected more needles from the black velvet interior. Stone watched silently as she took his arm and carefully inserted the needles in the same spots as before. She twirled them gently, one at a time, between her forefinger and her thumb.

"It still hurts," he said.

"A little impatience subverts great undertakings," she quoted sagely, her eyes intent on her task.

Stone scowled at her, but gradually his pain began to subside.

"Where did you learn to do that?" he asked, impressed.

"The needles have been used for healing in China for thousands of years."

Stone looked at her sapphire eyes and didn't want to look away. Suddenly he remembered that they weren't out of danger.

"Have you seen any sign of the Pawnee?" he asked, searching the trees alongside the stream.

Sister Mary shook her head. "I swept away much of our trail with a branch of leaves. This place is well hidden by the trees, and Jun-li will alert us if the red warriors approach."

"Jun-li?"

"My little friend there." She pointed at the monkey, who was busily grooming himself atop a flat rock. "Come, Jun-li!"

The capuchin quickly scurried forth to join them.

"Jun-li is very clever," she told Stone, stroking the monkey's soft black fur.

Stone began to feel as if he were inside some weird, unbelievable dream. Maybe he was. Maybe he was hallucinating.

"Do all Catholic Sisters carry monkeys around in their luggage?" he asked with not a little sarcasm.

"I do not know," she replied, her face set in utmost solemnity. "Jun-li has been my companion since I was very small. I have trained him to be my helper."

Stone also began to feel as if he were going to black out, and when he weaved slightly on his feet, Sister Mary took a firm hold of his good arm.

"Come, I have made a shelter for us. It is well concealed near the stream. You must lie down until your strength returns."

Stone allowed her to lead him to a small lean-to built of branches between two tree trunks. Amazed, he turned an incredulous gaze upon the nun. What kind of woman was she? And what the hell kind of order did she come from?

A couple of hours after dark, Stone was no less confused about the nun. He watched her across the fire she had built expertly in the opening of the lean-to. Earlier, she had concocted a poultice from a downy moss she carried with her, applied it to his shoulder, then set it afire until it smoldered upon his skin. Still, he had felt nothing because of the needles. Next, she had expertly bandaged his wound, then produced rice and tea leaves from a black silk bag tied at her waist and prepared them a meal. He was beginning to believe her talents were innumerable.

"You're not a nun, are you?"

Sister Mary looked up from where she sat cross-legged in a very un-nunlike position.

"You risked your life to save me from the red warriors," she said. "Why would you do such a thing?"

Surprised that she would ask such a question, Stone laughed. "Believe it or not, I thought you were helpless."

"Life is very different in China, so is it so strange that I behave in unusual ways? I have been taught many things you might find peculiar."

"Who taught you these things?"

Again she didn't answer, but rose in the lithe way she had demonstrated before. She cocked her head as a far-off chattering cry sounded from the treetops.

"That is Jun-li. I must see what has frightened him," she whispered softly.

Before Stone could object, she disappeared into the darkness outside the lean-to. Frowning, he moved to the entrance but could see nothing. He looked around for his guns, cursing his wound. His holsters lay where she had carelessly discarded them. He was in the process of strapping them on when the nun reappeared.

"What was it?" he asked quickly.

"There is nothing amiss now. You must sit down. The bleeding has started again."

Stone frowned, but he lowered himself to the ground as she filled a small wooden cup with water, then sprinkled a white powder over the surface. She swirled it carefully until it dissolved, then handed it to him.

"This will help you rest, but you must drink it all."

"I need to stay awake in case the Pawnee show up," he objected, pushing the potion away.

"Jun-li will warn me if there is danger. Please, drink, so you will feel strong tomorrow."

"What is it?"

"Ginseng and other healing herbs."

Stone took the cup. The brew, whatever it was, was not unpalatable, but it must have been highly potent because almost at once his muscles seemed to go limp. He lay back and closed his eyes. Within minutes, he slept.

4

When Stone awoke next, the fresh fragrance of pine trees and the damp smell of early morning mist assailed his senses. He sat upright and looked around. Sister Mary was nowhere in sight. He listened. The cheeps and trills of awakening woodland birds and the swift current of the rushing mountain creek were the only sounds.

Grimacing, he pressed the tender area around his shoulder wound. The injury had been freshly bandaged with strips of black cloth. He was still shirtless, but Sister Mary's miraculous silver needles were gone. His holsters were still buckled to his thighs, but both his guns were missing. A moment later, he found them lying together near the entrance of the lean-to. He spun the cylinders to make sure they were loaded, then felt better as he slid them into their well-oiled leather holsters.

Ducking out of the makeshift hut, he eyed the gurgling water of the creek. He licked his lips, suddenly aware of just how thirsty he was. The inside of his mouth felt as dry as desert sand. A few steps took him to a low portion of the bank, and he leaned down and dipped a palmful of the clear, cold water. While he drank, he scanned the rocky shore downstream from where he stood, wondering where the nun had gone. His hand stilled halfway to his mouth.

Several yards away, half hidden by a stand of cedar, two Indian braves lay spread-eagled on the ground. Both wore deerskin shirts and leggings, and both were bound to stakes and gagged with strips of black cloth.

"Sweet Mother of God," Stone muttered, pulling his revolver and going into a crouch. He glanced around warily.

Frowning, he moved closer to the two captives. Both looked very young, probably in their late teens. The one closest to him was handsome, lean, and hard-muscled; the other warrior was shorter of stature and heavier built. Each wore one wide horizontal streak of red war paint across the bridge of his nose, from ear to ear. These Indians didn't have the long braids of the Pawnee; their heads were shaved, except for a scalp lock running from the top of the forehead to the nape of the neck.

Osage, he recognized in relief, a southern branch of the Sioux who lived along the Arkansas River in Oklahoma. Several Osage scouts had worked for Kincaid railroad construction crews when Stone had been in charge of the Denver operations. But if they were Osage, they were a hell of a long way from home.

Both braves stared dispassionately at him as he knelt on one knee beside the thin one. He hoped to God they spoke English. He found in his dealings with the Indians that most tribes now spoke some of the white man's lingo. He hesitated, debating whether or not to try to talk to them.

He glanced around the clearing. Where was Sister Mary, and how the hell had she managed to overcome two well-armed braves? A twig snapped behind him, and, already on edge, Stone wheeled around, expecting to see the nun. Instead, he stared dumbfounded at a dozen more Osage warriors, every one of them carrying a weapon trained on his heart.

Stone knew he didn't have a chance in hell to escape. A helpless feeling rose in the back of his throat, and he let his gun drop to the ground. He raised his hands, palms out in the gesture of surrender.

The moment his Colt hit the dirt, three Indians rushed him. He was forced to his knees by a blow to the back of his wounded shoulder, and he grunted in pain as his head was violently jerked back. A razor-edged blade bit into his gullet. Held immobile, he watched as the two bound Indians were released.

Both young warriors sprang to their feet, speaking excitedly in their own guttural tongue. Stone couldn't understand them, though he knew a few words of their language, but he noticed the handsome youth did most of the talking. The respect with which the older warriors listened to the boy indicated he bore some importance to the tribe.

The agitated youth continued to gesture wildly as he spoke, pointing up into the trees and around the clearing, while his heavyset friend nodded agreement and added animated rejoinders from time to time. The other Osage began to glance around, their expressions fearful. Suddenly the young brave in charge moved swiftly toward Stone. To Stone's relief, he lapsed into English.

"Woman with hair like sun. Sun-On-Wings want know where her go."

Maybe, if he was lucky, Stone thought, he might be able to talk himself out of this mess.

"I don't know. I—"

The blade at his throat pressed deeper, drawing blood. Stone swallowed convulsively. Sun-On-Wings frowned, then pointed toward the dense forest behind the stream.

"Yellow-Haired-Woman move like spirit of night. No see her come, no hear her attack. Her strong medicine."

Stone detected the awe in the young Osage's voice, and he quickly used it to his own advantage. "The Great Spirit sent Yellow-Haired-Woman to tend my wounds."

Several of the Indians began to stir uneasily, but the young chief's eyebrows drew together in a deep frown.

"Woman not flesh and bone, like Sun-On-Wings," he said, raising a muscular forearm before Stone's eyes. "Her spirit of legends. Her will come for you."

After Sun-On-Wings' pronouncement, Stone was yanked to his feet. His hands were bound tightly in front of him with a thong of rawhide. He searched the trees for the nun. Was she hiding and watching? Or had she taken the mare and ridden for help? He hoped to hell she was somewhere far away, because once the Indians found out she wasn't a spirit, they would kill both of them.

High in the branches of a cottonwood tree, Windsor watched the band of red men mount their ponies. Stone Kincaid stumbled behind them, his hands tied to a rope secured to the tail of Sun-On-Wings' horse. Jun-li had warned her of their approach, but they had crept upon her with much stealth, and she had had no time to rouse Stone Kincaid from his sleep. Once they had surrounded him, she had known she could not overcome their numbers, not even with her fighting skills. Not when they had pointed so many weapons at the big American.

She must follow and free Stone Kincaid, no matter what the cost to herself. He had saved her life at the train wreck, had he not? Now she must do

the same for him—the Old One himself had read
the law from the sacred scroll.

While the red warriors kicked their ponies and
rode away with their captive, Windsor swung her
bamboo case across her back, then rearranged the
short bow and quiver of arrows she had taken from
the strong young brave she had subdued the night
before when he had discovered the lean-to.

When the Indians had attained a safe distance
from her, Windsor descended to the ground. She
whistled softly for Jun-li. The monkey appeared,
hanging by his long tail from a nearby branch, and
she held out her hand. The capuchin leapt atop her
arm, then quickly climbed to his favorite perch on
her shoulder. Without a word, she ran with a silent
tread to where she had hidden the white Indian
pony the day before.

Exhausted, Stone staggered after the horse, endeavoring to stay on his feet on the rocky mountain terrain. They had been traveling for most of
the day, moving fast into higher elevations, with
few stops to rest. Some of the stitches in his shoulder had already given way, and his shoulder felt
as if it were impaled by a heat-reddened poker.

He gritted his teeth and tried not to think about
the pain or what would happen to him when they
reached the Osage camp. The Osage were halfway
civilized, a lot more so than the Pawnee or Coman-
che, and there was little they could do to him that
would be worse than what he had suffered in Andersonville.

He didn't think they intended to kill him, anyway, at least not on purpose. If he lasted through
the grueling trek to their village, they would probably keep him alive until they were sure the nun
wasn't going to show up. He would have to find a
way to escape before they lost patience.

Near dusk, the Osage riders finally drew up atop

a low ridge. Rasping for breath, Stone fell to his knees, grateful for even a moment's rest. A wide valley spread out below them, ringed with high mountain peaks. Fifty or more lodges set up in circular patterns edged the shore of a large lake that shone like blue glass in the late afternoon sun. Almost as many cooking fires sent plumes of black smoke rising to blend with the purple of the evening sky.

Thank God, he thought, so tired he could barely move. But he forced himself to his feet again as the Indians urged their ponies down the steep hillside. By the time they splashed through the shallow creek that fed the lake, most of the camp had assembled to meet them. Dozens of women and children ran forth, hurling angry words at him and pelting him with rocks and clods of dog dung.

Fending off the attackers as best he could, he was eventually hauled to a standstill in front of a ceremonial lodge in the center of the village. Two of his captors roughly pulled him to a tall pole, lashing his hands and legs behind it as the tribe gathered around. A great deal of yelling and whooping began in honor of his capture, and as night slowly encroached over their frenzied celebration, wood was gathered and stacked into a huge bonfire a few yards in front of Stone's position.

Once the flames leapt high, a tall, white-haired chief appeared from behind the flap of the big lodge. The tribe separated respectfully for the old man, and he walked forward with a venerable bearing, resplendent in a long ceremonial headdress made of eagle feathers. A pure white buffalo robe was thrown over his aged shoulders.

At once, Sun-On-Wings stepped forth to speak. Again he used English.

"Grandfather, my eyes see spirit of night. Her come for white man."

The old chief slowly turned his head toward Stone. He stared silently at him for several moments, then returned his gaze to his grandson. When he spoke, his English was much better than Sun-On-Wings'.

"The spirits do not often show themselves to the Little Ones. How can Sun-On-Wings be sure of these things?"

"Sun-On-Wings see Yellow-Haired-Woman of legends. Her the one you, White-Spotted-Wolf, see in dream sleep. Her hair is gold like our grandfather, the sun. Her move through night like wind and shadows with no sound to warn our best warriors. Me see only small bit of her before her medicine make me sleep. It was so for Flat-Nose also."

Sun-On-Wings glanced at his heavyset friend for verification. Flat-Nose nodded in agreement.

White-Spotted-Wolf looked at Stone again. He frowned. "Who are you that Wah-Kon-Dah, the Great Spirit, sent Yellow-Haired-Woman to watch you?"

Before Stone could formulate an answer, a familiar, melodious voice floated out from the darkness behind him.

"The white man saved my life. I must do the same for him."

Stone jerked his head around and was astounded to see the nun step fearlessly into the circle of armed Osage. Jun-li sat on her shoulder, the flickering fire making his eyes glitter like those of a creature from hell.

A murmur of fear swept like a ghostly moan through the assemblage of Indians. Many backed away in alarm, but the nun stood unmoving, apparently unafraid as several braves set arrows upon their bowstrings. White-Spotted-Wolf raised his arm for quiet, his dark eyes focused on the small woman in black.

"For God's sake, get out of here," Stone hissed

to the girl, appalled that she had stepped so foolishly into danger.

At the sound of Stone's voice, Jun-li jumped from the girl's shoulder and scampered to Stone, quickly climbing up the front of his body and coming to roost atop his head. Stone cursed as the monkey's tail switched around his face. He tried to shake the animal off, but the capuchin clung tightly.

White-Spotted-Wolf looked visibly impressed.

"What strange manner of creature is this?" he cried. "A prairie dog who can climb like the squirrel?"

"Jun-li is my friend," Sister Mary answered calmly. "He obeys my commands."

"Dammit," Stone whispered, low so that only she could hear. "Run now, while you still can."

The nun ignored him. "I came here to challenge your best warriors to a contest," she then decreed, to Stone's horrified disbelief. "If I win, Stone Kincaid is mine. If I lose, you may do with us what you will."

"Oh, God," Stone groaned.

A look of absolute shock overtook the old chief's weathered face. He stared at the nun, then raised both arms to the sky.

"No woman of the earth would show the courage of the red eagle. You will fight our best braves when the sun wakes up and warms our lands."

"No, let me fight," Stone cried loudly. "She's only a woman."

Another frightened murmur rose among the tribe as the nun melted away into the night as swiftly and silently as she had appeared. Jun-li leapt from Stone's head and scurried after her, dissolving into the darkness as mysteriously as his mistress.

Stiff with cold, Stone leaned his head against the rough wood of the pole to which he was tied. The

Osage had danced and sung long into the night, celebrating his capture and calling on their spirit gods for courage in the coming contest. He frowned, twisting his hands behind him in an attempt to loosen the bindings. The rope held tight, but he felt another stitch in his shoulder pull apart, then the ooze of trickling blood.

The sun would come up soon, and Mary, or whoever the hell she was, would return. The little fool was on the verge of getting them both killed with her stupid challenge. Fury contorted his face, and he ground his teeth in frustration. What kind of game was she playing? She wasn't any nun, that was for damn sure. But who was she? She had more guts than most men he knew, he'd give her that much, but she didn't have a chance in hell of winning any contest of skill against battle-hardened Osage warriors. Instead, she would probably die some grisly, gory death right in front of his eyes.

With renewed determination, he struggled with the cords. If he could escape, he might be able to get both of them out of the valley alive. His arms ached from being stretched behind him all night, and his legs were so cold he probably couldn't walk, even if he did get loose.

Somewhere in the far-off reaches of the camp a dog barked, and the young brave guarding Stone shifted where he squatted nearby with a heavy buffalo robe thrown over his shoulders. While Stone watched, the boy yawned, his breath raising a frosty cloud in the cold morning air.

Stone glanced again to the east. The horizon was beginning to lighten, the blackness melting into shades of pearl and ivory. Both men and women were beginning to appear between the round lodges, and he watched as, one by one, they bent, rubbed dirt upon their foreheads, then began a keening song as they filed toward the lake. He had heard of the Osage Dawn Chant when he was in

Denver, but he had never expected to see it performed.

Perhaps their preoccupation with singing praises
to the sunrise would give the girl time to get away.
If she had any brains, she would have spent the
night putting distance between herself and the
Osage camp. Again he felt a sense of unreality
about the whole situation, half expecting to wake
up and find himself back in his chair in the passenger coach, the nun sleeping peacefully in her
draped berth.

"You have lost much blood. You will be very
weak."

The Indian guard next to Stone jumped to his
feet when he saw the girl, then ran shouting to
summon the chiefs.

"Untie me before they come. There's no way you
can fight them. Any one of them is twice your
size."

"You must trust me, Stone Kincaid," she answered calmly. "You must remember that the
smallest insect can cause death by its bite."

"Dammit, what the devil are you talking about?"
he said, his voice low with fury. "Cut me loose!
I'll have a better chance against them than you!"

"I am well versed in self-defense. I have no need
of weapons to fight the red men, while you must
use iron guns to protect yourself."

Stone cursed again, but the girl ignored him. She
turned her back on him, watching the Osage who
had begun to crowd around her. Wherever she
looked, the Indians grew quiet and adopted fearful
expressions, until White-Spotted-Wolf stepped
forth, his face solemn in keeping with the great
importance of the occasion.

"The spirits have spoken and told me many
things. They spoke of how Yellow-Haired-Woman
is strong medicine. They spoke of new ways you
will show our warriors to fight the pale skins who

take our lands and put their smoking iron beasts on the prairies to drive away the buffalo." He stopped, never taking his eyes off the girl.

"They spoke many words about Yellow-Haired-Woman, who fights as fiercely as great warriors. They spoke of how the Little Ones must prove courage or Yellow-Haired-Woman's medicine will turn sour and bring bad times to our people. They told me that our fiercest warrior, Hawk-Flies-Down"—he gestured to a tall, well-built brave standing behind him—"must fight you with his knife."

"I will fight him, but I will not kill him," she replied fearlessly, her voice calm. "And I have no need for a blade. I will best him without a weapon."

As a startled hum commenced among the onlookers, Hawk-Flies-Down stepped forth, his face creased with a scowl of disdain.

"I have heard enough of this talk of magic," he said contemptuously. "Look at her—she is nothing but a woman like those who tend our cook fires. Give me an opponent worthy of my strength. Untie the big white man and let me fight him."

"I will fight Hawk-Flies-Down!" Stone cried in a loud voice, still desperately trying to save Sister Mary's life. "I need no woman to protect me."

A faint smile curved her lips, and she bore Hawk-Flies-Down's scornful scrutiny without flinching. "I say that Hawk-Flies-Down is afraid to fight with me. He is a paper tiger who prefers a man wounded and bleeding and whose strength is sapped from the bite of a Pawnee arrow."

For one instant, Hawk-Flies-Down's face was frozen in astonishment; then it went red with anger. He reached out swiftly, bracketing her slender jaw and turning her face to White-Spotted-Wolf. "Use the eyes in your head. This is no spirit. This is a woman with white skin, nothing else—"

So quickly that those watching could barely comprehend the movement, the girl's hand darted toward Hawk-Flies-Down's throat, her fingers clamping hard upon the sides of his neck. Within seconds, the strong warrior was brought to his knees, his arms hanging limp at his sides.

Astounded, Stone watched her hold a six-foot-tall, two-hundred-pound Indian immobile for the space of a heartbeat. Then she released her hold, sidestepping agilely as he collapsed weakly upon his hands and knees. The brave recovered quickly, his face feral with rage as he leapt to his feet and drew a long-bladed hunting knife from a deerskin sheath at his waist.

Before anyone could move, he lunged at the girl, only to have his thrust blocked quickly by her raised forearm. Roaring with fury, he came at her again, but she ducked adroitly, spun gracefully, then jumped high into the air. Her heel hit Hawk-Flies-Down squarely at mid-chest, and he went sprawling backward in the dirt.

"Good God," Stone breathed incredulously, hardly able to believe his eyes. He tensed and tried to pull free as the humiliated warrior scrambled up again and whirled back toward the girl. Quick as lightning, he sent his knife flying at her heart. She dodged to one side with unbelievable agility, then stood waiting for her opponent's next move, her arms raised and moving in slow circles in front of her, palms out and fingers flexed tightly together.

A few yards away, Hawk-Flies-Down remained immobile, his eyes widened with fear. "The woman is not of this earth," he muttered gruffly. "How can our people fight a spirit they cannot touch?" Defeated, he faced the chief, who had watched the altercation without comment.

"Yellow-Haired-Woman has proved the courage of the great red eagle," the chief intoned in a voice that all could hear. "But she has yet to show her skill with the bow. Only then will we know she is the one of my dream sleep."

"I am ready," the girl said.

White-Spotted-Wolf gestured for his grandson to step forth. "Sun-On-Wings is the most skillful among us with the bow. His arrows are swift and sure."

"Sun-On-Wings set loose rabbit. Me shoot it before it run ten paces," he boasted confidently.

"No," the girl answered. "I will not kill a helpless animal only to demonstrate my skill."

Sun-On-Wings frowned; then, after a moment's contemplation, he drew a feather from his scalp lock. He held it high above his head for all to see. "Then me shoot feather of hawk from white man's head."

"Great," Stone muttered beneath his breath as Sun-On-Wings strode over to him and stuck the feather into the back of Stone's hair. As the young brave measured off one hundred paces, the girl moved close to Stone.

"You must stand very still," she whispered.

"Thanks. I probably wouldn't have thought of that," he said sarcastically.

She stepped away, and Stone leaned his head against the wood, watching Sun-On-Wings select a red-striped arrow from his fringed rawhide quiver. He's the best warrior with a bow and arrow, he told himself firmly. He ought to be able to do it. But his muscles tensed as the handsome young warrior took aim.

A moment later, the youth let the arrow fly. Stone barely heard the soft whistle of its flight before it thudded into the wood above his head, the feather impaled by its point. He released a long, relieved sigh.

"There!" Sun-On-Wings cried, his face exuberant. "Now Yellow-Haired-Woman must best Sun-On-Wings with a feat more difficult."

Warily, Stone waited for Sister Mary's response. He no longer put anything past her.

"I will use the same target as Sun-On-Wings," she pronounced with calm self-assurance, "except that I will shoot through the feather with a blindfold covering my eyes."

"Now wait a goddamn minute!" Stone began angrily, but she ignored him.

"If I succeed, he is mine," she finished, looking at the chief.

"Only the spirits would try such a difficult feat," White-Spotted-Wolf decreed. "It will be as you say."

The girl moved closer to Stone. "Do not fear. I am a good archer. I will rely on my inner strength to guide my shaft so that my sight will not be required. The Old One taught me well."

"I don't give a damn what the Old One taught you! Nobody can shoot a bow blindfolded!"

"What one knows not how to do is difficult; what one knows how to do is not," she admonished, her delicate brows knitted together as if his worries were unfounded. "You must have more faith in my ability, and you must not move a muscle as I draw back on the bowstring. I will not miss."

Stone was helpless to do anything but watch as she paced to the spot where Sun-On-Wings had released his arrow. She took the bow offered to her, weighed it in her hands, and tested the tautness of its strings. Looking at Stone, she had the audacity to present him with a smile. He was not reassured. Inwardly, he cursed the day he had ever laid eyes on her.

Stone's swallow went down hard as she wound a black strip of cloth around her eyes. She removed a pair of arrows from the quiver strapped to her back. She stood very erect, holding one arrow pointing straight up while she positioned the other across the bowstring.

For a long moment she remained completely still, as if absorbed in concentration. The crowd became hushed and wary, and Stone felt perspiration begin to bead his upper lip. He held his breath and uttered an inward prayer when she pointed the arrow in his direction. If she doesn't kill me, he thought, I'm going to kill her, and I'm going to do it the minute I get loose.

Long, heart-thundering moments followed as she pulled back on the shaft; then the arrow came, straight, swift, and true. He felt a bite of stinging pain as the arrowhead scraped across the top of his scalp, drawing blood, but the feather was impaled upon the point above his head.

A great roar of astonished approval echoed far out over the lake; then two braves ran forth to untie him. When the bindings dropped free, Stone rubbed his wrists, his chest heaving with anger and frustration. He watched the girl, now surrounded by the admiring Osage. He was not nearly as pleased with her as they were. Sister Mary had a hell of a lot of explaining to do.

5

Long after darkness had shielded the high mountain valley from the sun, Windsor sat cross-legged among the Osage chiefs. She had been given a place of honor between White-Spotted-Wolf and his favorite grandson, Sun-On-Wings. Blazing logs roared directly in front of her, warming her face against the cooler temperature and shooting glowing sparks into the ebony reaches of the sky.

Two rows of drummers sat across the fire, chanting and beating their tom-toms with painted, feather-adorned sticks. The reverberating throb of the skin-covered drums filled the night, and Windsor's brain, as dozens of warriors, dressed fiercely in wolf skins and long-horned buffalo headdresses, sang low, guttural praises to their spirit gods while they bent and stamped their moccasined feet in a slow, revolving circle around the fire.

"We call our songs wi-gi-ies. Our bravest warriors thank Wah-Kon-Dah for sending your strong medicine to us," the old chieftain said, leaning his hoary head close to Windsor's. "With Yellow-Haired-Warrior-Woman among us, we will be able to defeat the Pawnee in battle, and even the whites with their long knives and many guns."

Windsor nodded, thinking that White-Spotted-Wolf's slow, thoughtful speech and kind dark eyes reminded her of the Old One. The ancient chief had displayed great wisdom when he had spoken to her about his people, the Little Ones. After she had won the contest, he had kept her close beside him and told her the story of how the white men had forced the Osage from the home of their ancestors along a great river called the Mississippi.

Even after his tribe had moved east to a different stream called the Arkansas, white men had followed in hoards, even fighting a war amongst themselves over the Black White Man, such as the one Windsor had seen working as a porter aboard the train. White-Spotted-Wolf had moved among the blue-coated soldiers in the forts and tried to understand them, until he had been told by Wah-Kon-Dah in a dream sleep to take his people into the far, snowcapped ranges where the white man would not bother them. For eight winters they had lived peacefully in the mountains with only the Pawnee as their foe. As he had spoken, Windsor's heart had grown full with compassion.

Except for the coppery color of their skin, the simple, uncomplicated Osages reminded her of the people of China. Both the red men and the Chinese believed in the harmony that existed in nature. The Little Ones were honorable. They had proved their worth when they had kept their word to her once she had bested Sun-On-Wings in the contest of the bow. The white men she had met thus far in the United States had shown little honor.

Except for Stone Kincaid. He had displayed both honor and bravery. But she did not understand him. Turning her head, she found his place where he sat a short distance away. His silver-blue eyes collided with her own gaze, and an intuitive alarm rang inside her head. His eyes burned. He was very angry. Though he had said little to her throughout the day of feasting and ceremonial dancing, he had watched her incessantly and with such intensity that her stomach fluttered each time she became aware of his stare.

"When Yellow-Haired-Warrior-Woman become night wind?"

Sun-On-Wings' soft whisper interrupted Windsor's thoughts. She shifted her attention to him. The Osage youth sat so close to her that she could see tiny flames reflected like bright stars in the luminous jet-black depths of his eyes.

"I have already told you, Sun-On-Wings, that I am not a spirit. I move silently because I have been taught to do so."

Stubbornly, the young warrior shook his head. "Only wind so swift and silent. Wah-Kon-Dah hear song Sun-On-Wings sing, and me see strong medicine of Yellow-Haired-Warrior-Woman."

As he spoke, Sun-On-Wings enticed Jun-li from Windsor's lap with a pumpkin seed. The young brave had shown an irrepressible fascination with the capuchin, and he chuckled as Jun-li swung agilely atop his broad shoulder.

Windsor smiled as Sun-On-Wings fed the monkey several more seeds from his cupped palm, but she was acutely aware when Stone Kincaid rose to his feet. He moved away from the fire, pausing momentarily to look back at her before he disappeared into the darkness outside the firelight. A shiver danced down her spine, but the chill was not created by the cold wind. The buffalo robe Sun-On-Wings had draped around her shoulders kept her warm and comfortable.

Weary, she closed her eyes, sighing heavily. The evening before, she had retreated into the forest and meditated for long hours in order to prepare herself spiritually for the contests of skill. Her mind was dull with fatigue, as was her body. She knew she must sleep. She stood and looked down at the elderly chief.

"I am honored by your kindness, White-Spotted-Wolf, but I am very tired."

"The Little Ones are honored that you have come. Our warriors will grow strong with you among us."

"I will try to be worthy." Windsor bowed forward from the waist, her palms pressed together prayerfully in the Chinese tradition.

The old chief climbed to his feet. With great courtesy, he imitated her gesture of respect. Leaving Jun-li in the care of his new friend, Windsor headed for the lodge White-Spotted-Wolf had designated for her use. The small dwelling lay a good distance away from the ceremonial clearing at the center of the village, near where the waves of the lake lapped the shoreline. As she walked in the darkness, she stared upward into the sky.

High above, the vast starry firmament rose into infinity, stretching out over her like a diamond-spangled cloth of black velvet. How insignificant she felt in comparison, she thought, yet at the same time she knew herself to be a part of those spinning bodies of stars that traversed the night skies here and above her temple far across the wide ocean. The Old One had taught her that all life was integral to the harmony of the universe. She was a part of the night and the twinkling stars, and that knowledge gave her comfort.

She came to a standstill outside the entrance to her lodge. Instinctively, she knew that Stone Kincaid was inside the reed-covered hut. Steeling herself against the peculiar tingling sensations he was able to whip alive inside her body, she drew a long and steadying breath. Ready to face the anger she knew he harbored, she lifted the blanket flap and peered into the interior.

A small fire flickered in the center of the lodge,

bathing the woven ceiling with a faint reddish glow. Stone Kincaid was not there. Frowning, she ducked inside, then gasped as someone came at her from the dark shadows. Strong hands gripped her by the shoulders; then she found herself flat on her back, the big American's heavy body atop hers, his strong fingers locked tightly around her wrists, forcing her arms down on either side of her head.

"All right, Sister Mary, or whatever the hell your name is, it's time for confession." Stone Kincaid's words were low and deadly, each syllable ground out with lethal emphasis.

"You are angry," Windsor managed breathlessly, confused by the yearnings set astir deep inside her loins with his body completely covering hers and pinning her to the ground. Her heart began to pound, beating so hard she felt it would surely throw him off her at any moment. Dismayed, she suffered a slow, burning heat that suffused every inch of her flesh, as if she lay in a bed of fire. Her lips went dry, and she moistened them.

"Very observant, Sister Mary," he muttered, so close to her that their faces nearly touched. Her heart leapt and hammered as wildly as that of a cornered doe as his gaze wandered slowly and thoroughly over every inch of her face. His attention lingered on her mouth.

"I do not understand," she said, distressed at the way her voice was trembling. "I only sought to win your freedom. Does that displease you?"

"You're damn right it displeases me. I don't particularly like being lied to and made a fool of, and I sure as hell don't like you shooting at me blindfolded!" His hold tightened around her wrists. "Now, I want to know just who the hell you are, and don't give me any more lies about being a nun. You're no more a nun than I am."

"Please release me. You will hurt your shoulder."

"To hell with my shoulder! Don't think I'm stupid enough to let go of you and have you knock me out with one of your fancy Chinese kicks. I want answers, and I want them now."

Windsor lay still, trying to control her overwhelming reaction to Stone Kincaid. She could not understand why he made her feel so weak and strange. She wondered if he was similarly affected by her presence. She did not think so. His frown was black with rage.

"Talk, dammit!"

Stone Kincaid meant to have the truth, she realized, and the time had come to give him the answers he wanted.

"My name is Windsor Richmond, but in China I am called Yu-Mei. I traveled to Chicago to kill you."

Stone Kincaid's furious expression slowly disintegrated into one of pure astonishment.

"What? Why? I never laid eyes on you until that day at LaSalle Street Station."

"Because I was told that you killed my friend Hung-pin. It is my sacred vow to avenge his death so that his spirit can fly free and ride the heavenly dragon."

Stone Kincaid stared down at her for another moment, his black brows drawn together. "I've never known anyone named Hung-pin." Suddenly his anger returned. His grip tightened. "Quit lying and tell me the truth. Who are you?"

"To tell a lie is to dishonor oneself."

"Then I'd say you're as dishonorable as they come. You sure as hell lied when you said you were a nun."

"I did not lie."

"Dammit, girl, I'm losing patience."

"I am not a Catholic nun. I am a disciple of the

Temple of the Blue Mountain. I am a Chinese nun."

"You're not Chinese."

"No, but when I was orphaned at the age of ten, I was taken by Hung-pin to the priests of the temple. He was a disciple there, so I became one, too."

"And you think I killed this priest friend of yours?"

"The witnesses to his murder called you by name."

Stone Kincaid's eyes delved into hers, as if he doubted her words; then he abruptly released his tight hold on her wrists. He sat back on his heels, staring down at her. The moment his weight left her, Windsor began to feel in control of herself once more. He affected her in dangerous ways, this big American. She suddenly felt frightened of him, when she had never feared any other man.

"Why didn't you just kill me when you had the chance, instead of nursing my shoulder?"

"You saved my life from the Pawnee warriors. When you save a life, it belongs to you. It is the Chinese law."

"And do you still believe I killed your friend?"

"I no longer think you are capable of killing a man in the cowardly way Hung-pin was murdered."

"How'd he die?"

Windsor's throat clogged as her mind unwillingly conjured up the image of the way Hung-pin had been flayed alive. "He was hung by his arms from a tree limb, then struck with a whip until his spirit was driven to escape the earth."

"Good God," Stone muttered, his mouth twisting with revulsion. "Why would anyone want to do that to him?"

"Those who were there said that Hung-pin came to the aid of a white woman who was being abused by cruel and drunken men. He fought bravely, but there were too many of them for him to over-come."

"I didn't kill your friend. I haven't been to California in three years, I swear it."

"I believe you." The Old One had taught her to trust the voice that spoke inside her heart. It spoke to her now of Stone Kincaid's innocence, and Windsor felt an overwhelming gladness that he was not the one.

"You're awfully quick to believe me. Why?"

Their eyes seemed to fuse. "Because our souls have touched before. I knew of our kinship from the first moment we met. Did you not feel the hand of destiny binding us one to the other?"

Stone Kincaid looked so startled that Windsor smiled, but his answer was cold with cynicism. "I don't believe in destiny."

Windsor frowned. "That is very strange. If that is so, what is it that you believe in?"

"I believe in revenge. That's why I can understand exactly why you came after me. I'm on my way to San Francisco to get a man myself, one who likes to use a whip, too—" He stopped in midsentence, then grabbed her shoulders again, his eyes burning into her face, hard, consuming. "Tell me about the man who killed the priest. Did the witnesses describe him?"

"They said he was tall with blue eyes, but they could not see the color of his hair because he wore a black hat. And he wore a ring on one hand, in the shape of a coiled cobra with red, sparkling stones for its eyes—"

Windsor's words faltered as Stone Kincaid released her and lunged to his feet. His face twisted with hatred, his eyes so full of bitter loathing that she was taken aback.

"So now the bastard's using my name when he does his killing! Damn him! Damn him to hell!"

Windsor said nothing as he took several agitated

strides away from her. She could almost feel the waves of enmity flowing out of his body, like hot gusts of wind. He seemed a different man now, a violent one capable of terrible brutality. Some awful evil must have passed between him and Hung-pin's killer. Something that still dwelt deep in Stone Kincaid's soul, festering there like an ugly black tumor in a dying man.

"Hung-pin's killer is the man you seek, is he not? The man you call Emerson Clan?"

Stone swung around to face her. "Yeah, he's the one. He's worn that ring ever since I gave it to him at West Point. And you don't have to worry about avenging your friend's death anymore, because I'm going to do it for you. Your Chinese priest was only one of Clan's victims. He's murdered people before, during and after the war, and he's killed in even worse ways than with a whip, if you can believe that. But his days are numbered. I'm going to find him, and I'm going to kill him."

"We will find Emerson Clan together."

At her words, Stone Kincaid seemed to become aware of her again. "No, we won't. Killing him is one pleasure I mean to reserve for myself."

Windsor watched in silence as he jerked back the flap and exited the lodge, his face contorted by suppressed anger. His soul was very troubled. In the days to come, she must find a way to help Stone Kincaid attain inner peace.

6

Several weeks after Windsor had scraped an arrow across his scalp, Stone made his way slowly through the Osage village. The lodges were scattered over the wide valley in circular clusters, and as he walked, the Indians he encountered greeted him courteously, when they paid him any heed at all. Since the contest, Stone and Windsor had been treated well and given free rein to roam where they would. What was more, he didn't think White-Spotted-Wolf would prevent either of them from leaving the camp.

But Stone was not yet ready to escape. His shoulder was still sore enough to make his grip weak and hard to sustain, though Windsor's unorthodox medical treatment had certainly appeared to accelerate the healing. He knew he would be wise to bide his time and let his wound mend longer before attempting the long trek back to civilization. He had already pinpointed his approximate location, and if his calculations were correct, the railway line west lay a day or so south. He felt sure he could locate the track bed if given time.

His immediate concern was the weather. The snows were late in coming already. He sure as hell didn't want to be stranded in the mountains with the Osage all winter. Nor did he want to be forced to spend any more time than necessary with Windsor Richmond.

Stone had already decided he wasn't taking the girl out with him. There was certainly no danger in leaving her among the Osage. Hell, they treated her like some kind of goddess, and if she ever did want to return to California, he had no doubt she could get herself there. Windsor Richmond had made her way to Chicago by herself, hadn't she? She would be fine without him, and Stone would be well rid of her.

Pausing near the lake, he flexed his left arm, determined to keep his muscles strong. Lifting his face toward the sun, he basked in the warmth. The weather was unusually mild for early December, especially so high in the Rockies. Throughout the past weeks, the days had been sunny and pleasant, but the temperature dropped drastically when the valley was covered with darkness.

He scanned the rocky shoreline, his gaze stopping when he found Windsor. She stood at the edge of the lake with perhaps a dozen young braves, who sat cross-legged on the ground around her. The water behind her sparkled deep blue, without a ripple to mar the glossy surface. Sapphire, like her eyes, he thought, then shook his head impatiently, chagrined at himself. Despite all his resolve, Windsor Richmond continued to fascinate him. She was so strange. He never could quite figure out what she was going to do or say next.

At the moment, she was instructing the young Osage warriors in her unorthodox method of fighting. Curious to hear what she was telling the boys, he drifted closer. He leaned his shoulder against a cottonwood tree, far enough away to be unobtrusive but close enough to listen.

"I have come from a faraway, ancient land called China," she told them in her lilting voice. "When I was a child, even younger than you, a great master shared his deep wisdom with me. Like your people, the Little Ones, we of China believe that all creatures are sacred, be they great or small, weak or fierce."

Windsor paused as she caught sight of Stone. First she seemed surprised to see him, then she presented him with a lovely smile. Stone glanced away, not wanting her to think he was particularly interested in her discourse. She began again.

"So it is better to deal with force inflicted upon oneself by running away from the aggressor. For one of true wisdom prefers peace and quiet above victory."

Stone was not impressed. Windsor Richmond's turn-the-other-cheek philosophy didn't exactly ring true, not when she had journeyed all the way from San Francisco to stick a knife in his back.

A rush of anger, cold enough to chill his bones, swept over him. So now Clan was using Stone's name when he tortured and killed. Stone's jaw clamped tight. The idea made him sick to his stomach. If it was true, Stone had to be careful. Clan already had a warrant for treason on his head, one issued by the army right after the war. Now there could be a warrant out in Stone's name, too. But he wasn't surprised. Clan had always been clever, so clever in fact that he had managed to hide his real character from Stone during their years together at West Point. God, Stone had actually considered him a friend then—up until the moment he had caught Clan feeding information to the Confederates during the war. Dozens of their comrades in arms had died because of Clan's treachery.

Trying to suppress the rage spinning like a typhoon through his soul, Stone concentrated on what Winsdor was saying.

"You and I, and all living creatures, are one with nature, and it is of great importance for all of us to observe the natural laws of existence. If you do this, no force of man can harm you. The lessons the Old One taught me will help you learn to fight, if you will but listen and learn. There is one which is of particular importance, and that is this: never must you meet a wave head-on; instead, strive to avoid it. There is no need to stop a show of force; it will be much easier to redirect that force. To be victorious, you must learn more ways to preserve life, rather than try to destroy it. Always remember: avoid rather than check; check rather than hurt; hurt rather than maim; maim rather than kill. For all life must be considered precious, because none can be replaced."

Except for mine, Stone thought. You certainly made an exception to your fine rules in my case. Irony twisted his mouth. Windsor hadn't hesitated to track him down. And he would probably be dead right now if the Pawnee hadn't attacked the train when they did. Regardless, he had to admit the logic of her teachings. While he watched, she demonstrated several blocking procedures, her elbow bent to deflect an opponent's blow.

Slowly, deliberately, she moved within the circle of her enraptured students, her slender body graceful and sure-footed, her long, shiny blond hair braided into a queue down her back, snaking around her shoulders when she moved quickly, gleaming as pure as the golden rays of dawn. She still wore her odd black tunic and trousers, and each time she turned or bent, the soft, silky fabric molded provocatively against her high breasts and slim hips.

To his annoyance, Stone's body was profoundly affected by the slow, suggestive positions she was demonstrating. He muttered a string of low, self-disgusted oaths.

"Why Stone-Man-Show-Courage-When-Arrow-Parts-Hair say words to self?"

Stone stiffened. The low voice had come from somewhere close by, but when he looked around, he saw no one. Nevertheless, he knew who had spoken. His new friend Sun-On-Wings was the only one who continued to call him by the ridiculously long name with which White-Spotted-Wolf had saddled Stone during the celebration after Windsor's contest. Most of the Indians had abbreviated it to Arrow-Parts-Hair, which was embarrassing enough. A moment later, Stone was able to search out the boy's hiding place in some nearby bushes.

"What the devil are you doing, Sun-On-Wings?" he asked impatiently.

"Do not speak with loud voice, or Yellow-Haired-Warrior-Woman will find where Sun-On-Wings hide."

Irritated, Stone grimaced. "There's no need to hide if you want to learn how to fight, for God's sake. All you have to do is go over and sit down with the other boys."

"Sun-On-Wings no need learn to fight. Me a man, a fierce warrior." Sun-On-Wings sounded a mite insulted, but he went on in a low voice. "Me hide so me can see Yellow-Haired-Warrior-Woman change self into the wind."

Stone shook his head. Almost every day since Stone had been brought to the village, Sun-On-Wings had sought out his company solely to discuss his obsession with the idea that Windsor was the spirit of the wind. No matter what Stone said or did, the sixteen-year-old would not give up the absurd notion. Although Stone rather liked the impressionable young man, his patience with him was beginning to wear thin.

"Like I've told you before, Sun-On-Wings,

Windsor's a flesh-and-blood woman, just like any other woman.''

"You are wrong, Stone-Man-Show-Courage-When-Arrow-Parts—''

"Oh, for God's sake, Sun-On-Wings! Just call me Stone, will you?''

The handsome young brave nodded. ''Grandfather give big name for big man, but tongue grow twisted if say much.''

Stone felt an overpowering urge to laugh. How in the devil had he gotten himself into such a preposterous predicament? If he ever got out of the mountains alive, neither Gray nor Tyler, nor anyone else, would ever believe all that had happened to him.

"Tell me, Sun-On-Wings, just how long do you plan to skulk around in the bushes like this?''

"Sun-On-Wings watch until Yellow-Haired-Warrior-Woman ride on wind.''

Stone shook his head, but he didn't waste his breath trying to talk sense to the boy. Sun-On-Wings was not going to listen to him.

"Is Yellow-Haired-Warrior-Woman your woman?'' Sun-On-Wings demanded suddenly.

"No.''

"If woman share lodge with man, she him wife.''

"She's not my wife.''

"Then I want her for woman.''

Stone was annoyed with the whole conversation. "Look, Sun-On-Wings, I hate to tell you this, but Windsor won't take a husband. She considers herself a nun.''

"What is this nun?''

"A nun's a woman who serves the gods. Like your medicine man, I guess.''

"Medicine man take woman him want.''

"Well, Windsor won't. She told me.''

"Me make her feel love. Yellow-Haired-Warrior-Woman live in heart.'' Sun-On-Wings touched his

chest emphatically, shaking the two long white eagle feathers in his scalp lock. "Me play flute and
sing wi-gi-ie of love so her come to Sun-On-Wings'
lodge."

"Suit yourself," Stone grumbled, washing his
hands of the subject.

Intentionally not looking in Windsor's direction,
he headed for the rocky trail that led alongside the
water. After walking for a time, he rounded a curve
of the narrow beach that jutted into the lake and
took him out of sight of the village. A good distance away, he sat down and leaned back against
one of the big boulders that towered above the water.

A slight wind had risen, riffling the calm surface
of the water, making the afternoon cool and pleasant. The sun felt almost hot beating down on his
bare head, and the mountain lake was beautiful,
mirroring tall, craggy peaks crowned with snowy
caps.

He thought again about leaving the Osage. He
was eager to reach San Francisco and locate Clan
before he disappeared again. He had already decided that when he left the Indians, he would head
for Silverville. As far as he could calculate, the mining town lay a two or three days journey to the
south. If he could make his way that far while good
weather held out, he had friends there who would
help him. Hopefully, the western expresses would
still be coming through there to pick up shipments
of ore.

He smiled, thinking about the rowdy little town.
He had spent several months there before the war,
surveying track to the silver mines located high in
the mountain from the storage warehouses in
town. Sweet Sue had made his winter there mem-
orable, to say the least. He hoped she still ran the
Pleasure Palace.

Thoughts of Suzy Wright dissolved as Windsor

Richmond walked into view just below him. Not wanting to talk with her, Stone inched backward into the shadows of the trees, where she would have trouble seeing him. He wondered if she had followed him.

She glanced around, but she didn't seem to be searching for him. Then, to his utter shock, she suddenly swept her tunic up over her head. Unwittingly, he came to his feet, his jaw hanging slack. His gaze riveted like a magnet to steel on her naked back, just as she stepped out of her trousers. Completely nude, she dived into the frigid mountain lake.

When his astonishment had receded, Stone was furious with her. He stalked to the bank, palms planted on his hips. "What the hell do you think you're doing?" he shouted.

At the sound of his voice, Windsor jerked around in the water, obviously surprised to find him so near. "Why, I am swimming, of course."

"Dammit, I'm talking about you stripping down buck naked in front of anybody who might happen along! Don't you have any modesty?"

"No one is here but you, and I did not see you. Where were you?"

Stone felt a hot flush creep up his neck. "Never mind that. You shouldn't undress out in the open where someone might see you."

Her calm sapphire eyes searched his expression. "I have embarrassed you, I think," she ventured slowly, an expression of realization dawning across her face. "You have never seen a woman's unclad body before, have you, Stone Kincaid?"

"Of course I've seen naked women. Lots of them!" he snapped with more feeling than was necessary.

"Then why are you so upset?"

"I'm not upset, dammit!"

"You sound upset, and you look upset."

"Oh, for God's sake, do whatever you want! Just stay away from me!"

"Why do you avoid me, Stone Kincaid?" she called as he turned away. "We should have started making our plans to capture this man called Clan—"

"My name is Stone! S-T-O-N-E, Stone! Just one little word! Can't anyone around here just call me that?"

As he glared blackly at her, Windsor's delicately arched blond brows puckered. "It is the Chinese way to use two names. I do not understand why you are always so angry with me. Perhaps if you will tell me what I do that offends you so, I will stop doing it."

Against his will, Stone found his gaze drawn down through the crystal-clear water. Vaguely, he could just make out her nude body, her soft white breasts and long, shapely legs glimmering palely beneath the surface as she moved her arms back and forth to keep afloat in the deep water.

Suddenly a highly disconcerting thought struck him. He whirled around and scanned the thick tangle of bushes alongside the boulder-strewn bank, then swiveled around to confront Windsor again.

"And cover yourself when you get out, for God's sake! You never know who might be hiding in the bushes!"

For the first time since they had met, Windsor laughed, a soft tinkle of genuine amusement. "You Americans are really very peculiar," she said, then smiled up at him, looking so unbelievably beautiful that Stone's breath felt trapped in his throat.

Swallowing hard, he set his jaw and hastily took his leave with long, furious strides, swearing when he glimpsed a pair of white eagle feathers gleaming from the dark depths of a thick fir tree alongside his path.

7

Windsor opened her eyes, listening to the rain beating in a steady drizzle atop the mat-woven roof of the lodge. What had awakened her? She lay still for a moment, wondering if Jun-li had called to her. Raising herself on one elbow, she found the capuchin curled quietly at her feet. She glanced around and discovered that Stone Kincaid lay sleeping several feet away, half shrouded by shadows hugging the far wall. She was surprised. He had been so angry about her swimming in the lake that she had expected him to spend the night elsewhere.

A low rumble of distant thunder rolled and echoed through the stormy night, and Windsor realized the cold rain must have driven Stone Kincaid inside. Sitting up, she folded her legs into the lotus position and contemplated the man she had wanted to kill.

Stone Kincaid was a strange and silent man whose words and deeds baffled her, but he had shown much bravery. She wanted to become his friend, in the way she and Hung-pin had shared a close kinship. She wanted to help this big, troubled American find spiritual peace.

Like a silk scarf floating weightlessly to the floor,

a forlorn sadness settled over her heart. Of late her own spirit had been tossed about in turbulent seas, plagued by inexplicable conflicts she had not known before she had met Stone Kincaid. Tomorrow she must find a quiet, private place where she could empty her mind of conscious thought and seek inner solace.

A low, tortured moan brought her regard back to Stone. He no longer slept peacefully, but twisted and turned restlessly atop his buffalo skins. His breathing had become loud and labored, as if his lungs were obstructed. Then suddenly while Windsor watched, he raised both his hands and frantically slashed the air, almost as if he were digging a hole.

Mystified, Windsor frowned in concern, but before she could lean forward and awaken him, he lunged upward onto his knees, loosing a short, dreadful cry of terror. Wild-eyed, sweat covering his face, he stared at her as if he had never seen her before.

Windsor spoke gently, wanting to soothe him. "Your dream must have been very frightening."

Stone turned abruptly away from her, and Windsor watched as, obviously still agitated, he tunneled splayed fingers through his thick black hair. He didn't reply.

"Sorry I woke you," he said, his voice thick and unnatural. "Go back to sleep."

Windsor made no move to do so, observing him without comment as he pushed himself to his feet and stumbled to the flap. He swept back the hanging blanket, gulped several deep inhalations of the crisp, damp night air, then reached outside and trapped a handful of icy rainwater in his cupped hands. He splashed it over his whiskered jaw, then rubbed the back of his neck. He rotated his head, massaging his nape, obviously trying to regain his composure.

"Dreams can seem very real at times," Windsor remarked softly, aware that he was avoiding her gaze. "There is no reason to be ashamed of your fears."

Stone still said nothing, sitting down and staring wordlessly at the smoldering embers. Windsor's attention focused upon his hands resting on his knees. While she watched, he squeezed his long fingers tightly into his palms, making fists so hard that his sun-browned knuckles whitened. He was fighting a terrible internal battle.

"Is it the man we both seek who dwells in your nightmares, the one named Emerson Clan?"

"Emerson Clan is a nightmare all by himself," he muttered viciously, his gaze fixed on the fire. "Ask anybody who's ever laid eyes on him."

"The Old One taught that a man must make himself despicable before he is despised by others."

"Clan's better at that than most men."

"Together, we will find him and avenge his many innocent victims."

"I told you before, Windsor, I intend to get Clan myself. Alone. Just me and him. Understand?"

"Why do you not wish my help?"

When he lifted his face, the firelight caught his blue eyes, making them flash with silver, like sun striking a snowbank and setting aglow a brilliant light. He is a beautiful man, she thought. Her insides quivered, and she felt shame.

"Because I don't wish to see you get killed—or cut to shreds with a whip like your friend, the Chinaman. And don't be naive enough to think the fact that you're a woman will make any difference to Clan. He likes to hurt women. He threatened my sister-in-law, Tyler, back in Chicago—said he was going to cut her throat. That's just one more reason I'm after him."

"If my destiny is to die at Emerson Clan's hands,

there is little I can do to prevent it," Windsor answered, her manner as calm as his was disturbed.

"Well, I sure as hell can prevent it."

Never before had Windsor seen a man so eaten
with inner rage. The well-defined angle of his jaw
was clenched so hard that a muscle shifted convulsively beneath the tanned skin of his lean cheek.
While she watched, he raised his right hand and
kneaded his wounded shoulder as if it had begun
to ache.

"You suffer much, Stone Kincaid, in your mind
and in your physical body. I can help you, if you
will but grant me leave to do so."

"How?"

"I will show you."

"No. You'll tell me first."

"I will relieve the pain in your shoulder with the
placement of my needles. Then I will show you
ways to control your mind so it will find harmony
alongside your relaxed physical body."

When Windsor Richmond finished her explanation, she smiled so sweetly that Stone found himself wanting very much for her to help him. Since
his nightmare had awakened him, every muscle in
his body had been rock-hard, every sinew taut, and
the tension only made his shoulder throb worse.

For some reason he felt reluctant to submit himself to her unorthodox treatments—he still didn't
particularly trust her—but he finally nodded in
consent. Windsor moved around the fire until she
sat facing him, very close. While he watched, she
pulled the braided queue in which she confined
her hair over one shoulder and began to unweave
the thick plait.

Shimmering blond tresses cascaded in loose
waves around her shoulders, as long and glossy as
a length of fine gold satin. She reached up beneath
the luxuriant fall and pulled a necklace from inside
the collar of her black tunic. With great patience,

she unfastened the thin silk cord and laid the strand of round green beads flat on the ground between them.

"These stones are made from flawless mountain jade," she told him, separating a strand of her silky hair. Still speaking, she began to plait the long narrow lock into a tiny, tight braid. "In China, jade stones such as these are held in great reverence. Since the times of the ancients, men have found all excellent qualities in such jade." She captured his gaze, the corners of her soft pink lips drawing upward in a gentle smile. " 'Soft, smooth, glossy, it appeared to them like benevolence—fine, compact, and strong, like wisdom—bright as a brilliant rainbow, like heaven—esteemed by all under the sky, like the path of truth and duty.' Those are the words of the great master K'ung-Fu-Tzu," she explained. "You of the West know him as Confucius."

Mesmerized, Stone listened to Windsor speak— the soft flow of her voice rippling over his mind like notes of music—pleasing, dulcet, sweet, lulling his turbulent state. Silently he watched her retrieve her jade-encrusted black dagger, place the short, straight blade close to her scalp, then sever the tightly woven braid in one quick swipe. Eyes absorbed in her task, she removed three of the shiny beads from her necklace.

"Whenever you feel disturbed and wish to calm your restlessness, stroke the smoothness of these jade stones," she murmured as she slid them one at a time upon the cord she had fashioned from her hair. She reached for his left hand, then pulled it close and carefully knotted the bracelet of hair and jade around his wrist. "You will find that doing so will help to restore your mind to peace and harmony."

As she sat back on her heels, Stone caressed one of the green stones between his thumb and middle finger. It felt soft and smooth, almost silky, and he found himself understanding what she had described. While he fondled the jade, he looked at Windsor Richmond's lips, imagining they would feel much the same way. He flinched, automatically drawing back as she put her hands against his chest as if to unfasten his shirt. Immediately, she withdrew her touch, her sapphire-colored eyes reflecting surprise at his reaction.

"You must remove your shirt," she murmured, watching him closely.

"I can do it myself."

As soon as he completed the task, she leaned forward and helped push the garment off his shoulders, gingerly guiding it over his bandage. Her attention fixed on his naked chest, she came even closer, near enough for him to detect the fragrant scent that clung to her hair. Jasmine, he thought, at its sweetest when the blossoms still clung to the vine. His entire body tensed hard, his loins tightening dangerously as she began to touch him, her fingers creeping softly, knowingly, over the lean bands of muscle at his waist, then up over his rib cage to the bulging musculature of his chest.

"You are very tight and hard," she murmured, continuing her examination, her delicate brows set with intense concentration.

Stone wanted to laugh. Yeah, damn right, he thought, his lips thinning with a wry twist. In more ways than one. And the manner in which she was caressing his body wasn't helping much. He felt both relieved and disappointed when she stopped her intimate exploration of his torso in order to retrieve her black-lacquered needle case.

Moving behind him on her knees, she ran her open palms lightly over the skin of his back, just barely smoothing the surface and taking her time choosing the precise spot. When she inserted the first needle, Stone barely felt the tip pierce his flesh.

He was far too distracted by how close she was to him and by how sweetly exotic her fragrance was. Five additional needles were selected and meticulously arranged along the outer curve of his right ear. She molded the ends with a grayish substance and lit them with a twig from the fire. Gradually, miraculously, the dull, aching discomfort in his left shoulder began to subside.

"Why don't the needles draw blood?" he asked, endeavoring to distract himself from thoughts of the softness of her mouth.

"Because they are very fine and delicate. Their ends are not sharp, but rounded, so as to push aside the skin instead of puncturing it. And I apply the moxa to heat them and accelerate the healing process."

"I don't understand how sticking smoking needles in my ear and arm can keep my shoulder from hurting."

Windsor paused, her large expressive eyes searching his face. "It is a difficult concept to understand for you who are born in the West."

"Try me."

She seemed pleased that he desired an explanation. "The ancient healers taught of a vital life force which creates and animates the physical body. They called this life energy *ch'i*, which means breath. Ch'i is found in all things that breathe, even plants and animals. Do you wish to hear more?"

"Yeah."

"All things in the universe are composed of two complimentary forces called yang and yin. Yang is the active force. It is positive and outgoing. Yin is passive. Yin is the negative, soft element. Where yang is light, yin is dark. Yang is male, and yin is female. Yang is the heavens and brightness, and yin is the earth and darkness. Both are equally essential to make up the ch'i. When yin and yang are well balanced, the result is harmony, but an excess of one or the other in a person's body will make one ill."

As Windsor explained, she gently twisted the needles in his ear. He felt no pain.

"Ch'i moves along pathways in the body called meridians," she continued in her mellifluous voice. "It controls the blood and nerves, and all the organs, and it must flow freely. If this energy flow is blocked or impaired, illness results. So, you see, the pain in your shoulder is the accumulation of energy when the flow of ch'i is blocked. By stimulating certain points that lie along the meridian, as is done when I twirl the needles like this"—she showed him—"the flow is rebalanced and your pain is alleviated."

"Where did you learn all this?"

"From the Old One, my Master Ju of the Temple of the Blue Mountain."

Finished with the insertion of the needles, Windsor moved up close behind Stone, and he shut his eyes as her fingers began to stroke across his broad bare shoulders and down his neck, kneading, massaging, until the habitual rigidity of his body began to melt. Tension flowed out of his arms and legs, as if she had unstoppered a bottle and allowed it to drain.

"That does feel good," he admitted begrudgingly.

"I am glad you feel pleasure," she answered, moving around until she faced him once more. She smoothed her palms over the mat of black hair on his chest, tenderly rubbing her fingertips over his flesh in slow, circular motions. Stone realized he had not felt such total relaxation since before the war. Pure pleasure flooded through him, and he smiled. Windsor returned his smile, the fire enveloping her in a shining copper aura.

"Like a halo," he murmured, lifting his hand to touch the bright softness of her hair. He caressed the silky texture with his fingers as he had done earlier to the jade stone. He wanted to kiss her, dammit; he wanted to taste her mouth, stroke the smooth, flawless skin of her face. He raised his hand and trailed his fingers down the elegant curve of her cheek, then over her full lower lip.

Windsor's lips parted beneath his touch, but she made no effort to resist. Her eyes locked with his, she lifted her hand to his jaw in a similar caress, her fingertips tracing the firm line of his mouth in the same way he had done to her. Stone's heart accelerated dangerously, and he realized with dismay just how much he wanted her. He wanted to jerk her up against him and taste every inch of her. He wanted to push her backward onto the soft furs and possess her completely.

Appalled at just how close he was to doing that very thing, he grabbed her wrist and thrust her hand away from him. He could not let himself get involved with a woman like Windsor Richmond. She was too damn weird, and she had been nothing but trouble since the first moment he had met her. More importantly, she considered herself a nun. She had said so herself. For what he had in mind, nuns were definitely off limits.

"We better get some sleep," he growled, not looking at her. He turned away and quickly wrapped himself in a buffalo robe. Careful not to dislodge the needles, he lay down, rolling over until his back was to her. He clamped his eyes shut, but he sure as hell didn't go to sleep. Instead, he listened to her every movement, felt her soft skin and lips again, imagined them pressed intimately against him, and decided then and there that he would have to get away from her soon. Because, God help him, he hungered for her with a passion he had never experienced before, not for any woman, and he'd been with plenty who were both beautiful and desirable. He didn't like wanting her so much. Such feelings made him feel weak and undisciplined, and they were dangerous, to both of them.

Gauzy gray mist hung in a low, wispy haze over the calm lake surface, shrouding the mountain peaks usually mirrored there. The villagers had just begun to stir, the keening murmur of the Dawn Chant echoing in a low drone over the water, when Windsor ducked beneath the flap to join them. She looked around for Stone Kincaid. He had not slept inside the lodge with her for more than a week now, not since the night the rainstorm had driven him inside. He purposely avoided her, and she did not understand why.

"I have brought ponies for you, Yellow-Haired-Warrior-Woman. They are a gift from Sun-On-Wings, the son of my youngest brother."

Windsor recognized the speaker before her as an older brave known to the tribe as Buffalo Man. A tall warrior with a weathered face and a short, wide scar across the bridge of his nose, Buffalo Man held the reins of several ponies, all fine, sleek-coated animals that snorted and stamped their hooves in the brisk morning air.

"Sun-On-Wings is a good friend," she murmured, stroking the velvety muzzle of a spotted mare as the warrior wound the halter ropes around the lodge pole. "He is very generous to present me with such a fine gift."

Buffalo Man nodded without comment, then rapidly strode away. Windsor patted the horse's neck, but her hand stilled when she caught sight of Stone Kincaid. He stopped a short distance away, looking at her for a moment before he turned and strode off in the opposite direction. He was still angry. Windsor could see the emotion inside his eyes.

On the night she had massaged his tight muscles, she had hoped she could help him find relief from the pain he carried within himself. But since that time, he had seemed even more silent and withdrawn. He was not yet ready to open his heart and let the hard core of bitter hatred melt away.

He is well named, she thought, for he is a hard man, as hard as the granite stone so abundant in the mountains around us. But she had not given up. Someday she would find a way to help him. Someday, when she was deep in her meditation, the way to reach out and ease the hatred gnawing inside his soul would be revealed to her. She was patient. She had only to wait.

Stooping, she dragged her fingers over the cold ground, then rubbed the accumulated dirt across her forehead, as was the custom of the Osage before performing their Dawn Chant. Most of the Little Ones had finished their morning devotions to the sun, but she enjoyed their custom of obeisance to the fiery red globe that gave the land warmth and light. Murmuring praises, she removed the warm buffalo skins and walked to the edge of the lake. Kneeling, she dipped her hands into the clear, rigid water and bathed her face and arms. But even as she cleansed her body, unsettling thoughts disturbed her mind.

She felt so bewildered. She had experienced so many powerful, new sensations since she had met Stone Kincaid. When the big American looked at her with burning eyes that seemed to want to devour her, or when he touched her cheeks and lips with his fingertips as he had the night she had given him the jade stones, her flesh would shiver and grow bumps like the skin of the river toads along the great Yangtze. At such moments her heart would drum like the hardest downpour upon the temple roof, and her body would ache with intense, inexplicable longings.

Troubled by her own feelings, Windsor draped

the warm fur wrap around her shoulders and moved away from the shore. High atop a hill overlooking the lake, she had found a private spot where she could perform her chant of the ancient sutra in private. There, in the quiet of nature, she would delve deep into herself and find the answer to her perplexing dilemma.

The sun was bright now, glimmering off the water, and Windsor spread out her buffalo skin. She assumed the lotus position, propping her ankles atop the opposite thighs, her hands resting palms-up atop her knees.

"*Om Mani Padme Hum, Om Mani Padme Hum,*" she began in a low murmur, and the familiar intonations immediately gave her comfort. Concentrating on cleansing away all conscious thought, she focused her mind inward, looking deep inside her body, delving past her skin and muscle and bone, until she traveled the streaming pathways of her bloodstream, past her beating heart to the very core of her being, where the answers of all existence lay for the true disciples to discover.

Eventually, as she sang the soothing syllables of the sutra over and over, peace began to flow through her like a warm liquid oil, submerging her in a feeling of safety and contentment, a quiet place of love and tranquility. Then in the space of a heartbeat she saw herself with Stone Kincaid. He lay atop her, his long brown fingers tangled in her hair, his mouth moving slowly over her face, seeking her lips. Stunned by the revelation, she found that her trance was immediately broken. Her eyes flew open. Stone Kincaid stood a few yards away, his blue-gray eyes intent upon her face.

"I desire your body atop my own," she admitted breathlessly. "I looked into my heart, and the truth was revealed to me."

Stone Kincaid stared at her for a moment, then

gave a low laugh. "Yeah, the same thing was revealed to me a few nights back."

Very disturbed, Windsor drew her brows into a V-shaped frown. "But what does one do when confronted with such a problem?"

Stone hunched a shoulder, but his eyes glinted in a way that made Windsor feel he wanted to laugh again. "Well, in my case, I usually put my body atop the one I desire."

"What if one cannot do that?"

"Then one is in a helluva fix."

Dismayed, Windsor stared wordlessly at him. "The Old One taught us to guard against such desires of the flesh. He said that carnal acts would bring only suffering and pain. True disciples must be celibate and disregard earthly desires to achieve ultimate peace within one's self. It is the way to enlightenment."

"Then I seriously doubt I'll ever reach enlightenment," Stone answered, transferring his gaze out over the lake. He assumed a stance with his feet braced apart, thumbs caught behind the black leather of his gun belt. Windsor thought of the vision she'd had, thought of Stone Kincaid writhing atop her, naked, their limbs entwined. Her swallow went down dry and hard, and she tried vainly to banish the disturbing mental image.

"Sun-On-Wings sent me up here," Stone said a moment later, turning back to face her.

"Sun-On-Wings? Why did he not come himself?"

Stone hesitated. "I know you probably didn't realize what was happening earlier, but when you took the ponies from Buffalo Man, you accepted Sun-On-Wings as your husband."

Windsor's eyes widened. "But that cannot be. If I am to become a true disciple of the Dragonfire, I can never marry. It is forbidden."

"Disciple of the Dragonfire? What's that?"

Windsor looked down, astonished that she had let slip mention of the Dragonfire. Never before had she spoken of her temple's secret warrior sect aloud, not even the name! Oh, what was happening to her? Stone Kincaid made her say and do strange, unnatural things.

"I can say no more," she answered quickly.

Stone Kincaid didn't press her. "Then I suggest you let the kid know how you feel as soon as you can, or he'll end up being humiliated in front of his whole tribe."

"I will tell him the truth, and he will understand."

"He's waiting for you down by the lake. He wanted me to find out when you would be coming to his lodge to be his woman."

Stone's gaze captured hers again, holding her eyes against her will, but he said nothing else. Windsor was glad when he turned and strode away. Men made things difficult for women. She was finding that out more and more. The Old One had been right to teach her to avoid such temptations. She would have to explain such wisdom to Sun-On-Wings so that he would accept the fact that she could not be his woman, or any other man's.

Sun-On-Wings retraced his steps on the trail beside the lake. What was taking Arrow-Parts-Hair so long? He was so eager to know if Yellow-Haired-Warrior-Woman would share his lodge when Grandfather Sun slept behind the mountains that he was beginning to feel sick inside his stomach. The mere idea of taking her down upon his sleeping mat made his heart thud until it hurt his chest. Anxious to see her again, he shielded his eyes from the bright sun and studied the slope that rose to where she liked to sit above the lake.

Yellow-Haired-Warrior-Woman was coming swiftly toward him. As always when she approached, Sun-On-Wings' tongue felt thick and twisted up like a lariat of horsehair. At such times no words welled inside his throat to leave his mouth. He strove for the appropriate greeting when she stopped in front of him. But all he could think of was how beautiful she was. How white her skin, how soft and gold her hair, like the bright leaves of the aspen in the Moon of the Falling Leaves. All he wanted was to reach out and touch her, but he did not dare.

"I am honored that you wish me to be your woman, Sun-On-Wings."

At her initial statement, Sun-On-Wings' hopes soared heavenward like the red eagle for which he was named, but as she continued, his spirit plummeted back to earth as if pierced by a Pawnee arrow.

"But I cannot marry. I have pledged myself to seek the truth and the way of enlightenment. I must return to my home at the Temple of the Blue Mountain, where I can attain true peace and harmony."

"But can you not do such a thing here among the Little Ones?" Sun-On-Wings asked, swallowing back his disappointment. "Our mountains are high enough to reach into the heavens. Here you will be close to Wah-Kon-Dah."

"Your land is beautiful. I have been happy here in your village, but I must leave when Stone Kincaid's body has healed and he is able to travel."

"I will go with you," Sun-On-Wings decided on impulse, suddenly finding the idea very appealing. "I will go to your faraway land called China, where I, too, will find peace and harmony."

Yellow-Haired-Warrior-Woman smiled. She has to be a spirit, Sun-On-Wings thought, struck dumb with awe. No mortal human could be so beautiful and so wise.

"Before I return to my temple, I must travel far

with Stone Kincaid. We seek a man of evil—a man who has killed ones beloved to us. When he is punished, then I can journey across the great ocean and submit to my destiny."

"I am a brave warrior, and the best in the tribe with my bow. I can help you find this evil one."

"No. You belong here in your mountains with your own people. One day you will be a great chief of the Little Ones. White-Spotted-Wolf has seen it in his dream sleep. He told me."

"I would rather be with you," Sun-On-Wings muttered, his chest tight with a feeling of loss.

"You will care for another someday. I am not the woman of your destiny. But I will always remember you, and our contest with the bows."

Smiling, she placed her palms together as Sun-On-Wings had seen her do so often since she had come into his life; then she bent respectfully at the waist. Sun-On-Wings returned her bow in the same way, but as he watched her walk away with her silent, graceful tread, his heart was heavy with loneliness.

8

Crouched behind Windsor's lodge in the darkness, Stone shivered and pulled his buffalo robe tighter around him. The temperature had plummeted since nightfall, complicating his decision to leave while the Indians slept. During the month or more they had spent at the Osage camp, he had secreted enough food and supplies for the trek home. Now was the time; all he had to do was go.

Huddling deeper beneath the furs, Stone grimaced as the high notes of Sun-On-Wings' courting flute filtered out to him from inside the lodge. The damn kid was serenading Windsor again, and as much as Stone didn't want to admit it, he knew exactly why he had waited so long to leave. He cursed his own weakness.

Windsor Richmond was the reason, dammit. Leaving her behind did not set well with him. After all, she had saved his neck. And he liked her—even if he did think she was the weirdest person he had ever met.

Furious at himself for the guilt that continued to prick his conscience, he stood up and tried valiantly to shake off his nagging reluctance to strike out without her. She would be all right. She could take care of herself; she had certainly proved that more than once.

His face molded in determined lines, he slung his heavy hide-wrapped bundle over his good shoulder and, careful to edge the perimeter of the village, crept silently toward the trees where he had hidden a pony. There was no moon, which helped conceal his furtive flight, and the night was so cold and still that he could hear wolves howling, their melancholy songs echoing eerily far across the lake.

Within minutes he came upon the spot where he had tethered the horse early that morning while the camp was busy performing the Dawn Chant. He slung his supplies over the mare's back, then hesitated, glancing out across the quiet fields toward Windsor's hut. She'll be all right, he told himself firmly. The Osage treated her like a queen, didn't they? Nobody was going to hurt her. She would be in far more danger if she went after Clan with him, as she wanted to do. Stone didn't intend to see her get hurt. Besides that, she had a way of causing too damn much trouble for him.

Swinging up onto the woven blanket that acted as a saddle, he touched his heels to the mare's flanks and headed up the narrow forested trail that would take him out of the valley. I'm doing the right thing, he told himself, still struggling with his conscience. If Windsor wanted to leave the Osage, she would. He had to stop worrying about her and concentrate on his own problems.

Two days later, Stone was still reproaching himself for leaving Windsor behind. What if she did something foolhardy again, such as following him on her own? Even the survival skills she possessed wouldn't be enough to save her in the dead of winter. And the weather was worsening each day. He had waited much too long to leave. The snow was already deep at the higher elevations, and judging by the threatening sky, if he didn't reach Silverville soon, he might not make it at all. He urged his horse to a faster gait.

As he had feared, snow began to fall by late afternoon. Sporadic flakes swirled on gusts of wind, then gradually increased until the mountains around him were hidden by a white curtain that concealed the landmarks he needed to guide his way to the old mining town. Finally, when visibility was practically nil, he began to search the cedar-spiked slopes for some kind of temporary shelter. He pushed on, the snow falling harder, and was relieved when he glimpsed several caves above him on the side of a rocky slope.

As far as he could tell, the only way to reach them was straight up a steep hill studded with tall evergreen trees. The ascent looked rocky and as slick as frozen cobblestones. But he didn't have a choice. Guiding the mare upward, he prayed she wouldn't lose her footing.

Stone released a heavy sigh of relief when the mare lurched up the last few feet to the level stretch of ground in front of the caves. There were three caverns; one was large, with a smaller one on either side. Eager to get a fire started, he dismounted and pulled his horse toward the nearest opening. His hands felt frozen; his face was red and chapped despite the blanket he had wrapped around his nose and mouth.

The bite of the wind lessened once he reached the shelter, and he hobbled his horse, unloading her and wiping her down, then went outside again to gather kindling for a fire. Wood was plentiful, and he gathered an armload, then drew to a standstill when he glimpsed a couple of Indian ponies on the ground below, moving slowly against the driving snow.

Ducking down, he inched backward into the cave, not taking his eyes off the two riders. He had been lucky so far—he'd not seen any war parties or hunting bands. His good fortune seemed to be holding out, because the swift-falling snow had already obliterated the hoofprints of his horse.

"Damn," he muttered beneath his breath as one of the Indians pointed up toward the caves. He backed farther into the darkness. If the two braves had decided to wait out the storm in the caves, he was in trouble. Unless they were friendly—and he sure as hell couldn't count on that.

Pressing back out of sight, he drew his Colt and held it up against his shoulder, cocked and ready to fire. He didn't have long to wait. Within five minutes, the first heavily cloaked rider appeared, the second one a few yards behind him. Luckily, they chose to take shelter in the big cave, which lay about fifteen feet from Stone's position. Still gripped with tension, Stone watched the first man nudge his horse toward the mouth of the cave; then he turned his gaze to the other horse now cresting the slope. Stone's jaw dropped, his eyes riveted on the tiny black-and-white monkey clinging to the rider's back.

"Dammit, Windsor," he swore furiously beneath his breath. He stepped from his hiding place, certain now that the first rider was Sun-On-Wings.

"Windsor!" he yelled. "What the hell are you doing following me?" His words whipped toward her, tossed about on the howling wind.

Startled, she whirled to face him, nearly unseating Jun-li from her shoulder, but before she could respond, a great growling roar split the air. Horrified, Stone watched a huge grizzly bear plunge out of the cave toward Sun-On-Wings. The immense animal rose on its hind legs and attacked the boy's mount, its six-inch claws slashing downward to open long, bloody gashes in the horse's neck.

Seriously wounded, Sun-On-Wings' mare brayed and fell backward, flailing her hooves in panic. Stone ran forward as the terrified horse backed into Windsor's mount, sending both animals and riders reeling off the ledge and somersaulting down the steep incline.

Still enraged at the invasion of his den, his angry bellows echoing out over the snow-muffled valley, the grizzly went after his victims, plunging down the incline, half loping, half sliding on his hindquarters.

Stone reached the edge of the cliff and tried to take aim, but the trees and blowing snow blocked his gunsight. He scrambled down the hill after them, slipping, half falling, finally managing to stop his out-of-control descent by grabbing onto a tree branch with his free hand.

A few feet below him, Windsor's horse was galloping away, but Sun-On-Wings' mare lay struggling weakly on her back, screaming in agony as the angry bear clawed open her belly. The boy lay motionless on the ground behind the grizzly. As the bear turned on the Indian, slapping at him with sharp, blood-drenched claws, Stone was appalled to see Windsor scramble up from where she had landed, waving her arms and shouting in a suicidal attempt to distract the bear from her friend.

"Windsor, get back!" Stone cried, but his warning came too late. The bear veered away from Sun-On-Wings and after Windsor. She was limping heavily, and the grizzly caught her within moments, swinging one gigantic paw against her back and sending her sprawling forward.

Stone opened fire, pumping six bullets in rapid succession into the bear's back. The grizzly staggered but did not fall. Stone halted as the great gray beast turned on him; then he began to back away as he pulled his other revolver from his holster.

Growling in pain and rage, the wounded animal loped toward him. Stone fired again, once, twice, three times, but the grizzly kept coming. Dropping to one knee, Stone braced his arm and aimed at the beast's head. He pulled the trigger.

The slug hit, ripping through the lower jaw, but still the bruin came at him. When the bear was two yards away, Stone fired yet again. This time the lead ball hit true, smashing into the bear's brain and stopping him in his tracks. The animal fell forward heavily, and Stone scrambled out of the way, emptying his cylinder in the writhing carcass. Panting and gasping with delayed reaction, Stone sank to his knees, staring at the huge, bloody creature, realizing just how close he'd come to being mauled to a gory pulp.

Still shaky, he got to his feet and saw that Sun-On-Wings had come to and was sitting up, groggily rubbing the back of his head. But Windsor lay still, facedown in the snow. Jun-li was screaming shrilly and pulling at her clothing, and Stone's heart turned as icy as the ground beneath his feet. Then he was running to her, rolling her over, wiping the snow off her face. Frantically, he searched her body for blood, then heaved a sigh of relief when he heard her moan.

"Damn you, Windsor," he whispered. He pulled her gently into his arms and carried her back up toward the cave, shouting for Sun-On-Wings to follow.

"Windsor? Can you hear me?"

She opened her eyes and found Stone Kincaid's face very close above hers. She struggled to sit up, but his hand on her shoulder held her down.

"Better not move so fast or you'll be sorry. You have a bump as big as a goose egg on the side of your head."

Windsor obeyed, raising her hand to touch the spot above her temple. She winced as her fingers found the gigantic lump; then she suddenly remembered her friend's peril.

"Where is Sun-On-Wings?"

"Sun-On-Wings here," came the boy's voice.

Battling the pain slivering through her skull, she turned her head and found the Osage youth sitting near the fire. A blood-soaked white cloth was wrapped around his forehead, and his face was marked up with scratches. Makeshift bandages covered the long, shallow gouges across his naked chest.

"Are you all right?" she asked him. Sun-On-Wings nodded, but it was Stone Kincaid who answered.

"If you ask me, both of you are damn lucky to be alive."

His voice was more like a growl, and she knew he was angry from the way his dark brows were drawn together and his abrupt movements as he fed sticks into the fire. She shifted slightly, becoming aware of the pain throbbing in her ankle from where it had been pinned beneath her horse's leg when they had landed at the base of the cliff.

"You saved our lives, Stone Kincaid. We are grateful to you."

Stone gave her a sour look. "Frankly, I'm getting a little sick and tired of risking my life to save your neck. One of these days I'm not going to be around when you get yourself in trouble. Then what the hell will you do?"

"You will always be there for me, as I will be for you. Destiny has written our names together. You must learn to accept—"

"I don't have to accept a damn thing! Don't you understand, Windsor? You almost got yourself killed today! And the kid, too. If I hadn't picked this place to stop for the night, you'd be dead right now!"

"But I am not dead. And you did stop here. Is

that not convincing proof to you that our souls are connected?''

"All that tells me is that you're damn lucky. You should have stayed back at the camp instead of following me. How the devil did you find me so fast anyway? I had at least a day's head start on you.''

"One who wishes to hide his footprints should not walk upon the snow,'' Windsor pointed out sagely.

"Don't give me that. It sure as hell wasn't snowing when I left.''

"Trail easy to see,'' Sun-On-Wings announced, "Jun-li help follow.''

"Jun-li?''

"Jun-li watches for me,'' Windsor explained. "He alerted me when you left the camp, so we followed at once. Where do you journey, Stone Kincaid, that you sneak away in the dark of night?''

"None of your business. Tomorrow I want both of you to turn around and head back to the village. I'm not taking you with me, and I mean it.''

"I will not return to the village of the Little Ones,'' Windsor replied with calm resolution.

"Sun-On-Wings go with Yellow-Haired-Warrior-Woman,'' the Osage boy added, his face fervent. "Sun-On-Wings go to land of China and be nun.''

"Oh, for God's sake,'' Stone grumbled, massaging his brow, "you're both crazy. And I'll be damned if I take either of you with me when I go after Clan.''

"One flea cannot a coverlet raise,'' Windsor told him, disregarding his obvious wrath.

Stone Kincaid looked at her for a moment; then, to her surprise, he grinned. "Yeah, maybe, but Clan is not a coverlet, and I'm not a flea.''

"I can be of great help to you. And so can Sun-On-Wings.''

"No. I don't want to see you get hurt.''

"Let us fulfill our own parts and await the will of heaven."

"Hell, there's just no reasoning with you, is there? And you're already here, so I guess I don't have much choice. I'll take you along with me until we get to San Francisco. Then you're on your own. Is that clear?"

Not waiting for an answer, he lay down and turned his back to her. Windsor smiled. He would see reason soon enough, she thought, and together they would find Hung-pin's murderer, for that was the way it was meant to be.

9

By early the next morning the snowfall had diminished, but puffy layers of dark gray clouds still hung over the mountains, shrouding the jagged peaks and threatening another winter storm. Windsor gazed up at the sky, plagued by a nagging headache from her encounter with the grizzly. Her ankle was weak and sore, but she could walk without assistance. The clopping of hooves against rock brought her attention to Stone Kincaid, who was coming toward her, leading his horse by the reins.

"Let's go," he said curtly, not looking at her. "If it doesn't start snowing again, we just might make it to Silverville tonight."

"What is this Silverville?"

"It's a mining town where our railway company put down tracks a few years back. I still have some friends there who'll help us board a train to San Francisco."

Windsor looked around for Sun-On-Wings. "Will Sun-On-Wings be able to ride by himself?"

"Yeah. I caught your pony for him, but you'll have to ride with me. I had to shoot the horse the bear got." He finished tying his bedroll to his mare, then scowled at her. "I'm telling you that Sun-On-

Wings better head back to his own people while he still can. He'll hate being among the whites, and they sure as hell won't accept him.''

"Sun-On-Wings go with Yellow-Haired-Warrior-Woman," interjected the sixteen-year-old from a few yards behind them. "Me seek inner peace and be nun.''

Stone loosed a string of oaths beneath his breath, then trained exasperated eyes upon Windsor. "Tell him he's wasting his time, Windsor, so he'll go home. You know as well as I do that he can't be a nun. He doesn't understand what the hell he's talking about.''

Windsor hesitated, because Stone Kincaid's taut, angry words revealed his mood. "I cannot," she answered slowly, "for he can become a priest as Hung-pin was, if that is his desire. Such is an honorable quest.''

"He's an Osage warrior, for God's sake, not some proverb-quoting Chinese holy man! The only reason he wants to come along is because he's in love with you. I'm surprised you haven't seen the truth about him when you do all that damned chanting and looking into yourself.''

Shocked by Stone's scornful rebuke, Windsor remained silent as he led the mare a few feet away and swung onto the horse's back.

"Sun-On-Wings take Jun-li," the boy said to her, and Windsor nodded, watching the capuchin climb to the Indian's broad shoulder and hold on to his long black scalp lock. Troubled by Stone Kincaid's accusations, she contemplated his words while she draped the leather strap of Jun-li's bamboo cage across her chest.

"Come on, Windsor, we're wasting time," Stone Kincaid ordered, reaching down to her. Her heart trembled as his fingers closed around her hand in a strong grip. A moment later, she sat astride behind him, her arms locked around his waist.

"Here. You'll need this to keep warm."

As he urged his mount down the steep trail, she took the heavy buffalo hide he handed back to her and arranged it around her shoulders. The air was very cold, making her chest burn when she drew breath; the day was bleak and gloomy. Her own spirits felt dipped in lead, as they had ever since she realized Stone Kincaid had left her behind without saying good-bye. He didn't want her along now either; he had made his feelings abundantly clear.

Nevertheless, her heart told her that they were meant to hunt down the Evil One side by side. She was certain fate would allow neither of them to capture him alone—it was intended for them to work together. Why couldn't Stone Kincaid understand that? Why did he fight against her so hard when she only wished to help him in his quest for vengeance?

Her chest rose in a mournful sigh, and the way in which they rode made her distinctly aware of the broadness of his back and of the way his wavy black hair curled long against the nape of his neck. Her feelings for him were growing into emotions she could not understand. If only the Old One were here to explain what she was feeling, then she would know what to do. How she longed to return to the temple and kneel at his feet while he spoke his wise counsel.

Stone pushed hard throughout the day, and Windsor used the time to ponder her own problems. Sun-On-Wings traveled well with no complaint of pain in his mauled chest, and Windsor was glad his wounds were not deep. The bear could have ripped him apart, as he had done to the horse. All three of them had been lucky.

After many hours in the saddle, Stone finally pulled up on his reins and leaned forward to peer through the deepening dusk.

"There it is. Thank God I remembered the way. It won't take long now, an hour, maybe less."

Windsor peered around his shoulder when he raised his arm and pointed down the snow-covered valley before them. A good distance away, she could discern a cluster of small buildings where black smoke poured from a dozen stovepipes and chimneys. She could see no other sign of activity.

"Are there many people in this place?" she asked.

"Most of them work at the Ringnard Mine. If you look close, you can see the mine shaft up there on the mountainside."

High up a rocky road that wound like a serpent on the barren slopes rising above the town, Windsor finally found the mine settlement, but she could tell little about it. Stone dug his heels into the horse's flanks, and the animal lurched to a faster gait. Sun-On-Wings kept close behind them, but it took a good deal longer than Windsor had expected to reach the town. By the time they walked their mounts down the slushy, mud-sloppy major thoroughfare of Silverville, darkness had turned the valley black.

Just a few stores lined the street, with one large, two-story structure constructed at the far end of the road. Stone passed the smaller establishments without slowing, his obvious destination the brightly lit building straight ahead.

"I'll see if I can find my friend," he told them, dismounting in front of the place. Windsor remained on the horse as he flipped his reins over a wooden rail attached to the long covered porch. "Both of you wait right here, understand? Don't go anywhere. I'll find out if we can get a room for the night."

Stone's boots clomped hollowly as he moved across the wooden boards to the entrance. Sun-On-Wings slid off his horse, holding Jun-li in his arms.

He looked up when Stone opened the door and tinny piano music spilled out to shatter the quiet evening. Coarse laughter and raucous shouts could be heard as Stone disappeared over the threshold and shut the door behind him, muffling the loud noise. "Is this place Arrow-Parts-Hair's lodge?" Sun-On-Wings asked curiously, gazing up at the tall clapboard structure.

"No. His house is in a place called Chicago. I do not know this place." She dismounted, taking special care with her injured foot, then looked up at the second-floor windows, where shadows moved back and forth behind the sheer white curtains of the tall glass windows. "Those within this house appear happy and content," she said to Sun-On-Wings. "They are sure to welcome us with hospitality."

"The white man is strange creature," Sun-On-Wings observed quietly. "Loud and silly."

"Yes. I have found them odd and hard to understand since I crossed the ocean to the Western world. They are very different from my Chinese friends."

"Sun-On-Wings smoke pipe of peace with Old One and warriors of China," Sun-On-Wings told her. "Then Sun-On-Wings know peace and wisdom of Yellow-Haired-Warrior-Woman."

Before Windsor could reply, Stone reappeared in the doorway in the company of a lady. Once again the discordant sounds intruded into the street. He motioned with his hand for them to come inside, but Windsor's regard rested solely on the way Stone Kincaid was holding the woman close, one arm across her shoulder.

Never before, not in China or America, had she ever seen a woman walking around only in her undergarments. Stone Kincaid's friend wore nothing except a tight garment of black lace that left her shoulders and most of her breasts bare and reached only as far as her knees. Black stockings covered her legs, and she wore black boots with high heels that buttoned to her calves. Windsor thought her quite foolish to dress in such a way on a cold winter night. When Stone motioned again, impatiently this time, Windsor slowly limped to the board walkway, and Sun-On-Wings carried Jun-li close behind her.

As they stepped into the big house, Windsor stared around with great interest. Instead of being divided into small rooms, as were most homes she had found in the United States, this place had one immense rectangular room with many lanterns hanging from long ropes secured to the ceiling. A long platform was built across the back wall, perhaps the height of Stone Kincaid's waist. Many round tables covered with green cloth were placed about the floor, each one surrounded by several bearded white men.

And there were other white women, too, dressed in the same sort of odd, filmy clothing that bared much of their bodies for the view of the men. But she was sure they did not suffer from the cold. Several iron stoves made the room stiflingly hot. Up close, she found Stone Kincaid's friend to be pretty, with luxurious black hair curled and twisted into fancy ringlets held back by jeweled combs. Her face was heavily painted, her eyes lined with black kohl, her lips bright scarlet.

"Windsor, this is Sweet Sue. She owns this place. She's the old friend I was telling you about."

"Oh, you devil," Sweet Sue cried, slapping the flat of her hand playfully against Stone's chest. "We're more'n just friends, and you know it! You're the best man I ever took into my bed, and I've had a goodly supply of handsome miners, believe you me!" She guffawed loudly, then gave Windsor an exaggerated wink, but at the same time, her eyes seemed to take in every detail of

Windsor's face and body. "But as pretty as you are, dearie, I guess you know how good this one is, now don't you?"

Windsor looked at her blankly, very upset by Sweet Sue's words but not quite sure what she meant.

"Windsor's a nun, sort of," Stone was quick to explain, "so watch your tongue, Suzy."

Sweet Sue's big blue eyes grew enormous. "Oh, Lordy me, a nun, is it? Traveling with the likes of you, Stone Kincaid?"

Stone lifted a shoulder and grinned, and Sweet Sue turned back to Windsor. "Sorry, sweetie, but we sure as the devil don't get many Sisters through here, especially not inside the Pleasure Palace."

Windsor wasn't sure what sort of answer was expected from her, but the woman was obviously sincere in her welcome; she was smiling in a very friendly manner. "I am sure this house is a worthy abode," Windsor finally answered, pressing her palms together and bowing courteously from the waist.

Sweet Sue's expression went slack. She looked at Stone, who merely shrugged; then she threw back her head and gave the loud, raucous laugh that Windsor and Sun-On-Wings had heard while waiting in the street.

"Well, now, I don't know how worthy this here abode is, but my customers sure do go out that there door with great big smiles on their ugly mugs! Just ask Stone here. He brought his whole railway gang in near every night while they was building the trestle over Johnston's Canyon."

Sweet Sue's gaze moved past Windsor, obviously getting her first good look at Sun-On-Wings. Her amiable expression disintegrated. She whirled on Stone.

"What are you thinking about, bringing a wild Injun in my place?" Alarmed, she glanced behind her, as if afraid her customers would see him. "Lord have mercy, you're liable to cause a riot with all the trouble the Cheyenne and Pawnee've been kickin' up down south of here!"

"Oh, c'mon, Suzy, he's just a kid. He's not going to cause you any trouble. Nobody'll know about him anyway. If you put us up for a couple of nights, I'll make sure he stays out of sight. He'll behave himself, you have my word."

Sweet Sue looked unconvinced, but she finally smiled again, lifting herself to her toes and pressing her body close against Stone's chest. "You always could sweet-talk the devil out of hell, Kincaid. But tonight, I want you for myself, you hear?"

Windsor was most curious to hear what Stone Kincaid thought of Sweet Sue's idea. She found him smiling as if he was quite impressed with it. She frowned slightly as he gestured down a short hallway that led off to their left.

"You still operating the bathhouse, Suzy? I suspect we could all use a hot tub after riding all day in the snow."

"Sure thing. Charlie just filled 'em up for the girls, but you can use 'em if you want," she offered, lifting her hand to stroke the thick black beard covering Stone's jaw. "And do me a favor, honey. Take a minute to shave off those nasty old whiskers while you're at it. My skin's too tender to get all scratched up." She laughed. "Go on down now, and I'll fetch a couple of the girls to help." She kissed her fingertip and put it against Stone's lips, winked at Windsor, then swayed off toward a group of women at the back of the room.

Windsor watched her leave, but when she turned her gaze back to Stone, he avoided her eyes.

"C'mon," he said brusquely, "a good soaking's bound to help your ankle. Then I'll see if Suzy can find us something to eat."

Silently, Windsor and Sun-On-Wings followed

him down the hall. Stone opened the door at the
end and motioned for them to precede him. The
bathhouse was small and even warmer than the first
room. There were no windows, and two potbellied
stoves glowed red-hot in the corners, with wooden
tubs set in small, white-curtained alcoves along
both sides of the room.

Stone closed the door and walked to the wooden
hip bath nearest to him. It was full almost to the
rim, and he thrust his hand down into the water.
"Yeah, it's still nice and warm. Should feel good
after all day in the saddle, don't you think? Just
pick one and close the curtains."

A hot bath did sound nice, Windsor thought, her
gaze settling on the stacks of thick towels and
round cakes of yellow soap provided on tables beside each tub. In China, she had bathed her body
in the lake below the temple, both in the warm
summer months and in the cold of winter, but she
had used the American bathing tubs when she had
first arrived in San Francisco. The experience was
one Western custom that she found most enjoy-
able.

"What big cooking pots for?" Sun-On-Wings
demanded suspiciously.

"Just take off your buckskins and get in one of
them," Stone muttered, annoyance threading his
tone. He picked up a bar of soap. "This is called
soap. You wash with it."

Sun-On-Wings' expression was full of disdain.
"Brave warriors not sit in pots of hot water like
skinned rabbits waiting to be boiled."

"If you want to sleep in one of Suzy's nice, soft
beds, you will."

"No need bed."

"Now look, Sun-On-Wings, like I told you before, things are different among the whites. You
better get used to it." As Stone spoke, he unbuckled his gun belt and laid it on the table beside the

nearest tub; then he began to unbutton his shirt. "Now, if you'll pardon me, I'm going to take a bath. The two of you can do whatever you want." Metal rings scraped along the rod as he jerked the canvas curtains together.

"The Old One taught us that cleanliness of body is necessary for purity of being," Windsor told Sun-On-Wings. "The whites bathe in such places as this, just as the Little Ones wash themselves at dawn. But I will not tell you what to do. You must follow your heart in this, as you must in all things."

Sun-On-Wings gave a solemn nod. Windsor moved into the alcove across from the one Stone Kincaid had chosen. Carefully, she drew the drapes together and slipped out of her clothes. Stepping carefully into the hip bath, she emitted a soft sigh of pleasure as she sank naked into the heated water. Her limbs were still stiff and numb from the long hours of traveling, and every inch of her flesh prickled as the warmth began to invade her cold body.

Closing her eyes, she lay back and listened to Sun-On-Wings moving around the bath cubicle behind hers. She heard him mutter a few low words in his own language; then a slosh of water told her the Osage youth had decided to try the white man's bath after all. Very relaxed, she picked up a bar of the soap and lathered it briskly between her palms. She smoothed it over her skin, and finally felt really warm again.

Not long after, the calm of the bathhouse was destroyed as a group of young women entered the room, chattering and giggling among themselves. To Windsor's shock, her privacy curtains were swept aside, and she found Sweet Sue looking down at her while two other girls peered over her shoulder. Windsor sank deeper into the security of the water.

"I bet that feels mighty fine, now don't it,

sweetie? Openin' this here bathhouse was the best idea I ever did have." Suzy glanced toward Sun-On-Wings' compartment. "Joanie, you scrub down the Injun, and don't fuss 'bout it, 'cause he's right good-lookin' for a redskin. And, Shirley, you take on our little nun here. And why don't you go 'head and use a squirt of my special shampoo on that purty blond hair of hers?"

She presented Windsor with a wide smile, then turned and parted the drapes of Stone Kincaid's bath. Appalled, Windsor stared at them, realizing she could now look unrestrictedly inside Stone's bathing area.

"Here, honey," Sweet Sue was saying to him, "I brought you a smoke and a flask of my best whiskey. It'll sure take the chill out of them bones quick enough."

"Thanks, Suzy."

Windsor blushed when Sweet Sue leaned down and kissed Stone Kincaid full on the mouth. Wanting to look away, Windsor found she could not. An awful feeling erupted in the depths of her woman's breast, bringing out unwanted emotions as she watched him put his hand on the back of Sweet Sue's neck, holding her there for a more thorough exploration of her lips. The knot of sickness in the pit of Windsor's stomach grew tighter, but she dragged her eyes off the couple across the aisle as the girl named Shirley moved up beside her. She had light brown hair braided atop her head, lots of freckles, and a friendly smile. Her face was painted in a fashion similar to Sweet Sue's.

"Sweet Sue wants me to help you wash your hair," she said, holding up a stoppered blue bottle. "This hair soap smells real sweet, like real-live roses, and you just wouldn't believe how shiny and purty your hair'll look afterward when it gets dry again. All us gals use it near every day, 'cause

Sweet Sue gets whole crates of it sent up special
from Omaha.''

"You are kind,'' Windsor answered, modestly
covering her breasts as Shirley unbraided Windsor's long queue hanging down the back of the tub.
She carefully tipped a pitcher of warm water to spill
over the thick blond hair, thoroughly wetting it,
then applying the sweet-smelling shampoo.

Although Windsor really didn't want to watch
the couple across from her, she couldn't help herself. Sweet Sue was now scrubbing Stone Kincaid's broad brown back, but he wasn't paying any
heed to her attentions. He was smoking a cigar and
staring straight at Windsor.

His eyes didn't waver, and she felt frozen in the
intense burning revealed in their silver-blue depths.

The same oddly disturbing sensations began to
stir in her loins, deep in the core of her womanhood, more intense than ever before. She swallowed hard as his gaze left her face and went slowly
down to her bare shoulders, then even lower, to
where her crossed arms hid the soft mounds of her
naked breasts. Windsor shivered.

"I declare, I believe I could use a bath myself,''
Sweet Sue murmured across the way, her voice low
with sensuous promise. "What do you say, Kincaid?''

"Suit yourself. There's plenty of room.''

Sweet Sue laughed and reached out to jerk the
curtains together, effectively closing off Windsor's
view of whatever was destined to transpire between them.

Windsor bit her lip, at a loss for the deep sense
of desolation wounding her heart. Stone Kincaid
and Sweet Sue had lowered their voices, and
Windsor strained to decipher the intimate murmurs coming from their hidden alcove. Water
splashed and sloshed out until streams ran from
beneath the curtains, and when Windsor heard

Sweet Sue giggling, she knew the painted woman had joined Stone Kincaid in his bathtub.

The unwanted image of that scene branded itself on Windsor's mind, and she could almost see Stone Kincaid's arms around Sweet Sue's plump white body, his mouth pressing down on her red-painted lips. Windsor began to feel quite ill. Upset, she thrust away thoughts of what they were doing, concentrating instead on the conversation Joanie was having with Sun-On-Wings in the cubicle behind her.

"Brave warriors no need woman wash them." Sun-On-Wings sounded highly insulted.

"Oh, c'mon, hon, don't be so stubborn 'bout it. It'll feel right good, you'll see. And just look, you're all cut up and bruised, and scratched all over. Good Lord, what's been happenin' to you anyways? Did a jealous woman get hold of you?"

"No woman. Bear."

"Oooh, you must be as brave as a king to fight a big old bear, as young as you are!"

"Sun-On-Wings brave warrior, grown man. No need woman wash."

More splashing followed, and Joanie's voice became soothing, sugary, and persuasive. "Now there, don't that feel good? See, it don't hurt one little bit to let me do that to you, now did it? I never had one man yet that didn't like me to help him with his bath. It feels good, don't it?"

A short silence ensued before Sun-On-Wings gave his begrudging answer. "Feel good."

"You sure do have a pretty head of hair," Shirley suddenly said to Windsor, interrupting her eavesdropping as she tilted Windsor's head back and began to rinse away the soap. "Wish I had yellow hair. All the customers like yellow hair the best."

Windsor didn't answer, grateful that Shirley was being so kind. This was one custom that she understood well. In China, the wealthy households always had concubines and female servants to care for the needs of the males of the family. But Windsor was surprised that Sweet Sue sent Shirley to tend to Windsor's bath. Among the Chinese, only the first wife of the master would be so honored.

10

Stone sat at the bar, morosely clutching the handle of an empty beer mug. For the past hour he had been watching Windsor and Sun-On-Wings through the long narrow mirror in front of him. He fixed his eyes unflinchingly on where Sweet Sue had seated them at a corner table, where they could eat their dinner yet go unnoticed by the boisterous patrons of the Pleasure Palace. They sat quietly while all around them the saloon was becoming rowdier with rough scuffles and drunken arguments as the hour grew late.

Since Stone's party had arrived in town, more miners had trekked down from the Ringnard, despite the inclement weather. Most had wasted no time in laying out their hard-earned coin for the well-heralded talents of Sweet Sue's girls, but several dozen were happy enough to remain in the taproom swilling whiskey and playing poker. Stone frowned. He had already had too much to drink, and he knew it. It was rare for him to imbibe at all, much less to guzzle liquor like a landbound sailor as he had done for most of the night. In fact, he couldn't remember the last time he had overindulged. He had always considered it a sign of

weakness to crawl into a bottle for comfort, but tonight it hadn't seemed like such a bad idea. After
he had bathed and shaved, he'd felt the need for
a hefty dose of pleasure, and the brand Sweet Sue
peddled so ably at the Palace had sounded damn
good to him. He deserved it after all he had been
through since the train was ambushed.

Shoving his mug across the polished bar, he
watched George, the barkeep, turn the spigot and
fill the mug to the brim, then expertly blow off the
head of foam before sliding it back to Stone. Getting drunk just might get Windsor Richmond off
his mind for a while. Nothing else had worked to
rid her from his thoughts, that was for damn sure.
Now, with all the beer and whiskey he could down
readily available, not to mention a highly desirable,
skillful lover like Suzy willing and eager to please
him, maybe he'd be able to forget her.

Sweet Sue arrived and pressed up close against
him, and underneath the counter, he felt her fingers close over his thigh. He looked at her as she
slowly slid her palm higher. Stone smiled, lifting
her other hand to his lips.

Even as he did, his gaze strayed to Windsor, and
despite the further liberties Sweet Sue was taking
beneath the bar, his mind returned to the tantaliz-
ing vision of Windsor earlier that evening. She had
looked so small and innocent sitting in the big
bathtub across from him, and so beautiful she made
a man's insides ache.

Her hair had been wet and slicked back until it
hugged her shoulders like a rich mantle of dark
gold, and her white breasts had mounded above
the water, soft and glistening with droplets, enticing him, tormenting him. It had been she, not
Sweet Sue, whom he had wanted to pull into the
tub with him. The urge had been so powerful, he'd
had to consciously restrain himself from doing just
that. Each time the girl named Shirley had touched

Windsor's hair, Stone had watched with jealous eyes, coveting that pleasure for himself.

Frowning, highly aggravated with himself, Stone threw back his head and methodically set about draining his mug to the bottom. She's a nun, *a nun*, for God's sake, he berated himself with vicious self-disgust. Why couldn't he get that thought through his head? Why couldn't he quit dreaming about holding her, touching her?

Cursing his stupid obsession with the girl, he suddenly reached for Sweet Sue, pulling her to him and kissing her hard. Instantly, she pressed herself closer, rubbing her full breasts against his chest. Despite her ardent response, he released her almost at once and ordered another drink, resolving not to glance in Windsor's direction again.

"So you want the little nun," Sweet Sue murmured, incredulity coloring her words. "And don't you dare deny it, darlin', 'cause I happen to know you too well. You've got the most god-awful lovelorn look on your face that I ever saw." She startled Stone by booming out a hearty laugh. "For shame, Kincaid. You're a naughty one, to be sure, lusting after a religious gal like her."

Stone grinned. Sweet Sue was a good friend and perceptive as hell. "Yeah, you're right. And that's not even the worst part. She's not only an innocent nun, she's as crazy as the day is long. Not to mention the fact that she's nearly gotten me killed three times since I first laid eyes on her a month or so back."

Sweet Sue's amusement faded, and she leaned her elbow against the bar, observing him as he took a sip of beer. "She is a rare beauty, I have to say. Though, even as pretty as she is, I never would've figured her for your type."

Stone gave a derisive snort. "She's not anywhere close to my type. She's too weird. How many people do you know who carry wild monkeys around in their suitcases? Despite all that, I can't get her off my mind, no matter how hard I try." One end of his mouth curved up in a half grin as he caressed Sweet Sue's cheek with his thumb. "But now that I'm here with you, I'm counting on you to help me change all that."

"Maybe," Sweet Sue answered, glancing at her young blond rival, "and maybe not. But I'll tell you one thing, I'm sure willin' to give it a hell of a good try."

Stone smiled and out of the corner of his eye he saw Windsor and Sun-On-Wings rise from their chairs and move down the hall toward the bathhouse.

"Good," he muttered to himself, "now I won't have to look at her. C'mon, Suzy, show me how much you missed me."

He pulled her into his arms, eager for her full scarlet-painted lips to erase all his tormented thoughts of softer pink ones.

Windsor glanced over her shoulder just as Stone Kincaid began pressing his mouth against the black-haired woman's lips. He had kissed the woman named Sweet Sue many times since they had left the bathhouse earlier that evening. He must like her very much, she thought, and was alarmed at how low she felt about that realization, how her heart lay heavy inside her breast, so hard and cold that it hurt her to breathe.

The Old One had foreseen that her woman's body would betray her, that she would be tempted to lie with a man and give up her desire to reach fulfillment. She had not understood then, but she did now. And she hated it, because she could not control her body or her mind as she had always been able to do in the past. Clamping her jaw shut, she set about steeling her resolve, deciding then and there that she would subject herself to long, strenuous meditative trances in order to seek the strength to resist the constant yearnings Stone Kincaid set on fire inside her.

When she and Sun-On-Wings reached the bathing chamber, the room was deserted, but Sweet Sue had ordered several tubs to be pushed back so that narrow cots could be placed inside the cubicles nearest to the wood stoves. As they shut the door behind them, Jun-li swung down from the ceiling beams and hung by his tail, apparently tired of his lonely imprisonment in the small room. Sun-On-Wings knelt and fed the capuchin the handful of beans he had saved from his supper plate. Eager to perform the comforting lines of the ancient sutra, Windsor moved to the cot nearest the door.

"I am tired. I must go to my bed."

"Bed? What is bed?"

"The white man sleeps upon soft racks such as this," she explained, sitting down on the thin mattress.

Sun-On-Wings eyed the contraption. "Why need bed? Ground here warm and dry."

Windsor shrugged. "It is their custom. In the Temple of the Blue Mountain, the priests and their disciples lie on simple mats upon the ground. But in the great households, there are padded couches for repose. I have seen them."

"Sun-On-Wings need no rack. Sleep on buffalo robe," he told her, striding to the other end of the room and stretching out close beside the red-hot stove. Windsor watched Jun-li settle down beside the Indian youth, and feared her little capuchin friend had deserted her for his new companion.

Exhaling a heavy breath, she drew the curtains together, then sat cross-legged in the middle of the bed. Once she had assumed the lotus position, she began to block out the music and loud conversation filtering to her from the saloon.

Time passed, but she found concentration difficult. She felt too tired, too confused to subjugate her mind in the usual manner. Her inability to reach into herself alarmed her, for such a calamity had never happened before. Finally she gave up and stretched out on her back and stared up at the ceiling.

Stone Kincaid was probably upstairs with Sweet Sue, she decided despondently. He would have taken the pretty white woman there, as she had seen so many of the miners do with the other women while she and Sun-On-Wings ate their supper. Briefly, and for the first time in her life, she pondered why women had been created for the pleasure of men. That was the way it was in all the far provinces of China, and that was the way it was here among the barbarians of the West. Women were born to serve men, to please them with their looks and their actions. Women were made to obey. Women were weak; men were strong. Women were yin, men were yang. But why?

For long hours after she heard the soft whistle of Sun-On-Wings' snores, she lay still, her hands laced behind her head, contemplating ideas, new doubts, and questions that would have been alien for her conjecture before she had found Stone Kincaid in Chicago. Before he had come into her life, she had always slept calmly and deeply, without worry or plaguing dreams of men and women lying together in the carnal way. Now she rested uneasily, taking long to attain slumber and awakening often, as if she were waiting and longing for the impossible to happen.

She tensed when she heard the door open. She sat up quickly as it banged against the wall. Shuffling noises informed her that someone had come into the room. Then Stone Kincaid's voice came from the other side of the canvas curtains, the low-

pitched growl she was beginning to associate with
his ire.

"Where the hell are you, Windsor?"

Surprised, she quickly rose, but her privacy curtains were swept back with a squeal of metal rings
before she could speak. Stone Kincaid stood before
her, obviously very drunk and very angry, his fists
dug into his narrow hips. As he stared at her, the
thunderous frown riding his brow gradually loosened into puzzlement.

"Where the hell's the kid?"

"He sleeps by the stove. You are too full of spirits
to see him."

"Damn right."

Stone took a step toward her, staggered sideways, caught himself, then blearily tried to focus
on her face. "Except that it doesn't work that way
with you. You're always inside my head, making
me think stupid things and do stupid things."

Suddenly, with a quickness that surprised her
considering his state of drunkenness, he reached
out and grabbed her shoulders. Windsor could
have easily evaded his grasp, but she did not try.
She stood perfectly still as his long fingers tightened around her arms and drew her up toward
him until her face was only inches from his own.

"Tell me how to get you out of my mind," he
whispered softly, his eyes examining her face, his
breath strong with the odor of beer. He pushed her
backward, forcing her to sit down on the cot. Then
he went to his knees, leaning against her until his
chest pinned her back to the bed.

Windsor's heart went wild, thudding, skipping
beats, then racing out of control. Afraid of her own
response to what he was doing, she lay unmoving
beneath him as he threaded his fingers into the hair
at her temples, holding her face still while he spoke
to her in a low and tortured whisper.

"I put my hands in Suzy's hair, just like this,

and I kissed her mouth and held her body, and I didn't feel a thing. All I thought about was you. I wanted her to be you, damn you.''

Then his lips came down on hers, hard and eager, hotly, forcefully scattering any rational thoughts she tried to garner, warming her body until an alien sound was torn from her throat, a moan of both pleasure and despair. But her muffled cry seemed to inflame Stone Kincaid, and his fingers probed at the front of her silk tunic, pulling loose the shoulder tie enough to slide his hand inside against her naked flesh. At the same time, his lips sought the side of her throat, and she groaned helplessly, squeezing her eyes shut, breathless, intoxicated by what his lips were doing to her body as he pulled her top down so he could see her breasts.

Stone suddenly pulled back. Breathless, Windsor watched him stare down at her with burning eyes as he jerked open the front of his shirt; then he was pressing his chest against her, his black chest hair crisp and rough against her bare skin. He was panting hard and gripping her tightly, one hand clenched in her hair, the other sliding down over her bare stomach into the waistband of her silk trousers. He cupped her hips, bringing her violently up off the bed and clamping her against the hardness of his loins while he leaned back his head and groaned with pleasure.

''Nun no have man.''

Sun-On-Wings' accusing words came from right beside them. Windsor's eyes flew open, and Stone lunged off her and to the floor on the side of the cot, his Colt out of the holster and in his hand. The Osage youth stood his ground, staring defiantly at him. The shock of the moment seemed to sober Stone a bit, and he scowled blackly as he resheathed his revolver.

''You're gonna get yourself shot someday,

sneakin' up on a man like that," he warned the boy in slurred speech. He transferred his fury to Windsor, who had weakly pushed herself upright on the bed, and shakily righted her clothes. "And you, you stay away from me, you hear?" he muttered hoarsely. "I mean it. I don't need you. I don't want you. Suzy's upstairs waiting for me right now."

He proceeded toward the door in an unsteady gait, but halfway there, he changed course and collapsed facedown on one of the cots. He muttered angrily for a moment, then lay still, both arms hanging over the sides. Windsor and Sun-On-Wings eyed him for a moment, then looked at each other.

"White man's firewater bad medicine," the boy said, making the feathers in his scalp lock dance as he shook his head. "Arrow-Parts-Hair not act right."

Windsor took a deep breath and nodded. "The best cure for drunkenness is while sober to see a drunken man," she quoted with conviction, then moved to where Stone Kincaid lay in peaceful oblivion. With effort, she tugged an old patchwork quilt out from where it was neatly folded under his legs and used it to cover him. She pulled shut the curtains around his bed before returning to her own cot.

Stone Kincaid was very foolish to have drunk so much of the strong spirits, she thought, but in her heart she was glad he was sleeping here in the bed next to hers, instead of upstairs in the bed of the black-haired woman.

"C'mon now, darlin', wake up. I gotta open up for the customers."

Fuzzy-eyed, Stone squinted up at Sweet Sue. She smiled engagingly and waved a blue-speckled mug back and forth before his nose. The aromatic smell of strong, fresh-perked coffee filled his senses.

"You sure tied on a doozy last night, love. What on earth got into you, anyways? I never did see you down so much liquor."

Stone pushed himself up and braced his palm on the bed. He groaned and held both temples with the flats of his hands. His head felt as if a fifty-pound anvil sat atop it. He forced a swallow down a throat that seemed stuffed with thick, gritty gauze, cursing himself as the biggest fool who ever lived.

"Are you feelin' all right, honey? You don't look so good."

Still groggy, Stone focused his eyes on Sweet Sue's concerned face. He took the cup from her, his stomach rolling as he forced himself to take a sip. Even the slight movement of his head as he glanced around made his temples pound.

"Where's Windsor and the kid?" he asked, massaging the bridge of his nose.

"Why, they're gone. Didn't they tell you?"

Stone jerked his head up and immediately paid the price. Pain shot through him like a Fourth of July rocket.

"Gone? Where?" he mumbled, cupping his forehead in one palm.

Sweet Sue adjusted her frothy lace wrapper and sat down beside him. She shrugged. "They didn't say much to anybody. They just up and left after all the trouble—"

"What trouble?" Stone demanded, a terrible foreboding flooding through him. He waited tensely, half afraid to hear what she was about to tell him.

"Like I said, I don't rightly know where they went. But Mats—you know him, he's the big Swede who keeps everythin' peaceful 'round here. Anyways, he said the little nun and the Injun got

up real early before any of the girls were stirrin'
and went outside askin' around about some man.
I can't rightly recall his name just now—"

"Emerson Clan?"

"Yeah, that's the one, I think. Anyways, a couple of the boys knew somebody up at the mine
who'd been tellin' stories around the bunkhouse
about this Clan fella. But you know the boys—they
ended up pokin' some fun at the Injun kid. Making
fun of that strip of hair he's got running down the
middle of his head, and such as that. Most of them
hate all Injuns, anyways, since they've been pryin'
up the tracks and ambushing the expresses. You
should've known better than to bring him 'round
here with all that killin' goin' on."

"Dammit, Suzy, get to the point. Is Windsor all
right? Did anybody get hurt?"

Sweet Sue's eyes narrowed. "My, my, but that
pretty gal has turned your head all the way 'round
backwards."

Stone clamped his teeth together, tired of all the
chitchat and impatient for an answer. He glared at
her until she shook her head.

"Well, no need to get so riled. As far as I know,
she's okay. Mats says the two of them went outside, and he heard some sort of scuffle or something, but by the time he opened the door to see
what was goin' on, Johnny Holcomb and Dick
Foots were already lyin' flat on the ground,
knocked out cold. Mats said it took him half an
hour just to bring 'em around. I guess that Injun
kid can use his fists better'n most, 'cause Dickie's
known around here for his fightin', 'cause he used
to be a boxer back in Philly. And Johnny's as big
as a lumberjack."

Stone envisioned a different scenario. "More
than likely, Windsor got them with her feet."

Sweet Sue laughed. "Her feet? What on earth
do you mean?"

"Never mind. You'd never believe me, anyway." Stone drank more coffee, glad for something to cut through the clouds in his brain. He stood up, stuffing his shirttail into his waistband, then lifting the pitcher from its place on the bed-table and pouring wash water into the matching flower-sprigged porcelain bowl. He cupped his palms and splashed a generous amount of cold water on his face. Revived a bit, he glanced at Sweet Sue as he toweled off his jaw.

"You sure Mats doesn't have any idea where they might have gone?"

"All he said was that when they heard about this man they were lookin' for, they got their horses and rode outta here."

"Which way?"

"Up toward the mine."

Stone grimaced. "What time is it?"

"Near half past noon. I tried to get you up an hour ago, but you weren't hearin' nothin'."

Stone checked his guns, found them in order, then drank the last dregs of his coffee. "I better go find them before they get in trouble with the miners. Something tells me they aren't going to be exactly welcome up there. You have a horse I can borrow?"

"Sure thing. Just ask Mats."

"Thanks, Suzy," Stone said, stooping to kiss her cheek. "And thanks for taking us in last night. Sorry about the trouble this morning."

"Last night all you talked about was wantin' to get rid of the nun and the Injun as soon as you could. So why're you in such a hurry to go after them today?"

"I guess I feel responsible for them," Stone answered, but later that afternoon, as he urged his horse up the steep road that ran alongside the railway tracks, he knew better.

He had told himself a thousand times that he'd

be glad to be rid of Windsor, that he'd leave her at the first opportunity. His mouth twisted with derision. Instead, *she* had left *him* the first chance she'd gotten. Worse, she'd chosen the worst possible place to go, especially in the company of an Osage.

The men up at the mine hated Indians worse than rattlers, and Sun-On-Wings would be lucky if they didn't lynch him on sight. Suddenly more worried than before, Stone spurred his horse, his eyes riveted on the rooftops clustered around the mine, just barely perceptible in the distance.

The ugly incident with the two big bullies in front of the Pleasure Palace had caused Windsor much worry. She had found there was very much prejudice and hatred in the United States, much more than she had expected. As her beloved Hung-pin had been attacked without provocation, so now had Sun-On-Wings. If one's skin was red or yellow, he was to be hated and ridiculed. She was very worried for her young Osage friend.

"What about Arrow-Parts-Hair?" Sun-On-Wings asked suddenly. "Him be angry him left behind."

Windsor looked at her friend's swollen eye, which was beginning to puff out and turn black-and-blue. It still angered her to think how one of the men had come up behind Sun-On-Wings and held him while the other had hit him in the face with his fist until Windsor had come to his aid. "Stone Kincaid is still dull and lifeless with the juice of madness," she answered finally. "We will return to him after we have obtained the information about Emerson Clan."

"What happen to Evil One when find him?"

"We will kill him because of his crimes against our friends."

Her answer seemed to satisfy the youth, and they proceeded on, both content to embrace their own thoughts. Windsor's mind returned to Stone Kincaid and just how angry he would be when he found them gone. Or perhaps he'd be glad. He had made it clear that he considered them an unwelcome nuisance. But he would not be so intent on traveling alone when she brought back news concerning the whereabouts of his avowed enemy. Then he would appreciate her help, and he would be glad to have her along.

Vividly, she saw him the way he had looked in the saloon, his hands all over the black-haired woman, and she felt sick inside her stomach. She could have been the one in his arms. She had been, for a few minutes, and though it was hard to admit, it had felt good, more than good.

Consciously, she hardened herself against him. Such intimacy between them could not be. She must remain strong and fight her womanly instincts. If she were to become a true disciple of the Dragonfire, such desires were forbidden her. She could never lie with a man. Only the chaste of body and pure of heart could be initiated into the secret warrior sect of her temple. But now that she had met Stone Kincaid, it was very hard to remember those things.

Not far ahead, the shingled rooftops of the mining camp loomed into sight, and Windsor was relieved because the steep climb had been difficult in the snow and ice. She could see the shaft now, higher on the mountainside, and the workers laboring to bring out the silver ore. Somewhere far away, she could hear men shouting. Closer to them, a cluster of buildings hugged the rocky slopes, the wooden walls gray and dingy, several feet of snow still piled high on the rooftops. But the same gun-metal gray clouds that had brought so much snow several days ago now threatened to bring more, and she was glad they had almost reached their destination.

A quarter of an hour later, they walked their horses down the street of frozen mud. The entire camp was quiet and deserted. The narrow board sidewalks set in front of the half-dozen small wooden structures were empty, the store windows dark and dreary.

Stopping her horse, she looked around and wondered if everyone in town was at work in the mine. The wind had picked up, reddening her cheeks and nose. The sky pressed down harder, and, having lived in the mountains of Kansu Province most of her life, she knew the signs of a coming blizzard.

The sound of a door closing came to her, and she turned in time to see a bent, wizened old man appear from behind the nearest buildings. He carried a large metal pan, which, judging from the way he struggled with it, was very heavy.

Windsor dismounted and motioned for Sun-On-Wings to do the same. She led her mount toward the old man as he threw out the contents of the pan behind what looked like an outhouse. When he turned and trudged back toward them, Windsor's heart leapt with joy. The little old man was Chinese!

11

Ice pellets whipped by strong gusts of wind slammed against Stone's face. Night had fallen, and he bent his head against the punishing sleet, peering narrow-eyed into what little he could see of the dark, wintry landscape. Ahead of him, faint pinpoints of yellow led him like lighthouse beacons. Hunching his neck farther down into the collar of the heavy wool coat he had gotten at the Pleasure Palace, he pushed onward, hoping Windsor and the kid had made it safely to the mine before the blizzard hit.

Hell, he wasn't even sure they had come up to the Ringnard. Suzy hadn't known for sure, and neither had Mats. Chances were they had, and if somebody at the mine did have information concerning Clan, Stone was going to get it out of him. No doubt Windsor was going there for the same purpose.

For over an hour Stone fought his way up the mountain, following the snow-covered railbed as best he could. He knew the way well; his men had laid the tracks. When he entered the outskirts of the mining camp, the place seemed little changed since he had overseen the survey and construction operations. He rode directly to the most popular saloon and found it had in no way lost its appeal. Nearly every man in town was crowded shoulder to shoulder in the rough-hewn, one-room establishment. He remembered the lean-to stable built against the side, and he tied his horse there, his limbs stiff and half frozen as he dismounted and headed inside.

Pulling off his gloves and chafing his numb hands, he pushed open the door, welcoming the heated air that burned against his chapped face. Other than the warmth he found inside, the atmosphere of the saloon was not particularly desirable; the room was filled with the foul odor of unwashed bodies mingled with the smells of stale beer and smoke. The Staghead Saloon was certainly not in the same league with Sweet Sue's place. No wonder the Pleasure Palace did a booming business, despite its distance down the tracks.

Two dozen men stood around the twelve-by-four plank balanced atop two whiskey kegs that acted as a bar. There were no women; the Ringnard owners in Denver forbade ladies on the premises— no doubt another secret of Sweet Sue's continued success.

When Stone walked in, all conversation stopped as if on cue. Ignoring the curious stares his appearance aroused, he took off his hat and slapped it against his thigh to remove the snow. The buzz of gruff voices resumed as he stepped up to the bar.

Stone chose a deserted spot at the end, careful to keep his back to the wall. As the bartender ambled over, wiping his hands on a dirty white apron tied around his barrel chest, Stone scanned those around him for any faces he might recognize from his stint at the Ringnard. But he didn't expect to see any. Nearly eight years had passed since then,

and the men who worked the mountain mines
rarely stayed in one place that long.

"What kin I getcha, mister?"

"Whiskey."

The bartender, big, brawny, and long of limb,
looked like the kind of man who enjoyed beating
up people. As he dribbled whiskey into a shot
glass, Stone studied the enormous, detailed picture of a rearing lion etched into the skin on the
back of the man's hand.

"Nice tattoo," he commented, picking up his
drink.

"Yeah, got it done down San Francisco way.
Drunker than the devil, I was."

Stone didn't reply. He welcomed the path of fire
the first swallow of whiskey blazed down the
length of his gullet.

"Name's Jed," the man offered, leaning a massive elbow on the bar and staring openly at Stone.
"Bad night to be traveling, ain't it?"

"Yeah."

"What brings you up thisaway?"

"What's it to you?"

Jed squirmed under Stone's unflinching look.
"Ain't nuthin' to me. Just tryin' to be friendly-
like, 'sall."

"I have all the friends I want."

Jed sauntered away, picking his teeth with his
fingers. A ten-inch bowie knife hung from a fringed
leather scabbard on the back of his belt. In the past
few years, Stone had seen lots of similar men in
lots of similar saloons. Jed would plant his wicked-
bladed dagger in Stone's back without a moment's
hesitation. So would most of the other men in the
place.

Stone leaned back against the counter, examining the men crouching over their beers. The miner
who stood next to him was slump-shouldered and
small-boned, with long black hair tied into a greasy

ponytail. He wore round wire spectacles. The right lens was cracked into the shape of a Y. Stone decided to see if he could find out anything about Windsor.

"I'm looking for a blond-haired woman, small and real pretty," he said.

A heavyset, florid-complexioned man beside the bespectacled miner interrupted the conversation.

"Well, now, ain't we all?" The fat guy guffawed. "Tell you what, mister, if you find one of them pretty yellow-headed gals around here, I get her second."

"She's a friend of mine," Stone said, slicing him with a cold-eyed look. "So if she does show up here, I wouldn't like it if anybody bothered her." He put his hand down on his right thigh, close enough to draw. The red-faced man's cheeks grew a darker shade of crimson. He stared down into his beer mug without another word.

"There ain't no women a'tall in the camp. Ain't allowed," the man with the broken glasses told Stone. "We hafta go on down to the Palace when we want some."

"Yeah. Suzy's an old friend of mine."

At once, the tension surrounding their conversation lessened.

"Well, now, stranger, any friend of Sweet Sue's is sure as hell welcome up here. She's a real woman, that's for sure. She knows how to make a man feel good." He grinned and shook his head, apparently recalling past romantic interludes at the Palace. "Name's Buck Snodgrass," he said, proffering his hand.

Stone shook the man's hand, but he kept his other hand close to his gun. "Stone Kincaid."

Behind the marred lenses, Buck's amiable expression turned wary. His gaze darted down to the other end of the makeshift counter, and Stone tensed as a hush settled over anyone close enough to have heard his name. Several men stepped hastily away from him, but one man remained unmoving, his right hand resting on the base of a whiskey bottle.

Alert with the sixth sense he'd developed in Andersonville, Stone waited. He had never before laid eyes on the man, but there was a mean look about his pointed, fox-sharp features. When he uncoiled and pushed back his coat, an ivory-handled, strapped-down gun was revealed, slung low on his hip.

Shifting slightly so his own weapon was ready, Stone waited patiently for him to make the first move.

"Unusual name, Stone Kincaid," the man said in a deceptively quiet voice.

"My mother liked it."

"Don't suppose too many men would have that name hung on him, though."

"Unlikely."

"A man killed my partner over in Omaha a couple of months back," the gunslinger said very low. "Cut him up real bad with a bullwhip. People around there said his name was Stone Kincaid, too. I've been asking 'round for the bastard. Now I'm wonderin' if you just might be him."

"You've got the wrong man—" Stone began, but before he could finish, the man made a move for his gun.

Stone was faster. Before the man could pull the trigger, Stone had drawn and fired, the bullet striking the man's gun hand and sending his fancy pistol spinning across the floor. The gunslinger fell heavily against the bar, supporting his bleeding fingers with his other hand. The spectators pressed farther back against the walls. Everyone watched Stone.

"Like I said, you've got the wrong man. I didn't kill anybody in Omaha. And I don't want to kill

anybody here. The name of the man who killed
your partner is Emerson Clan. I'm after him, too,
for going by my name."

The gunslinger held up his good hand as if to
ward off further trouble, then bent to retrieve his
revolver before he threaded his way past the whis-
pering onlookers and out the door.

Stone glanced around to make sure no one else
wanted to use his back for a target, then ordered
more whiskey. A hubbub of voices filled the room
at once, and the saloon quickly returned to normal.
Stone was given all the privacy he wanted, and he
pretended to concentrate on his drink as he surreptitiously watched the people around him. They
were as tough and hard as men could get, and he
wasn't stupid enough to trust any of them.

If Windsor made the mistake of walking into such
a place, God help her. But apparently she hadn't,
or she'd be the talk of the place. Where the hell
was she? Unless she and the kid had taken his ad-
vice and headed back to the Osage village. Vaguely,
he remembered confronting her in the bathhouse,
and an even dimmer recollection of holding her
down on the bed came back to him, all very fuzzy
and indistinct. Again he cursed himself for getting
drunk.

The idea of them taking off on their own didn't
set well with him, not at all, and he couldn't believe they would just leave without a word, not
after all the trouble they'd had in tracking him
down. Besides, Windsor was as hell-bent to find
Clan as he was. She had to be somewhere in the
camp. There wasn't any other settlement for miles
around. He would just have to search the place.
There was a bunkhouse for the miners, a stable for
the freight horses, and a cookhouse and ware-
house. An Indian with a half-shaved head and a
weird girl with a monkey couldn't be that hard to
locate in an all-male mining camp. He would find

them first; then he would search out the man who knew Clan.

After dropping a couple of coins on the bar, he eased toward the door, trying not to cause undue attention. Gunmen bested in a confrontation had a tendency to want to put a bullet in your head. He'd have to be careful.

Outside, the night was black as a grave, but the sleet had turned to snow and the wind had died down, allowing the snow to drift earthward in soft white spirals. He stood still for a moment, drawing his Colt when he sensed a presence behind him.

"Follow Chen-Shu, please," came a heavily accented whisper.

Stone relaxed when he saw that the speaker was an old, white-haired Chinaman with a long thin beard. Chen-Shu hurried away, his hands tucked inside the folds of his long Oriental-style coat. Suspicious, Stone followed slowly at first, then picked up his pace when he realized the coolie might be leading him to Windsor.

A few doors down from the Staghead, the old man disappeared into the stable that housed the dray wagons and beasts of burden. Stone followed him, more cautious now, his gun still in his hand. He breathed a sigh of relief and quickly reholstered the pistol when he saw Jun-li sitting atop one of the stall rails. The Chinaman had disappeared as mysteriously as he had appeared.

"Windsor? Where are you? I know you're in here," Stone demanded softly, searching the darkness beyond the lamp hanging by the door.

"I am here." Windsor stepped into view at the far end of the center aisle.

Stone frowned. "Why the devil did you come up here by yourself? Is the kid with you?"

"Sun-On-Wings here." The boy appeared in the shadows just behind her.

Glad to see them safe, but also angry with them,

Stone strode quickly down the straw-covered floor. "Well? Answer me! Why'd you go off without me?"

"Because the gods do not help a man who loses opportunity," was Windsor's low reply, uttered with a look of censorious disdain.

"What the hell's that supposed to mean?"

Windsor's gaze was one of unwavering disapproval. "You were intent upon using the black-haired woman's flesh and muddling your head with spirits. You were useless in our quest, so instead of lying senseless in our beds, we came here to find a man who can lead us to the Evil One."

Stone felt a flush rising in his face, burning and embarrassing. Her calm rebuke was well taken, and he knew it. She was right. He had behaved like a fool.

"The Old One often said that drunkenness does not produce faults," she continued with mild condemnation, "it discovers them, for time does not change manners, it uncovers them."

Stone took a moment to digest that scrap of philosophy, and decided she was insulting him again. "All right, I admit it. I shouldn't have had so much to drink. I'm sorry. I don't usually get drunk like that. But you still shouldn't have come up here by yourself. It's dangerous for a woman alone."

"I am not alone. I am with Sun-On-Wings and Jun-li."

"It's dangerous for them, too, dammit!"

Stone's explosion of anger fled abruptly as he heard what sounded like a low, smothered groan. "What's that?"

"Yellow-Haired-Warrior-Woman and Sun-On-Wings capture white man," the Osage answered, looking down at the floor of the stall beside him.

Warily, Stone stepped closer and stared down at a burly man with a bushy red beard lying upon his back on the floor. His wrists were tied to one rail, his ankles to another. A strip of black cloth bound his mouth. His eyes were bulging, and he was making muffled, terrified sounds behind the gag.

Fists braced on his hips, Stone scowled at Windsor. "Windsor, you can't keep grabbing people and tying them up like this. It's going to get you in trouble. Who the devil is he, anyway?"

"He is the man who spoke of the Evil One. Chen-Shu told us he was the one, so we brought him here so he might answer our questions."

"And hog-tying him hand and foot was really necessary?"

"He did not wish to come with us."

Their captive squirmed against his bindings, his eyes imploring Stone to help him. Stone squatted beside him. "Can you tell me anything about a man named Emerson Clan?"

The man bobbed his head up and down with a good deal of anxiety. His eyes darted fearfully at Windsor, then over to Sun-On-Wings.

Stone pulled the cloth off his mouth. The man swiped his tongue out to wet his dry lips.

"Who is she?" he managed hoarsely. "She came out of nowhere, and the next thing I knew, I woke up here, trussed up like a pig."

"Yeah. She has a bad habit of doing this," Stone muttered, giving Windsor a sour look. "Tell me what you know about Clan."

"I'm not sure where he is now, I swear. When I was with him, he was hiding out in San Francisco, but I don't know where he is now."

"Where in San Francisco?"

"I don't know, I tell you! Clan'll kill me if he finds out I told you this much! He'll cut me up with that god-awful whip of his! He's a devil when he's crossed—you don't know him!"

"I know him better than you do. But right now, you'd better be more worried about what my two friends here have in store for you. The kid there wouldn't mind taking another scalp to hang on his lodge pole."

"I'm telling the truth, I swear to God I am. He was heading up a gang, a bunch of cutthroat bandits who robbed gold shipments and anybody else who got in their way. I rode with them a while, but I couldn't stomach the way he tortured people. God, Clan would kill men for looking at him wrong. I seen plenty of killin', I fought against the Rebs in the war, but I ain't used to that kind of cold-blooded murder."

Windsor dropped to her knees and turned the man's head around to face her. "Were you with him when he used his whip on a Chinese priest named Hung-pin?"

"No! No, I swear I didn't have nothing to do with it! Clan did it, though, I heard him braggin' 'bout it, more than once, too. He kept sayin' he flayed the slant-eyes until he looked like a skinned rabbit. Them's his exact words, I swear."

Stone watched Windsor's face drain to a paler shade, and he laid his hand on her shoulder. She sat back on her heels, staring silently down at the man. Suddenly angry to think Clan was still killing and maiming people, Stone grabbed the man's lapels and jerked his torso up off the ground.

"Damn you, tell me where he is!"

"I swear I don't know! You gotta believe me! The law's after him now in San Francisco, so he's on the run!"

"You've got to have some idea. Tell me, or you're a dead man."

"I don't know, I tell you! I was scairt of him, too, and the boys in his gang are devils, every one! I was afeard I'd get a blade in my back if I hung around, so I headed east. I didn't have nothin' to do with killin' the Chinaman!"

"Somebody's got to know where he's gone. Give us a name. Someone who might have seen him."

"I don't know—"

Stone put his hands around the man's throat and squeezed.

"There's a woman he keeps sometimes," he choked hoarsely out of his constricted throat. Stone released his grip slightly. "Name's Ruby Red. She works at one of the saloons in Frisco."

"Which one?"

"I don't know the name. It's down on the wharf somewheres. I don't know nothin' else, I swear on my mother's life—except he's mean, real mean, and he likes to hurt people."

"Yeah, I know," Stone said as he got to his feet. "Cut him loose, Sun-On-Wings. He's told us everything he knows."

The Indian went down on one knee and drew out his long-bladed hunting knife. The captive's eyes bulged fearfully, but the boy quickly sliced through the cords. The man rolled away and fell twice in his rush out the stable door.

"We must find this Ruby Red woman," Windsor said, "and she will lead us to Clan."

"Maybe. Maybe not. The first thing we'll have to do is get to California."

"And you will take us with you?"

Stone was silent. Even when he spoke, his answer was reluctant. "I'll think about it."

"We can be of much help. You will see."

Windsor picked up a blanket and wrapped it around herself, then settled down in one corner of the stall. Sun-On-Wings did the same, not far from her. Stone sat down and leaned against the wall, but he laid one of his revolvers atop his knee, just in case the man they had just terrorized came back with some friends.

"You are tired," Windsor told him. "You may sleep without worry. Jun-li will watch for us."

She closed her eyes, obviously trusting the capuchin as a sentry, and Stone swiveled his regard to where the monkey hung upside down by his long tail from the rafter just above his mistress. The creature peered back at Stone, his small black eyes shining beneath the black fur that grew like a widow's peak above his white face. Stone leaned his head back, but even after Windsor and Sun-On-Wings slept without worry, he kept a vigilant eye on the stable entrance, not yet ready to place his life in the hands of a damned trained monkey.

12

Windsor sat cross-legged, watching Sun-On-Wings partake of his breakfast. Chen-Shu was the bunkhouse cook, and he'd had no trouble smuggling the food left over from the miners' table into the stable for them. Ever since she had arrived in America, however, she had found the food unappetizing, especially the morning meal—fried eggs, potatoes, and greasy salt pork. Boiled rice and oujay tea were her usual fare and all she required to appease her hunger pangs.

"Yellow-Haired-Warrior-Woman not eat," Sun-On-Wings observed, wiping the back of his hand across his mouth. The young Osage warrior certainly had no aversion to white man's food, she thought. The scratched tin plate on the ground in front of him was already scraped clean.

"I need little food," she answered, noticing the way he was looking at her portions. "Here," she offered, handing her plate to him. "Waste is not good."

Sun-On-Wings looked pleased. Jun-li sat on his shoulder, and he fed the monkey a piece of bread, then ate the rest with his fingers. He was not yet ready for the use of the fork—she did not like it either, much preferring to use the chopsticks she carried in her black bag. With both hands, Windsor lifted her own small porcelain cup, savoring the warm, fragrant tea she had brewed over the lantern flame. Each time she drank, she felt transported back to China, in mind and in spirit.

It had been good for her to find Chen-Shu so unexpectedly and to speak with him in the ancient tongue of the Old One. He, too, had been eager to hear of China, especially Shanghai, the city of his birth. He had come to the Ringnard with a gang of Chinese workers to lay track, but when they had moved on, he had remained to prepare meals for the miners.

She shifted her gaze to the stable door, which Chen-Shu had unintentionally left ajar. The sun had risen, hurting the eyes with its dazzling reflection off the pristine snow. The storm had blown itself away, and the day would soon grow warm enough for them to set out on their journey.

She wondered when Stone Kincaid would come back. He had risen early and ordered them both to stay hidden in the stable. He had been particularly adamant about Sun-On-Wings keeping out of sight.

Windsor glanced at the young Indian. His eye was still purple and swollen. Anger rose swiftly, gripping her inside and out. The two big men had hit him because he was a red man. America was no different, though the Old One had taught her about the officials who had founded the United States and their declaration that all men were created equal. She had thought such a place would be a wonderful land in which to live. But it was not. Stone Kincaid was right. The miners would not like having Sun-On-Wings among them. They would persecute him.

The stable door creaked, and Windsor rose swiftly to her feet, ready to protect herself and Sun-On-Wings. Stone Kincaid appeared, his broad shoulders blocking out the sun. His great size never failed to astonish her. In comparison to the men of China, who were so slight of stature, he seemed almost a giant.

"I've decided to take you both along with me," he said, his tone brusque and impersonal, "but you're going to have to do exactly what I say, understand? As long as you tag along with me, I'm the boss."

"If you lead us well, we will follow well."

"You damn well better follow well." Stone reinforced his words with a hard look as he pulled the door shut behind him. "I found some clothes for you in the company store. They probably won't fit, but you'll have to make do."

"No wear white man's clothes," Sun-On-Wings decreed, rising. He crossed his arms in an arrogant stance, obviously proud of his fringed leggings and laced buckskin shirt.

"Oh, yes, you will. Or you'll be lynched before we get anywhere close to San Francisco."

"What is this lynched?" Windsor asked, unfamiliar with the word.

"Hung by the neck on a rope until dead," Stone answered curtly, thrusting a shirt and a pair of trousers into the boy's hands. "And, kid, you're going to have to shave off that scalp lock. People in the cities will gun you down if you don't. And get rid of those feathers in your hair. If you're going with me, you'll have to start looking like a white man."

Sun-On-Wings' chest puffed out as if he were mightily offended. "No cut hair. No rid feathers."

"Dammit, you aren't with the Osage now. You're with the whites, and they've already beaten you up once. It'll happen again as long as you wear buckskins. Now, either you act like a white man and do what I say, or you go back to your village and act like an Indian, because I don't have the time or the inclination to bail you out of trouble every time I turn around."

Sun-On-Wings looked askance at him. "What bail out?"

"Oh, for God's sake, just do what I say, will you?"

Windsor put a comforting hand on Sun-On-Wings' back. "The priests of my temple wear shaved heads. It is a sign of their humility. It will be so for you as well, my friend."

Sun-On-Wings did not look convinced. "No cut hair even for Yellow-Haired-Warrior-Woman—"

"And quit using Indian names!" Stone muttered, interrupting him. "Call me Stone and call her Windsor!"

Still frowning, Stone thrust a parcel into Windsor's hands. "And around mining towns like this where men have to travel for miles to have a woman, you need to dress like a man. If you don't, you'll draw too much attention, and I'll be the one who'll have to fight for your honor."

"I will fight for my own honor."

At her quiet statement, Stone stared at her for a moment; then his expression softened. When he spoke, the underlying anger and annoyance in his voice were gone.

"I know you will, Windsor. And I respect you for it. But I don't want you or the kid to get hurt. This is my country and my people, and I know how they think. All I'm asking is for you to trust me and let me make the decisions."

"Then I will trust you."

Her immediate acquiescence seemed to surprise him, but he said nothing else, instead moving to the coffeepot Chen-Shu had left. Windsor watched him pour a cup of the strong black brew; then she glanced at Sun-On-Wings. A stubborn scowl creased his face.

"Brave warrior. Hair sign of honor."

"You will be honorable with your hair or without it, will you not?"

Sun-On-Wings considered her question and nodded. He touched his scalp lock, then shook his head. "No cut hair. Wear white man's headdress." He took the brown felt hat that Stone had provided for him and jammed it down so far on his head that the wide brim nearly touched his eyebrows.

"Hurry it up," Stone growled, tossing the remnants of his coffee onto the ground. "I want to get out of here before something else goes wrong."

Windsor obeyed, slipping her arms into the big red flannel shirt Stone had given her. The fabric felt warm and soft, and she stepped quickly into the brown wool pants, leaving on her black silk tunic and trousers beneath the larger clothes. The heavy coat of navy blue wool was bulky and uncomfortable, but it would keep her warm on the journey down the mountain. Once she had it buttoned, she tucked her long blond braid beneath a brown hat similar to the ones Sun-On-Wings and Stone Kincaid wore. She didn't mind if people thought she was a man. She would get more respect if they did.

Although snow still lay deep on the ground, the sun had melted some of it, making travel easier. Stone knew if they followed the tracks long enough they were likely to reach a manned depot. He hoped the one his own crew had built alongside the trestle over Yellow Canyon was still in operation. Sweet Sue hadn't been able to tell him if it was. The Cheyenne had burned the trestle several months before, and all the expresses had been rerouted through sidetracks.

Glancing over his shoulder at his traveling companions, he frowned and shook his head. They both had put their new outfits on atop their own clothes, and both looked absolutely ridiculous. But if he kept his mouth shut and his hat on, Sun-On-Wings would pass for a white man, even if he had stuck his two white eagle feathers in the hatband and had a monkey sitting on his shoulder.

Windsor, on the other hand, was too damn beautiful to ever be mistaken for a boy. Even with her blond hair tucked out of sight, her soft white skin and long golden lashes gave her away. Feeling low, his guts all twisted up, he didn't look at her again. He just didn't know what to do with her anymore. He wanted her so much his body ached with the need to touch her, but he had a bad feeling concerning her, too. She was going to get hurt or killed if she persisted in going along with him. He felt it in his bones. But she was determined to follow him, come hell or high water.

Worse, he wasn't sure how long he could keep fighting off his desire to make love to her. God, he'd never been a lustful man; there had been too many beautiful women around who were willing to provide what he wanted. But his hunger for Windsor went far beyond mere lust—he was obsessed with her and dangerously near the point where he'd do anything to have her. He had already lost control once and made a fool of himself. What the hell was he going to do?

His only choice, he supposed, was to put up with both of them until they reached San Francisco. Then Windsor and the kid would be on their own. It would be easier to give them the slip in the city, and he could telegraph Gray for money and let him know he was all right. But getting there was still the problem. He just hoped they could catch an express west without too much trouble.

Hell, he thought, even if they did manage to catch a train, it would probably be blown up by Indians or held up by outlaws. Or both, the way his luck had been running. After all he had been through, he was surprised he was still alive.

For most of the day, they picked their way down the slippery, ice-coated trail that ran parallel to the railway bed. In several areas the Indians had been at work, prying up tracks or burning bridges. No wonder Silverville was so cut off from the rest of the country. It would take months for the construction crews to rebuild the trestles.

Forging on, Stone forced his mind to go blank, determined to reach the refueling station that used to lie at the fork of Wilson Creek. He didn't want to spend a night out in the cold where the Cheyenne could spot their campfire and where he'd have to listen to Sun-On-Wings serenade Windsor with his damned courting flute. The boy could talk all he wanted about becoming a Chinese priest, but the adoring looks he continually cast in Windsor's direction told Stone a different tale. The kid was in love with her, all right. Enough to leave his people, and go wherever she led him. Stone knew how that felt. He'd follow her to China and back to get what he wanted. Sexual frustration was a new experience for him, and he hated it. And with each passing day, it was getting worse instead of better.

Near dusk, Stone drew up his horse, relieved to see a building in the distance. The creek running beside it shone in the setting sun like a silver ribbon, and he was elated when he saw a wisp of black smoke drifting from the chimney.

"It looks like we're finally going to have some good luck for a change," he called back to Windsor, then urged his horse onward.

Not long after, he dismounted at the front of the depot. Before he could tie his reins to the post, the front door swung open, and he found himself looking into the double barrels of a shotgun.

"Hold it right there, mister."

Stone held it right there. He raised his hands.

"We don't want trouble. We just need some help. We've been stranded out here since our train was ambushed by the Pawnee a couple of months ago."

"Then why you got that Injun with you?" the voice growled suspiciously.

So much for Sun-On-Wings' disguise, Stone thought. "He's a friend. He's all right, you have my word."

"What's that he's got ridin' on his back?"

"It's a monkey, but it's tame," Stone answered, feeling stupid giving such an answer. "None of us wants to cause you any trouble."

"All Injuns is trouble. You ain't been 'round here much if you don't know that yet. So git. I ain't trustin' no Injun-lover in my place."

"Look, my name is Stone Kincaid. My family owns the Kincaid Railway Company out of Chicago. Surely you've heard of it. If you can get a telegraph through to Chicago, I can prove everything I say."

The gun lowered a degree. "Stone Kincaid, you say? I got an inquiry about that feller a month or so back. If you're him, seems your family's lookin' for you. I reckon if they's a reward out for findin' you, I oughta get it."

Relieved, Stone nodded. "That's right. I'll see that it's worth your while to help us."

"Then I reckon you can come on in."

The door opened to reveal a short, wiry man of about forty. His face was heavily lined and covered with deep pock scars, but he grinned, revealing long white teeth as Stone followed him inside with Windsor and Sun-On-Wings on his heels.

"Sorry for holdin' the gun on you," the stationmaster was saying, "but you don't live long out here in the mountains if you ain't real careful-like. The depot man afore me—he got done in by drifters and left outside for the buzzards to pick. They didn't find him for near a month. The name's Robinson, Mr. Kincaid."

The man held out his hand, and Stone shook it. It felt greasy. "We certainly appreciate your hospitality, Mr. Robinson. We've been up at Silverville and the Ringnard Mine."

"At Sweet Sue's, I reckon. Boy, ain't she some woman?"

"Yes, she is," Stone said, glancing at Windsor.

"You hungry?" Robinson asked. "I got some black beans and corn pone cooked up back there on the stove."

"Yeah. We all could use a bite to eat, if you have plenty. When's the next express coming through?"

"Don't rightly know." The man paused as he dipped up a ladle of beans and dumped it on a plate that looked none too clean. "Supposed to be one in the morning, but with the Injuns cuttin' up the lines and pryin' off the rails, we don't run true to schedule no more."

"Is it a Kincaid express?"

"Nope, it's running outta St. Louie."

"I don't have any cash, but I can telegraph for some as soon as—"

"I have much gold."

At Windsor's surprising revelation, Stone turned to look at her. She stepped forth and pulled a small black silk pouch from inside her clothing. She spilled the contents onto the scarred table, the heavy coins clattering loudly against the wood surface.

"I'll be danged. You's a girl, ain't you? I can tell by your voice." The man grinned as if proud of himself.

"She's a nun," Stone said quickly, aware of the way Robinson's eyes were now intently surveying the front of Windsor's body. "Where'd you get all that money?" he asked her.

"My mother gave it to me."

"Your mother? I didn't know you had a mother."

Robinson snorted out a chortle. "Near everybody has a mother at one time 'nother, I reckon."

Stone ignored him, more interested in hearing Windsor's reply.

"She is in San Francisco. Are the coins enough to buy tickets to go there?" she asked Robinson.

"You told me you were an orphan and that you were raised by priests!" Stone accused.

"Why, little lady, that there's enough gold to buy out half of St. Louie," Robinson answered.

"That is good," Windsor said, nodding at the stationmaster. "Then I would like to purchase three tickets. I will carry Jun-li in my bamboo case."

"No ride in belly of iron horse," Sun-On-Wings decreed from behind them.

"Why didn't you tell me you had a mother in San Francisco?" Stone demanded furiously. "Who is she?"

"You did not ask me, Stone Kincaid. She will welcome us into her household." Windsor then turned to address the worried Indian. "You will have to ride the train if you wish to accompany us. There is no other way."

"No ride in belly of smoking beast. Bad medicine."

"Then you'll have to get back to your village the best way you can," Stone snapped, his temper getting the best of him again.

"You must think long and hard through the night, Sun-On-Wings," Windsor said soothingly. "This is a great decision you must make. If you board the iron horse, you cannot return easily to your people, for it will take us far away."

"You're gonna hafta pay for the beans, too," Robinson chimed in suddenly, greedily eyeing Windsor's cache.

"Take all the gold pieces you wish," Windsor told him generously. "I have no need of money."

"Wait a minute," Stone intervened at once, stopping Robinson's hand as he reached for the small fortune lying on the table. Stone picked up one coin and tossed it to the stationmaster. "That's more than enough to pay for our fare and the beans."

Disappointed, the man wiped his nose with his forearm, then finished dipping out their supper. Stone carried his plate to the corner where Windsor and Sun-On-Wings had taken places at a rickety table. While he ate, he watched Robinson. The gold that Windsor had spilled out with such naive disregard was enough to provide a whole lifetime of luxury for the grubby, keen-eyed depot man. Plenty enough to kill three strangers for. Stone sighed, well aware he wouldn't get much sleep that night, either.

13

The high and barren hills of San Francisco were wrapped in the eerie fog that drifted nightly into the city to muffle the cold, deserted streets. As he left the Ferry House at the foot of Market Street, Stone peered through the creeping mist that swirled along the ground. He hadn't been to California in three years, and now that he had finally arrived, he found it difficult to believe the trip from Chicago had taken him nearly two months.

Exhausted from lack of sleep and constant hardship, all he wanted was a bed, a soft one with clean sheets. After a good night's rest, he would be ready to proceed. Windsor Richmond, on the other hand, looked and acted as fresh as a newly sprouted daisy blossom. She never seemed to tire or grow weary, even though she had spent most of the week on the train performing her monotonous, droning incantations while he had sat and watched her, all the while struggling desperately inside himself to keep his hands off her.

As for Sun-On-Wings, once they had finally persuaded him to venture up the iron steps and into the passenger car, he had shown a lively interest in everything he laid eyes on, from the black silk tassels on the window shades to the brass cuspidors beside each seat. At the moment, the kid was even more absorbed in the wonders of downtown San Francisco as he stared awestricken at the lamplight casting a yellow glow in the fog high above his head.

"The Concord Hotel is just up Market Street. It's late. We better stay there tonight," Stone suggested, not wanting to waste any time.

"No. We must go to the household of my mother. Sun-On-Wings will be welcome there. Come, I will show you the way."

Before Stone could object, Windsor hurried off down a dark sidewalk, Jun-li in the bamboo case slung over her back, her rapid pace disrupting the damp mists along the ground. Sun-On-Wings followed without hesitation, and Stone brought up the rear, beginning to wonder about Windsor's family. Lord, what kind of mother would a girl like Windsor have? Certainly not any run-of-the-mill lady, he thought. More likely she would be something novel, like a circus juggler or a gypsy fortune-teller.

His curiosity grew as Windsor led them down Market to the point where it forked into California Street, then traveled west a block or so. Before they reached Powell Street, she turned north on a road that rose on a steep incline. Nob Hill, he thought, an area he had heard was fast becoming one of the most exclusive in the city. Due to the late hour, many of the elaborate brick homes were dark, but the tall stone walls and ornate, iron-spiked gates bespoke wealth and power.

Whoever Windsor's mother was, she obviously resided in the most prestigious part of San Francisco, one equal to Lincoln Avenue in Chicago, where his own family had their palatial home. Or perhaps Windsor had lost her bearings in the murky haze obliterating the street markers and house numbers. He would be surprised indeed if she turned out to have a socially prominent relative in the city. Unless her mother was a servant in one of the houses, he realized suddenly. That would certainly be the most reasonable explanation.

"There. That is the house of my mother."

His expression dubious, Stone eyed the four-story, red brick mansion. At the higher elevation, the mists had dissipated enough for him to make out the Italianate facade with its impressive portico, six bay windows, and fancy gabled roofline.

"You're telling me that your mother lives up there in that house?"

"Yes. I do not understand. Your voice sounds as if you do not believe me."

"Who the hell is she? The Queen of Sheba?"

Windsor looked at him as if she thought he was very strange. "No. My mother is not a queen. Her name is Amelia Richmond Cox."

"Cox?" Stone furrowed his brow, trying to place the name. It suddenly dawned on him who her mother must be. "Not the Cox family who owns all the gold mines?"

"Yes. Do you know her?"

"I've heard of the family." Stone's brother, Gray, had once been interested in forming a partnership with Cox Mines when rail lines had first reached San Francisco. The deal hadn't worked out, but Stone remembered reading the report that had summarized the Cox holdings. The figures estimating their wealth had been mind-boggling.

"Aren't we showing up unannounced a little late?" Stone asked Windsor as they passed beneath the ornate scrolled pillars and stopped in front of an eight-foot-high front door of intricately designed stained glass. A huge Christmas wreath made of fir boughs and red ribbons decorated the entrance. Good God, Stone thought, he had forgotten all about Christmas. He wasn't even sure what day it was.

"My mother will wish to receive us despite the hour."

Windsor turned the doorbell key, which initiated a shrill ring inside the house. After many minutes had passed with no answer, she knocked loudly and rattled the door handle. Finally, a flickering light appeared dimly behind the thick crimson-and-gold panes. When the portal was opened, a young Chinese boy squinted sleepily at them, holding out a chimneyed oil lamp to light their faces.

Windsor smiled. "It is Windsor, Ning-Ying. I have returned."

Ning-Ying beamed when he heard her voice, laughing and performing a quick bow from the waist. "Enter, please. We have waited long for you."

Windsor bowed in turn. "Thank you, Ning-Ying. These are my new friends. This is Sun-On-Wings. He is a great Osage warrior."

Pleased at her complimentary description, Sun-On-Wings nodded, then bent in a newly learned Chinese bow.

"And this is Stone Kincaid, the man I wished to kill."

Stone wasn't nearly as thrilled with his introduction, but the Chinese boy bowed to him with every bit as much courtesy.

"Ning-Ying? Did I hear someone knocking at the door?"

Stone lifted his gaze to the massive mahogany staircase that rose at right angles at the rear of the spacious entry hall. A small woman stood at the corner landing, leaning over the glossy carved banister and clutching her black quilted wrapper together at the throat.

Windsor was the one who answered. "Mother,

do not be alarmed. It is I. Your daughter, Windsor.''

The woman moved around the newel-post and into the light cast by a gold gas lamp affixed to the wall. Even in the glow of the dim jets, Stone could ascertain both relief and joy written across the woman's face as she gazed down at her child. Amelia Richmond Cox loved her daughter very much, he knew that at once, and she was not as old as Stone had expected her to be, most likely somewhere in her late thirties. Stone could readily see where Windsor had inherited her delicate, patrician features. Amelia was a beauty, too.

As she moved down the stairs, she appeared graceful and elegant, though now her face was composed, making it more difficult for Stone to read her emotions.

"I'm very glad you have come home safely, Windsor," she said in a cultured, low-pitched voice. "Ning-Ying and I were beginning to worry about you."

"I am sorry if I caused you concern. As you can see, I am well."

At once, Stone noticed the stiff formality between the two women. Both of them acted extremely uncomfortable with each other. Why?

"Stone Kincaid and Sun-On-Wings are strangers here. They have nowhere to stay in the city," Windsor was saying now. "I beg you to extend an invitation to them. Both have come to my aid when I needed their help."

"Then, of course, they are more than welcome in my home." Amelia Richmond Cox inclined her head graciously in Stone's direction. Her eyes lingered an extra moment on Sun-On-Wings, but Stone could detect no scorn or distaste in her expression. Another short silence ensued, as if the two women were endeavoring to think of something else to say to each other.

"Are you hungry?" Amelia asked a moment later. "I'm sure Ning-Ying could find something good in the pantry. And perhaps while he prepares it, we could sit down together and you could tell me about your journey."

"We are very tired," Windsor replied, effectively curtailing her mother's idea.

"Of course. I understand. Come, I will show your friends to the guest rooms." Amelia smiled slightly, obviously unsure of how to deal with her daughter. Again Stone contemplated the strangeness of their strained behavior.

"I have a surprise for you, Windsor, a Christmas present," Amelia announced with a hopeful look. "I realize Christmas was several days ago, but I'd be pleased if you'd let me give it to you now."

"Of course, Mother. Thank you."

"Please follow me. And, Ning-Ying, don't forget to bolt the door."

Amelia led them up the steps, which were covered with a wide runner of black-and-gold Persian carpet, to the second-floor corridor, then up a narrower stair to the third story. At the top, Windsor's mother stood back and let her guests precede her. As Stone stepped through the doorway behind Windsor, he paused and stared in openmouthed disbelief.

The wide corridor stretching out before him could just as well have been a royal receiving hall of the Imperial Palace inside the Forbidden City of Peking. Every inch was hung with shimmering panels of the finest silk—crimson, gold, black—all embroidered with beautiful Oriental scenes. Shiny black-lacquered tables set with gold handles, their tops etched with Chinese symbols, lined the walls, placed among low divans with gold-and-black silk cushions. Through the nearest bedchamber door, he could see a gigantic ebony bed atop a draped dais, the canopy of flowing scarlet silk grand enough for an empress.

"Are you pleased, Windsor? Ning-Ying helped me with the decor. Everything came straight from China."

Amelia Cox's question sounded so eager and vulnerable that Stone almost felt sorry for her. He glanced at Windsor to gauge her reaction to the magnificence surrounding them. As far as he could tell, Windsor seemed even more astonished by the lavishness of the decoration than he was. And Sun-On-Wings' eyes nearly bugged out of his head.

In answer to her mother's question, Windsor put her palms together and bowed respectfully to Amelia. "I am most grateful."

The barest flicker of disappointment flitted across Amelia Cox's face, but she quickly hid her reaction by turning to Stone.

"There are several extra bedchambers on this floor, Mr. Kincaid, as well as a few on the second floor. You and Mr. Wings are welcome to whichever ones you wish."

Without a hint of a smile, Sun-On-Wings nodded, but Stone had an irresistible urge to laugh at the way she had addressed the Indian.

"Sun-On-Wings am most grateful," the Osage said solemnly.

Another awkward pause ensued as Mrs. Cox watched her daughter. Windsor remained silent.

"Well, then, I know all of you must be tired. I'll leave you now so that you can get some rest. The bedchambers are prepared, and the fireplaces are readied as well, in case you should become chilly during the night. We are certainly pleased to have you here. We've been waiting anxiously for Windsor to return."

"Thank you very much, Mrs. Cox," Stone answered politely, "and I apologize for barging in on you so late."

"Please don't concern yourself with that. You're most welcome. I'm just happy Windsor's safe at home again. I'll see you again at breakfast, I hope. Good night."

She hesitated, as if debating whether or not she should embrace her daughter; then she apparently decided against it and took her leave. After her mother had gone, Windsor moved into the luxurious bedchamber Stone had noticed earlier.

Stone and Sun-On-Wings followed her, watching her walk across the deep plush carpet to the enormous bed. She ran her fingertips lightly over the lustrous red silk coverlet embroidered with flying dragons and Chinese dancers.

"My mother doesn't know me very well. That is the reason she thought I would like this."

"She seems very eager to please you," Stone commented, his admiring gaze circling the flamboyant room.

"She need hang no silken draperies to please me."

Their gazes locked, but Sun-On-Wings could not hide his fascination with the vivid colors and fine, shiny fabrics. He reached up to finger the material covering the wall.

"What this made of? Smooth as beaver pelt."

"It's called silk," Stone answered.

"What creature come from?"

"Worms."

Sun-On-Wings' eyes narrowed, and he leaned forward and examined the material closer. "Take big worm make this," he said, shaking his head. "Worm big as buffalo."

"I'll explain it tomorrow, kid," Stone said, grinning. "Right now, let's get some sleep. Tomorrow I'll go down to the wharf and see if I can find Clan's woman." He gave Windsor a warning frown. "And I'm going alone. You hear me, Windsor? You're to stay here with your mother."

"I must come."

"Dammit, I said no. You'll only complicate things."

"If I remain here, will you give me your word of honor that you will not go after Clan without me?"

Stone hesitated, but he finally nodded. "I'll come back here first."

"Then I will trust you. Sun-On-Wings and I will wait."

Much relieved, Stone sighed, massaging his tired eyes. After so many weeks of struggling just to survive, he could no longer ignore the weariness that weighed so heavily upon him. He had to get some shut-eye.

"C'mon, kid, we'll take two rooms down the hall."

Minutes later, he left the Osage youth examining the contents of a second lush Chinese den, the walls and carpet of which were resplendent in vibrant hues of dark blue and gold. And when he entered his own bedchamber at the back of the house, he found yet another magnificent room, this one hung with silk panels of ebony and silver.

Tired to the bone, he unbuckled his holsters and hung them on the bedpost of the massive bamboo bed; then he pulled off his boots and lay back on the soft mattress, not bothering to undress further. He stared up at the woven tapestry of the canopy, admiring the fastidious needlework depicting blue mountains ringed with fluffy white clouds. A pagoda could be seen above a sapphire-colored lake, and just before he closed his eyes, he wondererd if it could be the Temple of the Blue Mountain, where Windsor Richmond had grown into such a beautiful, fascinating, infuriating enigma.

He drifted into sleep still hungry for her, his

imagination rampant with the pleasures she could give him if only she would curl her small body up against him, her arms wrapped tight around him, her soft pink lips opening beneath his mouth.

14

Stone was up early the next morning. Ning-Ying brought him hot water, and he took time to bathe leisurely and shave before venturing out of his sumptuous Chinese den. He paused before the open door of Sun-On-Wings' room and discovered that the young Osage had disregarded the soft bed and chosen instead to sleep on the floor.

A short distance down the hall, he passed Windsor's room and heard the sound that was now very familiar to him—the low drone of her chant.

As he descended the stairs, Stone shook his head. If Windsor was deep in her self-induced trance, he was glad. He didn't want her tagging along. Eager to be away before her inner wisdom instructed her to follow him, he hurried down a second flight of steps to the main floor. He had almost reached the front door when Amelia Cox slid back the white double doors that led into the dining parlor.

"Good morning, Mr. Kincaid. I do hope you'll join me for breakfast. I would really enjoy talking with you about my daughter."

Stone hesitated. Lingering over a meal with Windsor's mother was the last thing he wanted to

156

do. But she looked so hopeful and had invited him so graciously that he found it difficult to decline her invitation. And he had to admit that he was curious about Windsor's past. Her strange relationship with her mother was particularly intriguing.

"I'd like that very much, Mrs. Cox. Thank you."

Following the elegant lady into the dining room, he was impressed anew by her home. The dimensions alone were stunning. He was well accustomed to wealth and all its luxurious trappings. The Kincaid estate in Chicago, where Gray and Tyler lived, was large and elaborate, but it was clear that Amelia Cox had spent enormous amounts of time and money filling her home with the finest imported porcelain from the Orient and furniture crafted in the far reaches of the world. The table was a masterpiece itself, hand-carved of Chinese teak with twenty matching chairs cushioned in plush crimson velvet.

"Please sit here beside me, Mr. Kincaid, so we can talk. I never could understand why my husband wanted such a large, impersonal table." She smiled, and Stone realized her eyes were very much like Windsor's, although perhaps a shade lighter. "Actually, I prefer dining in the kitchen with Ning-Ying. Would you care for coffee or tea?"

"Coffee, please."

Stone sat down in the chair beside hers, which stood at the head of the table. Ning-Ying came forward with a large silver coffee server, and no one spoke as he poured the steaming brew into delicate blue-and-white cups painted with marvelously intricate portraits of Chinese gardens.

"Windsor prefers tea, a special kind called oujay. I had to look long and hard, but I finally ordered it all the way from Shanghai. As you can imagine, I sent for enough to last her a very long time." She murmured a polite thank-you to the servant as she took the cup and saucer Ning-Ying handed to her.

"My daughter grew up in China, you know. Or did she mention that to you?"

"Actually, she said she was an orphan. I must say I was surprised a few days ago when she told me she had a mother."

"I can imagine you would be."

"I'm afraid I still don't quite understand your relationship," he added, wanting her to elaborate further. Pain creased faint lines across Amelia's smooth brow, and Stone again noted her similarity to Windsor. He had seen the exact same frown displayed on her daughter's face. Amelia continued to look down and remained silent as Ning-Ying served them from a large platter of buckwheat pancakes and honey-smoked ham. After the Chinaman had departed the room, Amelia looked up at Stone.

"After I left last night, did Windsor say if she liked what I had done to her apartments?"

Stone glanced down himself, wondering if Amelia had the slightest inkling that Windsor would be much more comfortable in the austerity of a monk's cell than in the elaborate room she'd gone to such expense to provide for her. He tried to conceive of a diplomatic reply.

"She loves all things Chinese," he answered, endeavoring not to sound evasive.

"Did she tell you what happened to us all those years ago in China?"

"No. All I know is that she was raised by some kind of priests in a place called the Temple of the Blue Mountain."

Amelia settled back in her chair. Her sigh was long and deep.

"Windsor's father was a Methodist minister named Jason Richmond. We were so young when we married, and he wanted so desperately to save the world. It was his mission in life. He was a dear man, and I was hopelessly in love with him and his ideals.'' She shook her head, as if remembering. ''When he decided to go to China and talked about his mission with such glowing eyes and fervent words, I was enthralled. I was only sixteen then, and so very naive. I'm afraid the idea of becoming a missionary in a foreign land sounded incredibly romantic at that age.''

She smiled faintly. ''I'm sure you can imagine my shock when I got to China and saw the customs there firsthand. I found Chinese beliefs so heathen and uncivilized that I was simply appalled. Especially the way they treated their poor women. As long as I live on this earth, I'll never, ever forget how horrified I was the first time I heard a poor little girl crying in agony because her parents had her feet broken and bound tight so that they could not grow. Dainty feet are a sign of femininity there, you see. Have you ever been to China, Mr. Kincaid?''

Stone shook his head. ''No, but I realize the culture is very different from ours.''

''Yes. They called us the barbarians.'' She took a moment to stir her tea. ''I never got used to that, either. I hated it there, especially after Windsor was born. I couldn't bear to think of her growing up in a place where women were forced to deform their feet, and where newborn girls were thrown out into the street to die just because they were females. I myself picked up half-starved infants and took them to Western orphanages, more times than I like to remember.'' She shuddered slightly. ''Yes, my greatest fear was for Windsor to grow up in China, and that's exactly what happened to her. Ironic, don't you think?''

Amelia looked so terribly sad for a moment that Stone felt the need to comfort her. He gentled his voice. ''What exactly did happen to Windsor, Mrs. Cox?''

Amelia bit her lip, then rose and moved away

from Stone and stared out the front window. Keeping her back to him, she fixed her eyes on the street.

"In the beginning Jason was too intent on his work to listen to my fears. So we stayed. Windsor was born there, and we remained for nearly a decade before I could persuade him to take us home. All that time we lived apart from the Chinese and associated mainly with the Europeans, but there were very few of us. In all that time Jason managed to make true converts out of only a handful of Chinese."

Her voice changed pitch slightly, and her shoulders tensed. "Windsor was ten years old when we finally left. We took a riverboat down the Yangtze River. I'll never forget how beautiful it was, so wide and swift with hundreds of junks with their graceful sails, and even more of the small, covered boats that the peasants used to take their produce to market. We were to go to Peking, then on to the nearest seaport."

She put her hand to her throat as she continued. "We never made it. One night while our boat was anchored, a thunderstorm swept down on us. It was so sudden and swift, and the winds so high, that we overturned before we knew what was happening. Jason managed to get us out from belowdecks, but Windsor was swept out of my reach. I never saw either one of them again." She stopped, her throat clogging. "For years I couldn't speak of that night without going to pieces."

"What happened to you?"

"I managed to cling to a piece of the boat, and when I awoke the next morning, I had washed up on a dirty beach. Several Chinese fishermen were trying to revive me."

"What about Jason?"

"They found his body several days later, miles downriver. There was no trace of Windsor. I waited and searched for three months, praying and hoping, and I went into such a deep despair afterward that I couldn't function. Some British friends of ours sent me home and promised to keep looking for her. I thought she was dead, I truly did. If I'd had any hope at all, I could never have left her there alone.''

Her voice broke again. ''If I'd known she was alive, growing up in some cold, godforsaken place where she couldn't even understand the language, I would have gone mad. She's my only child, Mr. Kincaid. Even years later, when I met William Cox and married him, I never stopped grieving for my beautiful blond-haired girl. Then William died, too, and I was left with all of this.'' She carelessly swept her arm to encompass the spacious house. ''And still I had no one to love.''

''How did you find out Windsor was still alive?''

''The friends from England I mentioned before wrote to me last year and told me they'd heard rumors of a white girl living in an isolated monastery in the mountains.'' Amelia suddenly turned, her eyes studying Stone. ''You know, Mr. Kincaid, it's very strange. But the moment I read that letter, I knew that the girl was Windsor. I knew it here.'' She touched her breast. ''My heart told me it was her, and I was so filled with joy that I couldn't say a word.''

''Did you go there?''

''No. I wrote to my friends and told them to find this girl and tell her about me. I sent money for her to come home to me, if that's what she wanted. I knew I could not force her to love me, not after all these years.''

''You were wise to let her make the decision on her own.''

''Apparently so, because she did come to me. But it took her six months to decide whether or not to make the trip. She told me later that it was her good friend Hung-pin who persuaded her to come here. I've tried very hard to treat her like a daughter and show her how much I love her, but she's been so strange and reserved. Most of the time she looks at me as if I'm the barbarian. In her eyes, I guess I am."

"I imagine it'll take time for the two of you to get to know each other. But it'll happen someday. If it makes you feel any better, I find her hard to understand, too."

"I'm terrified she'll go back to China, Mr. Kincaid, and then I'll never see her again."

"Believe me, Mrs. Cox, she won't go anywhere until she finds the man who killed her friend Hung-pin."

"That poor young man died in such a horrible way. And he was one of the kindest, gentlest men I have ever met."

Amelia returned to the table and took her seat beside Stone. "When she left here in November, soon after Hung-pin died, she didn't even tell me where she was going. But I had a feeling she was searching for his murderer. She took his death hard, but she had a peculiar expression on her face, tranquil yet so filled with determination, I feared for her."

"Yeah, I know that look."

"Tell me, Mr. Kincaid, how did you meet my daughter?"

Stone grinned, wondering what she would think if he told her the truth. But he didn't want to upset her any more than she already was. "Let's just say our paths crossed because I'm after the same man she is. He's killed before. Some friends of mine died because of him."

"I'm very sorry to hear that."

"I'll get him."

Amelia suddenly reached out and put her hand over his, where it lay on the arm of his chair.

"Windsor seems to consider you her good friend, Mr. Kincaid; that's why I've told you all of this. Do you think you can help me persuade her to stay here in America? I am so frightened that I'll lose her again. And this time if she goes away, it'll be forever, I know it will."

"She'll have to make that decision herself, Mrs. Cox. Neither one of us can force her to care about us."

A faint look of surprise registered on Mrs. Cox's features. Her eyes searched his face. "Could it be that you love her, too?"

"I care what happens to her. She saved my life once," Stone answered carefully. But even as he did, he realized with some alarm that it was more than that. Lord, he hoped he wasn't stupid enough to be falling in love with Windsor Richmond. Nope, that wasn't it, he told himself firmly; he just felt the strongest physical attraction to her that he had ever experienced before. Nevertheless, the idea of never seeing her again didn't sit well with him. And the ramifications of that admission were frightening to contemplate. Abruptly, he pushed back his chair.

"If you'll excuse me, Mrs. Cox, I do have some important business to take care of. I'd really appreciate it if you'd do me a favor and try to keep Windsor and the Indian kid here with you, if you possibly can. Tell them I'll be back later on tonight and not to try to find me."

"Of course, Mr. Kincaid, I'd love nothing better than to spend the entire day with my daughter."

"Then I'll see you this evening."

"Good-bye, Mr. Kincaid."

Stone took himself away from the dining parlor with a good bit of haste, not in the least certain that Mrs. Cox could keep her daughter from following him, not if Windsor got it in her head to go.

15

Near noonday when the sun shone directly overhead, Windsor sat by herself on a low stone wall dividing the private garden from her mother's coach house. Sun-On-Wings and Ning-Ying stood a few yards away, practicing their marksmanship with the handcrafted bows Windsor and Hung-pin had brought with them from China.

Windsor wasn't surprised that the two boys had taken a liking to each other. They appeared to be close in age, though the Indian was much bigger and stronger. At the moment, Sun-On-Wings was exhibiting his impressive prowess at archery as best he could with Jun-li clinging to his shoulder, chattering and grabbing his arrows.

Stone Kincaid had not returned. According to Ning-Ying, he had risen early, breakfasted with her mother, then ridden away on a horse borrowed from the stable. He had gone alone to find the woman called Ruby Red, and Windsor was afraid he would not return. Her feelings for him were burgeoning with each passing day. No longer was her desire to find Hung-pin's murderer the mainstay of her thoughts. Her eyes longed to gaze upon Stone Kincaid; her body wanted to press close against him; her heart cried out with loneliness now that he had gone away from her.

Windsor's breaths grew shallow and rapid from just such thoughts, and she realized she was unprepared to handle these devastating new sentiments. Physical desire was a powerful force, but she had never expected to be afflicted with it.

Beholding the rear facade of the great house, she swept her gaze over the myriad of windows and wondered in which room her mother dwelt. Throughout the morning, Windsor had avoided the prospect of a private audience with Amelia Cox. Her disrespect for her parent was wrong—guilt struck her as she remembered the Old One's words: "Respect for one's parents is the highest of the duties of civil life"—but she could not help but feel the strain between them when they tried to speak together, each word dragged out with stiff awkwardness.

Although she still recalled bits and pieces of her childhood—primarily hazy glimpses of her parents strolling through the rooms of their whitewashed cottage on the outskirts of a Chinese village that Windsor could no longer name—she felt no blood kinship with her only living relative. Windsor considered herself as much Chinese as if she had been born with the yellow skin and slanted eyes of her friends. Her mother could never understand that.

On the other hand, Amelia seemed a wise woman in the ways of the Western world. She ran an immense household with many servants. She had been married to two different men. She had borne a child. Perhaps she could advise Windsor on the inexplicable needs that had taken control of her body since she had met Stone Kincaid.

"I must speak with my mother, Sun-On-Wings," she called, impulsively hopeful that her mother could help her understand her dilemma. "Please bring Jun-li inside when you finish with your practice.''

The Indian nodded, but he kept his eyes on Ning-Ying's red scarf, which had been tied around the trunk of a slender cypress tree to act as their target.

Windsor ran lightly up the wide steps that led to the rear gallery, past two huge copper urns overrun with trailing ivy, then through the back door of the entrance hall. She walked toward the front of the house, checking inside each room for her mother. Two maids were busily removing the garlands of evergreen that had been wound through the mahogany banisters. Both women paused in their work to curtsy, and Windsor pressed her palms together and bowed her head in a respectful response.

''I seek my mother.''

The older servant, a stocky, ruddy-cheeked woman whom Windsor's mother called Myrtle, pointed her finger toward the formal parlor. ''She be in the company room workin' with the tree, Miss Windsor.''

Windsor thanked her and crossed the black-and-white tiles to the front chamber. Her mother stood beside a round marble-topped table on which there was usually displayed a large green fern with thick, waving fronds. Now, however, a four-foot cedar tree had taken its place. While Windsor watched, Amelia stepped atop a footstool and removed a silver star from the topmost branch. As she climbed down, she glimpsed her daughter in the oval mirror suspended over the mantel.

''Windsor!'' she said, turning quickly with a smile. ''Please come in! Would you like to help me take down the tree? You used to love to help with the decorations when you were little.''

For a fleeting instant, Windsor's memory revisited a tiny kitchen adorned with a similar evergreen tree. She saw herself enclosed in her father's sturdy arms, heard her mother laugh merrily as she leaned forward to place a white paper star atop the highest branch. But now, a dozen years later, she could not even remember what religious significance the tree had. An aching sense of loss pervaded her heart, making her spirit dip with weariness.

"I will watch you, my mother," she offered instead.

A pained expression flitted across her mother's face. "Of course, I'd like that. I'm always glad when we can spend time together."

Feeling uncomfortable with the woman who had given her life, Windsor chose a spot by the hearth and sat down on the floor in her usual cross-legged position.

Windsor watched as her mother lifted a string of red cranberries from the branches and laid them on the table. She could not help but think that bringing a tree inside the house was a very strange ritual. Again she wondered what it could possibly signify. Perhaps a reverence for nature, she decided, but if that were the case, why would they sever the tree's trunk and allow it to wither?

"I like your new friends, Windsor," Amelia remarked casually when the silence grew to an embarrassing length. "Mr. Kincaid and I had a nice chat this morning before he left."

Windsor's interest sharpened. "Did he tell you where he was going?"

Her mother paused, carefully cupping a delicate crystal angel in her hands. "He said he had to see someone."

Windsor waited eagerly for her mother to elaborate, but Amelia busied herself instead with untying tiny silver bells from the swaying boughs. Windsor was finally forced to verbalize her greatest fear. "He *is* coming back here, isn't he?"

"Why, I believe so. Did you expect him not to?"

"I am not sure what he will do."

Amelia's dark blue eyes turned to study her, and while Windsor watched, her mother's gaze suddenly registered understanding. She put down the tray of decorations she had been holding.

"You care very much for this man, don't you, my dear?"

Windsor hesitated, feeling very humiliated at having to discuss Stone Kincaid with her mother, though she had sought her out expressly for that purpose.

"I do not know for sure," she admitted softly, "but I fear I do."

Her conscience-stricken admission brought a smile to her mother's lips, and Amelia moved across the floor toward her. To Windsor's shock, her elegant American mother lifted her stiff, rustling gown of maroon velvet and sat down cross-legged opposite Windsor.

"He is a very handsome man."

At her mother's remark, Windsor blushed hotly and stared at her folded hands, unable to meet Amelia's knowing eyes.

"There is nothing in that to be ashamed about, child," her mother said gently. "Bestowing your love upon another is a precious gift, especially if you are loved in return by that person."

Windsor raised troubled eyes. "But I have pledged to forsake such earthly desires. And I do not understand all that I feel. Such intense longings have never plagued me before. It only happens when Stone Kincaid looks at me or puts his hands on me. Then I tremble and burn from inside my skin, and I crave more, and I want to press myself against him." She stopped, nervously moistening her lips. "Surely this cannot be good."

Her mother gave a rueful laugh, then shook her head. "Oh, Windsor, it is good if a man and a woman love each other. I felt that very same way when your father touched me. There is nothing wrong with having such feelings. It is a wonderful part of being in love."

"But I have vowed to renounce any physical gratification."

At Windsor's distressed revelation, Amelia's manner became more serious. "And was this vow made before God, such as the one taken by the nuns of the Catholic faith, or to the Old One, of whom you speak with such fondness?"

"My pledge was to neither Master Ju nor the gods. I made it to myself so that I could more readily attain enlightenment."

"Then you must be true to yourself. You will have to search your heart and decide which course your life will follow—one of religious devotion or one in which you are a wife and mother. Both can give you great joy and happiness, but only you can decide which you will choose."

Windsor's breast rose and fell with a resigned sigh. Her mother's words were true. She reached out and grasped her hand. "Thank you, my mother."

Tears welled to glitter in Amelia's eyes. "I'm just so glad you came to me for this talk," she murmured, retrieving a white lace handkerchief from her full sleeve. She dabbed the corners of her eyes. "I never wanted to leave you behind in China. I hope you know that."

Her long-suppressed guilt began to tumble out faster as she continued in an anxious rush. "I thought you drowned in the river, or I swear I would never have given up the search for you. Please, Windsor, you must believe me. I loved you and your father more than anything in this world. I never would have left you there alone if I'd thought there was any hope of finding you alive. I die inside every time I think of you the way you were then, so little and innocent, all alone with the Chinamen who took you in. You weren't mistreated by them, were you?"

Her mother's face was so stricken with remorse that Windsor was startled. She hastily reassured her. "I do not blame you. I did not suffer but was well treated by the priests. They taught me much and with wisdom and kindness."

"Oh, I thank God for that. If you had been abused or hurt in any way, I don't think I could bear it!"

Her mother dissolved into a fit of quiet weeping, hiding her face inside her open palms, and as Windsor put her arm around Amelia's heaving shoulders, she felt compassion for her suffering. Deep inside her heart, the childhood love she had once felt for her parent began to stir again, awakening feelings that had lain cold and dormant for so many years of separation. Perhaps when enough time had passed, she and her mother could be a family again, she thought, her heart full of hope, because until that moment she had never considered that such an eventuality could come to pass.

On the wharf overlooking San Francisco harbor, Stone flipped his horse's reins through a hitching ring and parted the swinging doors of the White Albatross Tavern. A hundred or more saloons hugged the waterfront, all similar in construction and clientele, and he had visited nearly all of them since he had departed the Cox mansion early that morning. But he had turned up no trace of the mysterious woman named Ruby Red. Hell, how many girls could there be with a name like that?

His mouth tightened with mounting frustration as he threaded his way through the milling rabble and found a table on the outer perimeter of the merrymakers. The place was crowded and rowdy, even in late afternoon. He scanned the barmaids, who hung on the male customers or carried wooden trays loaded with mugs of beer. Eventually one of them sauntered up to his table. She leaned over, ostensibly to wipe the tabletop, and Stone's gaze lowered to the display of heavy white breasts that her bent position and low-cut bodice presented to him.

"Name's Milly. What would you like, mister?" she asked, straightening, and her inviting smile offered him a lot more than a drink.

"Whiskey and a girl named Ruby Red."

Recognition flared behind the woman's eyes, just long enough for Stone to know she was familiar with the name. "Don't know nobody by that name," she answered, shrugging indifferently. "What d'you want her for?"

"What do you care?"

When she started to move away, Stone grabbed her wrist and held her where she was.

"Hey, mister, let go o' me! I don't know nothin' about her, I tell you!"

"I think you do." Still holding her firmly, Stone divested a twenty-dollar gold piece from his pocket and slid it across the table toward her.

The girl's eyes latched greedily onto the money. She glanced around in a furtive manner, then spoke very low. "Who wants to know? If I tell you, you ain't gonna hurt her, are you?"

"I want to know, and I have no intention of hurting her. I just want to talk to her."

The woman continued to hesitate, frowning and chewing on her lower lip. "Look, she don't never do nothin' to hurt nobody. I don't wanna send no trouble her way."

Stone retrieved a matching coin and placed it beside the first one. The girl snatched them and tucked them between her breasts.

"She does the washin' 'round here. She's out back hangin' up the bed sheets, but don't go and hurt her or nothin', 'cause she's real frail and poorly. You know, jumpy and stuff.''

Stone let go of her. He stood. ''Thanks, Milly. Show me the way.''

Moments later, he was standing on a back stoop that overlooked a small yard enclosed by an unpainted board fence. Long clotheslines ran from one end to the other, the freshly starched bed linens flapping in the brisk sea breeze. For a minute he didn't see the girl where she bent over a cauldron of boiling water. Then he stepped down to the grass and made his way toward her through the hanging sheets. She heard him coming before he reached her and swiveled around, clutching a wet pillowcase, her face twisted with fear.

''Hello,'' he said, surprised by her fright. ''Sorry if I startled you. Milly told me I could find you here.''

As he spoke, Stone examined her face. Her dark complexion and black braided hair hinted of a Mexican heritage, and she was young, probably even younger than Windsor. But her eyes didn't display the tranquil innocence that so attracted him to Windsor. The expression in this girl's chocolate-brown eyes was old and jaded, dulled by God knew what, especially if she had been around Clan much. She had the look of a scared rabbit poised to flee. She hadn't moved a muscle or said a word. She just stared at him, her eyes huge and terrified. He had to be careful with her, very careful.

''Look, there's no need to be afraid. I'm not going to hurt you. I just want to ask you a few questions. My name's Stone Kincaid.''

Stone watched her dark eyes glaze over with stark horror. She started to back away, staring at him as if he were the devil come to claim her soul. He took a few paces in the same direction, afraid she was going to bolt. ''I'm looking for a man named Emerson Clan. Know him?''

Her face went slack, as if her facial muscles had turned to jelly. "Oh, *Dios, Dios,* senor, please don't make me go back to him, please don't, he'll hurt me again. *Por favor,* I beg you, I'll do anything you say."

Her pleading was so heavily accented with Spanish that he had trouble understanding her, but he was more appalled at the way her jaw was trembling. She was on the verge of hysteria. He gentled his voice.

"Hush, now, and listen to me. Don't be afraid. I'm not going to tell Clan anything. He didn't send me here, do you understand that? I'm looking for him, and when I find him, I'm going to kill him."

Stone watched as she wrapped her arms around her shoulders, trying to control her quaking. "He will kill me if I speak with you," she whispered, her voice ragged.

"Not if I kill him first."

Her chest heaved uncontrollably, and she said nothing.

"Is there somewhere we can go to talk?" he suggested, glancing around the yard. "Somewhere private? Do you have a room here?"

Nodding, she pointed a quivering finger to a shack built against the back wall of the saloon.

"We'll go inside where no one can see us. I won't hurt you, I promise."

She backed slowly toward the hut, her eyes never leaving his face. Once inside, Stone examined the tawdry place. Dark and windowless, it had a narrow cot with a washstand beside it. A cracked white bowl holding a pitcher stood atop it, and a broken oil lamp had been set on the floor near a large wicker clothes basket full of laundry.

"I understand you're called Ruby Red. Is that your real name?"

The poor girl pressed herself against the wall as far away from him as she could get. She shook her head in denial. "No, it's not. It's Nina, Nina Nunez. He just liked to call me Ruby Red. I don't even know why, but I hate it! I hate him!" Her voice was shaking so badly he could barely understand her. He had never seen anyone so terrified. "I beg you, *por favor*, go away and leave me alone. Don't take me back. Senor Clan nearly killed me the last time I saw him." She sobbed, an awful, hopeless sound.

Stone sat down on the bed, realizing he was going to have to calm her if he expected to get any information out of her. "You can trust me, Nina. Believe me, I hate that son of a bitch worse than you ever could. He killed some friends of mine, and he tried to kill me. He shot my brother and terrorized my sister-in-law while she was carrying a child. He would have killed her, too, if we hadn't gotten to her when we did."

Nina didn't answer. Her eyes were wide, focused unblinkingly on him.

Stone tried again. "I know he used my name several months ago when he killed a man here in San Francisco, a young Chinese named Hung-pin. He whipped him to death."

Nina crumpled to her knees, rocking back and forth, her chest heaving. "He's so evil," she muttered thickly. "He likes to kill people. He made me watch him whip the Chinaman, over and over with that terrible whip, just because the Chinaman helped me up after Clan slapped me. He smiled and smiled all the time he was doing it. *Dios*, it is so awful the way he can flick the whip with his wrist and make the skin fly off. It was the most horrible thing I've ever seen. When I tried to stop him, he got angry and beat me with the whip handle! See how much he hit me!" She jerked off the black shawl around her shoulders and loosened the drawstring of her top. She swept her hair away so he could see her back. "See! See what he did to me! And he'll do it again if I tell you things about him!''

Horrified, Stone stared at the intersecting marks on her shoulders, purplish weals, still raised and discolored from a ruthless beating.

''Good God, he's an animal,'' Stone muttered, hoarse with rage to think of Clan abusing the frail young woman. ''Is he still in San Francisco, Nina? You have to tell me.''

Nina drew her shawl over her shoulders again, her head moving from side to side. ''No, he'll kill me if I tell you. He will. I can't get away no matter how hard I try. He finds me every time I run away!''

''I'll protect you.''

''You can't! No one can. I'll never be free from him, never.''

Stone stared at her, shocked at her trepidation, but he understood her dread of the man. Clan had that effect on people, especially his victims.

''I'm a wealthy man, Nina. I can send you far away from here, where he can't find you. You've got to trust me. Tell me where he is, and you'll be free of him.''

''No, no, he'll come for me. I'm tied to him forever.''

Stone frowned. ''I don't understand. I know Clan. If you disappear, he'll move on to another woman. Tell me where he is, please, Nina. Let me get him for doing this to you. Let me get him before he hurts someone else.''

Nina looked at him, her face streaked with tears, her eyes filled with hopelessness. ''He'll come after me, I tell you, no matter where I go or what I do.''

''Why?''

Nina got up and moved to the clothes basket beside the bed. She stooped and picked up something. When she turned around, she was cradling in her arms a blond baby about six months old.

"He'll always come after me," she said softly, tears shining in her eyes, "because I have his son."

16

Her mother was trying very hard, Windsor decided as she watched Amelia, who sat beside her in the dining room. Sun-On-Wings also supped with them. At the moment, he was admiring one of the four ornate silver candelabra that graced the lace-covered table. Twelve white tapers burned in the elaborate holder, with a dozen identical flames reflected in its large mirrored base.

The entire room seemed to gleam and glitter in the flickering light—the heavy silver cutlery, the gold-rimmed, navy blue dishes etched with golden pagodas, and most of all, the long diamond pendants swinging and sparkling at her mother's ears. Windsor was caught by a brief curiosity as to why her American mother thought so many fine, fancy trappings were necessary to merely partake of nourishment.

No doubt Sun-On-Wings thought he was in a wonderland. He had seen something of the white man's world at the Pleasure Palace and aboard the train, but certainly nothing like her mother's extravagant estate. Windsor's lips curved slightly, remembering how she and Hung-pin had stared when they'd first been ushered into the Cox mansion.

Poor Hung-pin, she thought sadly. He had left the pathways of the earth at so young an age. It had been he who had encouraged Windsor to befriend her mother. Hung-pin would be pleased to know the two of them had become closer. But he would not be free to ride the dragon until Emerson Clan had been punished.

"Mr. Wings, you really must try cook's pudding. It's flavored with butterscotch, you know, and it's her very best dessert."

Windsor had to smile at her mother's attempt to civilize the Osage name. Sun-On-Wings sat crosslegged atop one of the tall-backed, red velvet chairs, and she realized that, like herself, he must find the soft-padded furniture useless. But he had been trying to learn the customs of the whites.

"The pudding tastes good, Sun-On-Wings," she urged him. "I know it doesn't look very good, but if you'll try it, you'll find that it tastes sweet."

Sun-On-Wings peered suspiciously at the orange paste swirled decoratively in the silver bowl before him. He reached out and dipped up a portion with his fingers. Windsor heard her mother gasp, but when Sun-On-Wings turned quickly to gaze at his hostess, Amelia managed a faint smile.

"Ning-Ying could dip some for you, if you wish," she suggested hopefully.

"What dip?" Sun-On-Wings asked, licking pudding off his fingers. Looking pleasantly surprised, he finished the first dab and helped himself to more. Smiling, he held out some for Jun-li, who clung to the back of the chair next to him. The capuchin fed with great enthusiasm, then leapt atop the table, grasped Sun-On-Wings' wine goblet, and in the blink of an eye, drained the contents.

"Jun-li like berry juice," Sun-On-Wings noted to Amelia. "Him like pudding, too, good."

"Yes, well, I am so pleased," Amelia answered with distracted graciousness. "Is there anything particular that you'd like cook to prepare for tomorrow's dinner?"

"Buffalo meat good."

Her mother looked so disconcerted by the Indian's suggestion that Windsor laughed. Amelia and Sun-On-Wings both looked at her in surprise.

"I am sorry. It is just so strange that the three of us who are so very different have come together in your house. My mother, you are kind to let us share your table. You must forgive us if we offend your customs. Sun-On-Wings is as new to the world of the white man as I am."

"Don't apologize, my dear. Having you and your friends here is wonderful for me. This house has been too big and empty for one woman alone."

Windsor was ready to answer when she caught a glimpse of Stone Kincaid standing in the doorway. She came to her feet, very glad to see him. Then she saw that he was not alone. He had a woman carrying a baby with him.

"Why, Mr. Kincaid, please do come in and join us," her mother said.

"Thank you, Mrs. Cox," he answered, drawing the woman forward. "This is Nina Nunez."

Windsor stared in dismay at the pretty young girl beside him. Nina said nothing, clutching her infant tightly as if afraid someone would snatch the child from her. Windsor frowned. Stone Kincaid had gone to find Ruby Red, so why would he bring this woman named Nina home with him? Unless she was Stone Kincaid's woman? If that were true, was her child Stone Kincaid's, too? Her unanswered questions set off a terrible churning in the pit of her stomach, and she fought the nausea rising as bitter as bile in the back of her throat. He was holding the woman's arm gently, treating her with much honor and respect.

"I was hoping you might let Nina stay here for a while, Mrs. Cox. She and her baby have nowhere else to go."

Windsor could tell her mother was shocked by the request, but she watched Amelia's good manners come to her rescue.

"Of course, Mr. Kincaid," she answered, glancing briefly at Windsor. "As you know, we have many guest rooms. Would you and Miss Nunez care to join us for dinner?"

"No, she's very tired. I'll show her up and help get her settled, if you don't object. There's no need to bother the servants when they're busy serving dinner."

"Well, if you're sure. But if you should need anything, please feel free to summon Ning-Ying or one of the maids."

"Thank you, ma'am." For the first time, Stone turned to Windsor. "I'll talk to you later about this."

Windsor watched him lead Nina out into the hall. He didn't have to explain. She had been taught the ways of men. He had found a woman to be with him the way Windsor could not be. Her heart was ravaged by sharp, cutting slashes, and she recognized her pain for what it was. She was jealous, she thought in bewildered humiliation. Jealous because Stone Kincaid had taken a concubine.

Even an hour later, when Stone had managed to settle Nina and her son, Carlos, in the bedchamber next to his own, he could barely contain his outrage after having witnessed the abuse the poor girl had received at Clan's hands. Inside his head, over and over again, Stone saw the young girl's disfigured back. A chill ran down his spine. Fourteen years old, taken from her family to be used and abused by nothing less than a monster. Clan was enjoying his whip. First Hung-pin, then Nina, and God only knew how many others had felt its bite.

His face hard and grim, Stone walked down the hall to Windsor's bedchamber. My God, what if Clan got his hands on her? What if the bastard scarred up her soft white flesh the way he had Nina's? The idea terrified Stone, more than anything he could ever remember. Despite all the times Windsor had proved she could take care of herself, he knew that Clan was different from most men, clever as hell and more dangerous than the devil. He had no feelings, no compassion, no scruples. And he would show no mercy just because his victim was a woman. He would wield his bullwhip upon Windsor's smooth flesh as lethally as he would upon a mongrel hound.

Just the thought of Windsor in Emerson Clan's hands made Stone sick to his stomach. If he had any brains, he would find out where Clan was and go after him right now, without a word to Windsor and Sun-On-Wings. If he thought doing that would keep her safe and sound in her mother's house, he wouldn't hesitate. But it wouldn't. Using her calm and methodical methods, she would find out exactly where Stone had gone, and she would follow him there, just as she had done when he'd left the Osage village.

Stone's lips tightened. She would no doubt drag Sun-On-Wings along with her, too, her damned monkey hanging off his shoulder. Stone wished he could lock them both up somewhere so that he wouldn't have to worry about them. As much as he hated to admit it, he had grown fond of them. He shook his head. Who was he trying to fool? He was falling in love with Windsor, dammit, as much as he didn't want to. Even Suzy had seen it coming. And Sun-On-Wings was beginning to grow on him, too. Lately the Indian boy seemed almost like a little brother.

Furious at himself for making everything so damned complicated, he stopped outside Windsor's bedchamber, debating whether or not he should knock. Hell, he'd never even considered taking a wife before; he hadn't had time for any kind of serious relationship, not as determined as he was to catch up to Clan.

Now he had found a woman who made him burn like a tropical fever, and he couldn't have her. Windsor had pledged herself to a spiritual life, and no matter how much he wanted her in his bed, it just wasn't going to happen. And he wouldn't stoop low enough to try to seduce her. Even if he succeeded, Windsor would end up hating him for compromising her principles.

A faint light glowed from the crack beneath the door. She was still awake. He ought to walk away, go back to his room, and forget about talking to her, that's what he ought to do. Instead, mocking his own weakness, he tapped a knuckle against the wood panel and was surprised to find the door ajar.

''Windsor?''

Only one tall candle burned in a copper sconce set at the end of the bed, cloaking most of the silken draperies and luxurious decor in darkness.

''Windsor, may I come in?''

Still she did not answer, so he quietly closed the door. When he neared the bed, he realized that she was sitting cross-legged atop the lush satin bedcover, just barely discernible in the shadowy bed. She no longer wore her black silk tunic and trousers; her body was draped in a beautiful robe of flowing scarlet silk, the sleeves and hem emblazoned with splendid fire-breathing dragons embroidered in shiny golden thread.

Even more unusual, she had unbound her long pigtail, allowing her silken hair to tumble in a soft, shimmering cascade over her shoulders and back. The flickering light rippled bright glints through the golden tresses, making Stone want to bury himself in their depths. He fought his overpowering reaction to her beauty, trembling all over with the desire to slide his fingers through her hair, his whole body awash with tenderness and need. With more willpower than he'd ever imagined he had, he resisted the urge to push her backward, to possess her for as long and as often as he wanted. Instead, he reached out and pushed away the flowing silk bed hangings that kept her face hidden from view.

His body stiffened, shocked to see the tears wetting her cheeks. He had never seen her cry; always before, she had been calm and composed, even in the most dangerous, hair-raising situations. Concerned, he sat down on the edge of the bed, facing her.

"What's wrong, Windsor?"

"Much is wrong." Her whisper was barely audible.

"What is it? Are you ill?"

"I am in pain."

"What kind of pain?" he asked quickly, alarmed. "Do you want me to call a doctor?"

She put her fingers against her cheeks and wiped away her tears. "It is my heart that hurts me, Stone Kincaid. I do not understand my own feelings. My meditation no longer brings me peace. Please, you must help me."

"Of course I will. I'll do anything you want."

Windsor shivered, closing her eyes. She sat very still.

"I think about you every minute of the day," she admitted in a husky murmur, hanging her head until a silky gold curtain veiled her face from Stone's gaze. "I dwell upon how I would feel if you would hold my body against your own, and how it would feel if we coupled together." Swallowing convulsively, she bit her lip. "My mother told me that such thoughts are not shameful, but I feel perhaps they are.''

Her head dipped even lower, as if the weight of the world lay upon it, but Stone's heart soared with hope.

''What you feel is not shameful,'' he told her, rigidly trying to hold his passion in check. He had to touch her, he had to. Gently, he brushed back a lock of her hair as a tear rolled down her cheek. ''It is love.''

''Do I love you? Is that what is wrong with me?''

Stone almost smiled, but he didn't. The moment he had been dreaming about for days and days was finally at hand. He wanted her so desperately. ''When you love someone, their touch gives you pleasure.'' His hand shaking with restraint, he stroked his fingertip lightly along the flawless contour of her soft cheek. ''Do you like it when I do this?'' he whispered, his voice hoarse.

She sighed, her tongue flicking out to moisten her mouth. ''Yes. I've wanted you to touch me many times, but I fight against myself because I have sworn to remain chaste.''

Bitter disappointment swept Stone, and he forced himself to let his hand fall away. ''I won't touch you if it makes you uncomfortable.''

Windsor's gaze remained on her lap. ''I saw you tonight with the woman named Nina. I saw you touch her with gentleness and look at her with tenderness in your eyes, and I knew you had taken her for your woman. That was when my heart felt as if it were breaking apart.''

''Nina?'' Stone said in surprise. ''But I only met her today.'' He gave a soft laugh. ''God, Windsor, you ought to know I haven't wanted any other woman since I first laid eyes on you.''

Windsor's expression remained somber. ''But you wanted Sweet Sue. You held her and kissed her many times. I saw you.''

"I kissed her because I couldn't kiss you. But I still wanted you. That's why I got drunk that night. I knew your vows were sacred to you."

Windsor lifted her sapphire gaze; their eyes locked. "I made no sacred vow. The Old One said that lying with a man would distract me and make deep meditation difficult to attain, so I decided on my own that I should retain my chastity."

A profound stillness descended over Stone. "Are you telling me that all these weeks I've been driving myself crazy trying to keep my hands off you, you were just trying to concentrate better?"

Her face set in misery, Windsor nodded. "But now I know that I must find out for myself what it is that happens between a man and a woman, what makes me want you to hold me and—"

Stone let her go no further. He grabbed her shoulders, his eyes burning. "Dammit, Windsor, all this time I thought you were bound by religious vows—"

He didn't finish. He was far too desperate to taste her lips, to make her his own, now that she was willing. Their mouths forged together, hot, hard, their breathing heavy and labored. Stone was seized by a thundering, mind-numbing brand of desire, a passion he'd never known before, one harnessed and kept at bay for months of waiting, hoping, and denying himself the woman he wanted most in the world.

Nearly out of control, he was like a man possessed, pushed into the depths of a frantically spinning world of pleasure and release. When Windsor moaned and put her arms around his neck the way he had dreamed of her doing for so long, he slid his hands beneath the thick, luxuriant fall of her hair, grasping silken handfuls and pulling her head back so that she had to look at him.

"This is what love is, Windsor," he muttered gruffly, his lips against the graceful arch of her throat where her pulse hammered beneath his mouth. "This is how it feels."

"And I must love you, too, because it feels so wonderful," she whispered, her voice shaky and indistinct.

Stone drew back and smiled, pleased by her quivering response.

"You are so beautiful," he said, his gaze lowering to the front of her robe as he threaded loose the silk sash hiding the rest of her from his hungry eyes. He inched the shimmering fabric over her slender shoulders, and Windsor sat still as it slid off her arms onto the bed, revealing to him the satiny perfection of her body.

"And you are like the great god-warriors of China," she murmured, breathless and trembling as she worked to unfasten the buttons on his shirt. Stone groaned when she smoothed her open palms over the hard, molded contours of his muscles. He slipped an arm around her waist and pulled her tightly to him until her soft breasts were flattened against his naked chest.

"I've wanted you for so damn long." His low words were muffled against her hair. "I've lain awake nights dreaming of holding you like this."

"Kiss my mouth again, Stone Kincaid. I like it when you kiss me."

He laughed softly, exultantly, but his triumph did not last long, so eager was he to show her how good it could be, how much they had denied themselves. He captured her mouth and pressed her backward against the pillows, bracing his elbows on either side of her head, controlling himself by force of will, endeavoring to kiss her slowly, to let her enjoy the soft melding of their lips.

Again and again their lips twisted together, then drew apart, his hands snarled in her hair, until all thoughts were stolen from him and he became like a man dying of thirst, her body the water to quench

the fire flaming inside him. His mouth possessed
her, bringing her alive, moving with greedy abandon from her cheeks to her throat, from the hardened tip of one breast to the other, until she
writhed and moaned beneath him. Stone felt himself swimming in an ocean of sensual bliss, the
need to possess her like a roaring blaze that
scorched his brain and made him unable to think
or speak.

Caught in her own roiling sea of newly awakened desires, Windsor gasped and protested as
Stone suddenly wrenched himself from her, lurching from the bed and throwing off the rest of his
clothes, his eyes burning like blue flames. He is
magnificent, she thought, her breasts rising and
falling with quivering anticipation as he came back
to her like a naked god, falling upon her, entwining his fingers with hers and pinning her arms
against the pillows. She reeled with pure pleasure
as their bodies molded one to the other, marveling
at the feel of him, hard and strong and forceful, his
sun-browned skin warm and smooth as his chest
slid over her naked flesh.

Windsor closed her eyes, a warm tranquility descending and dissolving any doubts lingering inside her. She belonged in his arms as she had never
belonged to anyone else in her life. She arched up
against him, wanting more, wanting to join with
him, wanting to become a very part of his own
existence. He made a muffled sound as he poised
to enter her, and when they did unite, man to
woman, dark to light, yang to yin, she gave herself
to the pain of her surrendered innocence with eager acceptance, pleased by his groans of joy,
pleased that he wanted her as desperately as she
wanted him, pleased that there was a way to express her love for him.

Finally, the pleasure he brought to her overrode
all else, and she forgot to think, could only feel,

quivering with desire and exertion with each slow thrust, until her body exploded with a magnificent fulfillment, bursts of pleasure rocketing through her until she cried out with the sweet wonder of it. Stone groaned from his own passionate release, then held her even tighter, his face buried in her throat, her arms wrapped fiercely around his neck.

Not long after their passion had cooled, Stone awoke to the sound of humming. Smiling, he reached for the warm softness that was Windsor, but she no longer lay snuggled against him. Disappointed, he sat up and looked around. She was seated at the foot of the bed, her limbs folded into the lotus position, her sapphire eyes hidden by long golden lashes, her lovely face serene as she chanted the singsong verse of her sutra.

Stone fought an overpowering desire to reach out and pull her back into his arms. He knew that would be a mistake. Her time of meditation was important to her, so he lay back against the pillows, placing his hands behind his head while he watched her. He could be patient; God knew she was worth waiting for.

His gaze wandered over her face and body; as always he was caught spellbound by her exquisite beauty. Her Chinese robe covered her, but the front had been left untied, providing him with a veiled glimpse of one curving breast. He drank in her loveliness, vividly aware of how sweet she smelled, of how good she had felt locked in his embrace. The mental images he was harboring were enough to make his loins ache with the need for her.

Never in his life had he been so consumed with such passion for a woman. Never had he felt the kind of pleasure Windsor was able to arouse in him. Once she had made her decision, she had shared herself eagerly, wanting all he had to give, giving herself to him without shame or regret.

Suddenly he craved her again, fiercely, wildly, hopelessly. He wanted to press deep into her, bury himself forever in her soft, fragrant flesh. No longer willing to stop himself, he reached out and placed his palm on her knee, then slowly slid it up the inside of her naked thigh.

Windsor's eyes fluttered open. She stared blankly at him for a moment, as if she were not truly awake yet. Then the spark seemed to reenter her eyes as she returned from a faraway, mysterious journey, coming alive once more right before his eyes. She smiled at him, and Stone's heart lurched when she unfolded her legs and came eagerly to lie atop him.

"I missed having you in my arms," he whispered, stroking his palm down the length of her blond hair.

"I had need to search my inner self," she murmured, wrapping both arms around his neck and pressing her lips into his ear.

"And did you?" Stone put his hands on her waist, lifting her until he could nuzzle inside her open robe and caress the base of her throat with his tongue. He smiled when he felt her pulse jump, then accelerate madly beneath his mouth.

"Yes," she breathed, shivering from what his roaming hands were doing to her.

"And?"

"And my heart is happy. I looked deep into my soul where one sees oneself very clearly. We are truly meant to be one, just as I felt from the first moment I looked into your silver-blue eyes." She paused breathlessly to enjoy the moment his mouth closed over the tautened tip of her breast. "But I didn't know it would be as wonderful as this."

Stone stroked her back, their lips mingling gently, softly, then gradually becoming an urgent quest for much more. Passion igniting, he rolled with her, capturing her body beneath him. He

stared down into the dark blue depths of her eyes,
now smoky with desire, and he knew he loved her.
Despite his every intention not to become involved
with her, he had grown to love her more than any
man should let himself love a woman.

Windsor's gaze seemed to draw him, body and
soul, into her spirit. "Make my heart sing with joy,
Stone Kincaid," she whispered, sliding her fingers
down the hard muscles of his chest, pushing him
over onto his back. "Teach me more about this
wondrous thing called love." Stone's breath caught
as she suddenly sat astraddle him, her hair falling
forward over his face as she pressed warm lips into
the hollow of his collarbone.

"You're doing all right at the moment—" he
managed, his voice hoarsening as she leaned forward, teasing him by barely brushing his chest with
her naked breasts.

"A novice at the first attempt, an adept at the
second. The Old One taught that as well—"

"Well, my love, you're proving yourself more
than adept," Stone muttered, pulling her head
down until their lips came together fiercely, possessively, making no other words between them
necessary.

Several hours later, Windsor opened her eyes
and gazed sleepily at the candlestand at the end of
the bed. The long taper had burned nearly to the
base. She lay on her side; Stone Kincaid pressed
close behind her, his right arm beneath her cheek,
the other holding her around the waist. The long,
hard length of him felt nice against her back. She
snuggled deeper into his embrace, wanting even
more intimacy. His fingers, loosely tangled in her
hair, tightened and pulled back her head as his lips
sought the base of her neck.

"I want you again," he mumbled against her

shoulder. "I don't think I'll ever stop wanting you."

Windsor closed her eyes as his hand slid up over her naked flesh to cup her breast. She sighed, her body growing aroused and hot, and she wet her dry lips, trembling as his palm slid downward over the smooth flat plane of her bare stomach, then lower still, fondling her until she pressed against him and moaned with helpless surrender.

Filled with a need that burned like a flame in her core, she turned quickly in the circle of his arms, overwhelmed to think that such intense pleasure could be sustained for so long, time and again, the mere touch of his hand inflaming her body until she lost control of her own desires. Overcome with the need to join with him, to have him inside her, she groaned and pressed her palms against the sides of his face, seeking his mouth in a frenzied attempt to communicate her feelings of wonder.

A similar sound came from deep inside his throat, and he gripped the sides of her head with equal passion, his tongue thrusting into her mouth, then out again, in a courtship dance similar to the one she craved their bodies to share.

"Oh, God, Windsor, I don't think I can ever let go of you again," he said, pushing her onto her back, and Windsor savored the words he uttered so desperately, their limbs entwined, their hearts beating wildly, their bodies joined yet again as they soared into the heavens and rode the dragon of destiny.

The next morning dawned bright and clear. When a bar of sunlight crept through the opened draperies to fall upon Stone's face, he opened his eyes. Windsor was already up, standing in the middle of the room. Still naked, she was practicing the slow, deliberate moves of her fighting skills. He sat up and smiled at her.

"You look very pleased with yourself, Stone Kincaid," she observed, slowly raising one leg, then pivoting and kicking out in slow motion, her arms held in a controlled posture of self-defense.

"No, I'm pleased with *you*," he disagreed, not exactly unaffected by the sight of her nude body performing the sensual movements. Every motion was graceful, lithe, and agile, but he well knew how lethal she could be.

"You had better quit doing that, or I'll have to have you all over again."

"I perform these positions every day for mental and physical strength."

"I'll teach you new positions."

"You already have." She turned, one arm straight out, the other bent, her left knee lifted high in front of her body, giving Stone a view he had once been willing to pay a sultan's ransom to have unveiled.

"I'm warning you, Windsor," he said, already hard with arousal. He rose from the bed. "I think I might want you again, right now."

She laughed, then spun around and performed a graceful kick, but Stone caught her and pulled her against him.

"Come back to bed. It's too early to get up."

"I am not finished with my exercises."

"Yes, you are."

Despite her objection, she turned in his arms, and he took her down on the bed with him, lying atop her and staring down into her smiling face. Again he realized how much he cared for her, with some misgiving as to just how vulnerable that made him. Always before, he had had no one but himself to consider, no one to claim his time or his heart, but now he would always have Windsor to care about and protect.

"Stay here when I go after Clan, Windsor," he whispered, holding her face between his hands so that she would listen. "I want you somewhere safe, where you won't get hurt."

"We are meant to go together. You must know that by now."

Stone shook his head. "Listen to me—"

"If you leave without me, I will follow."

Windsor's eyes looked into his, tranquil and knowing, and Stone sighed in defeat, well aware that she'd do just what she promised. Tenderly, he brushed back a silken lock of hair from her temples, not sure he could leave her anyway.

"If I let you come along, you'll have to promise to do exactly what I say, you hear me? I know Clan better than you do. I know what he's capable of. I make the decisions, is that clear?"

"When two partners are of one mind," she murmured with a sweet smile, "clay is into gold refined."

"Stop spouting your Chinese proverbs, dammit. I want your word on this."

"I will abide by your decisions because I love you."

Stone smiled in triumph. "Now we're getting somewhere."

"I am tired of conversing. I want to make love."

Stone laughed. "You're sure as hell not a novice anymore. What are you trying to do? Wear me out?"

"There is evidence that you are not worn out."

A gasp was torn from Stone as she reached out and proved her point.

"Will every night be like this one, Stone Kincaid?" she asked, smiling up at him. "Is it an acceptable custom to make love so many times?"

Stone gazed down into her eyes, then lowered his mouth to brush her parted lips. "Yeah, every night I spend with you will probably be just like this.''

"That is very good," she murmured, before her whisper was subjugated by the eager warmth of his kiss.

17

From where Sun-On-Wings hunkered down atop the veranda wall at the back of Amelia Cox's home, he had a splendid view of the shining blue waters of San Francisco Bay. His black eyes were riveted on the vast inlet dotted with sailing ships and the great steam-driven vessels that left clouds of smoke hanging over the surface. Low mountains, their barren slopes shadowed to royal blue, rose around the shores, reminding him of his mountain home. Except that the majestic peaks around his village would be white with snow and ice, and the Little Ones would be snug before their lodge fires, wrapped in warm buffalo robes while they listened to the old men recite the legends of their people.

Nostalgic longings swept over him, tightening around his heart like the wet leather strips with which he wrapped his lance to give it strength. He had wanted to leave his people, to travel to Yellow-Haired-Warrior-Woman's land, to witness her strong medicine and wondrous way of fighting. But now he only yearned to return to the quiet village and his relatives of the Sky Clan. He missed his grandfather the most, but he also hungered to see his best friend, Flat-Nose. He missed the excite-

ment of the buffalo hunt and the honor of being
the youngest scout in the war party. He missed the
eerie strains of the Dawn Chant when many voices
echoed out over the clear cold waters of the lake.

Living with the white man was more difficult
than he had expected. He had seen many marvels
in his journey to be a nun. He had bathed in pots
of warm water and slept on high soft racks, but
more than anything else, he was astounded by the
numbers of white men he had seen walking the
land.

Here, in the great village of Yellow-Haired-
Warrior-Woman's mother, his eyes had seen more
people with white skin than he had ever thought
existed. They lived and worked with no hardships
to overcome, no need to gather food or protect their
lands from enemies. Why, had he not witnessed
food being brought along the street in wagons so
that people had only to go outside and barter their
round coins for it! Even now, outside the high wall,
he could hear a woman calling that she had eggs
and milk in her basket for any who needed them!

White-Spotted-Wolf and the other warriors
would never dream of the strength of their greatest
enemy, the white man. Just as Sun-On-Wings had
done, the Little Ones would stare, their tongues
struck dumb, to see the night turned into day by
strange lamps that burned without bear fat and
great stone houses that rose into the sky like the
mighty yellow aspens. The magic of the white man
frightened even him, Sun-On-Wings, a fierce warrior. How could the Little Ones fight such a powerful foe? He should return to the mountains and
warn them of all he had seen, he thought, but he
knew he would not.

More than anything, he wanted to stay near
Yellow-Haired-Warrior-Woman. He longed for her
to love him in the way he loved her. She was so
strange and different from anyone else he had ever

known. But in his heart he knew she cared not for him. Although her tongue told him that she did not wish to have her own man, her eyes followed Arrow-Parts-Hair everywhere he went.

Sun-On-Wings shifted as Jun-li knocked over the bowl of oranges between them. He watched dispassionately as the strange round fruit rolled off the wall and fell to the ground. Despite his own feelings for Yellow-Haired-Warrior-Woman, Sun-On-Wings could not lay blame upon her for wanting the big white warrior. Arrow-Parts-Hair was strong and brave. He had proved his courage many times. He had saved Sun-On-Wings from the claws of the great grizzly.

Last night he had heard Arrow-Parts-Hair pass his room and enter Yellow-Haired-Warrior-Woman's door. All through the night he had listened and waited for him to leave, but he had not. They had been together, even after Grandfather Sun had risen over the distant hills and called Sun-On-Wings to prayer. He felt lonely because he was by himself while his two friends were together.

A slight sound broke into his melancholy thoughts. As he did when stalking elk, he turned only his head to listen. Below him at the turn of the garden trail a girl came into sight. He recognized her as the Mexican woman whom Arrow-Parts-Hair had brought back with him, the one he had called Nina. She carried her baby as she had the night before.

Sun-On-Wings remained motionless as she strolled slowly past below his perch. She did not see him, because she stared at the ground as she walked, as if lost in her own troubles. While he watched, her child began to cry, a thin, muffled wail. Beside him, Jun-li cocked his head with interest, and before Sun-On-Wings could react, the mischievous capuchin had wrapped his tail around a branch and dropped down unexpectedly right in front of the girl. Nina screamed in fright and backed away, clutching her child tightly to her breast.

Wishing to calm her fears, Sun-On-Wings leapt soundlessly to the ground just behind her. "Jun-li no hurt Nina."

Nina swung around, and Sun-On-Wings was startled at the terror so evident in her eyes.

"Don't come any closer!" she cried, her voice high and shrill.

Sun-On-Wings looked at the black revolver that had suddenly appeared in her hand. Where had the white man's weapon come from? Her hand was shaking so much, the barrel waved back and forth, but it was aimed at his stomach. Battle-hardened warrior though he was, Sun-On-Wings did not know what to do when facing an armed white woman with a baby.

"Nina, don't. Put my gun down. He's not going to hurt you."

Sun-On-Wings was very relieved to hear Arrow-Parts-Hair's voice. His words had been uttered very low and soothingly, and Sun-On-Wings stood unmoving, waiting for the fear and indecision to leave the girl's large brown eyes.

"Sun-On-Wings is my friend, Nina." Arrow-Parts-Hair had now moved up beside Sun-On-Wings. "He's an Osage warrior, but he would never hurt you or Carlos. Clan didn't send him here to get you. He's going to help us find Clan."

Sun-On-Wings watched Arrow-Parts-Hair inch closer to the girl, then reach out quickly and take the revolver from her hand. "It's all right, Nina," he said, sliding it into his holster and putting his arm around her shoulders, "I know you took the gun out of my room because you're so scared. But you're safe here. We're all your friends. We want to help you."

Nina didn't answer, hugging her baby close to

her face, shutting her eyes, and making a low moan that sounded like a sick coyote. Nina was very weak and full of fears. Sun-On-Wings felt much pity for her as he followed her and Arrow-Parts-Hair toward the house.

Inside the front parlor, Windsor glanced around to see if anyone was there. When she found herself alone, she fingered one of the fragile white angels lying on the tray of ornaments her mother had left upon the center table. Vaguely, in the murky depths of childhood memories, she recalled another such trinket and how gently she had stroked its gossamer wings with the tip of her finger.

That memory brought another, the way Stone Kincaid had caressed her bare skin, with both his fingers and his lips. She could almost feel the sensations again, could feel herself becoming hot and eager with never-ending chills rippling along her flesh from one end of her body to the other. Her mouth dried as she relived the intimacy they had shared, and she moistened her lips with the tip of her tongue, amazed that the mere thought of Stone Kincaid could bring alive the erotic tingling deep inside her woman's core.

Windsor closed her eyes, desiring to lie down with him again, to have him become a part of her, to feel him press his mouth on hers and whisper tender words. Physical love was a precious, wondrous thing that one wanted to experience over and over again. No wonder the Old One had warned her that it might distract her in her pursuit of higher wisdom.

"Windsor, come and let me introduce you to Nina."

Windsor turned as Stone led the brown-haired girl into the room. Sun-On-Wings followed close behind them, Jun-li riding on his forearm. A blush rose in a dark stain in Windsor's cheeks when

Stone smiled at her. The tickling sensations stirred afresh inside her loins, and she looked away from him and let her attention fall on the Mexican girl.

"Hello, Nina. I am Windsor."

The night before, Windsor had not realized how young Nina was. Probably even younger than Sun-On-Wings. Her eyes were widespread and timid, and Windsor could see the haunted expression that hovered in them. Nina didn't look like the kind of woman Windsor would have expected the Evil One to choose. And she didn't look old enough to have borne a baby.

The girl kept looking from one of them to the other, as if she were scared. Stone led her to a royal-blue-and-white figured wing chair near the fireplace. He motioned Windsor to an identical seat across from her. Windsor sat down, while Sun-On-Wings stood nearby, feet braced apart, arms folded across his chest. The Indian said nothing, but Windsor noticed that he never took his eyes off Nina.

"Nina, I know you don't like to talk about Clan, but we really do have to ask you some questions."

The girl chewed her lip and kept her gaze on the infant on her lap. Windsor looked at Stone, realizing with some alarm that she might have already conceived his child. The thought sobered her, and her eyes settled again on the tiny human being squirming in Nina's arms.

Windsor had never seen a baby at close range. At the temple the youngest disciple was never under ten years of age. Certainly she had never held a small child. Suddenly she wanted to cradle Nina's boy in her arms and see how it felt. But judging by the possessive way Clan's woman clutched her son, Windsor did not think the young woman would allow it.

"What do you want to know?" Nina's English was heavily accented and her manner so fearful that Windsor and Sun-On-Wings exchanged concerned glances.

Once more Windsor wondered why a man like Clan would choose a little girl like Nina to bear his child; she was so young and not even very beautiful. Or perhaps the fact that she was a frightened victim was the very attribute that had attracted so cruel a man to her.

"I'm sorry to put you through this, Nina," Stone said. "I really am. But if we're going to get him, we have to know where he is and what he's doing. Will you help us?"

Windsor doubled her attention, but she could see how tense Stone Kincaid had become. His handsome face was set in tight lines of concentration, his entire body strained forward in anticipation of Nina's reply.

"If you trust us now, you'll never have to suffer at his hands again," Stone added persuasively when she didn't answer. "And Carlos will be safe from him. You don't want Clan to get hold of your son, do you?"

Nina shook her head emphatically. At first Windsor thought she would still remain silent, but finally her words came, low and afraid. "He has returned to Mexico."

"Where in Mexico? Do you know?"

"At a village on the sea called Mazatlán."

Triumph lightened Stone's face, but his eyes remained determined. "What's he doing there, Nina?"

"He is smuggling guns from the Estados Unidos to the *guerrilleros* who fight against the Nacionales of the Juarista government. He was forced to flee after he killed the Chinaman. But he sent word that I am to bring Carlos to him at Mazatlán. He said if I don't, he will come back and kill me. When you came for me yesterday, I thought he had sent you."

Her mouth began to tremble. "He'll do it, too. He'll kill me if I don't go to him soon."

"Where are you supposed to meet him?"

"There's a cantina on the edge of the town, one with a big iron bell hanging out front. He said I was to go there and wait until someone came for me."

"Do you have any idea where he is hiding?"

"High in the sierra where they sell the guns to *guerrilleros.*"

"I've got the bastard now," Stone ground out viciously, rising to his feet as if he had forgotten all about Nina. His face hard and cold, he strode from the room without another word to any of them. He would insist that they leave at once for the place the Evil One had taken as his lair, Windsor thought, and she would go with him to avenge poor Hung-pin. The gods would surely help them to rid the world of one possessing such evil.

Amelia sat in her favorite rocker in the front parlor, observing those around her. Sometimes she couldn't believe the ironies of life. A mere month ago, she had sat in the very same room, hoping and praying for word from Windsor. Now her daughter was home again, along with three of her friends. Granted, Amelia had to admit that she found all of them a bit strange, but she had grown to like them during the fortnight they had been guests in her house.

Stone Kincaid and Windsor shared a tapestry-covered settee across the room. For several hours they had been discussing their impending voyage to Mexico. The two of them were so obviously in love that even Amelia was aware of their feelings. She wondered if they would get married. She blushed to think that they were already living as man and wife under her roof.

Windsor's father would turn over in his grave,

she thought with a guilty conscience, but her own misgivings fled quickly. As she had grown older, she had developed a great deal more tolerance than she'd had in the past. As long as Windsor was happy and safe at home, Amelia would say nothing and do nothing to drive her to return to China. She felt sure her daughter would marry Mr. Kincaid in time, anyway; they were too much in love not to.

Her attention was diverted from her daughter when Sun-On-Wings rose from where he had been sitting cross-legged before the bay window. Amused, Amelia watched as he sauntered nonchalantly toward the basket in which Nina's child was napping. The young Indian was absolutely fascinated with the baby, though Amelia knew he often tried to hide his interest.

Pretending she wasn't looking, Amelia watched surreptitiously as he squatted beside the crib. He glanced around, then pulled one of the white feathers from the brim of his hat. Amelia could see the baby's hands waving over the top of the basket, but when the Indian held the feather closer to the child, a tiny fist darted out and grabbed it. Sun-On-Wings gave a low chuckle, and Amelia smiled.

All of them were so very young, she thought fondly, children themselves, really. Except, of course, for Mr. Kincaid. He was certainly no boy, but a handsome, virile, self-confident man, probably no older than thirty. Windsor had only just turned twenty, and Sun-On-Wings could not be more than sixteen.

And then there was poor, mistreated, abused little Nina. Amelia turned her regard to the girl, who sat staring silently into the flames. Fourteen years old and the mother of a six-month-old infant. Amelia shook her head, filled with pity for the girl. Amelia herself had been only eighteen when she had borne Windsor, but she had been married and in love with her husband.

The baby began to fuss, and Nina started to rise. Before she could, Sun-On-Wings picked up the child.

"Carlos smell bad," he decreed at once.

Amelia had to laugh at the way the boy was holding the soiled baby an arm's length away. "Nina, I was just going upstairs to fetch my embroidery basket. I will be glad to change Carlos's napkin if you'd like me to."

Nina seemed hesitant to accept her offer, but Amelia had noticed before that the young mother didn't like her son to be out of her sight. Who could blame her? Emerson Clan had threatened to take her baby away from her!

"I'll be gone only a minute, and I'll bring him right back," she promised. "Why don't you finish your tea while I'm gone?"

Nina finally gave a reluctant nod, and Amelia crossed the room and wrapped a soft yellow blanket around the child.

"Carlos like Sun-On-Wings' feather," Sun-On-Wings told her. "Him not afraid of Indian."

"Of course he isn't," Amelia answered, presenting the Osage youth with her most reassuring smile. "And why should he be? You are kind and gentle with him, even though you are a fierce warrior."

Sun-On-Wings looked immeasurably pleased by her remark, and Amelia laughed to herself as she carried the child from the room. Yes, she was certainly growing fond of Windsor's new friends. She hoped they wouldn't leave for Mexico for a very long time.

As her mother left the room carrying Nina's baby, Windsor focused on Stone Kincaid again and how stubborn he could be.

"If I dye my hair to brown, I will look enough like Nina to fool the man Clan sends for her. And I can wrap Jun-li in a baby blanket and pretend that he is Carlos. He will lie very still if I command him to do so."

Stone's expression was incredulous. "That is the most absurd idea I've ever heard."

"There is nothing absurd about my plan. You cannot be seen because Clan will recognize you. He is expecting Nina, so I will become Nina."

"I said no, and I mean no."

"To spoil what is good by unreasonableness is like letting off fireworks in the rain," Windsor said with calm censure.

"I'm not being unreasonable. I'm being realistic."

"You are being stubborn."

"Dammit, Windsor, you said you'd let me make the decisions, and I just made one. You're not going to put yourself in that kind of danger. What if the man he sends knows Nina? Clan would have you killed before you got a word out!"

"What other way is there to seek out the hole in which he hides? Who else can lead us to him?"

"There's got to be another way. We'll just have to hide and watch everybody who goes in and out of the cantina until he decides to show up."

"You will not catch him. He is too clever." Nina's remark was uttered quietly, but it brought everyone's attention to her. Even Sun-On-Wings took a seat on the floor near her.

"Nina, don't worry yourself with this," Stone told her gently. "You'll never have to deal with Clan again. I promised you that, and I meant it."

"You have been good to me and my *niño*. I owe you much."

"You told me where Clan is. That's all I wanted from you."

"More than anything in this world, he wants his

son," Nina reminded him. "He has told me many times how much Carlos means to him. He will come after me as long as Carlos is with me. If I go away and hide, no matter how far I go, he will find me and kill me. Then he will have Carlos. I can never let him have Carlos to raise, never. He is too cruel. He will make my son into a devil, too."

Windsor sat down on the arm of Nina's chair and took her hand. "Do not be afraid. You are safe here in my mother's house."

"But what if he comes while all of you are gone to Mexico? What if he sends his men to get me? No one can protect me from them. He wants his son more than anything else in the world."

"Sun-On-Wings protect Nina." The boy's face was very serious.

Nina smiled gratefully at him, but she shook her head. "None of you understands what kind of man he is. I was only twelve when he saw me walking along the road of my village near San Diego, and he stole me away from my family. He does anything he wants, and no one dares to stop him. I ran away from him once, the day I realized I was going to have a baby. I went back home, but he came to my village and killed my mama and papa." Her bottom lip quivered uncontrollably. "He hung them from a tree, right in front of me, then told me that I no longer had any family to go home to. He told me he'd do the same thing to anyone who helped me."

"He has caused you more suffering than anyone should have to bear," said Windsor, "and he must be punished for his crimes."

"That is why I must come with you. I am the one he wants. He will come for me because I have Carlos. But you cannot trick him without me. He is too cunning."

No one said a word for several moments while Stone paced the room. He retraced his steps, frowning. "We just can't risk it, Nina. You might get hurt again. I don't want that to happen."

"I could go with her," Windsor suggested quickly. "I could protect her while we're at the cantina. I could pose as Carlos's nurse."

Stone knelt in front of Nina's chair, gazing into her eyes. "Nina, are you sure? You'll have to come face-to-face with Clan again. Do you think you can do that?"

Nina clasped her hands tightly together. Her lips trembled. "He murdered everyone in my family, in front of my eyes. On that awful day I swore to the Holy Virgin that if I ever found a man who could kill him, I would help him do it, for my mama and my papa. If I do not, if I let you send me far away from here, I would live in fear for the rest of my life. I would be afraid that he would find me and take my son away."

"I think you should leave the baby here with Amelia where he'll be safe."

"No, I cannot leave him. It is Carlos who Clan wants, not me."

Stone picked up her hand and sandwiched it between both of his. "I won't let anything happen to you, Nina. I swear it."

"I only want you to kill him, so he won't hurt people anymore."

"I'll kill him," Stone said with such savage vehemence that no one could disbelieve him. "But we must go to Mazatlán quickly, as soon as I can arrange passage on a ship, or Clan might decide to move on."

Windsor listened as Stone continued to solidify his plans, but a vague uneasiness was beginning to plague her. Nina was so vulnerable and easily frightened. Windsor was not sure she could face Emerson Clan without crumbling into terror. If that happened, they would all be in grave danger.

18

Nearly two weeks after she had agreed to help Stone Kincaid capture Emerson Clan, Nina Nunez found herself aboard a ship bound for Mexico. She sat on the starboard hatch of the *Trinidad*, shielding little Carlos's face from the brisk ocean wind. For two days they had sailed southward down the coast of California, and with each passing hour, she had grown more afraid.

A chill of revulsion undulated like an adder down her spine. In her mind she saw Clan's awful eyes again, so pale blue that they looked almost white. And his long blond hair always smelled like roses because he doused it frequently from the bottle of French cologne he carried in his vest pocket. Oh, *Dios*, she couldn't bear to be near him again! She had seen him do awful things, unspeakably cruel atrocities, since he had taken her from her parents' house nearly two years ago.

She still remembered how frightened she had been when he and three of his terrible men had ridden up to her small rancho outside San Diego. Her papa had offered him water from the well, but when Clan saw Nina on the porch, he threw a gold coin on the ground and demanded to buy her for his woman. He said he wanted a virgin, a girl young and pure enough to bear his son. Her parents refused and tried to protect her, to stop him, but he beat both of them. Eventually, he had killed them. He wasn't human. He was *el diablo* set loose upon the earth.

Her stomach fluttering, she looked down at her son. What if he took Carlos from her? What if he exploded with anger at her child the way he did with her? He could kill a small baby with one blow from his fist. She wanted to flee, to run and hide, but she knew Clan would find her no matter where she went, no matter how long it took him. She could never escape until he was dead. Dread gripped her, and she started to cry, hugging her child close.

"Nina no be afraid."

Nina whipped her head around, dashing her tears away when she saw Sun-On-Wings standing a short distance down the deck. Although the young Indian had been kind to her, she was still a little afraid of him. He seemed to watch her every movement, but he rarely said a word to her. She stared at him, intimidated by his size and the strength so evident in his hard, muscular body. He was almost as tall as Senor Kincaid, his coppery face handsome with high cheekbones and a square chin. His eyes were so black they seemed to shine with reflected light.

"Nina no need cry tears. Sun-On-Wings stay close and no let man hurt Nina and Carlos." Solemn-faced, Sun-On-Wings brought around something he had been hiding behind his back. "Sun-On-Wings make gift for little man."

Touched by his thoughtfulness, Nina smiled uncertainly as she regarded the object he was presenting to her. He held a board of about three feet in length. Covered with fringed rawhide, it had an opening at the top designed to form some sort of pocket. White feathers hung from a sturdy leather strap affixed to the upper end. Nina took it, trying to decide what it was. She had never seen anything quite like it.

"The beads are very pretty," she said, not wanting to hurt his feelings. He had no doubt spent many hours forming the elaborate red-and-black designs decorating the front panel.

"Yellow-Haired-Warrior-Woman's mother give me what I need. Nina like cradleboard?"

"Oh, *sí*, very much. *Gracias*, Sun-On-Wings." Nina had never used the Indian's name before, and the words sounded strange upon her tongue. "How exactly does it work?"

Sun-On-Wings took the contraption from her hands. "Tie little man in here and carry on back. No need hands. No get tired. Give little man to me and me show."

Nina hesitated, not liking to give up Carlos to anyone, but the Indian had shown gentleness in handling her baby during the past weeks. She held Carlos out to him, and Sun-On-Wings took the child with a great show of care. She watched him place the child on its back in the pocket of the board. He wrapped the rawhide bindings around the boy securely, leaving Carlos's head and arms free. The baby waved his hands and gooed happily as Sun-On-Wings held him aloft in his new carrier. "See? Carlos like. Nina like?"

Nina nodded, turning and allowing him to strap the baby upon her back. The cradleboard was comfortable and freed her arms, which ached from holding the weight of the baby all day.

"You are very kind to us," she said, genuinely grateful for the gift.

The young Osage warrior nodded, then trod away on silent footfalls that never gave anyone notice of his approach.

* * *

Belowdecks in the cabin Windsor shared with
Stone Kincaid, Stone rose naked from the bed and
paced the four steps that took him to the small
round porthole. He braced an arm against the wall
and gazed toward the distant coast of Mexico,
barely visible on the eastern horizon.

"It won't be long now," he said tightly. "I'll settle up with Clan, and we can get on with our
lives."

Draped only in her Chinese robe, Windsor sat
up and watched the man she loved. She sighed,
worried about him. His eyes were always afire with
the fury festering deep inside him, and even now,
so soon after their shared moments of intimacy and
love, his long fingers had clenched once more into
tight, hard fists. His anger and tension had become
worse since Nina had told him where Clan was.
He was so totally obsessed with his need for vengeance that he could think of little else. Hatred so
filled him that he had begun to awaken her
throughout the night with his bad dreams and
hoarse yells.

"He who is ruled by anger cannot overcome his
enemies," she told him gently. "You are too full
of anger to pursue the Evil One. You must let me
do the deed for you. My heart is calm, my hand is
steady. You will fail. I will not."

"I won't fail," Stone answered, turning quickly
to look at her. "Clan is as good as dead right now."

"You have never told me what he did to you to
make you burn so with rage. I pursue him because
he killed Hung-pin. He has killed friends of yours,
has he not?"

Stone prowled in agitation, absently twisting the
jade stones on the wrist bracelet she had made for
him, not looking at her. "It's different between us.
I thought he was my friend. We met when we were
assigned a room together at West Point."

"What is this West Point?"

"A military school. God, I was so stupid to ever get involved with him in the first place. I knew he had a mean streak in him from the beginning, but he never did anything bad enough to make me see through the civilized veneer he put on when I was around him. He's too damn clever for that. For some reason, he took a liking to me, and he seemed no different than anyone else at the academy. But, God, I must have been blind not to know he was playing a part. It wasn't until after the war started and we ended up in the same unit that I found out what a bastard he really was."

The planes of Stone's face went rigid, and Windsor realized he found it difficult to speak of his former relationship with Emerson Clan. "Anyway, he betrayed me, all of us, by passing information to the Rebs. Clan was from Alabama, and I would have found no dishonor in him if he had elected to join the South's fight. Instead, he was a goddamn traitor and caused dozens of my men to be killed, including friends from West Point whom both of us knew and liked."

"So you were the one who uncovered his treachery?"

"Damn right. I had the son of a bitch court-martialed and stripped him of rank myself, but we were attacked before we could hang him. We were captured by the Rebels and taken to Andersonville—that's a prison camp down in Georgia."

Stone's jaw tightened, making a angry tic jump in his cheek. "We were treated like animals there, worse than animals. Every day hundreds of men starved and died of exposure. We were crowded by the thousands in that goddamn swamp. But Clan managed to convince them he'd been a Southern spy in our ranks, so he was made a guard. You can probably figure out the rest. He made our lives a living hell. That's why I decided to escape."

He dropped into the straight-backed chair beneath the porthole. His voice went hoarse, and his face was so stricken that Windsor wanted to put her arms around him and comfort him. "He collapsed a tunnel in on us. My two best friends died, suffocated before I could dig them out. I came close to dying myself. That was the day I first swore I'd get him."

For several moments they were both silent; then Windsor crossed the cabin and straddled his lap, facing him. She laid her cheek against the top of his head while she massaged his tight shoulders. "You tremble with anger just in the telling, Stone Kincaid," she murmured. "You are dangerous to yourself and to others when you go into conflict in such a state. You will lose control if filled with such passion."

Stone's arms tightened around her, his hands seeking entry beneath the edge of her red robe, one sliding up her bare spine, the other cupping her hips close against his loins. "There's only one person on this earth who makes me tremble and lose control," he murmured, "and now she's mine."

Windsor's eyes closed as pleasure began to seep through her, melting her bones. She wrapped her arms around his head and held his face pillowed upon her breast. "But I am afraid for you," she whispered. "My heart tells me that danger awaits us in this place called Mazatlán."

"My heart tells me something else," Stone muttered thickly. "That I want you again, as much as I did the first time. God, I don't think I'll ever get my fill of you."

She felt his arousal beneath her as he deftly peeled off her silk garment and tossed it aside. His hands encircled her waist, and she gasped as he lifted her bodily and brought her carefully down upon him. Her sigh a whisper of pleasure, she braced her hands on his broad shoulders and arched her body until the silky softness of her unbound blond tresses swung down her back to brush his knees. She moaned aloud as he suddenly grabbed a handful of her hair and at the same time caught her breast between his lips, sending shock waves of desire raging through her blood.

Stone groaned himself, losing track of time and place and all thoughts of revenge, concentrating solely on Windsor—how she felt in his arms; how she was bending backward, her fingernails biting into the tensed muscles of his upper arms. Slowly, he brought her down upon him again, shutting his eyes and moving his mouth in a thorough exploration of her smooth white flesh, softer and silkier than he would ever have imagined. He treasured her body as a precious gift.

His head rolled back, a muffled sound forced from his throat as Windsor became the aggressor, taking over the cadence of their lovemaking, swaying toward him, lifting her body upward, then down, with unbelievably erotic motions, presenting her breasts for his pleasure as she brought him to the brink of fulfillment, slowly, sensuously, until Stone could stand the sweet torture no longer. He clamped her hips against his loins. He stood, their lips and bodies still joined, and carried her swiftly to the narrow bunk. He took her down with him, his breath ragged now with urgency, pleased by the contented murmurs filling his ears, pleased that she wanted him as desperately as he wanted her. He loved her, he adored her, and nothing would ever change that. Nothing could.

Her arms clasped tightly around his back, Stone let his passion take over, and they moved together, their hearts wild with exertion until the moment they left the earth and all things real, soaring together into the bright vastness of the heavens and trembling beneath the ecstasy of their love, a love

unparalleled, a love that would bind them together
forever.

Following Stone's plan, once the *Trinidad* reached
the port of Mazatlán, Windsor and Nina disembarked from the ship and boarded the freight
wagon. Leaving Stone and Sun-On-Wings behind,
they set off with Carlos toward the scattering of
small buildings hugging the edge of a curving sand
beach.

The weather was warm, and as they lurched
along in the wagon filled with salt pork and bolts
of velvet fabric, Windsor fanned her face. The cli-
mate of Mexico was very different from the cool,
moist days she had spent in her mother's house in
San Francisco. Here, even in late January, the sun
beat down hotly on their heads. She wished she
could take off the black shawl covering her blond
hair and remove the long cotton skirt she had been
forced to don over her silk trousers.

Windsor glanced back, trying to see Stone, who
had remained at the docking point with Sun-On-
Wings. They would follow soon, after dusk fell and
the cloak of night hid their arrival. No one must
see them, or their trap might be discovered. She
would certainly feel better once they arrived in the
town, and perhaps then Nina would be able to calm
her fears.

Nina's eyes continually darted around her,
searching the rutted road in every direction. She
was absolutely terrified. Despite the courage she
had shown thus far and her desire to avenge her
parents' deaths, her fright was beginning to communicate itself to little Carlos, whose usual contented behavior was disintegrating. He cried all the
way into the village.

The driver turned and spoke a few words of
Spanish. Windsor had no idea what he was saying,
but Nina answered him in a shaky voice.

"He said the cantina with the bell is a short way out of town," she whispered. "He asked me if we two women really want to go there alone. He said it is *muy malo*, a bad place."

"Don't be afraid, Nina. I'm right here with you. I know what to do. I won't let anyone hurt you."

Nina nodded, but her face was chalk-white, her mouth set in a thin, strained line. Windsor squeezed her hand. "You must trust me, Nina. I have been trained to fight. I can protect you."

"You don't know him, Windsor. You don't know what he does to people."

Windsor didn't answer, but she was beginning to understand just how evil Emerson Clan really was. Although she had never laid eyes on the man, he had played an important part in her life. He had taken Hung-pin from her, he had filled Stone Kincaid's eyes with fierce hatred, and he had turned Nina into a frightened, timid victim. He was surely a demon released by the gods, and she was determined to rid the world of him. He would die in the name of justice and honor, as well as revenge.

The cantina of the bell was very old, built of ancient adobe bleached white long ago by years of sea winds and torturous sun. The building was long and flat-roofed with tall windows opening onto narrow grilled balconies of iron. The walls were in disrepair, the plaster cracking in triangular patches along the front porch. As the driver pulled up before the doors, Windsor kept a cautious eye on the handful of men loitering around the front steps and guzzling beer from brown glass bottles. Nina gasped, and Windsor looked quickly at her.

"Did you see Clan?" she whispered, watching the ruffians in case one of them made a move toward them. She was not afraid; she could restrain all the men before they could lay a finger on her or Nina.

"No, but one of them rides with Clan. I've seen

him. Oh, God, what if he takes me away with him now, before Stone and Sun-On-Wings get here? What if he makes me give Carlos to him?''

''I will not let that happen. Which one is he?''

''The one with the black mustache that curves down around his mouth and the brown serape around his shoulders. His name is Parker. He was with us in San Francisco.''

As they climbed down from the wagon, Windsor watched the man Nina had described from the corner of her eye. He made no move to approach them, and she was relieved when he mounted a horse hitched at the rail in front of the cantina.

''Hold Carlos where he can see his face, so he will not ask to see him when he comes back for us.''

Nina pulled down the blanket and lifted Carlos, and Parker took a good look at him as he walked his horse past the two women. As they climbed the steps to the front door, Parker urged his horse into a gallop, headed toward the hills looming behind the beachfront.

''He's going to report to Clan,'' Windsor told Nina. ''Come, we need to get ready. Stone Kincaid and Sun-On-Wings will come soon.''

Inside, an old woman led them through a cool dim hallway where a blind man sat in a rickety wooden chair. While Nina spoke to him in her own tongue, Windsor examined the way the house was designed, just in case their plan should go awry. A moment later, they climbed the steps and entered a dingy room facing the rear yard.

While Nina locked the door, Windsor retrieved a small candle from her pocket, lit it, then hurried to the tall louvered doors that led onto the iron balcony. She set the candle on the rail, then peered down through the dusky light. The back of the cantina was dusty and unkempt, with much refuse littering the ground. There was a stable, and a chicken house with dozens of hens scratching and clucking inside a makeshift wire fence. There was no sign of Stone Kincaid or Sun-On-Wings.

"Do you see them? Have they come yet?" Nina asked anxiously.

"No, but they'll see the candle now and come for Carlos, just as we planned."

"Oh, *por Dios*, what if they do not? What if Clan has seen and killed them? He'll kill me for bringing you here!"

Nina's voice grew shrill enough to warn Windsor that the girl was close to hysteria. She went to her at once, gently placing her hand over Nina's mouth.

"Shh, Nina, you cannot do this. What if someone hears you? You have to be brave, for Carlos's sake."

Struggling to control her fears, Nina sat down on the bed, but her eyes remained riveted on the open doors of the balcony. Windsor sat quietly on a bench beside the interior door, where she could intercept intruders and watch the window for Stone. She was afraid Nina would not be able to go through with the eventual meeting with Clan. Even now the poor girl looked ready to collapse.

Outside, the night had darkened to black. When a sound came from the balcony, Windsor rose to her feet, then relaxed when she saw Stone's face appear over the iron rail. With one agile motion, he swung over the top and into the room. Sun-On-Wings followed without a sound.

"Did everything go all right?" Stone whispered to Windsor.

"Yes, but Nina is very afraid. She thought you weren't coming."

Stone knelt beside Nina. "We've been with you the whole time, Nina, watching and waiting. If Clan had made a move, we would have shot him down. You have to remember that. You can't ap-

pear too nervous, or Clan will suspect something.
Do you think he'll come here himself?''

Nina shook her head. "No, he'll wait somewhere safe while he sends someone for me. Now
that he's wanted by the Nacionales in Mexico, he's
very careful.''

"All right, then we'll have to follow you to
wherever he's holed up. And don't worry. We'll
be right behind you all the time.''

Nina nodded, but her chest heaved heavily from
her agitated breathing. "Hurry, *por favor*. Take Carlos out of here, before they come for him.''

Sun-On-Wings went down on one knee beside
her. He removed the cradleboard from where it
hung on his back. "Sun-On-Wings take little man.
Nina no need worry.''

Nina looked disconsolate at the prospect of sending her son away, but she settled the squirming
infant on his back upon the board. Hurriedly, she
strapped him in, then raised anguished eyes to the
Indian. "Take good care of him, Sun-On-Wings.
And you must promise me that you won't let Clan
get him. Never let him have him, no matter what.
Promise me.''

"No worry, Nina. Sun-On-Wings swear to great
Wah-Kon-Dah to take good care of little man.''

"*Gracias*, Sun-On-Wings. He should sleep for a
while now, but if he should cry, just put your face
close to his and hum a little song. He likes that. He
always quiets down when I sing to him.''

Sun-On-Wings nodded, and Nina helped him
arrange the cradleboard upon his back. Stone put
his arm around the girl. "We won't let anything
happen to him, so try not to worry. As long as he's
with us, Clan won't get his hands on him.''

Windsor was still standing guard by the window, and Stone paused beside her. "Are you sure
you can get Jun-li to lie still?''

"Jun-li always obeys me.''

"All right, then, we'll be outside watching. We'll intercept you before they can take you inside Clan's camp." He lowered his voice. "But if something should happen, and we don't make our move, you'll have to take care of the man guarding you and get Nina out. And don't wait too long to do it. I don't want either of you inside his hideout alone. Do you understand?"

"Yes."

"I mean it, Windsor. Clan's too dangerous. Once you find out where he is, find a way to escape from your guard. Then we'll take over. You just get Nina back to the ship, where you'll both be safe."

"I understand."

Stone stared down at her, continuing to hesitate. "Are you sure you want to do this? A lot of things could go wrong."

"Every task can be accomplished by a man of resolution."

"Is there anything you don't have a saying for?"

Windsor's lips curved mischievously. "Wait until the Yellow River becomes clear, and how old will you be?"

Stone gave a low laugh. "Is that your way of telling me to get going?"

"Parker will come soon. All will be lost if he finds you here."

"Remember, no heroics. Don't try to take him on by yourself, understand?"

"Yes. Please go."

Reluctantly, Stone motioned Sun-On-Wings to precede him. When the Osage was safely on the ground with the baby, he swung his leg over the rail. Windsor stopped him with a hand on his arm.

"You must be careful, too. Do not let your anger rule your head. Tonight you will be free of Emerson Clan. You will sleep peacefully in my arms with no terrible dreams of revenge to haunt you."

"If you'll remember, I rarely sleep at all when

you're in my arms.'' Stone smiled, cupping the
back of her neck to draw her closer. His lips explored hers gently, and when she made as if to pull
away, he prevented it, savoring their kiss for a moment longer.

"Don't worry about me, worry about yourself,''
he ordered, then he was gone.

Windsor watched the two men melt into the
night before she went to the bed and opened her
bamboo case. Happy to be free again, Jun-li jumped
onto her shoulder, and she affectionately stroked
his soft black fur.

"Much depends on you this night, my clever little friend. You must lie very still inside the blanket
and not make a single sound. Do you understand?''

The capuchin cocked his head, but his intelligent
brown eyes were much more interested in the
handful of almonds Windsor had retrieved from
her bag to feed to him.

19

The man named Parker came around eight o'clock the following morning. When he knocked on the door and called Nina's name, Windsor took a firm grip on Nina's shoulders.

"Don't be afraid. I will protect you if anything should happen. Don't say anything unless he asks you a question."

Nina nodded, but she looked terrified. Windsor drew in a lungful of cleansing air, then opened the door. Clan's henchman stood in the hall. He was alone, but he carried a rifle in one hand, and two ammunition bandoliers crisscrossed his chest.

"Clan sent me for his woman," he said in a low voice.

"Please enter," Windsor answered.

Nina stood up at once, nervously twisting her fingers together.

"Where's the kid?"

Nina stared mutely at him, so Windsor was quick to reply. "He is asleep. He has been very sick, and we must not awaken him, or he will start crying again."

"What's wrong with him?" he asked, glancing suspiciously around the room.

"It is a disease called measles."

"Hell, ain't that catchin'?"

"Yes, so you must be very careful not to get too close, or you will be infected."

"I don't know if Clan'll want to bring a sick kid into camp. Maybe you better wait here and let me tell 'im."

"He is his son, is he not? He will wish to see him."

The burly man stroked his thick mustachio, his eyes narrowing as he gazed at Windsor. "Just who the hell are you, anyways? Clan didn't mention no other woman comin' with Nina."

"I am the baby's nurse."

The man took a moment to contemplate her story. Afraid he would refuse to let her accompany Nina, Windsor looked up at him, making her words sound anxious.

"We must go now, while the baby sleeps." She turned to Nina. "I'll carry Carlos for you, Nina, so you can rest."

Quickly she crossed the room to where her bamboo case lay behind the bed. She opened the case, stroked Jun-li soothingly, then wrapped the capuchin inside Carlos's blue blanket. She whispered in Chinese for the monkey to stay still, then laid him in the bamboo case. She covered his face and lifted the suitcase, hoping her story about the baby's illness would keep Parker from getting too close.

"Hurry it up! Clan's riled anyways. The woman should've been here with the kid a long time ago."

The man's impatience was to their advantage, Windsor thought, feeling more secure when he frowned and motioned angrily for them to hurry.

"You are to wear these," he ordered, handing each of them a heavy knitted shawl. "Clan says to wrap up in these here rebozos so no one'll recognize you as Americans. The Nacionales have been

breathin' down our necks since they been bustin'
up the *guerrilleros'* strongholds.''

Nina immediately draped the black rebozo over
her head, and Windsor watched the way she
wrapped the ends around her shoulders, then arranged her red shawl over her hair in the same
fashion. She held the bamboo case horizontally in
her arms as Parker led them down the narrow
stairs, which led to the rear of the cantina.

A large, two-wheeled cart awaited them near the
back door. An old man sat on the driver's seat, but
a second *guerrillero*, a swarthy Mexican with long,
dirty black hair, held up the back flap for Nina to
step inside. As Parker preceded her into the wagon,
Windsor glanced around, confident that Stone and
Sun-On-Wings were somewhere nearby, their guns
trained on both of Clan's men. She knew they
would follow, but she was reluctant to step beneath the white canvas cover, where Stone could
no longer see her.

Keeping alert, she ducked through the back and
was surprised to find that two women were already seated inside with Parker. She sat beside one
of them. They stared impassively at her. Both had
the same brown face and dark eyes as Nina, but
both were older, the flesh of their faces coarse and
lined with many wrinkles, as if they had spent
many years working outside under the grueling
Mexican sun.

''Who are these women?'' Windsor asked the
Mexican guard, who had climbed in behind her and
closed the flap. Having others around would complicate her plan for getting Nina out of the wagon
and to safety before they reached Clan's secret
hideout.

''They are *putas*,'' the man said, spreading his
lips in an ugly smile that displayed his broken, yellow teeth. ''*Mis amigos* are hungry for women, so
we brought them whores.''

Windsor realized then that the two women were camp followers, such as she had seen used by the Emperor's guards in Peking. Hung-pin had pointed the painted women out to her when they had journeyed through the city on their way to America.

The wagon lurched forward, then the wheels began to turn. Windsor held the bamboo case tightly on her lap. Across from her, Nina sat beside Parker, her face as pale and stiff as a corpse's. She kept wetting her lips, and Windsor became alarmed when she saw Parker frowning at the way Nina was wringing her hands.

"How far must we go?" she asked him in an effort to alleviate his suspicions and bring his attention back to her.

He only stared at her, his dark eyes filled with an expression that made her uncomfortable. She tried to identify the look. What was it? Amusement? Or was it satisfaction?

Warier now, she returned her regard to the two Mexican prostitutes. Their flat brown faces were completely expressionless. The inner instinct that served her so well began to send her a warning that all was not as it should be inside the cart.

"I don't feel well," she said, putting a hand to her head. "Please, you must stop and let me get some air."

No one answered. Parker and the three Mexicans stared at her. Obviously frightened by Windsor's discomfort, Nina stood as if to flee. The *guerrillero* grabbed her arm and jerked her back down beside him. Nina cried out in pain when he caught her by the hair. Windsor shot to her feet, still holding Jun-li's case.

"Leave her alone," she cried, but before she could free her hands, she sensed Parker move up behind her. Something heavy came down against the back of her head, and she heard a dull thunk.

Then pain exploded, and she was plummeted
headfirst into a deep black well.

Stone reined up, careful to keep himself concealed in the trees. Below him on the narrow rutted
road that rose gradually into the mountains, the
cart in which Windsor and Nina rode creaked
slowly along. Despite the rugged trail, he'd had no
trouble keeping abreast with them. He had ridden
in a parallel line, higher in the foothills where his
progress was hidden by vegetation and rocky out-
croppings. Sun-On-Wings would be following a
similar path on the other side of the road.

All morning they had been following the wagon,
but he had seen neither Windsor nor Nina since
they had entered the back of the cart in the rear
yard of the cantina. Still, he wasn't particularly
worried. There were only two *guerrilleros*. If they
gave Windsor any problems, she would surely be
able to subdue them. With her quickness and fighting skills, she could single-handedly best more men
than that. She had proved herself more than once.

Shielding his eyes from the sun's glare, he
peered ahead at the narrow wooden bridge suspended over a steep-sided canyon about twenty
yards in front of them. Immediately, however, his
attention was drawn back to the wagon as the old
man brought the horse to a stop. The Mexican *guerrillero* climbed from the back, then helped Windsor
and Nina to the ground. Stone couldn't see them
clearly. Both were still wrapped in the long shawls
they had worn when they had left the cantina.
Windsor no longer carried her bamboo case, but
Nina had a bundle in her arms. Stone tensed, praying that Jun-li would make no betraying noise.

Stone watched the *guerrillero* point toward a path
that ran alongside the high rocky bluff that overlooked the swift-flowing river cascading over a series of rapids far below. Windsor began to walk

quickly in that direction with Nina behind her.
Their *guerrillero* guard followed them, and the cart
rolled onward, leaving them behind and rattling
over the rough planks of the bridge.

Grimacing, Stone urged his horse back the way
he had come. Damn Clan, he thought. He should
have known he would be especially cautious. He
was just glad Sun-On-Wings was already on the
other side of the road. Even if Stone should lose
sight of the women for a while, the Indian youth
would be able to keep close enough to help them
if something happened.

To his relief, however, the *guerrillero* did not herd
them into the thick woods, where it would be hard
for Stone to follow. He kept the two women walking away from the bridge and parallel to the river
at the top of the cliff. What the devil was Clan up
to? Was there a hidden cave somewhere nearby?
Or perhaps a different cart to take them along a
different road?

Growing more concerned, Stone urged his horse
across the road and into the opposite tree cover.
He caught up to the women within minutes, then
stayed out of sight as he followed them. A quarter
of an hour later, he jerked back on the reins when
he saw Sun-On-Wings suddenly burst from the tree
cover just in front of the *guerrillero*. When the out-
law went for his gun, Sun-On-Wings raised his rifle and shot him in the chest.

As Windsor and Nina began to run in opposite
directions, Stone spurred his horse down the hill
and through the trees toward Windsor. Frowning,
not understanding what had gone wrong, he tried
to cut off her panicked flight. Moments later, he
caught her, reining up and leaping to the ground
before the horse had stopped prancing.

"Windsor! Wait, it's me!" he yelled, but she
didn't turn until he managed to catch her skirt and
drag her to her knees. He went down beside her,

but she still struggled to escape as he turned her
over. He froze, staring down into the face of a
stranger. His face lost all color as he realized what
had happened. He lunged to his feet as Sun-On-
Wings dragged the other Mexican woman, kicking
and cursing, toward him. Oh, God, Clan had
tricked them, Stone thought in horror, bile rising
in his gullet to burn like acid. Clan had Windsor
and Nina.

Mindless with panic, he leapt upon his horse and
spurred it into a gallop back toward the bridge. He
rode hard, only half aware that Sun-On-Wings was
racing after him. He had to catch up to the wagon.
He had to get to Windsor. He had to stop the in-
conceivable from happening. Finally, after what
seemed like an eternity, he rounded a curve that
brought the bridge into sight. On the opposite side,
he could see the cart.

Hope surged, and he kicked his horse into a mer-
ciless gait, but a moment later, the morning quiet was
obliterated by an ear-shattering blast. Stone's horse
shied and pranced backward as the bridge went up
in a cloud of smoke and flying debris. Splinters of
wood shot high into the air and rained in a steady
stream into the rushing river below.

Fighting to control the spooked mare, Stone
forced the animal on, but his eyes were riveted on
the far bank in absolute terror. Oh, God, now he
saw Clan. The bastard was leaning into the back of
the cart and roughly jerking Windsor out. She lay
lifeless in his arms, and Clan turned and lifted her
up so that Stone could see her better.

"Look what I've got, Kincaid," came his faraway shout of triumph.

"You bastard! If you hurt her, I'll kill you!"
Stone yelled, his voice strident with rage.

Clan's laugh echoed out over the canyon.
"There's a cantina in the plaza in Durango. If you

still want her after I've had my fill of her, meet me there in a week."

"Wait, Clan!" Stone shouted desperately as Sun-On-Wings rode up in a thunder of hooves. "I've got your son! We can work a trade! Right now, goddammit!"

Clan hesitated, then slung Windsor's limp body over his saddle. He swung up behind her and, holding her in place with one hand, called across the canyon to Stone.

"I'm calling the shots now, Kincaid. Bring the boy to Durango a week from now, and don't try any more tricks if you want me to keep her alive!"

Paralyzed with helpless, hopeless horror, Stone watched Nina struggle with one of the *guerrilleros* before she, too, was subdued and hoisted onto his horse. As the band of outlaws rode away in a cloud of dust, Stone wasted no more time. In a reckless, desperate pursuit, he plunged his horse headlong down the steep cliff toward the raging river far below.

Nearly twenty-four hours later, Sun-On-Wings guided his horse blindly through the darkness, unable to see the trail. He was so tired he could barely grasp the reins, but he dared not stop or he would be left behind. Arrow-Parts-Hair was like a man possessed. He didn't say anything, didn't stop for anything, but rode on and on, endlessly, with the inhuman stamina of the spirit warriors who galloped on the night wind. Now that the moon had gone down, the rocky terrain was nearly impossible to navigate, yet Arrow-Parts-Hair continued without pause, dismounting and leading his horse on foot over the loose shale and slippery rocks.

All day and all night, they had been riding as hard as they could. It had taken a long time to ford the river—they'd had to go downstream several miles before they found a place they could cross;

then they'd picked their way up the other side of the towering canyon wall. Both their horses had become lathered and exhausted long ago, and still Arrow-Parts-Hair pressed on. Strapped to the cradleboard upon Sun-On-Wings' back, Carlos cried pitifully from hunger and fatigue, but Arrow-Parts-Hair did not stop, did not hear when Sun-On-Wings called out to him.

Clan and his men had left the road and ridden up steep and dangerous mountain paths. Sun-On-Wings was one of the best trackers of his village, yet he could no longer see traces of the *guerrilleros'* flight. He was not sure if they were still following the Evil One's trail or not. As much as he wanted to find Yellow-Haired-Warrior-Woman and Nina, he had to stop soon. He had to rest, or just stretch his legs a bit. The pace they had set was too grueling. Even the horses could not go on much longer without collapsing. He had to make Arrow-Parts-Hair listen.

In front of him, his white friend had hunkered down in the darkness to examine the path, but how could he see, without the light of the moon to show him the way? Arrow-Parts-Hair was not thinking straight. He thought only of getting the two women back. He did not realize they must stop until they could find the trail again.

"Too dark now," he said, pulling his horse up beside Arrow-Parts-Hair. "Wait for Grandfather Sun to show us way."

Without answering, Arrow-Parts-Hair rose and pulled his horse forward by the reins, the hooves ringing loudly on the rocks. Sun-On-Wings hurried to catch up with him.

"Arrow-Parts-Hair tired. Ponies need rest," he insisted, reaching for the horse's reins.

Before Sun-On-Wings could halt the animal, Arrow-Parts-Hair turned furiously on him, grabbing the front of his shirt and jerking him up close.

His words came out harshly, bitterly, through clenched teeth.

"Leave me the hell alone, goddammit! Do what you want, but I'm not stopping until I find her."

Sun-On-Wings staggered backward a few steps as Arrow-Parts-Hair thrust him away; then he watched as the big white man swung onto his horse and rode on. Sun-On-Wings stood still, feeling guilty for wanting to stop, feeling as if he were betraying his friends, but he was so tired. He could barely stand up. He had to stop for a little while, just long enough to rest his horse and feed Carlos; then he would ride hard to catch up with Arrow-Parts-Hair.

Carlos whimpered, and Sun-On-Wings sank to his knees and slipped the cradleboard off his back. He unlaced the bindings, lifted the child out, and held him against his shoulder.

"Shh, little man," he whispered, using the language of the Little Ones.

The infant quieted at once, soothed by the Indian's soft voice. Sun-On-Wings looked down into the tiny face and felt the most terrible sorrow constrict his heart. The white child's mother was in the hands of his evil father. His blood ran cold when he remembered the terror in her eyes the first time Nina had seen Sun-On-Wings in the garden of the big house in San Francisco, when she thought Clan had sent him to get her. He swallowed hard, frightened to think what was happening to Nina and Yellow-Haired-Warrior-Woman. He wished he were as strong and determined as Arrow-Parts-Hair so he could ride on without food or drink or rest.

His every muscle aching with weariness, he tied his horse to a branch and lay the baby on the ground. Carlos crawled around until Sun-On-Wings retrieved a piece of bread from his fringed rawhide bag. Carlos took it and gnawed on it while

Sun-On-Wings lay back on the ground. He should go on, he thought. He should be there if Arrow-Parts-Hair needed him. He would get back on his horse after just a short rest, he decided as he put his blanket around the baby and held him tightly against his chest. He would close his eyes for just a moment, and then he would ride as hard as he could after Arrow-Parts-Hair.

When he awoke next, it was nearly dawn. Appalled that he had slept, he quickly secured Carlos in the cradleboard and struck out again, feeling revived after his short nap. He rode as quickly as he could, tracking Arrow-Parts-Hair's horse. The narrow winding trails led through the rough mountain terrain, and it took most of the day before he crested a slope and saw a horse grazing in the meadow below. Arrow-Parts-Hair was slumped forward in his saddle. He didn't move as Sun-On-Wings rode up alongside, and Sun-On-Wings realized his friend had ridden himself to exhaustion.

Dismounting, Sun-On-Wings carefully dragged the bigger man from the mare, and still Arrow-Parts-Hair did not awaken from his dead sleep. Sun-On-Wings covered him with a blanket and sat down nearby, trying not to think about Yellow-Haired-Warrior-Woman being with the man named Clan. She was so wise and strong, surely she could find a way for Nina and her to escape. She would use her magic and wonderful fighting skills to gain her freedom.

For a while, he sat guard while his friend lay like a dead man. Carlos played with sticks and pebbles, until Arrow-Parts-Hair suddenly lurched upright with a terrible cry of despair, his face drawn and ashen.

"We've got to go on," he muttered thickly, climbing to his feet and grabbing the reins. He swung back into the saddle without another word.

Sun-On-Wings fetched Carlos and galloped after him as hard as he could.

Somewhere far away, Windsor heard someone scream. She struggled to make her mind work but found she could not think clearly. Her arms hurt, as if someone were pulling on them, and her head throbbed mercilessly, causing her thoughts to jumble all around in her head like disjointed pieces of a puzzle. She heard a loud crack, and another horrific yell pierced the fuzzy clouds inside her mind. It's a woman, she realized groggily, slowly becoming aware that she was swaying back and forth.

Again she heard frightening sounds—the deep rumble of a masculine voice, a sharp crack, a shrill cry. She tried to concentrate. She must still be on the ship, the *Trinidad,* but they had disembarked at Mazatlán, hadn't they? Where was Stone? And Nina and Sun-On-Wings? What had happened to make her so confused?

"Stone Kincaid?" she mumbled incoherently, then listened as the screaming began again.

Windsor forced open her eyes, but the room around her was wavery and indistinct, as if she were swimming under the sea. Groaning, she struggled to alleviate the aching of her arms, then realized in a burst of lucidity that she was hanging by her hands from a ceiling beam. She remembered the plan to capture Emerson Clan; remembered riding in the cart with Parker, the *guerrillero,* and the *putas.* Fear ran rampant in her blood, and she began to squirm against the ropes, causing herself to swing back and forth. Blinking hard, she wet parched lips, endeavoring to clear her vision. When she was able to focus on the scene in front of her, she wished she couldn't see.

They were in a barn. Nina hung across from her, strung up by her hands in the same way Windsor was. Windsor couldn't see her face, but her eyes became riveted on the girl's back. Her gown had been torn to the waist, revealing the awful scars of her previous beatings, but now there were new streaks of split muscle and streams of blood that ran down her spine in rivulets and spread dark crimson stains over the back of her white skirt. There was only one man, and he stood with his back to Windsor.

"You should never have betrayed me to Kincaid, Nina, my love. You really hurt my feelings," he said, each word uttered as smooth as oil and deceptively gentle. "Lucky for me, wasn't it, that we happened to be watching the waterfront for a new shipment of arms, and I saw you with Kincaid before you left the ship. Otherwise, his little trap might have succeeded."

"Oh, *Dios, por favor*, don't hit me with the whip again." Nina groaned, her voice ravaged by pain. "I can't bear any more, I can't."

"You should have thought of the consequences of your disloyalty before, my dear. Then we wouldn't have to go through all of this."

"I'm sorry. I'll never do it again, I promise. I'll do anything you say, oh, *Dios*, anything you want—"

Every muscle in Windsor's body tensed as he drew back his long black whip. The knotted thong made a soft whistling sound as it slashed through the air. The lash struck hard into the soft flesh in the small of Nina's back, and she shrieked in agony, the horrible sound echoing off the walls.

"Stop!" Windsor cried, trying to twist her body so she could use her feet to subdue the man torturing her friend, but her ankles were lashed together, making it hard for her to get any kind of leverage. "She can't stand any more! Look at her back! You're going to kill her!"

The man turned around, and Windsor tensed all over as the monster with the whip stopped directly in front of her. The light from the lantern shone on him, and Windsor got her first look at Emerson Clan's face.

His hair was very long, hanging freely down his back well past his shoulders: snow-white like an old man's, but as finely textured as a young child's. The strong fragrance of roses emanating from him was enough to choke her. He wore a mustache, neatly trimmed atop his upper lip, the same silvery color as his hair. His face was unlined and handsome, tanned deeply from months in the Mexican sun, but his eyes were what Windsor stared into— her whole body gripped with dread at the cruelty she read in their ice-blue depths. Never in her life had she seen such a look—only a demon could harbor such innate evil. In that one moment when their gazes locked together, she understood Stone Kincaid's nightmares, and Nina's terror of the man staring at her with such malevolent menace.

"So you've finally decided to join our little party, have you? I was beginning to wonder if I'd have to bring you around with my good friend here." He held up the bullwhip, coiling it loosely as he spoke. The ruby eyes of his cobra ring shone in the lantern light, and Nina's blood still dripped off the knots of leather. Windsor could hear Nina sobbing. She swallowed hard, but she forced herself to gather her strength and remain calm. Stone Kincaid and Sun-On-Wings had followed them. They would come soon. She would have to reason with Emerson Clan until they were able to rescue them.

"If you kill us, you will never get your son back," she told Clan, forcing all fear from her mind. She was pleased that she sounded unafraid.

Clan smiled, his teeth looking as white as his hair in his sun-burned face. "I do hope you're as brave as you seem. I like courageous women the best. They're more fun to break." He glanced over his shoulder at Nina. "Take Nina there, she has no tolerance for pain. Half a dozen lashes, and she passes out. Then I have to go to all the trouble of reviving her. It's a waste of time and energy, don't you think?''

"I'm not afraid of you, Emerson Clan. And I am not afraid to die, because I will only leave this body and enter another. But you will be punished for your evil deeds in the next life and for all eternity. I feel only pity for you.''

Emerson Clan threw back his head and laughed with hearty abandon. "You're a woman after my own heart, to be sure,'' he said, his eyes narrowing into malicious slits. "No wonder Kincaid made you whore for him. Yes, that's right, I know all about the two of you being lovers. Nina told me—and you know what, Miss Windsor Richmond? I only had to hold up my whip and let her see it, and she spilled out all kinds of interesting information. You see, little Nina knows me a lot better than you do, or you wouldn't be trying to annoy me like you are.''

"You don't scare me,'' she said again. "I have been trained to disassociate my mind from my body. You can whip me all day long, and I will tell you nothing. I will not cry out in pain. I will not make a sound.''

"Very interesting.'' Clan walked closer and grabbed the front of her shirt. He ripped it down the middle, baring her breasts. "And what about this sort of thing? Do you like this better?''

Windsor's expression did not change as he rubbed his hands over her body. "I feel nothing but contempt for you.''

Clan stepped back, his pale eyes gleaming; then suddenly he looped the whip around her neck, jerking it so tight that her breath was cut off. He held it secure, staring into her eyes, smiling, until she began to struggle, her face turning blue. Finally he released his stranglehold enough for her to draw one shallow breath. He bared his teeth again, a slow, cruel twist of thin lips.

"We'll just see how different you are from Nina and the others who've felt the bite of my whip, my dear. There are all sorts of ways to inflict pain. I've discovered them all over the years. Some people can't stand physical torture, some can't stand having their bodies violated. And some, my pretty little love—some grow to like what I do to them. You might turn out to be my greatest challenge, I can see that already."

Sliding his whip from around her neck, he chuckled, then raked his fingers down the length of his long hair. "What's more, I'm going to enjoy everything I do to you, because I know that Stone Kincaid loves you. I find that in itself extraordinary, because for years he's thought of no one but me. We were actually friends once, you know, before he got all righteous and moral, and turned me over for court-martial. Yes, he'll hate you being in my hands. He'll hate thinking about what I am doing to you. And listen carefully, for this is the very best part"—he snarled his fingers in her hair and wrenched her head back until she was forced to look at him—"he'll hate you, too, once I'm done with you, because every time he looks at you, he'll remember you were with me, and it'll make him sick to the depths of his soul."

"Stone Kincaid will kill you."

"I don't think so. He'll do anything to get you back, maybe even turn himself over to me. But you know what, Miss Windsor Richmond? I don't want Kincaid anymore. I'd rather have his woman, because I know that will hurt him far more than anything I could ever do to him."

When Windsor met his gaze dispassionately, he laughed again as if delighted by her defiance. "Oh, by the way," he said then, "using your little pet monkey to pose for Carlos was a nice touch. Too bad I had to wring its neck.''

Inside, Windsor cried out with grief, but she tried not to show any reaction as Clan leaned very close to her face.

"I do love a challenge," he murmured, his breath fanning her cheek. "So enough talk. Let the fun begin."

20

Durango lay nearly a hundred miles east of Mazatlán. Surrounded by the towering Sierra Madre, the village hugged a central square, a meeting place where Indians and mestizos met and talked, courted and haggled. As in most Mexican cities, a massive Catholic cathedral dominated the town, its towering walls dented and worn by the centuries.

Alongside the enormous symbol of faith, the main plaza was lined with tall, narrow houses with red-tiled roofs, the railed balconies a reminder of the Moorish influence of the Spanish conquistadors. Large terra-cotta pots of geraniums decorated the windowsills and hung from knotted ropes to brighten the dusty pedestrian walks.

Other than the church, the most frequented establishment was the cantina, a neatly whitewashed brick building erected where three busy streets converged upon the plaza. One evening as the sun painted the sky with melting streaks of pink and violet behind indigo peaks, Stone Kincaid sat by himself at a secluded table on a flagstone-paved patio outside the busy cafe.

Half concealed by a potted aguava tree, he drank alone, his back against the interior wall. His right

239

hand was curled loosely around a half-empty bottle of tequila. He appeared indolent, his bloodshot eyes heavy-lidded, but behind the pose his mind raced and his eyes darted constantly among the bundle-laden townspeople hurrying past him. His handsome face, now deeply tanned and covered with an unkempt black beard, was composed; the strength in his massive muscles was leashed. But deep in his gut, his emotions were shredded and raw, alive with anxiety and despair, twisting in and out, over and under, like a bed of swarming vipers.

It had been nine days since Clan had taken Windsor. For five of those days, he and Sun-On-Wings had followed Clan's trail across the mountains to Durango, but they had found no trace of the *guerrilleros* or their hideout. For the past four days, using Durango as a base, they had ridden up into the rugged mountains all day, every day, searching the canyons and villages, questioning the campesinos, following every lead, every clue. Stone no longer slept, no longer thought of food. Only when the sun went down did he return to the cantina that Clan had designated and sit by himself, suffering through the long, endless hours that crawled by while Clan kept him waiting.

Oh, God, what had that son of a bitch been doing to her? What awful things had he put her through? Stone's stomach took a forward roll, quivering with repugnance as he remembered the ridged scars on Nina's back. Windsor's skin was so soft and smooth, so vulnerable and easily bruised. He squeezed his eyes shut, clamping his lips in a strained, tight line. He felt sick with a guilt that weighed down on him like a granite coat. What if Clan had managed to find out what Windsor meant to Stone? He'd delight in transferring every caustic drop of hatred he felt for Stone onto her.

Don't, he thought, don't think about it! Concentrate on something else, anything! He pressed his

fist against his mouth and consciously turned his
mind into an empty slate, a brand-new black one,
as fresh as the ones he had used as a boy on the
first day of school. When he had been incarcerated
at Andersonville and the hardship and pain had
threatened to overwhelm him, he had learned to
mentally take a rag and erase his thoughts, eradi-
cate the torture and grief, until his mind became
black and empty, a total blank. The slate inside his
head had saved his sanity in the prison camp, and
he would use it again to help him survive the horror of Windsor's capture. No, don't think about
Windsor, he told himself again, not even her name.
Don't dwell on the pain and guilt eating away your
heart. Don't think at all.

Instead, he focused his energy on the need to
remain patient and in strict control of his emotions
so he would be ready when Clan finally showed
up. Despite his resolve, frustration stubbornly rose
to the surface again, like a bubble in a boiling ket-
tle, trying to take over his mind. What had her last
words to him been? *Tonight you will be free of Emerson Clan. You will sleep peacefully in my arms with
no terrible dreams of revenge to haunt you.* Oh, God,
oh, God.

Wipe the slate clean, he thought determinedly.

Clan was late on purpose. Stone knew that. He
had not come in a week, as he had said, because
he wanted Stone to suffer for as long as possible.
Stone was well aware of how the son of a bitch
thought. Clan was confident that time was on his
side. Stone would never hurt his son, and he knew
it. He also knew that Stone would do anything to
get Windsor back.

Oh, Windsor, where are you? How could I have
gotten you into this? His guilt-ridden mind
screamed the agonizing accusations before he could
subjugate them, and he shook his head and wet
cracked lips. No, don't think about her, don't do

it, goddammit! *Wipe the slate clean, wipe it clean!* But oh, God, he missed her! He needed her back so badly he wanted to die! He'd kill himself if he could stop what was happening to her! What if Clan didn't show up? What if he just kept Windsor for himself?

Gritting his teeth so hard that his facial muscles ached, Stone took up the cerebral eraser and rubbed away Windsor's beautiful face, her smile, the sweet fragrance of her hair, until his mind was blank and dark and dead. His grip on the bottle of tequila tightened, and he concentrated solely on taking a drink. Consciously, he performed the motions—lifted the bottle, put it to his mouth, drank, swallowed, forgot, didn't think. The tequila tasted warm and potent and bitter as it slid down his throat into a burning stomach.

Clan would come. He wanted Carlos enough to put Nina through hell and back. And he would know that Stone would never let him have the baby while he was holding Windsor and Nina. Oh, God, how could he give up poor little Carlos to the murdering bastard? But he mustn't think about that either. It had to be done; it was the only way he could keep Windsor and Nina alive.

Scanning the crowded street again, Stone tipped the bottle to his mouth. He drank deeply, wishing he could get drunk, the way he had at Sweet Sue's. Windsor had looked so beautiful that night in the bathhouse, and he had wanted her so desperately. God in heaven, how could he have let this happen? He should be shot for being such a fool. *Wipe the slate, wipe it clean, don't think.*

His gaze slid over the town fountain located in the center of the square. Every inch of his body went stiff. Clan was standing next to the well. The bastard was smiling. While Stone watched, Clan began to move in his direction, weaving his way among the men and women loitering in front of the

cantina. Stone drew his gun and laid it atop his
knee. Never in his life had he wanted to kill anyone as much as he wanted to murder Clan at that
moment. He wanted to put the Colt revolver
against Clan's temple and pull the trigger. His finger itched with the need to kill.

"Hello, Kincaid. It's been a while since we
shared a bottle, hasn't it, *amigo*?"

Stone stared at the man he had pursued for so
long, the man he hated with every ounce of his
being. His whole body quivered with the craving
to grab Clan by the throat and choke the life out of
him. He forced himself to remain motionless. He
must not let Clan use his weaknesses against him.

Instead, he studied Clan's appearance. He had
changed since last October in Chicago when Stone
had nearly captured him in the fiery lobby of the
Star Hotel. Now he wore a black frock coat and
trousers, and a white shirt with a stiff, starched
collar encircled by a black string tie. He was dressed
like an undertaker, Stone thought, noting that
Clan's hair was longer than he remembered, falling
in lanky strands over his back and shoulders. He
walked with a slight limp, Stone noticed with triumph, pleased to see that the bullet he had fired
into his leg the last time they'd met still caused him
pain. But his eyes were the same, pale and lifeless,
frighteningly cold and cruel.

"Sit down, Clan." Stone's words were clipped
off, terse and impassive. He forced himself to relax.

Emerson Clan took a seat across from him. They
stared at each other without speaking, then Clan
smiled lazily as he slid a hand inside his black frock
coat. Stone's fingers tightened around the ivory
handle of his gun, but Clan merely withdrew a gold
cigar case.

"Care for a smoke, Kincaid?" he offered, striking a match on the wooden tabletop. He leaned

back, coaxing the expensive square-tipped cheroot into flame.

Stone shook his head. "Where are they, you bastard?"

Clan leaned back his head and exhaled a cloud of bluish smoke. He took his time answering. "I must compliment you on your taste, my friend. Your lady is quite a beauty. And brave, too. At least, she was at first."

Stone went rigid, but, well aware of the power Clan would wield over him if he detected a hint of vulnerability, he deliberately acted unaffected. He shrugged, forcing a nonchalant smile. "She's a woman, like any other."

Clan cocked a silvery eyebrow. "Indeed." He paused, reaching again into his inside coat pocket. "Then I don't suppose this will bother you much." He tossed something onto the table, and Stone looked down at the long fall of silky blond hair, still braided into the queue that had hung down Windsor's back.

"I thought you might like something to remember her by, in case we can't come to terms—"

Clan's smug grin disintegrated as Stone lurched to his feet, his face contorted with rage, and grabbed Clan by the neck. His fingers encircled his throat, his thumbs clamping hard atop Clan's bobbing Adam's apple.

"Go ahead," Clan croaked out hoarsely, "kill me and you'll never see her again."

The strangled threat brought Stone back to his senses as nothing else could. He released his death grip. Clan collapsed weakly backward into his chair, and Stone fought for self-control as the other man coughed and held his hand against his bruised, aching throat.

"You always did let your temper get the best of you," Clan muttered. "It's still getting you in trouble. That's why we made such a good team when we were at West Point. I kept you under control. Just think what we could have done together by now if you hadn't played the hero."

"You were a goddamn traitor, feeding information to the Rebs."

Emerson Clan didn't answer. He drew in a deep lungful of smoke, then held the cigar idly between his thumb and forefinger as he gazed out over the crowd. "I have to admit I'm rather surprised that you've kept after me for so long. How many years has it been now? Six? More? Just think, Stone, old buddy, if you'd given up on catching me, your lovely little Miss Windsor Richmond would still be writhing under you in bed." He nudged Windsor's braid with his fingertip. "And all this would still be attached to her pretty head."

Stone's hands knotted into hard fists. Clan saw the way they were clenching and unclenching. He gave a satisfied chuckle.

"My goodness, Stone, you should see the look on your face. You must be in love. But don't worry, none of my men had her. I kept her for myself." His white teeth flashed in the deepening dusk.

A vein throbbed visibly in Stone's temple. "Don't push me too far, Clan. Remember, I have your son."

Clan's amused expression remained in place. "But you won't hurt him. You're much too honorable."

"Get down to business, goddamn you, before I lose patience and enjoy putting a bullet in your brain."

"Temper, temper, Kincaid." Clan bent his neck and blew an unbroken ring of smoke toward the sky. "I'm ready now to trade your woman for Carlos."

"I want Nina, too."

Surprise flickered across Clan's handsome features. "Nina? Whatever would you want her for?"

"You've abused her long enough."

"Nina's a betraying bitch. If my men and I hadn't been watching the incoming ships, your little scheme to capture me might have succeeded. But we both know that I'm just a little bit more clever than you are, don't we, Stone? That's why you just can't seem to catch me, no matter how hard you try. You really ought to give up and go home." He stubbed out his cigar, scarring the tabletop.

"When and where do we make the exchange?"

"You get that dirty Injun to bring my son here, then I'll tell you where you can find the women."

"Yeah, Clan, like hell." Stone's laugh was contemptuous.

"What? You don't trust me?" Clan's lips stretched into a mocking grin.

"It's got to be a neutral place. And I want proof that both of them are alive before I hand over your kid."

"My, my, but you do drive a hard bargain, Kincaid."

Stone waited in silence.

"There's a town called Saltillo farther up in the mountains. There's a bridge across a deep river canyon just before you reach the outskirts. Be there at dawn, three days from now. I'll bring the women to the eastern side of the bridge, and you have my son on the western side. They'll cross at the same time."

Clan made as if to rise, but Stone grabbed his forearm, his grip viselike. "If you've hurt her, I'll kill you—even if it takes me the rest of my life."

Clan jerked free. "I've heard that threat before, and it still doesn't scare me."

Tight-lipped with impotent rage, Stone watched him move away. He wanted to follow, to use his fists to wipe the confident smile off Clan's face, but he couldn't, not yet. Sun-On-Wings was waiting with Carlos in the mountains, well hidden from Clan's men. It would take him a long time to get there, because he would have to travel a slow and circuitous route to make sure no one was following him. But at least the waiting was almost over. Three days from now, he would have Windsor back.

He picked up the braid from the table and held the softly woven blond hair close to his face. The fragrance of jasmine lingered, and pain hit him with the force of a doubled fist. Grinding his teeth, he cursed Clan again, then turned and strode purposely for his horse.

"They're coming now," Stone hissed in a low whisper from where he lay on his stomach near the edge of the cliff. Below him, morning mists were just rising off the surface of the narrow, twisting river to shroud the bridge where they would make the trade. He squinted and peered hard into the wafting grayness. "Damn this fog. I can't see well enough to recognize Windsor. We'll have to wait until it lifts some."

"Nina not want Evil One to have little man," Sun-On-Wings said in a low voice from where he lay nearby. "Her say so."

Stone twisted his head around and looked at him. Guilt burned a brand of shame on his conscience at the thought of sacrificing the innocent baby, but he couldn't let himself think about that. "We have to. Clan won't hurt him, but he'll kill Nina and Windsor if we don't give him the boy." Sun-On-Wings looked unconvinced. He had become very attached to Carlos. Stone glanced at the baby strapped inside the cradleboard, heard his soft coos, and felt sick. He hardened his heart and looked away. "We have to do it," he repeated, "as soon as the fog lifts."

The sun gradually rose higher to become a ball of flame in the clear blue sky. The morning warmed, and birds trilled and flitted among the branches of the trees, as if nothing were wrong. Stone shielded his eyes with his hand, his gaze glued to the far end of the bridge, where he could detect five horses and a small, two-wheeled wagon with two figures sitting in it. "There they are." His voice grated harsher. "I can see them better now. He's got them in the donkey cart. Look for ambushers up in the rocks above them. I don't think he'd risk setting a trap, not with his son within firing range, but we mustn't underestimate him."

"C'mon, let's go, before he changes his mind," Stone ordered a moment later as he got to his feet.

Reluctantly, Sun-On-Wings slipped the cradleboard onto his back, mounted his horse, and followed Stone down the hill toward the meeting place. When Stone reached the narrow wooden bridge, he drew his gun and dismounted.

"I want to see them," he shouted across to Clan. His voice echoed hollowly in the rising fog.

Anger boiled through him as Clan jerked up Windsor's head to reveal her face, then did the same to Nina. He couldn't see them well, but he knew it was them.

"Send them over!" Stone yelled, his voice quivering with rage.

"Show me my kid first," came Clan's voice from the other side.

Impatiently, Stone turned to Sun-On-Wings. The boy's face was stricken as he held up the cradleboard to show Clan the towheaded baby.

"Tie him to the horse, and let him go on the count of five," Clan yelled back.

"Go ahead, kid, do what he says," Stone ordered. When Sun-On-Wings continued to hesitate, he walked over and took the baby out of his arms. "I'm sorry, but he's got to go. We'll get him back, I swear. As soon as Windsor and Nina are safe, we'll go after him."

Sun-On-Wings stepped back as Stone strapped the cradleboard securely to the saddle horn. Carlos began to cry and hold out his arms to Sun-On-Wings, and Stone's throat closed up. He clamped his teeth together and slapped the horse's flank. In the distance, they could hear the donkey cart rattling over the bridge. The riderless horse carrying Carlos passed the wagon near the middle, then clopped slowly onward to the opposite side. As soon as the old Mexican driver brought the wagon close enough, Stone ran to meet it. He rounded the end of the cart and froze in absolute horror.

"Clan, you bastard! Goddamn you to hell! Goddamn you!" he cried, his voice so shrill with anger and anguish that his strident curses reverberated far down the river, his words sending Clan into the fires of damnation over and over again.

21

With Stone's agonized shout still ringing against the canyon walls, Clan and his men galloped away toward Saltillo. A sob constricted Stone's lungs as he looked down at Windsor, her face so battered and bruised he hardly recognized her. She was naked except for a red rebozo wrapped around her. As he gathered her limp body into his arms, his heart filled so full of grief that he wanted to die. He lifted her until his face pressed against her cheek.

"Windsor? Oh, God, Windsor—"

"Please, don't hurt me anymore," she mumbled through cracked lips. Agony pressed down on Stone's soul until he felt he could not breathe. He fought to control his shattered emotions as Sun-On-Wings came running up beside them. He looked at Windsor, and his face crumpled with horror.

Stone buried his face in her cropped hair, unable to speak. From where she lay on the floor of the cart, Nina groaned, and Stone watched Sun-On-Wings turn her over. His stomach revolted when he saw the bloody shawl covering the young girl's back. Clan had brutally beaten Windsor, but he had used his whip to cut up poor Nina.

Infuriated, Stone turned his eyes on the peasant driving the cart. The old man looked terrified, and he held up his arms as if to fend off Stone's wrath.

"No, senor, no. I had nothing to do with this work of *el diablo*! I only drove my cart to market this morning, and the gringo paid me ten pesos to drive two sick women in my cart!"

Stone had no reason to disbelieve him. His dress and speech indicated he was a campesino. He did not have the hard, callous appearance of the men who followed Clan. "We need help, *comprende*? *El doctor*, and a place to stay. We can pay you, *muchos pesos*."

"Only doctor is far away in Durango," the man answered, obviously eager to help, "but there is a healer near here. He lives in the mountain with his *niñas*. He will care for the poor senoritas."

"Which way is it? We've got to hurry!"

Stone looked down at the cart and found he couldn't bear to lay Windsor back onto the blood-stained boards. Instead, he mounted his horse and let Sun-On-Wings hand her gently into his arms. He held her carefully, but she moaned in agony each time he shifted her. All the while they rode toward the healer, he cursed Clan over and over, swearing to send him to the very depths of hell.

Although they traveled for only an hour before the low white hacienda came into view, to Stone it seemed that hours and hours had passed. They had to force their horses to ascend an impossibly steep slope to reach the house, and Stone's patience was stretched past its limit by his inability to spur his horse into a gallop. Sun-On-Wings had taken Nina upon his horse when the path became too rocky for the cart, and now his fringed rawhide shirt was covered with her blood. Nina was going to die,

Stone thought helplessly. No one could lose so much blood and recover.

As they approached the well-tended, rambling adobe structure, an old hound began to bark and run alongside the horses. The howling brought three girls dressed in colorful cotton skirts and loose white blouses running out onto the front veranda. They were all young, with long braids of black hair. As Stone reined to a halt, the youngest one ran away, yelling for her papa.

"Please, can you help us? *Por favor*?" Stone asked, trying to remember Spanish as he slid carefully off the saddle with Windsor cradled in his arms. "Do you understand English?"

"*Sí*, senor. What has happened to the senora?"

"She's been beaten. The other girl's been whipped."

The girls gasped and exchanged frightened glances.

"Who did these terrible things?" said a deep voice, and Stone turned to find a gray-haired man rounding the side of the house. He was probably sixty or more, his brown face deeply wrinkled from age and exposure to the sun.

"A man named Emerson Clan. *Muy malo*. He and his *guerrilleros* have been running guns to Saltillo."

The old man nodded. "The rebels were strong in the mountains for a time, until they were crushed at the mission of San Miguel. Now the Nacionales patrol the roads between Saltillo and Monterrey." His gaze found Windsor, and his voice became urgent. "Quick, you must bring her into the house. I am Gilberto Gomez. My *niñas* will help you."

Stone strode rapidly in his wake, allowing one of the children to hold the door for him while Sun-On-Wings carried Nina inside. Gilberto led them through a low-ceilinged front room with an adobe fireplace, past a long dining table covered with a red-and-blue blanket, then through an arched opening and down a short hall that led to a small bedroom.

"Put her on the bed, then go help with the other girl. Margarita will help me with this one."

"No. I want to stay with her."

Gilberto glanced at him as he finished rolling up his sleeves. "Is she your senora?"

Stone hesitated. "We're not married, but I—"

"Then you must go. We will look after her, and I will come for you. My examination will not take long."

Stone frowned, unwilling to leave, suddenly gripped by an unreasonable fear that he mustn't let her out of his sight or she'd be in great danger again. He looked back at where Windsor lay on the bed as the girl named Margarita took his arm and led him out of the chamber. Sun-On-Wings was similarly dismissed from where he had lowered Nina upon a bed across the room from Windsor.

"Yellow-Haired-Warrior-Woman not die," Sun-On-Wings said firmly, once they both stood in the narrow hallway. He clasped Stone's wrist in the sign of friendship.

Stone nodded, not at all sure Sun-On-Wings' optimism could be believed. "Nina's in pretty bad shape."

"Her very bad. Lose much blood."

"Papa says you are to drink pulque. He said it will help to calm your fears." The smallest of Gilberto's daughters stood beside them, holding a tray set with two metal mugs and a brown bottle. The child looked to be around six years old.

"*Gracias*," Stone muttered, gratefully taking the bottle and one of the glasses. He stared at the closed door of Windsor's room. He could hear the low murmur of Gilberto's voice, then that of one of the girls answering him.

Not prepared to retreat far, he lowered himself

into a squatting position beside the door. Sun-On-Wings took the other mug and did the same. Stone poured them both a portion of the liquor, then tossed down his drink with one swift motion. The wine was sweet and potent. Sun-On-Wings drank from his mug with more discretion.

Stone leaned his head against the wall and shut his eyes. His mind was so full of fear, he felt numb, as if he were only a shadow of himself, a dead man who still drew breath. Ten minutes passed, then fifteen. Stone began to pace. He stopped in his tracks when Gilberto finally opened the door.

Stone looked at him without saying anything.

Gilberto's dark eyes were somber. "The man who did such a thing could only be the seed of *el diablo.*" He sighed, searching Stone's face for answers. "They have both suffered terrible injuries. The one called Nina is much worse, for her flesh has been cut until little of her back is left to mend."

Sun-On-Wings made a strangled sound, and Stone felt a caustic taste in the back of his mouth. "What about Windsor?" he managed to say.

"Only *Dios* and his angels know such things," the healer answered, placing a comforting palm upon Stone's shoulder. "Someone has abused her badly. The many marks upon her body tell me that he used his fists, or perhaps the handle of his whip. One of her arms is broken just above the wrist, and several of her ribs are cracked." He hesitated, sorrowfully shaking his grizzled head. His eyes avoided Stone's anguished ones. "Her body will heal, but she was used in worse ways, I fear."

Stone's face went white. He clenched his fists, wanting to smash them into Emerson Clan's face and body, to pummel him as brutally as he had Windsor.

"I am sorry for you, my *hijo,*" Gilberto said softly. "It is a hard thing for a man to hear, I know. But she will recover in time, at least from the injuries to her body. You must remember to be very gentle with her when she awakens. She was used vilely by a man who is no better than an animal. She will not forget it soon.'' He sighed, glancing at Sun-On-Wings. "As for the other girl, I am sending my Margarita to the village for the priest. I am afraid she will not last much longer, though I will continue to try to stop the bleeding."

After Gilberto had reentered the sickroom, Sun-On-Wings and Stone stood silently across from each other, their expressions stricken. Stone rubbed his hands over his face, desperately wishing he would wake up and find he had been having one of his bad dreams about Clan. But none of his nightmares had approached the terror of this reality.

"I'm going to sit with Windsor," he mumbled, turning away. He entered the room. Gilberto and his daughters were working on Nina. Windsor lay on her back in the bed beside the door. She was restless, moaning and muttering indistinguishable words. A straight-backed wooden chair stood at the foot of her bed, and Stone dragged it close beside her.

He stared down at her face. The dirt and blood had been washed away, but the bruises remained, dark blue and swollen into puffy mounds. A cry of desolation rose in his throat, and he struggled to stifle his despair.

His heart aching, he lifted her right hand to his lips. Her other arm was bound to a makeshift wooden splint with strips of bright red cloth. More bruises covered her bare shoulder and upper arm, as if strong fingers had held her in a brutal grip. Stone was suddenly so filled with rage, he wasn't sure he could control it. He wanted to yell, to beat his head against the wall, to kill someone with his bare hands.

Windsor moved fitfully, weakly trying to pull her

arm away from him. Stone let go, then leaned
closer, tenderly brushing dirty strands of hair from
her forehead. He gritted his teeth. Clan had
sheared off her hair at random, leaving hunks of it
long while other parts were cut nearly to the scalp.
Stone shut his eyes. He cursed himself, deeply,
bitterly, for allowing this to happen.

He groaned, the sounds becoming muffled when
he dropped his forehead onto the mattress beside
her. He ought to pray, he thought. He ought to
beg God to help her get well. But he couldn't. He
couldn't do anything but sit and watch her suffer
and know he had caused it to happen. He was responsible for all her pain. A sob caught in his
throat, a cry of guilt that plunged like a sword into
his soul and embedded itself so deeply there that
he knew he would never be the same again.

Three days after they had arrived at the hacienda, Nina lay very close to death. Sun-On-Wings
knew that soon she would follow the path of the
spirits to the shadow world where the footsteps
traveled in only one direction. He had seen many
die, both from battle wounds and from disease. But
Nina was not a woman fighter like Yellow-Haired-
Warrior-Woman, nor did she suffer from sickness.
She should not have to die so young, lying on her
stomach, her lifeblood leaking from her back.

Wincing, he remembered how her back had
looked when he had lifted the sheet a moment before so the old medicine man could apply his salve.
Very little of her skin was left there. The Evil One
had felt no mercy for the mother of his child.

The thought of Carlos caused an emptiness in
the pit of Sun-On-Wings' stomach. He had to get
the baby back for Nina. The longer he waited to
pursue Emerson Clan, the farther away the bad
men would take Nina's boy. Sun-On-Wings would
have to follow alone, because ever since they had

brought the women to the healer, Arrow-Parts-Hair had been like a man grieving. He would not leave Yellow-Haired-Warrior-Woman's side. He would not sleep. He would not eat. He sat motionlessly, waiting for her to awaken, saying nothing, doing nothing, just staring at her.

"Carlos, Carlos," Nina was mumbling, and Sun-On-Wings leaned closer to listen to her words, though he knew she called only for her son.

"Sun-On-Wings here. Nina not alone."

"Sun-On-Wings?" Nina's cheek lay against the pillow, her eyes glassy with pain and disorientation. "Where's Carlos? Where's my baby?"

Sun-On-Wings did not answer. He could not bring himself to tell her that he had broken his promise to her. He could not bear to speak of his dishonor.

Nina raised her head slightly, desperately attempting to focus her gaze on his face. "Take care of Carlos, *por favor, por favor . . .*" She lapsed into a few weak words of Spanish that Sun-On-Wings could not understand. He clasped her hand when she reached out to him.

"Sun-On-Wings take care of Carlos. Sun-On-Wings not break promise," he whispered close to her ear, embarrassed when his voice caught and hot tears welled up in his eyes. Nina should not have to die. Nina was his friend.

"Gracias, mi amigo, gracias . . ."

Sun-On-Wings swallowed over the big lump that had risen in his throat, then stood back as the black-robed shaman of the white man's world entered the room and went to Nina's bed. The old medicine man named Gilberto put his hand on Sun-On-Wings' arm.

"Come, the padre is here at last. He will prepare her to enter the gates of heaven."

Sun-On-Wings nodded, though he didn't understand all the low murmuring and hand signs the priest was doing over Nina's tortured body. The chanting reminded him of Yellow-Haired-Warrior-Woman. But she would not die. Arrow-Parts-Hair would not let her. Sun-On-Wings was glad for that, but his heart could not soar on the wind like the eagle as long as Nina suffered or Carlos remained in the hands of his evil father. Sun-On-Wings knew what he must do. No one could stop him.

22

Windsor did not want to wake up. She could hear the man's voice calling her name, but she didn't want to hear. It was him. He was waiting for her to open her eyes so he could hurt her again. But she wouldn't, no matter what he said or did to her. She would stay in the deep, dark world of blackness where there was no pain and no screams of terror.

For a while she waited to be overtaken by the wonderful peace that provided a safe haven for her. What was wrong? Why couldn't she sink into oblivion where no one could harm her? She lay as still as death, listening.

"Windsor, please come back to me, please hear me. I know you can do it. You're a fighter. Fight like you did against Hawk-Flies-Down—"

Windsor's mind was muddled and confused, but she tried to think what he could mean. Then she remembered. He liked for her to fight him. He always laughed when she did; then he punished her. Her entire body tensed with dread. Vaguely, she became aware of low whimpering sounds, then realized, horrified, that the moaning was coming from her. He'd know! He'd know she was trying to trick him! She must lie very still and not move a muscle. But her arm hurt so much. He must have kept her hanging from the ceiling beam all night. If only he would let her down for a little while. Then maybe the feeling would come back into her hands again.

"Windsor, try to open your eyes. Try, my love. I know you can do it. Just open your eyes and look at me."

My love, Windsor thought. Clan never said that. He liked to call her bad names, like "Kincaid's whore" and "Chinese bitch." He told her he had killed Jun-li, she remembered, a wail of grief mushrooming up inside her. And he had used his terrible whip on Nina, over and over again, until Windsor had screamed for him to stop. He might whip her, too, if she stirred. She couldn't let him know that she was awake, not ever.

Grim-faced with exhaustion, Stone leaned back in his chair. For days he had sat beside Windsor's bed, trying to reach down and destroy the black chains that held her from him. He wanted to take her hand and lead her out of her coma into the light of day, into his arms. But she still lay unconscious, for much longer than Gilberto had expected she would. Still, Stone couldn't give up. He had to keep trying.

He massaged the bridge of his nose with his thumb and forefinger, so tired he could barely think anymore. Dimly, he became aware that someone had entered the room behind him. He lifted weary eyes, red-rimmed and bleary from lack of sleep, and tried to focus on Sun-On-Wings' face.

"Nina die."

"I'm sorry, Sun-On-Wings. I know how much you cared about her. We all did." Stone rubbed his whiskered jaw and shook his head despondently. He had killed Nina, too. He had involved her, promised to protect her from Clan when she had been so frightened. Nina was dead, and Windsor lay as if dead before him, like some battered, broken rag doll.

"Sun-On-Wings go for little man. Sun-On-Wings promise Nina."

"No!" Alarmed, Stone stood and faced the young Indian. "You can't get a man like Clan by yourself, and there's no way I will go off and leave Windsor alone right now. When she's better, when she wakes up and I know she's going to be all right, then we'll get him together. I swear it, Sun-On-Wings. You've got to trust me."

"The Evil One take Carlos too far if no go now. Sun-On-Wings go now. Arrow-Parts-Hair follow."

"Dammit, Sun-On-Wings, don't do this to me right now! You'll get yourself killed if you go by yourself, and I can't let that happen! Nina's already dead because of me!"

Sun-On-Wings was silent, his black eyes delving into Stone's bloodshot ones. "Yellow-Haired-Warrior-Woman need Arrow-Parts-Hair. Her no need Sun-On-Wings. Me go for Carlos."

Stone grabbed him by the arm, his face furious. "You're not going, Sun-On-Wings, is that clear? Clan will kill you! Why the hell can't you understand that?"

Sun-On-Wings' expression remained impassive, his angular jaw set in a determined angle. "Sun-On-Wings get little man. Sun-On-Wings kill Evil One for what him do to Nina and Yellow-Haired-Warrior-Woman. No worry. Me brave warrior."

"It doesn't matter how brave you are! Clan will kill you if you try to take Carlos. Listen to me, listen to what I'm saying! Take a good look at Windsor! She thought she could take care of herself, too!"

Silently, the Indian gazed deep into Stone's eyes.

"Sun-On-Wings come back with little man. Me give word of honor to Nina."

Helplessly, Stone watched him turn and leave the room, his moccasins silent on the wooden floor. Gripped with the uncanny sensation that he would never see the young Osage warrior again, Stone collapsed heavily into his chair as the galloping hoofbeats of Sun-On-Wings' horse died into the distance. He felt exposed, all his emotions lying on the surface of his skin. Bereft, exhausted, he sat alone beside the woman he loved, sinking deeper and deeper into the darkest depths of despair.

Windsor started violently as something cool touched her lips. She opened her eyes and looked into the face of an old man. He seemed startled, too; then he smiled widely. At that point, she remembered.

"No, don't, please don't—"

"Hush, my child, I am not here to hurt you. See, I will not even touch you if you do not wish it."

Staring at him, Windsor swiped her tongue over her dry mouth. Her eyes darted to the right of the bed when she saw a movement. A young girl gazed down at her. She looked very sad and concerned. Dazed and disoriented, Windsor pushed away from them.

"Who are you? Where am I?"

"I am called Papa Gilberto, and this is Margarita."

Windsor's heart began to thud as she thought of Clan. "Where is he? Is he here?"

"Sí. He is outside by the river. He only just left your side a short time ago. I will send for—"

"No! No!" Windsor was terrified. "Please don't tell him I'm awake. Let me pretend to be asleep. Please, help me escape from him. He's so cruel—"

"Shh, my child, you are safe here. Senor Kincaid will not hurt you. He cares for you very much. He took you from the bad ones and brought you here to us so you could get well.''

Windsor didn't know whether to believe him or not. She felt suspicious, but gradually the hope she had thought to be dead began to kindle inside her heart. "Stone Kincaid? Is he really here?''

''*Sí*, senorita,'' the little girl answered, kneeling beside the bed. "He brought you to Papa nearly a week ago. He was very worried when you would not awaken.''

''Would you like us to send for him?''

Windsor nodded, tempted now to believe what they were telling her. They both seemed so kind and gentle. But as Margarita ran from the room to summon Stone, she remembered what Emerson Clan had done to her, the terrible things he had made her do. Nausea came swiftly, and she turned her face into her pillow. She was so full of shame, she wanted to die. She wanted to shut her eyes and never open them again.

''The senorita's awake, senor! Come quickly!''

Down near the creek, Stone whirled around, then threw down his cigar and ran toward the back veranda of the hacienda, his heart thundering. He tore headlong through the kitchen, down the hall, then halted in the doorway, panting with exertion.

Smiling, Gilberto and Margarita stood beside Windsor's bed. Stone's gaze centered on the frail figure swathed in the white linen bed sheets. Her beautiful sapphire eyes were open, watching him cautiously. Slowly, he moved toward her.

''Oh, Windsor, thank God,'' he muttered gruffly, overcome with emotion. He sank down on the edge of the cot and took her hand. He pressed his mouth against her fingers, his words muffled. ''I was so afraid you wouldn't wake up.''

Filled with joy and relief, he was shocked when she pulled away, turning from him and hiding her

face with her hand. "Go away, oh, please, go
away."

Stone's face fell, and he glanced at Gilberto. The
healer shook his head sadly. Stone frowned. Concerned, he motioned Gilberto and his child out of
the room, and as soon as the door clicked shut,
turned his regard back to Windsor. Sobs shook her
shoulders, harsh sounds of misery.

"Windsor, don't cry, please," Stone whispered,
leaning closer. "Let me hold you and comfort you.
I've waited so long to have you back."

"No," she cried, scrambling jerkily across the
bed, "I don't want you to touch me."

Stone wasn't sure what he should do. He certainly didn't want to force her, but he couldn't endure sitting back and watching her suffer without
doing anything about it. Not after all she had been
through. He needed to touch her. He wanted her
in his arms where she belonged.

"I love you," he muttered thickly. "More than
anything in this world."

For a moment, her weeping stopped. Her answer was muffled by the pillow. "Go away."

"I'm not going away, Windsor. I know that what
happened to you was very bad, but it's over now.
I'm here with you. I'm going to take care of you
and make sure nothing like this ever happens
again. Tell me what you're feeling . . . let me help
you."

"I don't want to talk about it," she whispered,
so low and wretched that he could barely hear her.
"Not ever."

"You won't have to, I promise."

Ever so gently, Stone laid his hand on her back,
wincing when she flinched away from even that
gentle contact. He took his hand away, afraid she
would lurch off the bed if he touched her again.
He listened as she began to cry, damning Clan,
damning his own stupidity for putting her into

such danger. He should have left her in San Francisco. He'd regret not doing that for the rest of his life.

After a time, her heartbroken weeping diminished somewhat, but she kept herself away from him until she fell asleep again. He stayed beside her all day, staring at her shorn head, aching inside as she alternately slept, then awoke, not talking to him, not looking at him.

By late afternoon Papa Gilberto persuaded her to try some chicken broth, and afterward she seemed a bit stronger and more alert. Outside the window, birds flitted from branch to branch, their chirps and calls loud in the peaceful mountain air. Farther away, Stone heard the creek rushing down the mountainside toward Saltillo.

"Is that a river I hear?" Windsor said after another long silence.

"Yes. It flows behind the hacienda."

"Will you take me there?"

Startled by her request, Stone frowned. "Why?"

"Please."

"You're too weak to walk that far. You need to rest and mend longer."

"I want to go now."

"I'll have to carry you."

"All right."

He watched her lean over and take something from the bedside table, which held a washbowl and pitcher. When she turned back, Stone saw that she clutched a bar of soap tightly in her hand. His guts twisted into a knot of compassion when he realized what she needed to do.

Standing, he moved around the bed, picked up a clean blue-and-white quilt, and wrapped it gently around her. He lifted her into his arms, very careful not to disturb her injured arm. He shut his eyes, grieving at how tiny and frail she seemed now, when always before she had been so strong and agile. Margarita had trimmed off the ragged strands of hair Clan had left, and the bruises on her face had begun to fade. Thank God. Stone wanted Windsor never to know how bad she had looked when he had found her.

Windsor laid her head weakly against his shoulder as if already fatigued, and Stone was silent, afraid to speak, afraid he'd say the wrong thing while her feelings were so brittle.

Four of the Gomez girls were on the porch playing with a new brood of frisky brown puppies. They called happy greetings to Windsor as he carried her past them. He strode swiftly down the hill to the creek, then hesitated on the bank, not sure what she wanted him to do.

"Put me down in the water."

"Do you want me to help you take off your gown?"

She trembled in his arms and shook her head.

Stone stepped into the shallows where the water was clear and clean, then carefully lowered her to a sitting position there. She shivered as the swift current washed over her bare legs, swirling up the edge of her white nightgown and making the wet fabric below the surface cling to her thighs. Windsor said nothing, and Stone moved a few steps away. He squatted down.

"Please don't look at me," she said, with downcast eyes, her murmur nearly obliterated by the splashing water.

Stone, feeling awful, transferred his gaze to the pine trees spiking the opposite bank. Despite her request, he could not keep his eyes off her. He looked back and saw her rubbing the bar of soap across her face, as if she wanted to scrape her skin away.

For a long time she weakly continued her frantic cleansing, her broken arm held against her side as she used the other hand to wash every inch of her body. So long did she keep it up that Stone felt he couldn't stand it much longer. Her ribs weren't healed yet. What she was doing had to be painful. He wanted to jerk her up and hold her close and tell her that what had happened had not been her fault. That everything would be all right. But he didn't.

After a long time, her motions slowed and she finally sat still, staring downstream as the creek rippled over her arms and legs.

"Nina's dead, isn't she?" she asked finally, not looking at Stone.

"Yes."

"And Sun-On-Wings? Is he dead, too?"

"No. He went after—" Stone stopped, afraid to use Clan's name for fear she'd go to pieces. "Carlos. They have him now."

Tears began to roll down Windsor's cheeks, terrible, silent tears, and Stone could not stand her suffering. He went to her, picking her up and holding her close, and was pleased when she did not pull away. She cried against his shoulder as he carried her back up to the hacienda.

It was going to take a long time, he thought, but she would be all right. He would do anything, whatever it took, however long it took, to rid her of the pain Clan had inflicted upon her.

Until she was well and whole, his own heart would remain in pieces.

23

A low-slung net hammock was stretched across the rear veranda of the hacienda, and late at night Windsor sat cross-legged within its wide, roomy depths. Desirous of retreating deep into the far reaches of her mind where she wouldn't have to think, she began to murmur the familiar chant. Since she had entered the temple at age ten, the ancient words had never failed to provide her with the inner repose that gave her peace and tranquility. But now serenity was elusive.

No matter how hard she tried to focus her thoughts, her mind would not disassociate from the world around her as it had in the past. Pain and bitter humiliation struggled inside her—thoughts of the terrible things that Clan had done to her beat against the walls of her brain as relentlessly as moths upon a lantern's glass.

Stifling a sob, she opened her eyes and stared bleakly into the dark night. She sat motionlessly, listening to the faint rustling sounds. Evening breezes stirred the pine boughs just above the porch, making them scrape against the roof, and hidden in the dense foliage surrounding the house, crickets chirped a strident, buzzing serenade.

The damp, leafy smell of impending rain permeated the thick pine forest and reminded her of the Temple of the Blue Mountain when the spring rains dripped off the eaves near her pallet. She had always liked the sounds and scents of nature. Now she liked the darkness where no one could see her.

Not far away, on the long veranda that overlooked a vast mountain valley, she could hear the baritone rumble of Stone Kincaid's voice. The murmured answers came from Papa Gilberto. The old healer had been very kind to her during the past weeks of her illness.

While Windsor listened, Stone gave a low laugh, then said something she couldn't hear. He had been gentle with her, too, always attentive and sensitive to her feelings. He acted as if he didn't care what Clan had done to her. But she knew her days with Clan had changed her forever. Her body and soul were no longer pure. She didn't feel the same about herself, or about Stone Kincaid, or about the things she had been taught to believe.

No longer did the wise words of the Old One give her counsel and direction. She felt as if she had been betrayed by them, as if she were floundering on some storm-tossed, demon-haunted sea of doubt and confusion. She shivered, distraught by her loss of faith.

The chill mountain air penetrated her lightweight clothes, and she tugged the warm black shawl over her head, then wrapped the long ends around her shoulders. Little Margarita had given her this shawl, as well as several full cotton skirts of bright colors and low-necked white blouses that had belonged to their oldest sister, Juana, who was visiting friends in Mexico City. Papa Gilberto and his family, especially Margarita, had been good to her.

In the kitchen behind her, Windsor heard the youngest Gomez girl attempting to coax a tune

from Sun-On-Wings' feather-decorated flute. As if
wrung by invisible hands, her wounded heart was
squeezed tightly, painfully. She missed her brave
Indian friend. She hadn't even been able to say
good-bye to him.

A moment later the wind brought the acrid scent
of cigar smoke wafting across her awareness.
Windsor's entire body went rigid. A dread memory pulled free from its shackles and flew unfet-
tered down the dank, hidden corridors of her mind
where she had locked away her worst fears. Stiff
with fear, she saw Emerson Clan again, striking his
match and staring into her eyes as he puffed his
cigar into flame. He had always smiled when he
was about to hurt her, she remembered with a
shudder of revulsion, biting her lip to keep it from
trembling. His teeth had been so white, as white
as his long, sweet-smelling hair.

Her pulse accelerated, thumping out of control,
her breath coming in short, labored gasps. On edge
with nerve-tingling apprehension, she peered into
the blackness that no longer seemed comforting but
filled with macabre malevolence. What if he were
out there, smoking and watching her? What if he
captured her again? Her jaw clamped hard, she
fought to steady jangled, raw-edged nerves. But all
she could think about, all her mind would conjure
up, was how Clan had laughed when he pressed
the glowing, red-hot tip of his cigar against her bare
breast. Swiftly, powerfully, panic rose inside her.
She shot to her feet, heart racing, poised to run.

"Windsor? What is it?"

Starting violently, she screamed, short and
clipped, then whirled and found Stone Kincaid
standing close behind her. He took a step backward, holding both hands out in front of him as if
to placate her fear. Windsor's gaze riveted on the
smoking cheroot he held idly between his fingers.
He seemed to realize the cigar had frightened her,

because he immediately flicked it out into the grass. Trembling, Windsor watched the lighted end curve in a wide red arc to the ground.

"Forgive me, sweetheart. I didn't mean to startle you. I thought you heard me coming." Stone's voice had taken on the low, soothing tone he had adopted since they had been living in the mountains.

Nerves still quivering, emotions shredded, Windsor backed away from him. She was afraid he might try to touch her. To her relief, he didn't make any threatening movements in her direction. Instead, he sat down on the wooden steps, a few feet away from her.

Still shaken, Windsor inched farther into the darkest corner where the lamplight coming from the window fell not upon her but illuminated Stone's position. Squatting down, she leaned her back against the wall, hugging her arms tightly around her waist.

"Do you feel any better today, Windsor?" he asked a moment later. "Papa Gilberto told me that your arm is healing well. He said that in a few more weeks, we'll be able to travel."

Alarm filled her. She did not want to go anywhere. Clan wouldn't be able to find her here in an isolated hacienda high in the Sierra Madre. Margarita and her sisters had often assured her that only a few of their neighbors, those requiring medical attention, ventured up the steep, rocky road that led to their casa.

Stone turned sideways and stretched out his long legs. He still wore his black pants and tall leather boots, but since they had come to the hacienda, he had taken to wearing the loose white shirts called *camisas*, as Papa Gilberto did. Both of his revolvers lay in their holsters, tied down atop his muscular thighs. He never took off his guns. His beard had grown heavy, a black, thick shadow on his chin

and jaw. At the moment, his eyes were searching
the shadows where she hid.

"Did I ever tell you that my sister, Carlisle, is
down here in Mexico visiting a friend of hers?"

"No."

"A friend of my brother's is escorting her. His
name is Chase Lancaster, and he's got a ranch
down around Monterrey somewhere, a place called
the Hacienda de los Toros. Well, I found out a moment ago that Papa Gilberto and the girls know
him, too. In fact, he said that both Chase and Carlisle visited them a couple of months ago. Apparently they got caught up in some kind of trouble
with the *querrilleros* before the revolution was put
down." He paused momentarily. "I'm a bit worried about Carlisle, because Papa Gilberto said she
was sick with malaria the last time he saw her."

"I am sorry she was ill." Stone had never spoken to her about his family before, and Windsor
wondered how it would feel to be like Carlisle and
have a brother who worried about her. Hung-pin
had been almost like a brother, and Clan had killed
him with his whip, as he had done to Nina. She
screwed her eyes shut, unable to think about Nina.

"Papa Gilberto said Chase's ranch isn't far from
here. I know we'd be welcome there, especially if
Carly's staying there, too. Even if she's not, I could
probably find out if she's well again."

"I will stay here and wait for you," she told him,
alarmed at the prospect of venturing out of her safe
haven.

There was a lengthy pause, then Stone spoke,
very low. "You can't stay here forever, Windsor. I
want to marry you and take you home to Chicago
with me. I can protect you there, I swear it."

Hot tears welled, burning like flames behind
Windsor's eyelids. How could he contemplate such
a thing? He must suspect the terrible things Clan

had done to her. She couldn't bear the thought of
a man ever touching her again, not even Stone.

"When I leave here, I will return to the Temple
of the Blue Mountain."

Stone's sigh was heavy, defeated. "If you're sure
that's what you want, then I'll take you there."

No other words passed between them, the distant rushing of the river and the chirping of insects
the only sounds in the quiet night.

Stone sat on the low bed called a *catre*, which
Papa Gilberto had provided for him soon after their
arrival at the hacienda. He had moved it into
Windsor's room during the first days when she had
still been unconscious. He hadn't slept much in the
beginning but had kept a constant vigil at her bedside, terrified she was going to die. Now, weeks
later, her body was finally beginning to heal, thank
God, but her mind was still gouged by deep emotional wounds that he feared would never leave
her.

He studied her as she lay sleeping in her bed
across the room. She lay in peaceful repose at the
moment, but he knew her nightmares would begin
soon. Every night was the same. Still, during those
first moments just after she had lunged awake, terrified and trembling with fright, she would let him
hold her. He took advantage of those precious op-
portunities because it was the only time she could
bear having his hands on her.

Grimacing, he shut his eyes, his gut churning
with anger. She had been so strong before, so self-
assured and in control of her life. Clan had taken
all that away from her. He had broken her spirit as
well as her body.

Stone's jaw clamped, and his fingers curled so
tight inside his fists that his fingernails bit painfully
into his palms. Clan had perfected the art of de-
stroying people. How many more would he torture

and kill before he was stopped? Stone's mind conjured up Sun-On-Wings' young face, and he forced the image from his thoughts, praying the boy wouldn't suffer.

Consciously relaxing his grip, Stone shifted to a more comfortable position. He had to concentrate on making Windsor well again. She needed him now. He was pleased she was slumbering so peacefully. Maybe she'd even make it through the night this time. While she lay so quietly, he ought to try to get a few hours of sleep himself. Physically, he was bone tired. But it was even worse to watch her and want her, to relive the times he had held her in his arms and kissed her, had made love to her. He felt so damn powerless. All he could do was wait and watch, and hope that someday she'd get over all she'd been through.

Strangely enough, his own bad dreams had ceased. He rarely even thought much about what Clan had done to him at Andersonville. The uncontrollable thirst for vengeance he'd nursed for so long seemed unimportant.

Though he hated Emerson Clan more than before, he was tired of thinking about him, tired of chasing him for years on end. Most of all, he hated himself for bringing Clan's evil into the lives of the people he loved. John Morris and Edward Hunt had been victims of his feud with Clan. They both had died at Andersonville. Then when Clan had been enticed to Chicago, Gray had been shot, Tyler terrorized. A maid had been hurt and another servant killed.

And now because of Stone's obsessed pursuit of Clan, Windsor's lovely sapphire eyes were empty, her youthful innocence and idealism extinguished, as surely as if he'd reached inside her and pinched out the flame of her spirit.

Stone's cheek worked spasmodically, and he fought to control his roiling anxieties. He loved

Windsor. He didn't know all that she had been forced to endure while under Clan's control, but he could guess. He didn't want to hear about it, and he didn't want to think about it. He only wished he could wipe away all her memories of her suffering. But he couldn't.

Windsor had to be the one to find the strength to survive. All he could do was help her, gently, without pressuring her. If he tried too hard, he'd end up losing her completely. Despite what he'd told her a few nights ago when they'd sat on the back veranda, he didn't want her to return to her life in China. If she went back, she might decide to stay there, to become a monk like the Old One she held in such esteem. But how could he stop her?

All he could do was bide his time, be patient and understanding. Time was needed to cleanse her mind of the torment plaguing her, lots of time. Maybe if he could persuade her to go to Chicago with him, Gray and Tyler could help him get through to her.

Despair overrode his hope, and Stone bent his head to stare at the jade stones encircling his wrist. He stroked one of them out of habit, wishing it would relax him the way Windsor had once believed it would. Regardless of how either of them felt physically, they had to move on as soon as they safely could. He wanted Windsor out of the mountains, out of Mexico, and as far away from Clan as they could get. Perhaps taking her home to visit her mother would help. She and Amelia had developed a closer relationship during the weeks they had spent together in San Francisco.

Stone came out of his thoughts and to his feet when Windsor suddenly bolted upright in her bed. Before her strangled cry had faded, he was with her, catching her flailing arms as she beat ineffectually against his chest.

"It's all right, baby. It's me. You're having a dream again. I've got you now. You're safe."

He had said the same words the night before, and the night before that, and her reaction was no different this time. She stopped fighting once she realized it was him and not Clan; then she wept harshly against his shirtfront. But she did not pull away from him. She stayed in his arms, and that's where he wanted her. When morning came, he knew she would sink back into the deep well of misery and distrust in which she took refuge. But until then, he would hold her close and dry her tears, and enjoy the soft warmth of her body pressed tightly against his own. Time would heal her, inside and out, he told himself firmly. He had to keep believing that.

"There is no mistake, Papa Gilberto?"

"No, my child. You will have your baby in the winter."

Windsor looked away from his kind dark eyes. She had suspected that she was with child, but she hadn't wanted to believe it. She sat with the old man on the bank of the stream and stared down into the clear water at a small fish lying motionless on the bottom. Slowly, she moved her gaze downstream to where Stone stood.

Shirtless, the muscles of his back rippling, he lifted the ax over his head. The sun caught the steel blade, making it glitter like silver for an instant before he brought it down to thud against a log. He bent and threw the split pieces into a basket, saying something to the five little girls who sat on the ground watching him.

"Will you tell Senor Kincaid about your child?"

Windsor felt her face burn with color. "I am not sure he is the father."

"Sí. But you are not sure he is not, no?"

"I want him to be. It was awful when—" She

stopped, her throat growing tight. She sought to control herself.

Papa Gilberto propped his elbows on his bent knees. "Your child is a part of you. He is not at fault for what others have done to you. Newborn babies are innocent of the world and what went before. They cannot be blamed for the good or evil possessed within their father."

Windsor looked at him. "I would not blame a baby for what happened to me. Nina did not hate Carlos because of his father. She died to protect him."

"Then you must give Senor Kincaid the same opportunity. He will want to know if he is to be a father. He cares very much for you. I have seen the way he treats you. He will be good to your child."

"I do not know what I will do," she murmured. "I do not think I would make Stone Kincaid a good wife."

Papa Gilberto smiled kindly and patted her hand. "You must let your heart listen to the words he speaks to you. Then you will know what to do."

Windsor watched him get up and move off toward the hacienda, but she was very afraid. The idea of having Emerson Clan's seed growing inside her filled her with revulsion. She did not want to have his child, she thought, and then a new terror enveloped her. If he found out, would he come after her? Would he threaten to hunt her down the same way he had done to Nina after she had given birth to his son? She put her hand over her mouth, fighting her growing panic. They had to leave! Now, today! Stone had to take her somewhere far away where Clan could never find out that she might be carrying his baby.

24

Despite the broiling sun of late June, the tree-dappled patio of the Hacienda de los Toros was cool and shady. Dona Maria Jimenez y Morelos sat in a white wicker chair drawn close beside a double-tiered fountain, the high-arcing jets tinkling in a merry cascade into a octagon pool built of blue mosaic tiles. Soft pillows handcrafted with yellow-and-black Aztec designs made her straight-backed chair comfortable against her spine, and her dark head, crowned regally with graying braids, was bent tenaciously to her task.

Little heeding the hot weather, her brow furrowed into deep lines of concentration, Dona Maria drew a silver needle through the fine oyster-colored linen stretched inside her embroidery hoop. She pulled the ivory thread tight, then reinserted it, each stitch done with practiced precision. She paused, smiling as she examined the tiny lace-edged collar of the baby's gown.

Finally, after months of waiting and hoping, her two brand-new grandsons were on their way home from America. At last she would see their darling little faces and hold them in her arms as she had longed to do since last April, when her older son,

Chaso, had written to her with the announcement of their births.

Even more wonderful, Chaso had reconciled with his beautiful gringa wife, Carlita. When Dona Maria's coppery-haired daughter-in-law had sailed away from Veracruz several weeks before Christmas, Maria had feared she would never see Carlita again. But Chaso had followed her to the *norteamericano* city called Chicago, and they had managed to work out all the problems plaguing their stormy marriage. By the sounds of her son's letters, they were very happy together now, just as Dona Maria had always known they could be.

The swift, silvery flash of her needle commenced once more, and Dona Maria's soft sigh was vastly contented. All the hours spent upon her knees before the altar of the Holy Virgin had not been in vain. She felt truly blessed.

Even her younger son, Tomas, was now behaving himself. She glanced at where he sat at a glass-topped table on the veranda. He was supposed to be studying from his law books, but instead, he was mending a leather lariat, his young face rapt. Dona Maria did not reprimand him.

At least he had finally outgrown his infatuation with Carlita, his own brother's wife! Nothing good could have resulted from that, and she was acutely relieved that he had finally come to terms with Chaso and Carlita's marriage, especially now that the couple had had their twins. And ever since Dona Maria had brought Tomas north to the Hacienda de los Toros, he seemed much more content.

Nearly a month ago, they had arrived at Chaso's sprawling rancho. During the past weeks, Tomas had spent nearly all his waking hours in the bullring, practicing with his scarlet cape. In time she hoped he would realize that wedding little Marta Moreno was in his best interest, as both their fam-

ilies had agreed. Indeed, everything seemed to be
working out for the best, and perhaps now she
could attain the peace of mind that had eluded her
earlier in the year when both her sons were so un-
happy.

Now she could stop worrying and spend her
days sewing infant sacques and knitting tiny boo-
ties. Whoever could have thought Carlita would
give Chaso *two* healthy baby boys, requiring a *second* layette? Twins, christened with fine Spanish
names. She was so eager to see little Esteban and
Enrico that her heart beat like the wings of a hummingbird just from thinking about it!

"*Perdón*, senora, but visitors have come."

Surprised by the announcement of guests, Dona
Maria looked up at her maid, then her heart
soared. "Is it Chaso and Carlita, Rosita?" she asked
breathlessly.

"No, senora. They are both *norteamericanos*, a
man and a woman. The senor says that Papa Gilberto has sent them to us."

Dona Maria was disappointed but also intrigued.
She rarely received visitors when she was here at
her son's house. "Papa Gilberto? Indeed? Well, *va-
mos*, then; bring them to me. I would like word of
my dear old friend. I do hope Papa and his *niñas*
are well."

"Who has come, Mama?" Tomas asked, joining
her as she creased her grandson's shirt into careful
folds, then carefully laid the garment in the large
hinged sewing basket on the floor beside her.

"We shall soon see, *mi hijo*. I only know they
have come from Papa Gilberto's," she answered,
smoothing her hands over her lustrous skirt of
black silk as two people entered the patio from the
front salon. As Rosita led the strangers across the
narrow flagstone path, Dona Maria studied them
with interest.

The gringo was quite big, every bit as tall as

Chaso, who was several inches over six feet. But this man was as dark as her own son was fair, with jet-black hair that hung long against the back of his neck, and a thick black beard clipped close to the lean contours of his jaw. He was dressed like the vaqueros, the cowboys who tended the cattle and bullrings. His long, muscular legs were encased in dark pants and tall black boots set with jingling spurs, and he wore a travel-stained, olive-and-tan striped serape slung over his shoulders.

The dusty blanket-coat of the campesinos did not conceal his heavy, ivory-handled Colt pistols. The black leather holsters decorated with fancy silver designs were strapped to his thighs. He carried his weapons as an experienced gunman would. He was a handsome man, she decided, but in a tough, dangerous way. She was suddenly glad that Tomas stood beside her, even though the stranger led his female companion gently. Why, he was holding her arm as if she were made of porcelain and he feared he might damage her, she thought, then was astonished at her uncharacteristic flight of whimsy.

Her interest truly piqued, she next studied the gringa he escorted with such extraordinary care. She was a little thing, not much taller than Dona Maria's own five-foot height. The girl kept her eyes planted on the paving stones as they walked, so Dona Maria could not see her face clearly. She wore a full skirt of bright scarlet cotton and a white blouse with a drawstring neck that exposed her slender collarbones. Her head was bare of rebozo or hat, her hair a shiny pale gold color and shorn to lay in loose curls close to her scalp—certainly a fashion Dona Maria found most scandalizing! Never before had she seen such a coiffure upon a woman, not even among the poorest campesinos.

''Bienvenida,'' Dona Maria greeted them as they stopped in front of her. She was careful not to stare at the gringa's peculiar haircut, though she felt the urge. "I am Dona Maria, Don Chaso's mother. And this is my son, Don Tomas. Rosita said that Papa Gilberto sent you here."

The big gringo inclined his head toward Tomas, but he looked her straight in the eye when he answered. She immediately detected the fatigue hovering in the blue-gray depths.

"*Sí*, senora. We've been staying at Papa Gilberto's hacienda for several months now." He glanced at his blond-haired companion, but she didn't look up. "This is Windsor Richmond, and my name's Stone Kincaid. I believe that both my brother and sister are acquainted with your son, Senor Lancaster. Actually, I was hoping to find Carlisle here. Papa Gilberto told me she'd been sick with malaria."

"Kincaid! Why, you are Carlita's brother, no?" Tomas asked excitedly.

For the first time, Stone Kincaid's dark-bearded face flashed with a white smile. "Yes, I am."

"Carlita often spoke of you and your brother, Gray, when she and Chaso lived at my casa in Mexico City," Dona Maria explained, examining his face with renewed interest but deciding he bore no resemblance to his flame-haired sister.

"Is she here now?" he asked.

"No, I am sorry to say she has gone home to America for a visit. But we expect her to return to the Hacienda de los Toros any time now with Chaso and their children."

Stone Kincaid frowned slightly, looking at Tomas, then back to Dona Maria. "Children? I'm afraid I don't understand, senora."

"Why, you do not know, then, Senor Kincaid? Your sister was wed to my son, Chaso, back in the autumn. She recently bore him twin sons." Maria smiled, noticing that the girl looked up at the mention of the babies.

"Well, I'll be damned," Carlita's brother swore, shaking his head, then quickly looked apologetic. "Forgive my language, senora, but that news comes as quite a shock. I've been out of contact with my family for months now, and I had no idea Carly had married, much less had a child. Last November, when I left Chicago, we knew she was down here on a visit with the Perez family, but no one suspected she was considering marriage to your son. In fact, I was under the impression she didn't like him."

Dona Maria was reluctant to relate all the tragic incidents that had led to her son's hasty marriage to Carlita. "I fear Carlita's story is a long one, senor, and I am sure you are much too tired to listen to all of it just now. Forgive my saying so, but the senorita looks exhausted."

At Dona Maria's mention of her, the silent gringa raised her large, golden-lashed eyes. The expression in the sapphire depths was so full of sorrow that Dona Maria was startled.

"Sí, I am very tired, senora," Windsor Richmond answered. Her low words were uttered in English, but were threaded with some accent other than Spanish. Dona Maria wondered where she came from.

"We've been traveling hard for several weeks now," Stone Kincaid explained, draping his arm protectively around the girl's shoulder. When she flinched slightly, he was quick to remove it. Dona Maria became even more curious as Stone Kincaid continued. "I was hoping Senor Lancaster would put us up here for a while, until I can arrange passage to New Orleans. But if he and Carlisle aren't here—"

"Oh, sí," Dona Maria interrupted swiftly, "you must remain here. Carlita would be most disappointed if I were to let you leave before she arrives. As I said, she will be here shortly." She swept her arm up toward the arched gallery running along the second floor. "And as you can see, the Hacienda de los Toros is very large. Tomas and I will be honored to entertain you until my son and daughter-in-law arrive."

"*Gracias*, senora."

Smiling at him, Dona Maria nodded, appreciating Stone Kincaid's attempts to use her own language. He was not fluent in Castillian by any means, but the Spanish words he did use were understandable.

"There is another thing, Dona Maria. I do need to send a message to my brother, Gray, where he lives in Chicago. Is there a place near here where I can find a telegraph office?"

"We often send riders to Monterrey for just such a purpose. If you'll write what you wish to wire, I will see that the message leaves here in the morning." Dona Maria smiled, but she was a little worried about the senorita, who was swaying on her feet as if ready to drop. "My son and I were just about ready to partake of a meal, senor," she offered, still eyeing the poor girl. "We would be pleased to welcome you to our table."

"I don't wish to be rude," Stone Kincaid replied, "but Windsor has been very ill for the past few months. I'm afraid our journey here has been hard on her. Would you be offended if we retired for the night and then visited with you again in the morning?"

"*Sí*, the journey down from the sierra *fría* is a grueling one. I will show you to your apartments myself. Tomas, would you summon Rosita to bring warm water for baths, *por favor*?"

"*Sí*, Mama."

Stone Kincaid watched the boy hurry away. "You're very kind, Dona Maria, but please don't go to the trouble to ready two rooms. I'll stay with Windsor in case she needs me through the night."

Again Dona Maria was shocked. Nodding, she hid her reaction and preceded them toward the steps leading to the upper floor. When she glanced behind her, Stone Kincaid had picked up the frail young woman and was carrying her in his arms. Dona Maria lifted her long rustling skirt and swept up the white adobe staircase to the second-floor bedchambers, instinctively aware that something most dreadful was wrong between the *norteamericanos*.

Windsor sat across from Stone, looking as still and fragile as the porcelain vase filled with white roses on the crystal-laden, linen-festooned table between them. As he studied her face, he knew it was imperative to find a way to reach her. They had been at the Hacienda de los Toros for nearly two weeks now, and though she seemed more rested, she was still as edgy as a trapped cat. Any sudden move or unexpected noise sent her jumping with fright. Stone's stomach contracted, his emotions as tangled as a knotted skein of thread.

More than anything, he had hoped her shattered nerves would improve in the relative safety of Chase Lancaster's ranch. That was one reason he had decided to make the strenuous journey down from the mountains. Stone had never felt secure in the sierra where Clan and his filthy band of cutthroats rode unopposed. God only knew where the bastard had gone.

Here, on the other hand, Lancaster had over a hundred armed vaqueros patrolling the sprawling estate night and day. No intruder could get past them, not even one as clever as Clan. The house, with its tall walls and barred gates, was also manned by a battery of servants and as fortified as a castle keep.

Physically, Stone felt a hell of a lot better than he had in a long time. He had shaved and bathed the first night they had come, and since then, Dona Maria had been an unparalleled hostess, making sure they had everything they needed. She had even instructed her cook to prepare plain dishes for Windsor, steamed rice without the tomato sauce and chilis Mexicans depended upon for their spicy cuisine. And he slept on a real bed for a change, one with a comfortable mattress. But not with Windsor. She still would barely let him touch her.

At the moment, she was poking at her food with a heavy, engraved silver fork. At least she was eating something. At Papa Gilberto's, she had partaken of food only when Stone had insisted. Yes, she was better here. She stayed in her room most of the time, but she did rise early each morning to walk by herself in the interior garden. He considered that a victory in itself. Still, she wouldn't discuss what had happened to her or what the future would bring.

Lightning flashed behind him, and Windsor looked up. When their eyes met, her mouth curved in a softly entrancing smile. He thought of the first time he had ever seen her, when she wore a nun's habit and carried Jun-li hidden in her bamboo case. Even then, garbed in dreary black, she had been the most beautiful woman he had ever seen. They had been through so much together since they had boarded that train in Chicago. It was hard to remember what his life had been like before he had met her.

Now, in front of his eyes, she was wasting away, in body and in mind, and it was killing him to watch.

Tonight he was going to make her remember the way it had been between them, the way it could be again. But the idea was as terrifying as it was desirable, because he knew he had to be careful not to sabotage the painstaking progress he'd made with her.

Outside the tall white slatted doors, which stood open beside him, rain beat upon the scrolled, wrought-iron railing on the balcony of their bed-chamber. It had been raining all day, filling the terra-cotta geranium pots with water and pelting the bright red blossoms until they bent their heads in defeat. The drenching deluge drummed relentlessly against the curving red Spanish tiles of the roof and dripped in slow, hypnotic rhythms from the overhanging eaves.

Lifting his stemmed goblet of wine, he observed how her white embroidered shirt had fallen off one shoulder. Her slender collarbone stood out as a prominent reminder of her ordeal, making her smooth ivory skin appear fragile and translucent. But she had regained some of the weight she had lost and was still undeniably beautiful, her lovely face smooth and soft again, free of the bruises and scrapes left by Clan's abuse. The only scars now were those inside her head. Anger gripped him for an instant, hot, intense, overwhelming. He would never forgive himself for allowing Clan to abuse her, not as long as he drew breath.

After the horrors he had survived at Andersonville, he had thought of little but his own obsession to kill Emerson Clan. He had skimmed over the surface of his life like a water bug darting over the still surface of a pond. Hunting down Clan had been his life. He hadn't cared about anything or anybody else. He had gone through the motions of living, with his family, with the handful of women he'd wanted enough to make an effort to be civil with, but he hadn't really lived, not like other people did.

Although he had to go after Clan again someday, now he found himself wanting a peaceful life. He wanted Windsor at his side, the wonderful, enigmatic Windsor that she used to be. If God would give him that, he would never ask for anything else.

Windsor sighed again, her attention focused on the spattering rain, and Stone's gaze lingered on the bluish circles beneath her eyes. She was resting better, but she had yet to make it through the night without being awakened by nightmares.

Thunder growled threateningly, rolling across the night sky, recalling to Stone the night he'd awakened in the Osage lodge, sweating and heaving from his own brand of hell. He glanced down at the jade bracelet Windsor had given him. He hadn't taken it off his wrist since she'd knotted it there months ago.

If only he had known then what he knew now, he would have wintered there among Sun-On-Wings' people. If he'd done that, Windsor would still be the woman who shot arrows blindfolded and defeated hardened warriors barehanded. Bitter regret gouged into him, puncturing deeply, but he quickly pushed his remorse away. She would be that way again someday, he told himself firmly.

"Do you remember the night you gave me these jade stones?" he asked, lifting his arm so she could see them.

She nodded, but her sapphire eyes were clouded. When she put her fingers to her throat where her own jade necklace had once hung, Stone realized she was probably remembering when Clan had taken it from her. He didn't want her to think about Clan anymore, not tonight, not ever.

"The jade stones have helped me, but now you need them more than I do."

Stone slipped the bracelet off his wrist, then slid it over her hand. Windsor stared down at the smooth round stones, twisting them between her fingers. "Thank you, Stone Kincaid. These are the only things I have left that I brought with me from

China." Her voice broke, and she bit her lip. "Even poor Jun-li is lost to me."

Stone fought his need to touch her, hold her close, stroke her hair, bury himself inside her. That's what he wanted and that's what she needed if she was ever going to forget.

"You rubbed my neck that night and stuck a bunch of needles in me." He grinned. "I wasn't so sure about you then."

"You did not like me much. You did not trust me."

"I trust you now, Windsor," he told her quietly. His eyes captured hers. "Do you trust me?"

"Yes. Thrice you have saved my life."

"Then let me hold you, let me touch you. I need you, sweetheart. I miss having you in my arms. Is that so much to ask?"

Her thick golden lashes lowered to shield her eyes; then she stood and walked to the open doors. Stone rose as well. Moving up behind her, he cupped her shoulders with his palms, felt the tension in her body. "I won't do anything you don't want me to, Windsor. Surely you know that by now."

As he spoke, he slid his hands up beneath her short, silky hair, pressing his palms firmly against her scalp as she had done to him that rainy night in the Indian lodge. How strange life was, he thought. How ironic that their roles had reversed so completely. How could one evil man disrupt so many lives? Why were such things possible?

He flexed his fingers, drawing them down from the center of her head to her temples, then back up again. Windsor emitted a soft sound of contentment and relaxed against his chest. After a time, he lowered his hands to her shoulders, kneading the tight muscles until they became soft and pliant beneath his touch.

"Feel good?" he whispered, his lips caressing

the delicate curve of her ear. His own self-control was slipping, fast. God, how he wanted her. But he couldn't force her, couldn't push her too soon. He swept a handful of silken curls behind her ear so he could nuzzle the side of her throat.

"Yes." Her head lolled weakly back against his shoulder. Stone shut his eyes, struggling to contain his desire for her but mindlessly intoxicated by the sweet fragrance emanating from her hair.

"I love you, Windsor," he muttered, his voice so thick as to be nearly incomprehensible. "I don't give a damn what happened to you. I want you for my wife. Let me show you how much I care. Let me make love to you the way I used to."

Windsor's head rolled back and forth, denying him, but as his palms moved down her shoulders, teasing loose the ties of her blouse, she did nothing to stop him. Stone's heart began to thud. God help him, he had never wanted anything as badly as he wanted to carry her to the bed, to let the softness of her wrap around his loneliness and need. But he knew only too well that he could not. She needed his gentleness and understanding much more than the thundering passion which held him in its fist, making his hands tremble.

She pulled away, clutching her loosened bodice against her breasts. "No, I can't do what you want, not ever. Please don't. You know I can't bear to feel your hands on me!"

Her words hit him hard. "I'm not going to hurt you. I'll never hurt you, never," he muttered hoarsely, turning her around and forcing her to look up at him. He took her by her wrists and gently placed her open palms against his face. "Look at me, Windsor. It's me, not him. Let me love you. Let me help you remember how good it is between us."

Tears pooled in her eyes, dripped over her long lashes to run down her cheeks. "I can't, Stone Kincaid. When you hold me like this, all I can think about is him and what he did—"

Stone stared down at her, not wanting to force her but afraid that if he didn't break through her barriers soon, he never would. Tortured by the thought of losing her, he pulled her up until his face was buried in her hair. "Please don't do this to me, Windsor. I don't think I can stand it if you keep pushing me away."

"Oh, Stone, he hurt me so much. He hurt both of us," she moaned, her voice cracking with agony, her despair flooding out. "He laughed when he hurt us! And I thought I could stand it. I thought I could control my mind so that he couldn't torment me, but when I did that, he would turn on Nina instead and use his whip on her! He'd hit her over and over, and she'd scream and scream and beg me to do whatever he wanted. I can still hear her terrible screaming. I can still see the blood running down her back until she was covered with it—"

Stone's mind recoiled. This was the first time she had revealed anything of what had happened to her, and he wasn't prepared for the rage that roared inside him as Windsor twisted away from him. Distraught, she fell upon her knees, hiding her face in her hands. "He kept me with him all the time," she muttered, her words muffled by weeping. "When we traveled, when we stopped, every minute, he wanted me close so he could taunt me and hurt me. At night he'd take us to a barn or a stable, just Nina and me, and he'd keep us there for hours, hitting her with his whip, making me crawl on my hands and knees and beg him for things. And, oh, Stone, he made me tell him about you, about what we did together, about how you touched me and made love to me. He made me tell him that he was a better man, a better lover, that I never really loved you—"

Stone turned to granite, every muscle as hard as rock. The anguish that gripped him was so powerful, so all-encompassing, that it completely consumed him. He couldn't move, couldn't answer, couldn't even comfort her. All the fury he had suppressed and held inside himself for months could no longer be contained. The tight rein with which he had harnessed his boiling emotions slid from his grip, and extreme, unbridled horror flooded over him, despair and guilt gushing upward from the bottom of his soul to take possession of his body.

Shaking all over, he took a few jerky steps to the supper table and clutched the edge until his anger exploded. He gave the table one vicious heave, overturning it and sending plates and cups shattering against the wall. Still blind with rage, he staggered to the bed and braced both hands on the bedpost. He leaned his head against it, gripping the wood so hard that his fingers hurt, fighting an internal battle to stop the terrible pictures inside his head, the visions of the woman he loved with Emerson Clan, of Windsor being touched and tortured and defiled.

A moment later, he went rigid when Windsor put her arms around his waist. She laid her cheek against the quivering muscles of his back. "I'm so sorry, Stone Kincaid," she whispered softly, her words low with regret. "I have closed my eyes to your pain and have thought only of myself. Forgive me for being blind to your suffering."

Groaning, his eyes shut, Stone turned and crushed her against him. "What happened to you is my fault. I did it to you," he muttered, his voice rough. "Oh, God, Windsor, I'll never get over letting him hurt you."

"I blame you for nothing," she said in a soft voice. "You came for me when I had given up hope. You brought me here and took care of me. I love you."

Stone sought her mouth, anxiety grating the words he uttered against her lips. "I can't go on without you. You've got to think about us, the way it was before we came to Mexico. Think about me, Windsor. Think about how much I love you and need you. Empty your mind the way you used to do. Reach inside yourself and feel with your heart." His breath rasped raggedly as she put her arms around his waist and laid her head against his chest.

"I love you more than life itself. I swear I won't hurt you," he whispered, trying not to rush her or frighten her. He kissed the top of her head and pressed his mouth to her temple, then to her cheek, then at last to her trembling mouth. Her lips tasted sweet and soft, the way he remembered, and he forced himself to hold her lightly, gently. But he had to fight his own battle for self-control, steeling himself against the passion that ignited like lightning in his heart and rushed through his blood like a stream of fire. With iron restraint, he scattered kisses along her bare shoulder, then lifted her off her feet, bringing her up against him so that his lips could find the soft swell of her breasts.

When she did not pull away, he swung her into his arms, lowering her to the bed, lying beside her, holding her close but making no move to do more. Instead, he savored the feel of her pressed against him after so many long weeks of hoping and dreaming for just such a moment. Then, when she grew relaxed in his embrace, when she slid her arms around his neck with a contented sigh, he began to stroke her back with his open palm, slipping his hand beneath the blouse to rest against skin that felt like smooth, hot velvet.

In time he raised himself on one elbow, leaning over her, bending down just enough to brush her lips. He fit his mouth against hers, tasting, teasing her lips apart until she began to kiss him back. His heart pounding, he almost lost sight of reason, kissing her harder, wanting her so desperately that he thought he'd die if he couldn't have her.

Then Windsor arched against him, her breasts heaving, her breathing short and shallow, and Stone grew bolder, sliding both hands beneath her skirt and tracing a path up her bare legs to cup her hips. Windsor moaned, a pleasured, helpless sound, and Stone pulled her tighter against him, his lips seeking her naked flesh, stroking her body gently with both his hands and his mouth until she writhed and clutched him to her.

His pulse pounding in his temples, pumping through his veins, he rolled atop her, his fingers sliding into the silk of her hair, his mouth forging down on hers as he joined himself to her, overjoyed when at last they became one the way they were meant to be, the way he wanted them always to be. When her release came she cried out, her body going rigid as pleasure rolled over her in undulating waves. His own moment of ecstasy came swiftly, powerfully, shaking him to the core, finally leaving him limp and sated.

Even then he kept her possessively against him, her soft arms clutched tightly around his neck, the thumping of her heart merging into a single beat with his own. And in those moments of tenderness, with his love come back to him, he knew that never in his life had he experienced such unparalleled joy.

25

Hours after the candlewick had sputtered and extinguished in a puff of smoke, Stone was awakened by the clatter of wheels rolling across the cobblestoned drive just below the balcony. Windsor's warm body was lying intimately against his side, and he eased carefully out of bed, not wanting to disturb her.

Exhausted by the heat of their passion, she slept peacefully at last, unplagued by endless tossing and strangled cries of fright. Stone, too, felt content, for they had eliminated one of the major barriers left separating them. The rest would come down in time. Gently, he covered her bare shoulders with the soft coverlet, then dressed quickly, fervently hoping the newly arrived coach had brought his sister, Carlisle, back to the Hacienda de los Toros.

The moment he stepped onto the patio veranda, he heard the commotion going on in the front salon. Voices filtered up the main staircase as he stood gazing over the railing.

Dona Maria stood beside the large adobe fireplace. She had obviously just awakened, for she still wore her long white nightgown, covered by a brown velvet wrapper. She was in the midst of a rather impressive bout of cooing and gushing over the two babies being held up for her inspection by a dark-cloaked nursemaid. Stone smiled. Such behavior seemed a bit astonishing from such an elegant, imperious lady, but he had grown fond of her during the weeks she had been so gracious to Windsor.

But it was his sister's face that he sought with great eagerness, and he grinned when she entered his line of vision. She put her arm around Dona Maria, laughing and giving the older woman a hug. At that moment he realized with some surprise just how much he had missed his feisty little sister. He had not seen her often enough lately.

Until a year or so ago, she had been in the Sacred Heart Convent in New Orleans, to which his brother, Gray, had sent her for her schooling after she had marched with a women's suffrage parade and exhibited various other acts of female defiance. For the most part, however, he hadn't seen his sister because he had been more interested in pursuing Emerson Clan than in spending time with his family in Chicago. Only lately had he begun to realize just how misguided his priorities had been.

While he watched, Carlisle flipped back her hood, tucking a wayward strand of golden-red hair into the thick coil secured at her nape. As she removed the storm-spattered, blue serge cloak draping her shoulders, a tall man took the wrap and shook the rain from its folds.

"Oh, Chaso, Carlita, your *niños* are so beautiful," Dona Maria was saying as she lifted one swaddled bundle from the arms of the Indian nursemaid. "And they're such big boys. Why, anyone who sees them will think they're at least six months old, and they're barely three! Tomas, aren't they precious?"

"They look just alike," their sixteen-year-old uncle observed, peering at the baby his mother was holding.

"Twins have a tendency to resemble each other, Tomas," Chase Lancaster said dryly, chuckling as he settled his other son in the crook of his arm.

Eager now to speak with Carlisle, Stone moved down the steps, his hand sliding along the black wrought-iron rail. When he had almost reached the bottom, Dona Maria caught sight of him and turned at once to Carlisle.

"Oh, Carlita, how could I forget to tell you! Look who is here! Your brother Stone. He and his friend have been my guests for several weeks now."

"Stone's here?" Carlisle cried, grabbing hold of Dona Maria's arm.

"I sure am, and it's about time you arrived," Stone answered in Dona Maria's stead. Carlisle whirled around; then, with a cry of joy, she flew toward him. Stone laughed, opening his arms for her usual enthusiastic greeting.

"Oh, Stone, we've been so worried about you!" she scolded. She hugged him tight before demanding, "Where have you been? And why haven't you gotten in touch with us before now? So much has happened to all of us, I don't know where to start!" Her bubbling words slowed down as she leaned away and peered accusingly up at him. Her onslaught of questions renewed the moment she regained her breath. "And what on earth are you doing here in Mexico? The last we heard, you were heading for San Francisco! And what about Emerson Clan! Did you find him?"

"Maybe if you'd let the poor man say something, Carly, you'd get a few answers," suggested her husband with a low laugh.

Stone turned to Carlisle's husband. Chase Lancaster was tall, his six-foot frame lean and strong. His dark blond hair was bleached lighter on top from the sun, and he wore it combed straight back from his forehead. His face was deeply tanned, making his dark blue eyes look even more intense and assessing. He didn't in the least resemble his dark-haired, dark-eyed mother and younger brother.

As Chase joined them, he settled an arm around Carlisle's shoulders and smiled down at her. With that one loving gesture, Stone had no doubt that they enjoyed a happy marriage.

"I'm sorry, Stone, but I'm just so thrilled to see you!" Carlisle exclaimed, her green eyes glowing in the affectionate way Stone remembered so well. Ever since she was a little girl being raised by Gray and him, she had been full of brass and high spirits, which had gotten her in trouble more often than not. "Stone, this is my husband, Chase Lancaster. I bet you didn't even know I was married, did you?"

Finally, for the first time since Carlisle had caught sight of him, Stone was allowed to speak. "No, I didn't, not until Dona Maria told me. But I didn't know about Gray's wedding either until after it happened, so don't feel guilty."

"I'm glad to finally meet you, Stone," Chase said, extending his hand to shake. Stone clasped it, suddenly remembering Chase's relationship to Stone's sister-in-law, Tyler.

"Thanks. I've heard a good deal about you, too, from your cousin, Tyler. When she and Gray returned to Chicago last summer, you were just about all she talked about. How is she?" His eyes sought Carlisle. "And Gray? I telegraphed them when I arrived here and asked them to come with you if they could, but I haven't received an answer yet. Have they had their baby?"

Instantly, Carlisle's happy expression faded into sadness. "Their baby lived for only three days, Stone. Last February, Tyler and I were in an accident. A coach hit our sleigh, and Tyler went into labor too early. It was a little boy. All of us were devastated when he died."

Stone saw the way she looked at her own healthy children and understood her sorrow. His insides tightened into a hard curl when he remembered how eagerly Gray had looked forward to the birth of his first child.

"I'm sorry. They must have taken it awfully hard."

"Yes, they did, especially at first, but after the twins were born, they seemed to accept things a little better. The good news is that Tyler thinks she might be with child again. We're all hoping she is."

"That goes for me, too." Stone smiled at Carlisle. "I'm glad you're all right. I couldn't believe it when Dona Maria said you already had two children."

Carlisle's laugh veritably bubbled with happiness. "Chase and I couldn't either! But come, you haven't even seen your nephews yet." She pulled him with her to where Dona Maria was still crooning over the blanket-swaddled infants.

"This is Enrico," Carlisle told him, pointing to the one in his grandmother's arms, "and this little fellow is Esteban. We named him after Chase's good friend, Esteban Rivera."

"How in the world do you tell them apart?" Stone asked as Carlisle tenderly arranged a soft blanket more securely around one of her sons.

"Well, I'll tell you. Enrico's always fussing, and Esteban is as good as gold."

Chase laughed, agreeing with his wife, but as Stone looked down at the tiny boys, both happy and content in the loving care of their parents, all he could think about was poor Carlos. Again Stone cursed himself for delivering the innocent child into the care of a madman. Even though Stone knew Clan wouldn't hurt his son, he found it impossible to live with the knowledge that he had betrayed Nina's trust. Suddenly he turned as cold as winter inside. His face must have revealed his feelings, because Carlisle reached out and took his hand.

"What's the matter, Stone? Aren't you feeling well?"

A brief silence ensued until Chase seemed to notice Stone's reluctance to answer. "Maybe your brother would like to visit with you alone for a while, Carly. You two certainly have a lot of catching up to do. Mama and I can help Juana put the boys to bed. I'm sure you wouldn't object to that, would you, Mama?"

"No, I certainly would not. I have waited many long months to hold these precious little ones in my arms."

"*Gracias,*" Carlisle murmured to her mother-in-law, then smiled as her husband bent and pressed a kiss to her cheek. "I'll be up soon, after Stone and I have had a long talk."

"All right," Chase said, and turned to Stone again. "You don't know how happy you've made my wife by showing up here so unexpectedly. I hope you're planning a lengthy visit."

"I don't know yet how long I'll stay, but I'm grateful for your hospitality."

As the others carried the children upstairs, Carlisle looped her arm through Stone's. "Now you come along with me, because I want to hear everything you've done all these months you've been away."

Carlisle sat on the tufted cushions of the maroon leather sofa that faced the hearth. She watched her brother walk to the fireplace, then waited for him to speak. When he continued to stare silently into the flames throwing reddish lights against the grate, she realized he was, as always, reluctant to share his problems with her.

Although they had always been close—Stone had been her ally against Gray's stricter discipline—he had rarely confided in her, even before the Confederates had thrown him into the awful prison camp down in Georgia. After all the suffering he had endured there, he had grown even more aloof and hard to reach.

Now she sensed that he had changed in other ways. The first moment she had gazed into his eyes, and despite his smile, she had seen the shadow of pain. Even that was better than the horrible cold, bitter look he'd worn just after the war when he'd come home, wasted away to a human scarecrow. Suddenly she felt anxious for him. What on earth had happened since she'd seen him last?

"Stone? Please tell me what's wrong. Is it something to do with Emerson Clan? Did you find him?"

Stone's shoulders stiffened. "Yeah, I found him."

Carlisle saw the way his jaw was working. It took him several minutes to control his agitation. Carlisle waited patiently.

"He captured someone I care about," he finally managed to get out. "He hurt her." The last few words were gruff with pain. Carlisle's compassionate heart went out to him. She shivered, remembering how terrified her sister-in-law was of Clan, even now, months after he had accosted her in Chicago.

"We understood that you were traveling with a nun," she said gently. "Was she the one who got hurt?"

Stone nodded.

Again quiet descended over the room. Carlisle's brows furrowed with worry as her brother paced across the room and back again. "What happened to her? Can you tell me?"

Stone stopped where he was, and she watched

his face change, taking on hard, angry lines. "He beat her up, and he"—he choked on the next word—"raped her. And it was my fault, goddamn him to hell."

"Oh, no, Stone, I'm so sorry," Carlisle murmured, but inside she felt true horror. Clan had threatened Tyler with the same thing when he had held her against her will, but Gray and Stone had managed to save her. "Is she all right now?"

"She's better. We made some progress tonight."

"She's here with you?" Carlisle asked, surprised until she recalled that Dona Maria had mentioned another houseguest.

"I needed a safe place to bring her, and I remembered you were supposed to be visiting Lancaster's ranch. She was in pretty bad shape at first, but she's trying to get over it."

Carlisle waited for him to elaborate, but instead, he leaned his elbow against the stone mantel, his eyes fixed on the fire.

"Who is this girl?" she asked after a lengthy pause. "Is she someone special to you?"

Stone didn't turn around. His answer was low. "I love her. I want to marry her, but she won't. I don't know what's going to happen between us."

Carlisle sighed, wondering why life was always so hard. "Don't give up hope, Stone. Chase and I went through some terrible times just before the twins were born. I left him and went home to Chicago because I was afraid he couldn't forgive me for some of the things I'd done. Did Dona Maria tell you that I got involved with the *guerrilleros* when I first came here?"

Stone turned to look at her, a frown on his face. "No, she didn't. What happened?"

"Do you remember the girl I shared a room with at Sacred Heart Convent, Arantxa Perez? Her brother, Javier, told me lies about Chase and President Juarez, and I was naive enough to believe him." She lowered her eyes, still racked with guilt over all the pain she had caused by her youthful foolishness. "Chase's best friend, Esteban, was killed trying to rescue me from the *guerrilleros*. I didn't think Chase was going to get over that either, but he's finally accepted it."

"It's different with Windsor. She was brought up in China. She does things differently than we do. She thinks differently than we do."

Carlisle frowned. "I don't understand, Stone. Is she a nun, or what? Where did you meet her?"

"She's not a nun. She was disguised as one the first time I saw her. Believe it or not, she thought I was Emerson Clan."

"Emerson Clan! How can that be?"

She listened as Stone began to relate his story to her, starting on a day in Chicago when he and a woman named Windsor Richmond had boarded a westward-bound train. He prowled restlessly around the room as he spoke, his voice sometimes so full of anger that his words actually trembled. Carlisle's horror grew as the tale progressed, especially when he described what Clan had done to Windsor and the Mexican girl named Nina.

"When I got them back, we were in the mountains near Saltillo, and a campesino took us to the Gomez hacienda."

"Papa Gilberto? Why, I was there, too! Did he tell you?"

"He's the one who suggested I come here."

"My God, I just can't believe how strange all this is. Who would have thought Clan would have gotten involved with the revolution down here? But the uprising is over now, Stone. Chase and his Nacionales destroyed the major stronghold of the *guerrilleros* months ago."

"It's not over for me as long as Emerson Clan's heart is still beating," Stone ground out savagely.

"You're not going after him again, are you? Not after all that's happened!"

"As soon as I know Windsor's all right and safe where he can never get to her again, then I'll go after him. And I'll do it alone this time, the way I should have in the first place."

Carlisle didn't try to dissuade him. His eyes had burned with vengeance for years. "What about Windsor?"

"I was hoping you'd help me, Carly. I think there may be some things she can't come to terms with on her own, but she can't seem to bring herself to tell me, either. Maybe she'll be able to talk to you. She needs a friend."

"Of course I'll be her friend. She must be very special if you care so much for her."

"Yes, she is."

"Stone, please don't go after Clan again. Don't you see that Windsor will need you here with her after all the terrible things she's been through?"

"I don't intend to go anywhere until she's better." He strode across the room and sat down on a low hassock in front of her. His eyes searched her face. "You'll like her, Carly, I know you will. You'll find her a lot different from anyone you've ever met, but she's smart and beautiful and good—"

"You're in love with her, all right," Carlisle said, then laughed and nodded her approval.

Stone gave a rueful shake of his head. "I think I fell in love with her the first moment I ever saw her, even though I thought she was a nun at the time."

Carlisle laughed again, but her brother's face retained its somber lines.

"You've got to help me, Carly. You've got to convince her to marry me."

"I'll try, I promise I will. You know how persuasive I can be when I set my mind to it."

"Most mornings she gets up early and takes a walk in the patio."

"I'll be up with the boys anyway."

"Thanks, Carly. You don't know what this means to me."

Brother and sister shared a smile, and then Carlisle hugged him tightly, so glad he was home again. She hoped Gray and Tyler had received his telegraph message and would come soon. Both of them had been very worried about him. Once they arrived, surely the four of them together could convince Stone not to go after Emerson Clan.

26

When the pearl-hued mist of dawn drifted like gossamer over the night, Windsor rose naked from the bed. In the cool air of early morning, she hurriedly bathed her face and donned her clothes. Before quitting the bedchamber, she paused with her palm resting lightly atop the curved brass door handle. Stone lay motionless, half concealed by the smoky darkness of the draped tester bed. He slept on his stomach, the arm he had curled protectively around her throughout the night still outflung where she had slipped from beneath it.

After their lovemaking, he had pulled her tightly against the warm, muscled length of his body and kept her there, sweetly, possessively, her head cradled in the hollow of his broad shoulder. He had told her in whispers how much he loved her, and Windsor had wept because he had been so tender, because she knew he loved her as much as she loved him.

Yet she still had not told him about the baby. She couldn't, not while filled with the fear that he would never be able to accept the stamp of evil Emerson Clan had left upon her body. How many times had Clan leered into her face and reiterated why he was abusing her? To torment Stone, to make sure Stone would never forget that Clan had taken his pleasure with her body. *No matter how much Kincaid says he loves you, he'll never get over me touching you like this*, Clan had said with his evil laugh. *Not as long as he lives.*

Pain cut into her, slicing through her heart like jagged glass. If only the gods would allow the child growing inside her body to have sprung from Stone's seed, she thought, gripped by an awful burden of helplessness. Hot tears burning, she turned and left the room.

She wouldn't weep, she decided, resolutely attempting to rid her mind of such thoughts. She leaned over the wall supporting the arched stone colonnade that ran along the upper gallery. Below her in the quiet patio, the trees were barely visible, hidden in the mists of dawn. It seemed as if she was peering into her own eerie dreams, and she wanted to walk into those murky shadows by herself, alone.

Descending the steps, she ducked beneath the low-hanging limbs of a gigantic mimosa tree, the feathery pink blossoms enveloping her in sweet perfume. She avoided the path of flat tan stones, stepping instead across the yard where neatly tended beds of geraniums were set apart by whitewashed rocks, and pink hollyhocks bloomed on tall stalks to disrupt the neutral shades of daybreak. Although the grass was still damp from the night's rainstorm, she knew the heat of the day would soon dry it.

All around her was deep silence. Only occasionally did a bird flutter awake and erupt into sleepy song. Like the Osage, Windsor had always praised the sunrise and risen to watch the sun burn away the night. When she was little, she and Hung-pin had padded barefoot over similar cold, flat stones and knelt with reverent respect at the knees of the

Old One. Now both her dear friends were gone from her, neither one able to impart the calm and quiet wisdom she needed so much to hear.

Sighing with a regret that plunged to the bottom of her bruised soul, she moved beneath a long arbor constructed of willow twigs bent over a wooden frame. A different, delicious scent floated from the thick honeysuckle vines clinging to the curving bower, carried on a wisp of breeze, so gentle it barely stirred the soft petals. Somehow she felt secure behind the tall white walls of the Hacienda de los Toros. She felt more at home here than in any other place since she had left China. The peacefulness and isolation of the old adobe house reminded her of her beloved Temple of the Blue Mountain.

When she came to a gushing fountain, she sat down on a stone bench, watching water pour from a cornucopia held by a matador fashioned from shiny black stone. She felt better that morning than she had in a long while. She had rested well lying close inside Stone Kincaid's embrace, her mind at peace because she was where she belonged.

How she wished she could retreat into herself as she used to do. Perhaps there, staring into the white light, her mind would open and hear the soft words the Old One might have murmured to soothe her fears. He would have understood how much she had changed since she had traveled to the land of the Western barbarians. Before she had come to America, she had diligently practiced her fighting skills and trained to become a disciple of the Dragonfire, but now her desire to be with Stone Kincaid overrode her dream to join the warrior sect.

And although the Old One had warned her of the temptations of the flesh, he would not have condemned her love for Stone Kincaid. Love was the answer to all things, he had taught. He would have been more eager to help her accept what she had suffered at Clan's hands. He would have preached forgiveness. *Hatred is never ended by hatred but by love,* he had told her often, his gnarled, blue-veined palm resting gently atop her head.

Folding her legs into the lotus position, she closed her eyes and pressed her palms together. She longed for the day when she could once again attain the inner tranquility so necessary to her existence. Every day since she had been with Emerson Clan, she had tried to reach that plane of tranquility. Every day, she had failed.

The ancient sutra rolled easily from her lips. She had performed the slow, resonant hum many hundreds of times in her life, but she broke off almost at once as a violent heave lurched across her stomach. The nausea brought each morning by her unborn child lasted only a moment, but it would return, a reminder of her fears.

Molding the slight mound of her abdomen with her palms, she sought to use her mind as she had been taught, to travel through her own skin, to penetrate muscle and bone, to seep into her own rushing bloodstream until it took her into the body of her unborn child.

With quiet desperation, she longed to feel maternal love for the life growing inside her womb, to experience the warm kinship a mother should feel for the baby. Instead, a vision of pale hair and eyes, of screams and blood, filled her head, and sharply, like puncturing claws, she felt pangs of revulsion to think that the child might be the offspring of a demon.

Appalled at herself, she squeezed her eyes shut, slamming a mental door on Clan's horrid image, forcefully pushing all conscious thought inward to her core, to her beating heart, to the beating heart of her baby. She fought for peace of mind, for understanding of her dilemma, for hope for her confusion. But though she groped in the darkness of her despair, searching for the light, she found it not. Instead, she felt empty, floundering in a chilled, stagnant vacuum as if her body were a brittle shell. It was as if the purity of her soul had flapped away like a frightened crow the first time the Evil One had touched her flesh with his unspeakable cruelty, tarnishing its brightness until it was forced to cower in the shelter of darkness, blackened, torn, and bleeding.

Her skin grew clammy, her body cold to the bone, as if her internal organs were crusted with frost. She remembered how Clan had looked at her, how he had smelled when he put his hands on her—as sweet as the rose-oiled concubine of a Peking nobleman.

One vertebra at a time, an awful, debilitating shudder rolled down her spine. The baby could very well be Clan's, she thought, feeling her panic rise. It could look like him, could act like him. The child could grow up filled with his inherent evil, could torture and maim innocent people the way Clan had hurt her and Nina and Stone, and many others known only to the demon-gods who roamed the earth.

Her teeth dug into her lower lip. She had to stop thinking such things, she told herself, tightly entwining her fingers to check their trembling. Even if it were Clan's child, she was still the mother. She would bring it into the world and teach it the truths she had been taught.

"Near vermilion one gets stained pink, near ink one gets stained black," she whispered firmly to herself, finding comfort in the words taught to her many years ago when the Old One had demonstrated his adage by gently dipping her small fingers into first one pot of dye, then another. She must cling to his teachings. She must not dwell on the evil, but on the good.

She would try to think of the baby as Stone Kincaid's. She had been with him first; they had touched each other with tenderness and respect; they had created this child together as a testament to their love. Stone Kincaid was a good man, strong and kind and honest. The baby would have hair as black as a raven's wing and a smile that melted her heart. The baby had to be his, she thought. The baby *was* his.

Windsor looked up as a sound filtered through the quiet garden. As the sun rose to warm away the mists and dry the dew, someone was humming a lullaby. A moment later, a figure approached, a young woman whose slender form was wrapped in flowing pink nightclothes, her long hair woven into a braid the color of fire. She carried a small white bundle in her arms.

"You must be Windsor," the stranger said as she shifted the swaddled infant until it lay propped against her shoulder. She smiled, setting aglow her pretty heart-shaped face until Windsor thought she looked quite beautiful. "I'm Stone's sister, Carlisle. You were sleeping last night when we arrived."

Windsor studied her face but saw no resemblance between Carlisle and her brother. "Stone Kincaid will be very glad to see you," she told Carlisle. "Does he know you're here?"

The young woman laughed, a merry, infectious sound. "Do you always call my brother that? By both names, I mean."

"I am from China. It is the Chinese way."

The baby began to squirm inside the fluffy white blanket, and Carlisle rocked him.

"I'm sorry if I offended you," she apologized, "but it sounded so strange. And, yes, Stone heard our coach on the drive last night and came downstairs to see us. We had a nice long talk." Carlisle sat down beside Windsor, turning the child to face her while she gently bounced him on her knee.

"Your baby is very pretty," Windsor remarked,

gazing down into a round little face dominated by enormous green eyes.

"Yes, he is, isn't he?" Carlisle answered, beaming a proud smile. "And he's the best little thing you could imagine. He just has a nasty habit of getting up before sunrise. I brought him out here so we wouldn't wake up his brother."

The words had barely left her lips when several sharp wails pierced the upstairs gallery, inducing several birds to flutter off the wall in frantic flight.

"Oh, dear, that's Enrico now," Carlisle said, jumping to her feet. "He's not the least bit quiet when he wakes up, not like Esteban here. Rico will yell at the top of his lungs until he gets what he wants. My husband, Chase, says he gets that from my side of the family." She laughed as she plunked her child into Windsor's lap. "You don't mind holding him for me, do you? Please, it won't take but a moment for me to fetch Rico. Then you and I can get better acquainted."

Windsor had little choice, because Carlisle hastened back through the arching, vine-hung bower without awaiting an answer. Windsor studied the tiny man-child she held. She had never seen a baby so young. She cupped the back of his head in one hand, his bottom in her other, awed to think there was barely enough of him to fill her lap.

Wordless with wonder, she stared at him until the infant grew impatient and began to twist his shoulders. Afraid he might squirm out of her hands, she knelt on the ground, carefully spreading his blanket and placing Esteban upon his back in the middle of it. As soon as she did, he began to fuss and grunt, kicking his feet and angrily waving his tiny fists.

"Ga-ga-ga," he gurgled, drooling and sucking on his fingers.

When Windsor leaned down close, he grew still, focusing bright, unblinking eyes on her face.

"Shh, little one. Your mama will come back for you soon," she whispered softly. He began to gurgle again as Windsor straightened his rumpled gown around his feet. He wore a long white shirt embroidered with miniature yellow ducks and a soft, snowy swaddling cloth, but his legs were bare. As she held one tiny foot and examined an even tinier toe, he kicked hard, freeing his heel from her gentle grasp. "You are a strong little man. You will grow up to be long of limb and tall of stature."

Esteban seemed to consider her words with great solemnity; then he stretched his small mouth into an impossibly wide grin, exhibiting toothless pink gums. A tender smile was forced from Windsor, a deep reverence overwhelming her as she realized she would soon give life to another human being. Inside herself, she would create a tiny person with two eyes and two ears, and ten fingers and toes, and perhaps even a happy gurgling chuckle like Esteban's. How could one so little and untried be anything but innocent and pure? How could a tiny newborn babe be otherwise?

Astir with new motherly feelings, she lifted Carlisle Lancaster's child and tenderly held his head close to her neck as she rocked him to and fro. Her unborn child was a part of her. She would breathe life into him and she would love him. How could she have ever doubted that?

"I'm sorry I took so long, Windsor, but Rico was all wet and as mad as a whole nest of hornets," Carlisle said, coming up behind her. She knelt beside Windsor and held her son so that Windsor could look upon his face. "You see, they're identical twins. Isn't it amazing to think they're exactly the same in every way? It's like a miracle."

Windsor agreed, stroking Enrico's pudgy hand. He grabbed her finger tight in his fist and shook it as fiercely as a puppy with a sock. Windsor smiled at Carlisle. "You are lucky to have given your husband two fine, strong sons."

"Maybe you'll have a baby someday, too." At Windsor's startled look, she went on quickly. "Stone told me last night that he's going to marry you or die trying." She laughed. "I have to warn you that Stone is the most determined person I've ever met. When he makes up his mind about something, he never, but never, gives up." Smiling, Carlisle continued in the easy, companionable way she had about her. "And I must say that I'm very glad he found you to fall in love with. I was beginning to wonder if he planned to stay a bachelor all his life."

Windsor remained silent. She wondered if Carlisle knew what Clan had done to her. Windsor looked up as a man appeared on the path leading from the gallery.

"So here you are," he said, taking several long-legged strides to Carlisle, then bending down to kiss her.

Carlisle laced her fingers through his long ones, then introduced him to Windsor. "Windsor, this is my husband, Chase Lancaster. Chase, this is Windsor Richmond, the woman Stone is going to marry."

"*Buenos días*, Senorita Richmond," Chase said, politely inclining his blond head toward her. "Welcome to my rancho. I see you've met my sons." He reached down and picked up Enrico, who had begun to cry. Again, forcefully, Windsor's feelings were touched by the sight of a father so obviously proud of his children. Would Stone be able to look so fondly upon the child she carried? If its hair was white, could he bring himself to touch it?

Chase shifted the crying infant comfortably in the crook of his elbow, chucking him under the chin with his knuckle. Enrico's whining stopped at once.

"He just wanted a man to hold him," Chase explained, winking at Windsor. "He's tired of you women exclaiming over him all the time. He's no sissy."

"As you can see, Chase is a doting father," Carlisle teased.

"There is an old Chinese adage which says that the father in praising his son extols himself," Windsor said.

"Stone picked himself a smart lady," Chase observed to Carlisle, grinning.

"Don't encourage him, Windsor. He already thinks he's the best father who ever lived."

"Well, I am."

"I hope so, *mi hijo*," Dona Maria interjected as she joined them from a different pathway. "But where are my precious ones?" The eager grandmother had no trouble finding the babies and immediately took Enrico from his father. She nuzzled his neck with her nose, then held out her other arm for his brother. "Come, Chaso, and you, too, Carlita. I wish to show off my grandchildren to Rosita and cook." She paused to smile at Windsor. "Would you care to join us, *niña*? Breakfast will be ready soon."

"Thank you, but I must go and awaken Stone Kincaid. He is still abed."

"Well, that's a good sign," Carlisle remarked. "He hasn't slept this late for years. You must be very good for him. Wake him up soon so we all can have breakfast together."

Windsor nodded. With a wave of her hand, Stone's sister moved off down the path after her husband and mother-in-law, leaving Windsor alone by the fountain. She sat quietly for a moment, reflecting on what was in her heart. Suddenly, by looking upon the innocence of a babe, she had found peace. Now was the time for her to speak of the child with Stone Kincaid. Her face resolute, she walked down the flagstone path toward their bed-chamber.

Hummingbird

Windsor came forward on the bed to [illegible] the chill with a warm blanket. He held [illegible] it pulled closer to [illegible]

27

When Stone opened his eyes, Windsor was sitting cross-legged at the end of the bed, intently watching him. He smiled, remembering how good she had felt cuddled close to him throughout the night. He lifted the sheet and held out his arms to her.

"Come, I want to feel you against me."

Windsor came forward on her hands and knees, stopping beside him. Instead of lying down, she picked up his hand and pressed her lips against his tanned knuckles.

"I love you, Stone Kincaid."

Pleased to hear her whisper the words, Stone clasped her hand and tugged her toward him, wanting her in his arms, wanting to make love to her again. When she resisted, his eyebrows curled downward into a frown. "What's wrong, sweetheart?"

"I am with child."

Stone's muscles went stiff. Even though he had known there was always the possibility that she might become pregnant, he hadn't wanted to think about it. A worm of dread slithered nervously along his stomach. Her sapphire eyes held him in unblinking scrutiny—serious, searching, waiting patiently to measure his answer. He had to be careful, he thought, had to choose just the right words so as not to hurt her. Her emotions were so mixed up, he couldn't risk saying the wrong thing. He pushed himself upright, threading his fingers through his hair as he decided what to say. He took her hand and pressed her palm against his cheek.

"I suspected you might be."

"Why have you not asked me about it?"

"I didn't ask you because I didn't want to upset you."

"Are you upset?"

Stone paused once more, not sure what she wanted him to say. "I want our baby," he murmured, his gaze locked with hers, "and even more than that, I want you to be my wife."

"And if it is not our baby? Then will you want me for your wife?"

"It *is* our baby, Windsor. Mine and yours. I don't want you to think anything else. Promise me you won't."

Windsor's gaze slid away from his face. "It could be his," she muttered huskily, staring at her lap. "We cannot know otherwise until the child is born."

The lean muscle beneath Stone's tanned cheek jumped as he gritted his teeth. "No. It's mine. Do you understand me, Windsor? The baby's mine."

Tears welled, glittering blue in Windsor's eyes. Her face tormented, she carefully framed both her hands around his hard-tensed jaw. Her words were uttered gently, but honestly. "Since the first moment I saw you, my beloved Stone Kincaid, your eyes have burned with hatred for the Evil One. Your heart was filled with thirst for vengeance then, and you are even more obsessed with the desire to kill Emerson Clan now. If my child is born with hair like snow and eyes like ice, I will be able to love him because he will have formed within my womb. But can you look upon the face you suffer within your nightmares and still love him? Can you call him son and forget his father's sins against you?''

For a fraction of a moment, time stood still between them. Stone remained silent, struck by her wisdom, not sure how he could answer. Another tear escaped to wet Windsor's face, and he pulled her against him, holding her tightly, desperate to reassure her.

''I'll love you, Windsor, always, no matter what happens. For God's sake, say you'll marry me.''

Every nerve on edge, he waited, but long moments passed before her lips quivered against his chest. ''I will wait until my child is born, then I will give my answer. If he is your child, I will marry you. If he is not, I will take him and return to China.''

Stone clasped her shoulders and held her out from him so that he could look into her face. His fingers tightened. ''No. I won't let you do that. I'll never let you do that.''

Windsor's tears fell afresh, and Stone pulled her back against his chest. ''If you want to go to China, I'll go with you. Just don't leave me. I don't care whose child it is, I swear to God I don't. Give me the chance to prove that to you. Don't you understand, Windsor? Without you, my life won't mean anything.''

At his earnest entreaty, Windsor sobbed, a terrible, lost sound. ''But I'm so afraid,'' she whispered miserably. ''I'm afraid that if I stay with you, you will hate my baby. I'm terrified that your face will grow hard every time you look at him, the way it does when you think of Clan. Every day of your life, my child will remind you of everything you detest.''

Stone stroked her hair. He shut his eyes, but his voice was gentle. "And can you honestly say, Windsor, that you wouldn't be reminded of the hell he put you through?"

"My baby is a part of me."

"And that's why I'll love him," Stone muttered into the cropped blond curls lying against her temple.

Windsor laid her cheek against his chest and let herself weep. "He's so evil," she mumbled through her tears, finally putting into words her greatest fear. "You know how Emerson Clan feels about his son, how determined he was to have Carlos. What if I do have his child? What if he tries to take him away from me, as he did to Nina?"

"That'll never happen," Stone ground out. "He'll never lay a finger on anyone I love, not ever again. I swear it to you, Windsor."

His shoulder dampened by her grief, Stone crushed Windsor tighter against him, the fire of iron resolution turning his heart to steel. Whether the baby was his own child or not, Windsor would not leave him. Whether the baby was his or not, Clan would never come anywhere close to Windsor or her baby. Because no matter how long it took, no matter how far he ran, Stone was going to kill the murdering bastard.

For the next week or so, Stone lived with the roiling emotions his thirst for blood vengeance kept stirred up inside him. He hid his inner turmoil from Windsor, and he achieved his purpose, because with each day that passed, she seemed better. Since she had spilled out her fears and misgivings to him, she acted more relaxed, more resigned to all that had happened to her. And Carlisle, bless her heart, was treating her like a long-lost sister. Stone would always be grateful for that.

One night as the family gathered in the main salon, Stone watched Windsor from where he stood with his back to the windows. She sat quietly on a nearby settee, listening to Carlisle's chatter, looking beautiful and serene with her hands folded together in her lap. Gazing at her, he felt sure that in time everything would be all right. Since she had told him about the child, much of the tension had gone out of her. She was going to survive her nightmare.

As usual, thoughts of the baby she carried caused ropes of fear to twine around his chest. The baby is mine, he told himself firmly for the thousandth time; he has to be. He refused to let himself think anything else.

"Windsor, if you have a boy, I will lend you all my baby clothes, so you'll have double of everything," Carlisle was telling her generously. "But if you have a girl, then you and Stone will have to pass all your little lacy dresses down to me, because Chase and I are going to have a girl next time."

"Sure of herself, isn't she?" her husband remarked, smiling at Windsor.

Windsor's soft laugh made Stone feel good all over. He had been concerned about leaving her when he went after Clan, but she obviously liked both Chase and Carlisle. And Dona Maria treated her like a favorite niece. As soon as Sun-On-Wings returned with word concerning Clan's whereabouts, Stone would be ready to ride. Windsor would be safe here with his family, and that was his main concern.

"Which do you want, Stone?" Carlisle asked him, bringing him into the conversation. "A boy or a girl?"

Stone thought of his sister's sons with their green eyes and black hair. What color eyes would Windsor's child have? He looked at her and smiled. "All I want is for Windsor to marry me, the sooner the better."

"That's a good idea. We could make it a big family affair! Wouldn't that be fun? We haven't all been together for a wedding yet."

"Sounds good to me."

The deep baritone voice that answered had come from the patio doorway, startling all of them. Stone swung around to see his older brother, Gray, grinning at him. His wife, Tyler, stood beside him.

"Surprise!" she cried, making Carlisle squeal with delight. She ran to her sister-in-law, and the two women hugged, then danced around in a circle like excited children. Everyone began talking and laughing, all at the same time, but Stone walked forward and clasped his older brother's hand.

Stone felt a lump thickening at the base of his throat as they embraced. He was very glad to see his brother. All through their lives they had been close. They had raised Carlisle together, when they hadn't been much more than boys themselves, and they had fought to scratch out a living on the streets of Chicago after moving there from Mississippi, long before they had made their family fortune in the railway business.

"Thanks for coming, Gray," he said, his voice gruff with emotion.

"We left Chicago the day after I got your telegraph. I'm just damn surprised you've hung around here long enough for us to make the trip. You sure as hell haven't exactly kept in touch," Gray complained, but he was smiling when he continued. "Now where's this nun who finally got you hog-tied?"

Stone glanced at Windsor, who had quietly watched the affectionate round of greetings from her place on the settee. He led her forward to meet the rest of his family.

"This is Windsor Richmond, and she's going to

marry me as soon as you and Tyler can help us talk her into it.''

Bowing low, Gray captured Windsor's fingers. "How do you do, Miss Richmond? I'll warn you now that I'm much more charming and persuasive than my brother can ever hope to be, so you'll certainly need to put in an order for your wedding gown."

Windsor smiled. "I am pleased to see you again. I met you in Chicago when I boarded the train for San Francisco."

"Yes, I saw you," Tyler MacKenzie Kincaid told her, coming up to them. "I told Gray then and there that I was certain you weren't a nun. And I was right. I've got very good instincts about such things."

"Yes, now I remember," Gray replied. "You told us your name was Sister Mary, but Tyler said you were much too young and pretty to be a nun. Now that I see you again, I must agree with her. But tell me, Stone, how long did it take you to notice?"

"About two minutes," he admitted, putting his arm around Windsor's waist. "But it was a hell of a lot longer than that before I knew she wasn't a nun."

"I want to hear all about your experiences," Tyler said, "but first, I absolutely must see the boys. I can't wait another moment, I've missed them so much! Where are they, Carly?"

"They're out in the patio with Tomas and their grandmother," Carlisle answered, taking her arm. "Come along with us, Windsor. I can't wait for you and Tyler to get acquainted! Now that she's here, she can help us plan your wedding! And, Windsor, you mustn't wear black at the ceremony the way Tyler did," Carlisle teased, laughing when her sister-in-law blushed.

"Oh, don't tell anybody about that! I'm still mortified to admit I did such a thing," Tyler cried as Carlisle dragged both her and Windsor from the room.

The three men were left to smile after them. Chase shook his head. "Carlisle will definitely lead them into ruin. We'd better keep a close eye on all three of them."

"Tyler's good at finding trouble all by herself, if you'll remember," Gray replied, glancing at Stone. "You've got a lot to fill me in on, I believe."

"Yes. Quite a bit has happened since I saw you last."

"I gathered that by what little you said in your telegram."

Chase swung an arm toward the door leading into the next room. "Let's go into my office, where we can have cigars and brandy. We won't be disturbed there."

Half an hour later, Stone was finished relating the details of his story. For some reason, he found the telling easier this time, much more so than the night he had shared the sordid tale with Carlisle. Maybe because Windsor was now on her way to recovery.

Gray sat back in his chair, his face sober and subdued. "Damn that man. He's got as many lives as a cat. Sometimes he seems almost invincible."

"He's not invincible," Stone said, hatred steeling his words. "He's a dead man waiting for me to get the job done."

Gray leaned forward, his eyes intent on his brother. "So you're going after him again? Even after all this?"

"Wouldn't you? If he'd abused Tyler that way?" he asked Gray. "Or if he'd done this to Carlisle?" he added to Chase.

"I'd want to choke the life out of him with my bare hands," Gray admitted slowly, "but I get the impression that Windsor's still a bit shaky. You don't want to give her a setback by leaving and making her worry about you.''

"Look, Stone," Chase interjected, setting his brandy snifter down on his desk, "I have high political connections in Mexico City. If Clan is involved with the *guerrilleros*, I might be able to get you the use of Nacional troops while you're in my country. We could help you capture him and lock him up, once and for all.''

"No. I want to do it alone.''

"For God's sake, Stone, now you're being unreasonable," Gray said angrily. "Clan's proved himself too dangerous to be taken by one man. Let the three of us get some help, and then we'll go after him together.''

"Every time I get anyone else involved in this mess, they end up getting hurt. That's not going to happen again. I go alone. This is my fight. I want to kill him myself.''

"And what if you don't come back? Then what happens to Windsor and your baby?''

Stone gazed steadily into his brother's face. "I'll be back. And until I am, both of you will be here to protect Windsor.''

Chase and Gray exchanged concerned looks, but their serious conversation was effectively curtailed as the three women burst into the room with the two babies, a doting grandmother, a smiling nursemaid, and a sheepish-looking Uncle Tomas.

28

Just over a week later, Windsor performed the last of the slow, methodical motions of her Dragonfire fighting skills, then sat upon a blanket spread out on a grassy knoll overlooking the Santa Catarina River. She had begun practicing again to make her muscles strong and supple. The physical exercise helped her when she became tense and tired.

Below her, most of the other picnickers milled among the grove of shade trees growing along the bank. Windsor watched Stone, who was conversing with his brother, Gray, at the water's edge. From the beginning Windsor had sensed that the Kincaid men were very close friends as well as blood kin. Unlike their sister, Carlisle, Stone and Gray strongly resembled each other in appearance, both dark and good-looking, both tall with broad shoulders and long legs.

Since Gray and Tyler had arrived, they had been unfailingly kind to Windsor, as had Carlisle and the rest of Chase Lancaster's family. Nevertheless, Windsor felt very much the outsider of the group. The rich Americans came from a world diametrically different from her own. Their lives were filled with laughter and happiness and good fortune, while a heavy cloud of fear and doubt hung like a funereal pall over Stone and her, and would remain to darken their happiness until after her child was born. Afraid to contemplate what the future might hold, Windsor rested her palm upon the growing swell of her belly.

"Did your baby just move?" Tyler asked from where she had come up into the shade cast by a thick-limbed pecan tree.

Windsor turned to look at Stone's sister-in-law. The two of them had not conversed together at length, but Windsor had heard Carlisle speak sorrowfully of Tyler's recent miscarriage of her firstborn child. Now as Windsor looked into Tyler's pretty face, she could see the veil of melancholy still lingering deep in the young woman's cinnamon-brown eyes.

"No. I have felt no movement yet."

"You will someday soon, and it will be quite a miraculous moment," Tyler predicted with a smile. "Would you mind if I sit next to you for a while? Carlisle and Dona Maria have already taken the twins back to the house for their afternoon nap, and Tomas is off to fight the bulls, but it's so pleasant and warm out here by the river that I'd like to stay and walk home with Gray."

"I would enjoy sitting with you."

Tyler wore a fine silk gown, the same lustrous saffron yellow as the robes worn by Buddhist priests, Windsor observed as she returned her gaze to the dark silhouette of the Sierra Madre rising against the sky, as jagged and blue as the towering peaks behind the Temple of the Blue Mountain. As Tyler sat down and took several moments to arrange the voluminous folds of her wide skirt, Windsor wondered if the Old One was even now sitting in his favorite spot of meditation before the glowing candles.

"I wonder what Gray and Stone are talking about for so long," Tyler said when she had settled herself comfortably. "They're certainly engrossed in their conversation."

They're talking about Emerson Clan, Windsor thought. Stone is thinking of going after him again. Her heart constricted, and dread filled her.

"It's wonderful to see Stone again," Tyler went on amiably. "Gray and I have been awfully worried about him, though Gray has always said that Stone's perfectly capable of taking care of himself. Still, Stone is very special."

Windsor swiveled slightly toward Tyler. "Stone Kincaid is a good man, but he is still filled with hatred. It perches on his soul and eats it away like a vulture feasting on carrion."

Tyler looked slightly disconcerted by Windsor's gory analogy. "Well, yes, I think you're right, but I was hoping your marriage would help him."

Windsor was aware that Stone had told everyone how he felt about her, but she had not swayed in her decision not to marry him until after her baby was born. "I pray that destiny will allow us to intertwine our lives. But I am afraid for Stone Kincaid."

Tyler hesitated for a fraction of a moment, as if reluctant to speak; then she touched Windsor's sleeve. "Carlisle told me what happened to you. I am so sorry. I know how cruel Emerson Clan can be. He killed one of our servants when he broke into our house. He came there for me because he thought I was Stone's wife. Every time I remember the look in his eyes when he spoke Stone's name, I get chills up and down my back. Perhaps, though, when enough time has passed, you will be able to forget."

Windsor nodded, though she knew it would take a very long while for her to rid her mind of the torment. Regardless, she felt comforted by Tyler's understanding. She hadn't been able to bring herself to speak of her ordeal, except to Stone, and she had stopped confiding in him because she saw rage flame behind his eyes each time she did.

"I was terrified at first, even in the days after Stone Kincaid rescued me. But with each day that passes I, too, feel more the way I was before. Time will heal my spirit as well as my body, for iron long fired becomes steel."

"You are very brave," Tyler murmured, her eyes full of compassion.

"A wise man adapts himself to circumstances as water shapes itself to the vessel that contains it. We must do the same while we walk through this life."

"Oh, yes, I feel the same way. It's comforting somehow, isn't it?" Tyler looked down and plucked at a blade of grass. "I lost my baby, you know, just a few months ago." She stopped as if overcome by emotion, but then she went on, her words earnest. "But I had him for a while, and I treasure that gift. I believe that God may have already given us another child, though I'm not sure yet."

"I hope you will have another soon."

"The longer Gray and I have to wait, the more precious our baby will become to us. Don't you think so?"

"All life is precious, no matter how great or small."

The two women shared a meaningful smile, and Windsor suddenly felt a closer kinship with Tyler Kincaid. She sensed they were alike, in their hearts where it mattered.

While Windsor gazed upon Tyler's face, the other woman glanced past her, and her expression suddenly changed to one of fear. She put her hand to her mouth, stifling a scream, but before Windsor could spin around to see what had frightened her, a shrill cry split the air.

"*Chee, chee, chee, chee,*" sounded close to her ear; then something warm and furry grabbed her around the neck and scrambled up her arm to her shoulder.

"Jun-li!" Windsor cried, rising to her knees as the small monkey clung to her. She hugged the capuchin with both arms, overcome with joy to find him alive.

Tyler scrambled away as the monkey screeched loudly again and jumped to the ground, but Windsor's gaze was now riveted on the horse picking its way along the sandy riverbank a short distance downstream. The rider was slumped weakly against the horse's neck, but she could see the white eagle feathers in his black hair.

"It's Sun-On-Wings, Tyler! Run and get Stone Kincaid! Quickly!" she urged, already sprinting toward the Indian with Jun-li scampering madly to keep up.

Windsor vaguely heard Tyler calling to her husband, did not see Stone and Gray racing toward them, saw only her weary friend, still astride but barely able to hold on.

"Sun-On-Wings!" she cried when she reached him, grabbing the dangling bridle. The young Osage warrior's cheek was pressed against the mare's mane. He opened bleary eyes at the same time that Windsor saw his leg. "You're hurt!" she exclaimed, reaching up to him, her frightened eyes on the blood-drenched deerskin of his fringed leggings.

"Yellow-Haired-Warrior-Woman . . ." he mumbled, but his face crumpled with pain as he endeavored to swing his leg over the horse and slide to the ground. "Carlos sick—"

When Tyler ran up behind Windsor, Sun-On-

Wings was painfully shrugging the strap of the cradleboard over his shoulder. He collapsed onto his knees, still protecting the child in the carrier. Windsor went down with him, trying to support his weight, and Tyler quickly took the child as Stone and Gray rushed up to help.

"He's been shot in the leg," Windsor told Stone. "We've got to get him to the house. Hurry! Look how much blood he's losing!"

The boy groaned as Stone and Gray lifted him between them and carried him off toward the hacienda with Windsor running alongside them. Tyler stood where she was and stared down at the poor little creature strapped to the board. The baby's dirty face was streaked with tears, and the white-blond hair on one side of his head was crusted with blood from where Sun-On-Wings had touched him.

While she gazed down at him, he cried out, a thin, sickly wail that tore at Tyler's heart. She laid the cradleboard in the grass and unlaced the leather thongs that held the baby inside the beaded buckskin. Very gently, she extricated the child and cuddled him close against her breast. He lay still against her, as if too tired to move.

"It's all right, you sweet little thing, I've got you. You'll be all right now," she murmured in a soft croon. Then, with tears gathering in her eyes at the thought of how he must have suffered, she snuggled him securely in her arms and followed the others back to the hacienda.

As soon as Sun-On-Wings was stretched out upon the bed, Windsor took the scissors Dona Maria had fetched and began to cut free the fringed leggings so that she could tend the gunshot wound.

"What happened to you, kid?" Stone asked,

leaning close and helping Windsor gingerly peel away the bloody material.

"Where Carlos? Him sick. Him need Sun-On-Wings."

"Carlos is fine. Tyler's taking care of him. Did Clan do this to you?"

"No kill Clan. Him not with Carlos. Him ride away from mountains with many men and leave little man at house with woman. Sun-On-Wings take Carlos then."

"Who shot you?"

"Two men guard Carlos and woman," Sun-On-Wings answered, breathing heavily and wincing each time Windsor probed his leg. "Sun-On-Wings not hurt bad. Weak. Bleed much." He turned his face to Windsor. "Sun-On-Wings bring Jun-li and Yellow-Haired-Warrior-Woman's medicine sticks. The Evil One left them with Carlos and woman."

"You have my needles?" Windsor asked. "Where, Sun-On-Wings? I can use them to stop your pain."

His face contorted, Sun-On-Wings shifted his torso and pulled Windsor's black silk bag from where he had tied it at his waist. Windsor took it quickly and spread the contents across the bedside table, relieved to find it still contained all her precious possessions. She lifted the lid of the black lacquered box and took out three needles and the pouches containing the moxa with which she could cauterize the wound.

"This needs to be boiled in clean water. I'll dress the wound with it so it won't become irritated," she told Gray, thrusting one of the drawstring bags into his hands. Gray left the room with it, while Stone poured water into a bowl and began to dab at the blood and dirt surrounding the gaping gunshot hole in Sun-On-Wings' upper thigh.

"Sun-On-Wings want to kill Evil One, but could not follow with Carlos."

"Do you know where he went?" Stone demanded, bending closer to listen to Sun-On-Wings' hoarse words.

"Sun-On-Wings make woman tell. Him go to village on big river in north. Her call place Matamoros."

"Clan's in Matamoros?" Stone's voice went taut with intensity.

Sun-On-Wings nodded, and Windsor paused in her insertion of the needles to look at Stone. A cold feeling swept her skin at the look of determined hatred in his features. Now he would go, she thought with a sinking heart. But as Sun-On-Wings groaned, she bent again to her task, knowing she had to close the wound before her friend bled to death.

As she probed the deep laceration with her fingers, she began to relax. "The infection has not yet turned black, Sun-On-Wings. I will be able to help you. We must stitch your wound together, but first my needles will take the pain away."

With long-practiced expertise, she inserted the sharp pins in his arms, twirling them to heat and stimulate the flesh, both relieved and happy to have her young Osage friend safely with her again. She leaned close, brushing his hair from his forehead.

"Thank you, Sun-On-Wings. You are very brave and kind to bring Carlos back. I've been worried about you."

"Sun-On-Wings gave Nina sacred word. Little man not know father be Evil One."

Windsor nodded, cleaning his wound, then packing the newly stitched flesh with the moxa that Gray had returned to her. She held a candle flame to the soft, downy substance and let it smolder atop the skin.

"Tyler's tending to the baby," Gray told them. "The poor little boy was nearly starved, so she and Dona Maria are feeding milk to him down in the kitchen. I'll go and see if I can help."

As Gray left the room, Windsor dampened the moxa and wrapped clean bandages around Sun-On-Wings' leg. The young man now slept in exhaustion, and she gazed down on him fondly, her heart lighter than it had been for some time. But then she turned and found Stone near the wardrobe, strapping on his gun belt.

As he finished tying down his holster, he opened his arms to her. Without a word she went into his embrace.

"Must you do this?" she asked, but she already knew the answer.

"You know I do."

"I'm afraid for you. He is a demon."

"He's no demon. He's a man who doesn't deserve to live among civilized people."

Windsor bit her lip. Once, she had been as determined as Stone to kill Clan. Even now she longed to go along, to help the man she loved in his quest for vengeance. But she would *not* endanger the life growing inside her for want of revenge.

"Hatred is never ended by hatred but by love," she murmured, her heart full of fear.

"Not this time," Stone muttered. "Not with him."

Windsor laid her head against the soft white linen of his shirt. He was so strong, his heartbeat so steady beneath her cheek. "Come back to me, Stone Kincaid. I cannot go on without you."

Stone held her away from him, but his face was hardened with somber lines of resolve. "You'll be safe here until I return. Promise me you won't come after me. I have to do this alone."

"I promise," she whispered, though her mind rebelled at letting him go. She locked her arms around his waist, afraid that if he walked out of the room this time, she would never see him again. But she also knew she had no choice except to let him go.

He would come back. He had to.

29

Bracing the padded end of his crutch under one arm, Sun-On-Wings leaned heavily upon it as he limped painfully across the patio to where Yellow-Haired-Warrior-Woman sat outside on a stone bench, her gaze fixed upon the strange water hole the white man had built where water poured down like rapids in a mountain stream. Since Arrow-Parts-Hair had left the big house to kill the Evil One, she had often sat there with Jun-li, staring into the shallow pool.

Slowly he moved toward her, dragging his leg slightly, still unable to put much weight on his foot. Even now when he was so much better, each step razored pain from the ragged bullet hole in his thigh down his calf to his foot.

Despite the constant dull ache that plagued him, the wound was healing well. He had returned with Carlos only ten suns ago, but the strange silver sticks that Yellow-Haired-Warrior-Woman had pricked into his skin and the leafy substance she had burned upon his flesh had worked their magic and made him better. He would soon regain the strength in his leg, and then he would make the

336

long journey back to his people. He was tired of being with the white man.

As he drew near to Yellow-Haired-Warrior-Woman, she heard the scrape of his crutch and was roused from her pensive mood. Her face set in serious lines, she immediately slid to one side of the seat, welcoming him to join her. Jun-li jumped upon his shoulder, and as Sun-On-Wings maneuvered his leg into position and eased down beside her, he looked sadly at her short golden hair, still finding the sight difficult to accept, even after so long. He missed the woven braid of shiny yellow hair that had swung against her back the first time he had seen her. Even more strange to see, her slim body was now swollen with child. She worries much for Arrow-Parts-Hair, he thought. Sad songs dwelt deep in the dark blue of her eyes.

"Arrow-Parts-Hair brave warrior. Him return soon," he said in a low voice, trying to console her.

"I know," she answered. "But I wish we were with him, in case he should need help."

Silence prevailed for a few moments while both of them stared thoughtfully into the tinkling jets of water. Sun-On-Wings remembered Emerson Clan's face and the evil acts he enjoyed. In the pictures of his mind, he saw Nina's tortured back. He knew that Yellow-Haired-Warrior-Woman suffered from the same frightening thoughts of what could happen to Arrow-Parts-Hair.

"Sun-On-Wings go home as soon as Arrow-Parts-Hair come. No like way of white man. Bad medicine. Sun-On-Wings go to mountains where Little Ones sing at dawn. Man named Tomas say he will take me to north to river between Mexico and land of the Little Ones."

Yellow-Haired-Warrior-Woman turned quickly as if surprised. "I'll miss you, Sun-On-Wings," she said, her eyes earnest, "and so will Stone Kincaid. You're like a brother to us."

"Sun-On-Wings feel honor to be brother. Yellow-Haired-Warrior-Woman someday be Arrow-Parts-Hair's woman, then him be happy."

She looked down at her lap, twisting the bright braid that edged the neckline of her loose top. "I cannot, Sun-On-Wings. Not until my baby is born."

"Baby be Arrow-Parts-Hair's son."

"I ask the gods for that every day and every night," she replied softly.

Sun-On-Wings could easily read the uncertainty in her eyes. He spoke swiftly and with resolve. "Wah-Kon-Dah make him son of Arrow-Parts-Hair, Sun-On-Wings know."

"If that comes true, then I will gladly marry Stone Kincaid," she said. "I wish you could stay. I'll miss you."

"Go soon. Tired of white man's world."

"I will never forget you."

"Arrow-Parts-Hair and Yellow-Haired-Warrior-Woman live in Little Ones' legends. Me tell to children when winter make the mountains white."

"I think you will be the one to live in the legends of your people, Sun-On-Wings. Someday you will become the great chief whose destiny was revealed to White-Spotted-Wolf in his dream sleep."

Sun-On-Wings wondered if she could be right. Whether she was or not, he would leave as soon as he could. He hungered for the simple, good life of the Little Ones.

Across the patio, he caught sight of the white woman who was called Tyler. She moved from beneath the covered portico with Carlos propped on one arm. While he watched, she cuddled the child against her shoulder, kissing his cheek and brushing her fingers through his blond hair.

"Woman named Tyler like Carlos," he commented, returning his attention to Yellow-Haired-Warrior-Woman. "Her no care that Evil One his father."

"No, she wouldn't. She lost a child of her own not long ago. She still grieves for him, so having Carlos here is good for her."

"Me give Carlos to Tyler woman. Me no can take white child back to village. Carlos no belong there. Him belong with own people."

Yellow-Haired-Warrior-Woman smiled. "She would like that very much, Sun-On-Wings, and I can promise you that Tyler and her husband, Gray, will treat him as their very own son. They already do. Carlos will grow up well loved. Nina would like that."

Deep inside, Sun-On-Wings felt a terrible stab of loss. The white baby was a brave little man. Sun-On-Wings loved him, but he knew he should not take him back to the mountains. The Little Ones would welcome him into their clan, but Carlos belonged with others of white skin and pale eyes. Across the grassy lawn, Tyler Kincaid looked up from her bench seat and saw them. She smiled and waved.

"Why don't you go tell her, Sun-On-Wings? She's been worried that you might decide to leave soon and take Carlos with you."

Sun-On-Wings nodded, then pushed himself upright, taking time to position his crutch. Leaving Jun-li behind, he made his way toward Tyler Kincaid. When she saw him approaching, she stood to welcome him.

"Hello, Sun-On-Wings," she greeted, wearing the warm smile she always had for him. She turned Carlos around in her arms until he faced Sun-On-Wings. The baby grinned in delight and reached out his arms. "I do believe Carlos is glad to see you," Tyler noted with a laugh. "Here, we'll sit down so your leg will be more comfortable," she invited, perching on one end of the garden bench.

Sun-On-Wings sat beside her, straightening out his leg and propping his crutch against the seat. He grasped the little boy's hand. Carlos gurgled and laughed, his small fingers tightening around Sun-On-Wings' thumb.

"I think he wants you to hold him," Tyler said, immediately offering up the child to him.

Sun-On-Wings took the baby in his arms, and Carlos immediately grabbed a hunk of Sun-On-Wings' hair, which had grown long all over his scalp since he had left his tribe. The babe jerked it, and Tyler protested with a laugh, trying to disentangle his tight hold. When the child heard her soft voice, he twisted in Sun-On-Wings' arms and reached for Tyler again, his little face screwing up in readiness for a loud yowl.

"Him want you," Sun-On-Wings said, quickly handing the little man back to the white woman.

Tyler smiled as she took him, her voice as gentle as her strokes upon the child's back. Tyler looked at Carlos the same way Nina had looked at him, with the wonder and love of a mother aglow inside her eyes.

"Him think you his mother now," Sun-On-Wings told her, watching as she hugged the baby close again. "Him like you."

"That's because I'm the one who takes care of him most of the time," Tyler murmured in reply, pressing her lips to Carlos's head. "He's a little angel, so good that he's no trouble at all. Isn't that right, my little sweetheart?"

"Sun-On-Wings think you be Carlos's mother when Sun-On-Wings go back to Little Ones."

Tyler's gaze flew to him. She gasped with surprise. "Why, I assumed you would take him with you, or that Stone and Windsor would want him—"

"Him son of white man. Him belong with white man. You be better mother. His father hurt Yellow-Haired-Warrior-Woman. Her not forget easy. Arrow-Parts-Hair hunt down father to kill. Him too full of hatred to forget. Carlos better if him with you and white man name Gray."

Her eyes glittering with a sheen of tears, Tyler looked down into Carlos's upturned face.

"Oh, Sun-On-Wings, thank you. I do love this little boy so much. And so does Gray. From the first moment I saw Carlos, so dirty and tired, his hair all caked with blood, my heart went out to him."

Sun-On-Wings nodded. "Me know. Him nice little man. His mother much like you."

"Are you sure you want to give him up like this? I can see how much you care for him." Tyler's eyes were troubled. "I know how hard it is to let a child go."

"Carlos little. Him need mother."

Tyler withdrew a handkerchief from her sleeve and dabbed the corners of her eyes. "I'm sorry, I shouldn't be crying like this, but I'm just so happy. I thought I'd have to give him up, and I didn't think I could bear it." Sun-On-Wings waited patiently as she struggled to get hold of her feelings. Finally, she took a deep breath and gave him a tremulous smile. "Would you mind if I go tell Gray? It's just such wonderful news. He's been worried that I was getting too attached to Carlos."

Sun-On-Wings nodded, and Tyler put her arm around his neck and gave him a quick hug before she hurried away with Carlos. His own heart felt heavy, for he thought that once he left the hacienda, he would probably not see the small man-child again, not for many winters. But Carlos would be better off with the pretty woman with the red-brown hair. And Sun-On-Wings would be better with his own people. As soon as Arrow-Parts-Hair

returned, he would make the long journey back to
the snowcapped mountains far to the north. He
hoped that day would come soon. He had been
gone long enough.

Inside a dingy, back-street cantina in the border
town of Matamoros, Emerson Clan leaned back his
head and exhaled a ring of blue smoke toward the
ceiling. He glanced around the barroom, his slender cigar held loosely between his fingers. The
place was crowded with Mexicans, but his table in
the back corner was fairly deserted. The men in his
group of bandits had spent most of the night
drowning themselves in tequila and *aguardiente* and
pawing the low-cut blouses of the coarse Mexican
whores plying their well-worn bodies for a few pesos.

Let the fools have their good time, he thought
with scorn, because tomorrow, as they slept off
their drunken night, he would ride back across the
border into Texas with his saddlebags full of the
gold they had helped him accrue. Now that President Juarez had sent his Nacionales to stamp out
the revolution in Mexico, there was little reason for
him to remain among the filthy, ignorant louts he
had been riding with. His bandit band had earned
him a fair amount of gold, and he intended to put
it to good use in the States.

First, though, he would ride back to the rancho
where the old woman was taking care of his son.
Once he had Carlos, he would set out for home.
As far as he knew, he wasn't wanted by the sheriff
of New Orleans. There were plenty of rich women
and lots of money floating around the gambling
halls and whorehouses of the old French part of
that city.

Grimacing with distaste, he watched a fight erupt
between two of his men and quickly escalate into
bloody violence. He was damn sick and tired of

them all. None of them had the intelligence to find their way down a mountain trail. If it hadn't been for him, most of them would already be hanging from a gallows or rotting alive in filthy Juarista jails by now. He would be glad to get rid of them. He looked forward to traveling alone with his son. He was proud of Carlos. The boy would carry on his name, ride at his side, and enjoy the wealth Clan meant to accumulate for them.

The only problem was finding a woman to take care of the baby, one willing to do exactly what Clan told her, like Nina had when he had first gotten her. Hell, he'd never had any trouble finding women—they were drawn to him like flies to molasses. But only a comely one; he never could stand an ugly woman. And she had to be timid enough to be controlled without much effort. Then he could use her to warm his bed when he wanted, as well as to take care of the boy. He would be on the lookout for someone as young and innocent as Nina. God, toward the end, Nina had gotten so that she shook from head to toe if he merely looked in the direction of his whip.

Frowning, he placed his hand on the leather-thonged bullwhip he wore curled neatly on his hand-tooled gun belt. She had deserved to die, the bitch, for betraying him to Kincaid. He smiled, a cold, hard tightening of the lips, at the memory of how he had repaid his old friend for enlisting Nina's aid.

Clan's pale eyes narrowed, glinting with pleasure as he recalled his meeting with Kincaid in the cantina in Saltillo. Stone's face had turned white. Clan had actually watched the blood drain down his neck and the pain glaze his eyes when Clan had flung the woman's braid on the table. That one entertaining moment had made worthwhile all the trouble Kincaid had caused him.

Never before had he broken through Kincaid's

inscrutable facade to bloody up his emotions. He chuckled, amused just thinking about it. And despite her initial courage and resistance, Windsor Richmond had turned into a cowering victim by the time he was finished with her. Like so many others, her defeat had come when he had made Nina suffer in her stead.

Although he had triumphed over Kincaid once again, Clan wasn't stupid enough to think their game was over. Kincaid would come after him, like he always did. Kincaid's actions were incredibly easy to anticipate because he lived by his ridiculous code of honor, by his saintly conscience that upheld truth, honesty, and morality. That's why Kincaid always came out the loser. Goodness might prevail inside the pearly gates of heaven, but it sure as hell didn't on earth. How many times had Clan proved that?

As the hours lengthened, he grew tired of the noise and guitar music. He strolled across the saloon, stepping over a couple of his Mexican followers who were already too inebriated to stand. Let them have their good time, he thought. Tomorrow he'd be gone with the money.

He went outside, letting the swinging doors creak back and forth behind him. The narrow street was dark and deserted. Indeed, all of Matamoros seemed uninhabited, the night a warm velvet blackness all around him. He puffed desultorily on his cigar, then flicked it into the dirt and sauntered across the street to the livery stable. If he rode hard enough, he could get his boy and be across the border before the sun came up. He looked forward to being on his own again. He had ridden with a gang too long this time. Maybe he'd even settle down somewhere for a while. Marry a rich widow, if he could find one who pleased him in bed, one he could control without a lot of squawking and whining.

As he pushed the stable door ajar, a horse shifted restlessly, snorting and stamping a hoof. The odor of dust and straw mingled with horseflesh hung heavy in the dusky building, and loud wheezing snores alerted Clan to the whereabouts of the old Indian who cleaned out the stalls. As usual, he slept on his belly in the hay, an empty bottle of whiskey overturned on the floor near his head.

Clan picked up the lantern resting on an upright nail keg. The chimney windows were so dirty that only a dim glow escaped to guide him through the darkness. He held the lantern out in front of him as he walked slowly to the stall where he had quartered his bay mare. Maybe he would take all the horses, too, and sell them to the first rancho outside Matamoros, just in case any of the Mexicans tried to follow him and get their share of the loot. He doubted any of them had the guts, though; after months in the mountains together, they knew him too well. They had seen him wield his whip. He wouldn't mind killing them; in fact, he'd enjoy it. And they knew it.

Clan had never cared if those around him lived or died, at his hands or by the hand of another. Except for Stone Kincaid. Kincaid was different. He was smart, too, as smart as Clan himself. Clan had actually admired him when they were roommates at West Point. That had changed the day Stone had had him court-martialed for aiding the Confederates. Again, honor had ruled Kincaid's actions, the dumb bastard.

Clan lifted a leather bridle from a stall hook and draped it over the horse's ears, patting the animal's velvety nose as he buckled the straps in place. Suddenly he froze as something cold touched the side of his head. A soft click followed, the deadly turn of a pistol cylinder.

"Hello, Clan."

The hairs rose on the back of Clan's neck, undulating a cold chill down his spine. Stone Kincaid's low voice was uttered very close to his ear. Clan turned slowly, furious with himself for being so damn careless. He'd known Kincaid would come, but he hadn't expected it so soon. It was the first time he had underestimated him.

Their eyes locked. Clan smiled. Kincaid smiled back.

"So we meet yet again, old friend, and sooner than I expected," Clan ventured conversationally, inching his hand toward the vest pocket where he kept his derringer concealed.

"Move your goddamn hand another inch and you won't have a head anymore," Kincaid murmured in the same casual tone. "I hope you're stupid enough to go for that little gun of yours."

Clan grinned. "So, *amigo*, we're still playing the game, aren't we? We've gotten good at it over the last six years, you and I. We take turns besting each other, cat and mouse, mouse and cat, but I always end up the winner. Have you ever wondered why, Kincaid?"

"Tonight the game ends."

Clan gave a derisive snort. "You think so? Well, you're wrong. Let me tell you why. You're too goddamn moral. That honor you like to carry around pinned to your chest like a big, shiny gold badge does you in every time. You can hold that gun to my head, you can make threats, and you can beat me to a bloody pulp like you did up in Chicago when your pretty little sister-in-law tricked me into coming there, but you'll never pull that trigger." He paused, letting his taunts find their marks. He knew Kincaid so well, he had no doubt his words were true. He smiled into Kincaid's eyes. "Nope, you haven't got the guts to blow my brains out. You'll turn me over to the law again, like the fine, upstanding citizen you are, because it's the *right* thing to do. It's the American way—you know, God's way, the good Major Stone Kincaid's way. Yeah, you'll put me in jail just like you did last time, and I'll escape just like last time. Maybe I'll even come after your woman again, Kincaid. After all, she liked what I did to her. She got down on her knees and begged for more. Of course, my whip here had a little to do with that—"

Clan's words faltered, his pale eyes bulging slightly as he heard the soft scrape when Stone's finger pulled back on the trigger, but that was the last thing he ever heard on earth as the gun exploded and he was hurtled into hell.

30

The tiny chapel of the Hacienda de los Toros was nestled behind an ivy-hung corner of the inner patio, the heavy wooden door set with a large gold cross and half hidden by the heavily laden branches of an orange tree. The interior was dimly lit by a wall of arched stained-glass windows etched with Moorish designs. Bars of vividly hued light slanted through the beautifully painted panes onto plain wooden pews. Windsor stood motionlessly in the dusky shadows, her new black silk tunic and trousers blending into the darkness.

Early after her arrival at the hacienda, when Dona Maria had shown Windsor and Stone around her son's large estate, she had led them into the holy place where she practiced her faith. At the time, Windsor had wondered why Dona Maria had preferred a dark, hidden chamber to the lush beauty of the mountains and canyons beyond the walls of her house. But now that Stone had been gone for so long, the peace and solitude of the place seemed to beckon her.

At the front of the narrow vaulted room, the ornate altar rose in grand, gilded stairsteps, much like the graceful pagoda shrines along the Yellow

River. But Windsor was drawn to an alcove at one side of the nave where rows of squat white candles in glass bowls flickered on invisible air currents. In the Temple of the Blue Mountain, similar racks of tapers had burned throughout the day and night, the soft yellowish glow mingled with the pungent sweetness of smoldering incense.

Kneeling on the red velvet cushion atop the bench in front of the votive stand, she gazed up at the statue set in a wall niche above her. The woman was Mary of Nazareth, the Blessed Mother of Jesus Christ. Stone had told her about Mary once when he had explained Catholicism to her. Mary's carved face was beautiful, serene and smooth, a faint smile etched upon her gentle face. Windsor was more strongly drawn to her than to the poor, tortured figure atop the Christian crucifix. Mary of Nazareth was a woman, a mother, a wife. Perhaps she would understand Windsor's pain and grief.

Stone Kincaid had been gone for over a month. He had kissed her good-bye and left without a word to anyone else, and now she longed so much for his return that her heart seemed wounded beyond repair. Sun-On-Wings tried to comfort her, but there was little he could say. He was fit again now, probably well enough to depart upon his long journey, but he lingered in hopes of Stone's return, wishing to bid good-bye to his friend.

All of Stone Kincaid's relatives were good to her, making her feel very much a part of the family, and like Windsor, each of them knew and understood why Stone had gone and why he had chosen to go alone. But now that so much time had passed, they were concerned about his well-being.

Closing her eyes, Windsor braced her elbows on the praying stand and clasped her hands together. She sighed, thinking how strange and violent their lives together had been, ever since they had stepped aboard the train in Chicago. How many times had they entered danger together and saved each other from harm? But if Stone should need her this time, she would not be there to help him, and that thought troubled her more than anything. If it were not for the child inside her, she would follow now as she had always done in the past. But she had another life to consider, an innocent babe yet to be born.

Stone was strong, she told herself. He was smart, and he knew the Evil One well. Had he not survived every encounter with Clan in the past? Unwanted words from the Old One came echoing through the cavern depths of her mind.

"Fortune wearies with carrying one and the same man always," she said aloud, trembling with renewed fear for the man she loved. She looked up at the benign face of the statue, her heart full. Mary of Nazareth, she prayed silently, I am not one of your flock like Dona Maria. I have my own gods. But I ask you to bring Stone Kincaid back to me. Her throat clogged, making her eyes burn. I need him so much. I love him so much.

For a long time she sat there unmoving, thinking, hoping, remembering; then she froze as a voice spoke her name from the back of the church.

Windsor came to her feet as Stone strode down the center aisle toward her. Wordlessly, she went to him, torn by emotion, her heart high in her throat. When she reached him, his arms closed tight around her. He smoothed her hair with his palm as she lay her cheek against his shoulder.

"It's over. Clan won't come after our baby. He won't hurt anybody ever again."

No other words were necessary. They stood together in silence, content to hold each other, relieved and thankful that the long nightmare had finally ended. Now, together, they would await the birth of the child growing inside her. Then, the gods willing, they would join their lives, and live in peace.

Stone paced back and forth in the front salon, his boots clicking a steady rhythm across the marble tiles until he stopped abruptly and stared up the stairs toward the upper hallway. He couldn't stand it much longer, he thought, clamping his teeth down until his jaw ached with the strain. Windsor had been in labor for hours. How the hell long was it going to take?

"Stone, I think you'd better let Chase pour you another drink," Gray suggested. "Good God, the way you're prowling around and wringing your hands is making nervous wrecks out of all of us!"

Stone growled an oath, then stood with arms akimbo, still staring up the steps. "Windsor's pains started last night, for God's sake, and now it's nearly dawn! She can't go on like this forever, dammit! Why can't I go up and see how she's doing? She might need me."

Chase splashed a liberal portion of brandy into a glass and handed it to Stone. "Quit worrying. We've all been through this. It'll be over soon."

"I don't see how you stood it when Carly had the boys! My God, I'll go crazy if they don't tell me something soon."

"Actually, I helped deliver the twins," Chase replied equably, sitting down on the sofa in front of the fireplace. "Actually, Tyler did most of it, because I was in a state similar to the one you're in now. Believe me, Stone, you're better off down here with us. You don't want to watch her suffer when there's nothing you can do to help her."

His face a tight white mask, Stone stared at him, then tossed back his brandy in one deep draught. He resumed his nervous pacing, pausing now and then at the base of the stairs to listen. All was silent. At least she wasn't screaming from the pain; he tried to draw comfort from that thought.

But what if something had gone wrong, like it had with poor Tyler when her baby had come early? What if Windsor was too small to deliver the child? She was so slender, with delicate, fragile bones, and she had grown huge during the past few months. He had heard about women dying in childbirth when the child was too large. The idea made his blood run cold. Swallowing back the hard lump of fear, he returned to the brandy decanter. He helped himself to another shot, downed it in one gulp, then partook of a third portion as quickly as he could pour it.

"Sit down, Stone. You're making things worse for yourself, and if you keep drinking at this rate, you'll be too drunk to know whether your baby's a girl or a boy," Gray predicted calmly.

Ignoring the other two men, Stone continued to roam, his nerves more on edge with each passing moment.

She'll be all right, he muttered inwardly. After all they had been through together, surely they deserved this chance. Clan was dead now. They could be happy.

Hell, he didn't even care if the baby turned out to be Clan's. A long time ago, he had resigned himself to the fact that it could well be that way. If so, he would raise the child as his own. He just wanted Windsor to get through this ordeal alive.

Regardless of what she said, he was going to marry her, tonight, as soon as the child was born. He had waited this long only because she had asked him to. He had instructed Chase to summon a priest, and even now the padre waited out on the patio with Dona Maria and Tomas, ready to perform the ceremony. Even if Windsor protested, there was little she could do about it in her weakened condition. She wanted to marry him, anyway, he knew that. She was just afraid about the baby.

Moving to the window, he stared out into the night where rain fell in hard, slanting arrows. He rubbed his whiskered jaw. Fear gripped his heart, twisting, wrapping itself around every nerve ending in his body until he wanted to hurl something through the panes of glass and yell out his frustration. He had to do something to alleviate the terrible uncertainty. Oh, God, if anything happened to her, what would he do?

"Stone? Come quick, Windsor wants you! You've got a new daughter!"

Carlisle had cried out the happy tidings from the top of the steps, smiling from ear to ear. Gray and Chase called out their congratulations as Stone hurled himself up the steps three at a time.

"Is she all right, Carly?" he demanded, not slowing his pace as he bore down the upstairs gallery toward Windsor's room with long, eager strides.

"Yes, yes, they both are!" Carlisle cried, running to keep up with him.

"Then go get the priest," he said, and his sister laughed delightedly as she turned and darted off in the opposite direction.

Stone thrust open the bedchamber door and found Tyler and the doctor bending over the bed. They both looked up as he entered, but his eyes sought only Windsor, where she lay in the midst of fluffy white pillows, a small bundle resting in her arms.

"Congratulations, Stone," Tyler said, hugging him as he came near. "Your daughter is beautiful, and big and healthy."

Stone moved to Windsor's side, barely noticing as Tyler and the doctor left the room.

Windsor smiled up at him, and Stone sat down

on the edge of the bed, taking her hand in his and pressing his lips against her cool skin.

"Are you all right?" he muttered, his words gruff with emotion.

"Yes, now I am."

"Thank God. You've been up here so long, I was beginning to get worried."

Windsor raised her other hand and laid it against his cheek. "Don't you want to see your daughter? She looks just like you."

Their eyes held for a long moment, all the unspoken fears they had harbored finally dwindling to dust. Stone fought to contain his pure relief, half reeling beneath a hot rush of joy that burned his eyes as Windsor tenderly unfolded the blanket and allowed him to gaze upon his firstborn child.

Stone stared down at the tiny red face framed by a wealth of thick black hair. His newborn daughter blinked sleepily back out of dark blue eyes so like his own that he had no doubt she was his, his and Windsor's. His throat swelled, thickened with indescribable pride and love.

"Now you're going to marry me, you hear?" he mumbled, his words muffled against Windsor's hand.

"Oh, yes, I am. Right now, holding her in my arms."

She smiled, and Stone threw back his head and laughed without restraint, suddenly so filled with happiness that he wanted to shout at the top of his lungs.

"You wait right here," he cried. "Don't even move."

It was Windsor's turn to laugh as he rushed to the door and flung it wide.

"Come on, everyone, it's time for a wedding!"

Then he was at her side again, pulling her up and holding her and their child gently as his family gathered around them. The priest came forth, smiling broadly, and Stone held Windsor's hand tightly in his, reaching out with his other to touch the soft dark hair of their child.

Gazing down at his wife and daughter, his eyes serious as Windsor reached up to lovingly caress his cheek, he hardly listened to the padre's words.

"Do you, Stone Kincaid, take this woman to be your wife?" the padre asked at length.

Stone brought her palm to his lips, his eyes full of love and commitment. "Oh, yes, I do. Forever."

"And do you, Windsor Richmond, take this man to be your husband?"

"I do," she murmured wearily. "At last."

Stone gathered her into his arms, content now that they were one. He whispered his love to her and tenderly stroked his daughter's soft cheek, while the others tiptoed out of the room, leaving them to share quiet murmurs of wonder and delight, to savor together their long-sought joy.

Epilogue

Two years later
December 1874
San Francisco, California

Amelia Richmond Cox had never been so happy. The great empty mansion in which she had lived alone for so many years was full of family and friends. Her daughter, lost to her for so long, led a happy and contented life with a fine husband and a beautiful daughter. Yes, all Amelia's prayers had been answered. Her life had taken on new meaning. Smiling, she glanced around her drawing room at the turmoil of laughing children and lovely young couples.

Across from her, Stone Kincaid was helping Windsor set a white, porcelain angel atop the Christmas tree. His two-year-old daughter, Nina, was perched in the crook of his arm, clapping with delight as he set the ornament in place. Amelia's only grandchild was a complete joy to everyone she met, and each day she looked more and more like her father, with raven hair that curled softly down her back in silken waves and eyes of silver-blue that exactly matched her father's. Thank you,

God, for that gift, more than any other that you've bestowed upon us, Amelia thought with a grateful heart.

But there were many other gifts, so many that Amelia felt bountifully blessed after a lifetime of loneliness. The fact that Stone and Windsor had settled in San Francisco, in a magnificent new house near her own estate, was wonderful in itself. Stone had taken charge of the new offices of the Kincaid Railway Company in San Francisco, and since railroad lines had begun to spread all through California, he had already quadrupled the family interests in the state.

She heard laughter, and turned to look at Chase and Carlisle Lancaster, who had come out to visit for the holidays, along with Stone's older brother, Gray, and his wife, Tyler. Amelia joined their amusement as Chase grabbed up one of his sons, who had stolen a candy cane from his brother's stocking. The twins were two and a half, and rambunctious to say the least, especially Rico, who loved to run and shout, and pull his cousin, Nina's, long black curls. Nevertheless, Nina spent most of her time toddling around after the two boys like a little shadow, her mother's pet monkey in her arms.

Of all the visiting children, Gray and Tyler's adopted son was the most subdued. Older than the rest, he was a quiet child who often sat and watched the others or played with his new baby sister, Veronica. He is Emerson Clan's son, Amelia thought sadly, glad the family had elected never to tell him of his father's evil ways. Such a burden would be difficult for anyone to bear, much less a small child. While Amelia watched them, Tyler pulled Carlos onto her lap and kissed his flaxen hair, and the little boy lifted his arms around her and snuggled closer. Yes, Amelia thought, he would be all right, too. They all would.

"Me want to open presents," Enrico said loudly across the room. His protests soon brought Esteban up from his mother's lap with similar complaints. Carlos eagerly joined the circle of children around the Christmas tree, and Amelia took Nina from Stone's arms and carried her forward to join the excited little ones.

Oh, yes, Amelia thought, everything had turned out well for all the Kincaids, despite the many troubles they had faced. The three married couples before her were happy, all very much in love and ready to share their love and contentment with their children. And that's the way it should be, she thought, joining in the laughter as the children tore into their gaily wrapped packages. After all was said and done, what greater gift was there in this life than love given freely to others? And here, among the Kincaid family, love was everywhere.